MIDNIGHT
WOLF

COPYRIGHTS

MIDNIGHT WOLF

BOOK 2

S.V. SMITH

CHAPTER 1

VIOLET

"Oh, Goddess! I love this song!" I squealed with happiness.

I pulled Dylan to the middle of the gigantic living room, packed with sweaty teenagers, and started moving my hips in time with the beat. Catching my hand, he spun me around once before pulling me into his chest. I giggled as he tried to land a kiss for the third time tonight.

"I told you; I'm saving myself for my mate!" I grinned.

"It's just a kiss, Vie," he smirked.

I shook my head. "I want my first to be with my mate, every first."

He rolled his eyes and groaned. "You torture me, woman!"

I took a step back, shaking my hips again. I swear, he almost drooled. We danced for a while more, every so often Dylan trying to sneak a kiss. When it started becoming more annoying than funny, I excused myself to go find the bathroom. Finding an empty one, finally, I locked the door and sat on the edge of the tub.

Dylan was a nice guy, and he had been my friend since third grade when his parents had joined the pack. I knew he'd always had a crush on me; He wasn't very subtle about it. Yet, he didn't always respect the boundaries I'd put in place about waiting for my mate. He was captain of the football team, the typical jock. His gold, wavy hair, and clear blue eyes, coupled with his flawless skin and fantastic physique, made him a magnet for most of the girls at school.

There was a time when I'd swooned over him, too. Until he'd started making out with more than a few girls and slept with at least four that I knew about. And that was when I started to lose interest in him. He thought I was weird for waiting for my mate, but did I want to end up a notch on someone's bedpost? Hell no.

I knew it was silly to want my mate to be a virgin like me; Guys had needs, and teenage guys today? It was highly unlikely whoever my mate was would be a virgin. But that didn't mean *I* couldn't wait. It was, after all, my body and my decision.

Thinking all this through, I decided I was going to stop flirting with Dylan. Of course, it was harmless on my end, but he was right. Obviously, I was giving him the wrong impression. And I really didn't want to hurt him, either.

With that thought in mind, I opened the door, apologizing to the girls who'd been waiting outside, and made my way to find him. I took the stairs quickly down, scanning the crowd until suddenly, my eyes landed on him.

Dylan was tucked away in the corner of the living room with Sarah, the biggest hoe in school, in a heated make-out session. Her hands moved to the front of his pants, grabbing him. I almost gagged. This is why I wanted to wait! One minute, he was all over me, and the next, he moved on to the next girl.

Boys! I thought, shaking my head as I descended the rest of the stairs. Locating my jacket from the front closet, I left the house. I pulled out my phone and called Isa.

"Heya, where you at!" she yelled into the receiver.

I laughed. Isabelle was a few years older than me but one of my best girlfriends. She was a witch, so unlike us wolves, alcohol affected her way more.

"I'm leaving. Heading home," I told her.

"Whaaat? Why?"

"Just not in the party mood tonight." I checked the time quickly. It was almost midnight. "You'll be okay to get home, though?"

"Oh yeah! Trevor is giving me a ride later."

"Alright. I'll see you tomorrow. Love you."

"Love you girl!"

Tucking my phone into my pocket, I made my way down the long driveway and onto the sidewalk. The wind was blowing nicely through the trees, my long black hair lifting in it. My eyes scanned my surroundings, an automatic reflex now. Training with my Dad, Alpha of the pack, had caused my twin brother Garrett and me to be cautious, even inside the pack boundaries. It's not that I didn't feel safe here at Blood Moon, but as we were taught, you never knew when rogues might attack.

As I walked, my anger grew towards Dylan. Was I jealous? No. I knew it seemed that way, but honestly, I was more upset with him than jealous. I could only hope his future mate hadn't seen him shamelessly making out and being groped by another girl. His eighteenth birthday was in two days; He was going to find his mate sooner rather than later, I was sure. I ducked my head as the selfish thought ran through my head that I hoped it wasn't me. Again. I know, I was horrible. He was my best guy friend, and yet I hoped he wasn't my mate. Stupid.

SNAP

My head whipped around. I eyed the area around me slowly, holding my breath.

"You should try looking up, princess."

I groaned aloud but looked up anyway. Perched on a low-hanging branch was Jasper, my least favourite person in the world. He shot me a sarcastic smile while I glared at him.

"What are you doing up there?" I asked him.

He shrugged. "Does anyone own this tree?"

"No?"

"Then I guess I can be up here."

I rolled my eyes. Okay, honest disclosure time: Jasper was hot. Like, *hot*, hot. He had short brown hair that was thick and slightly wavy but not as wavy as Dylan's. His eyes were a gorgeous silver-grey, and his body? Damn. I'd seen him shirtless on the training grounds. He had a fully

11

stacked six-pack and was toned in all the right places, with just the right amount of facial hair to bring his look together into your typical sexy bad boy. But his attitude? Ugh. Jasper had this way about him, this "I don't give a fuck about anything" attitude that was a total turn-off. Plus, rumor had it he'd slept with more than half the school. Gross.

"Why are you staring at me, princess? Like what you see?" he grinned cockily.

"I'm not staring at you." I averted my eyes quickly. "And don't call me princess."

Swinging his legs over, Jasper jumped from the branch, landing lightly on his feet. I craned my neck back to look up at him. He stood over six feet tall, dwarfing my five-foot-four figure.

"Alright." He stuck his hands in his pockets. "What are you doing out here?"

"Walking."

"Alone?"

I folded my arms across my chest. "Yes. Is that a problem?"

"No need to get so defensive. I was just asking." He looked over my head before looking back at me. "Want some company?"

"Uh, no, thanks."

I turned and started walking again, but he fell into step beside me anyway. What was it with these boys? None of them listened to me.

"Jasper, I said I'm good."

"We're close to the border. It's not safe for you to be out here alone at night."

I stopped and shot him another glare. "Do you not remember who my parents are? I've been well trained to handle any rogues who might attack. Plus, the border is still fairly far from here. But thank you very much for your concern."

This time he crossed his arms. "Oh really? So, hypothetically, let's say that twenty or so rogues come out of the forest right now. How do you plan to handle them all by yourself?"

My mouth opened, ready to argue, but the words caught in my throat. I'm sure I looked very attractive, jaw opening and closing like a fish. Finally, I shot him the finger and turned away.

"That's what I thought," he said.

"I hate you," I mumbled. He laughed quietly beside me.

It took twenty-five minutes to get back to the packhouse—twenty-five minutes of awkward silence and annoying whistling from Jasper. When he started walking up the drive, I pulled him back sharply. He gave me a confused look.

"What?"

"You can't just walk up to the front door!" I hissed.

"Why not? You live here."

I bit my lip, watching as his face went from confusion to amusement with a hint of awe.

"You're not supposed to be out, are you?" he asked.

"That's not your business!" I snapped.

"Wow. Never would have thought *you* would break the rules."

"Would you just go?"

"How did you get out?" he asked instead. For the millionth time that night, I groaned out loud.

"Out my window. Okay? Now, will you leave?"

He laughed, trying to cover it with a cough. "Damn, Violet. Okay, okay. I'm gone." He patted my head like I was three years old and walked back the way we'd come.

I took the opposite way, scurrying around the bushes lining the sidewalk and into the shadows of the front lawn. I'd done this way too many times now, and in no time at all, I was at the back of the house, climbing the tree that led to my window. Slipping in carefully, I let out a breath of relief, smiling to myself. The lamp beside my bed clicked on, and the smile fell from my face. Mom sat on my bed, her face the personification of anger.

Shit.

CHAPTER 2

VIOLET

Mom stared at me, possibly too angry to speak. Her aura was growing by the second; I was surprised I hadn't felt it coming in. I decided to break the silence. I opened my mouth to speak, but she held up her hand. I closed it and waited. Finally, she spoke, her voice as cutting as ice.

"Where. Have. You. Been?" She said each word distinctly, gritting them out between her teeth.

"Uhm. . . out," I muttered. She raised her eyebrows. "Out with some friends," I clarified.

"Do you have *any* idea what time it is?"

"Uh. . . midnight?" I guessed. It had been close to then when I checked last.

"Midnight. And you were out. With friends." She blinked for the first time. "And drinking?"

There was no point in lying. "A little."

"And?"

"And what?"

"And what else?"

"And nothing else," I cocked an eyebrow at her.

"Violet." She looked away, her eyes scanning over the walls of my room. "Don't lie to me."

"I'm *not*. What else do you think I was doing Mom?"

"You were out with Dylan?"

"Yes," I admitted.

She gave me *that* look, the same look she gave me every time Dylan was around. I caught on to what she was implying and cringed visibly.

"Goddess Mom, I didn't do anything with Dylan! I didn't do anything with *anybody*!"

"You snuck out, *again*, you were drinking, and you were with a boy. What am I supposed to think?"

"I was with *friends*, not just Dylan. Isa was there, too. You have to stop assuming him and I are a thing!"

"Where were you, exactly?" she asked.

"I was. . . out." Smooth.

"Yes, but where?"

I sighed. "I went to a party, okay?" I crossed the room and flopped onto my beanie bag chair.

She stared at me. "Whose party?"

"Someone from school, Mom."

"Drop the attitude, Violet." She stood up, pacing in front of me. "Do you have any idea how worried I was? You're lucky I didn't wake your Dad. He would have sent people out to find you!"

I shuddered, because I knew she was right.

"This has to stop," she continued. "We can't keep doing this! We set certain rules for you to follow, and you just can't seem to follow them! Why? Why is it so important to disobey us? To make us worry about you?"

"I wasn't trying to worry you. I just wanted to have some fun," I said.

"You'll be eighteen in two weeks. It's time to start acting like an adult Violet."

My anger was burning. I threw her a glare. "Maybe if you didn't keep me locked up in here, I wouldn't feel the need to sneak out."

She met my tone. "I don't keep you locked up. You can go anywhere you want."

I scoffed loudly. "Right! As long as I tell you three days in advance, give you everyone's contact information, a GPS location, and take one of Aunt Clara stupid locater pendants! You want me to act like an adult, yet you treat me like a child!" I practically yelled.

"There are things out there that are worse than rogues Violet! I make you carry those pendants so we can always find you!"

"Why not just lock me in the dungeon Mom? At least I can't climb out the window there!"

"Ugh!" She sat heavily on the bed, her head in her hands. A wave of guilt washed threw me. I knew I wasn't an easy child; I never had been. At the same time, I felt like I had a valid point. Growing up, Mom and Dad would occasionally leave the pack for business, leaving us in the care of our grandparents. My friends talked endlessly about trips they'd taken, places they'd been. Me? To this day, I'd never been outside the pack. Not even to Uncle Killian's pack, which was practically merged with ours. What stung more was Garrett *had*. Because he was taking over as Alpha someday, he had to learn the ins and outs of the job and title. But I couldn't go to one freaking party? How was that fair?

As if he'd heard my thoughts, the door opened and my brother poked his head in, looking between Mom and myself.

"What's going on?" he asked.

"None of your business," I snapped. His mouth pressed into a thin line at my tone. He took in my clothes and my shoes and our mother still on my bed.

"You snuck out again, didn't you?"

"Again, not your business."

"Why do you have to be such a bitch?"

"Why do you have to be so nosey?" I threw back.

"Enough!" Moms' aura washed over us, effectively shutting us up. "Garrett, don't call your sister names. Violet," she raised her head to look at me, ", is there even a point in grounding you?"

I shrugged, not answering. Mom sighed.

"Fine. I'll talk to your Dad in the morning about this."

"*Great,*" I replied sarcastically. Shaking her head, she ushered my brother out the door and left. I kicked off my shoes and checked my phone. Three missed calls from

Dylan, and eight texts. I scrolled through them quickly, not really reading them before shutting it off. I wasn't in the mood to talk to anyone now. I stood up and stripped out of my clothes before going to my bathroom and turning on the shower. I washed quickly, removing what little make-up I had on and trying to release some of the tension in my body.

When I felt a little better, I threw on whatever pajamas my hands touched in my dresser and crawled into bed, turning off the light.

***

I woke up to the sound of someone knocking on my door. I rolled over lazily, calling that it was open. When my Dad walked in, I simply lay in bed and stared at him.

"Have you come to haul me away for my punishment?" I asked.

"Breakfast is ready."

And he shut the door. I got up and made my way to the bathroom. Apparently, this morning wasn't going to be any better than last night.

After I was presentable, I joined my family in the dining room. The room was converted from a bedroom on our floor, because Mom wanted a place to have family dinners other than in the cafeteria. I took my seat at the table and started to fill my plate with bacon, eggs, pancakes and hashbrowns. Garrett eyed me over the table, but I ignored him. Mom was sitting in her chair, sipping her morning coffee while Dad turned off the stove. I forked a piece of pancake into my mouth as he sat down; Mom put down her cup and Garrett leaned back in his chair. Everyone stared at me.

"Just get it over with," I grumbled around another bite.

"You know you're in trouble," Dad got to the point without any preamble.

"Obviously," I retorted.

"But we're not grounding you."

My fork stopped halfway to my mouth. I looked between the three of them.

"Last night I asked you why you refuse to follow the rules we've set down for you. I want an answer," Mom said.

I looked at her and decided to tell her the truth. "Because it's not fair."

"What isn't fair?" Dad asked.

I set down my fork. "You guys don't let me have a life. Garrett can do anything he wants, and you never say anything. I can't even hang out with my friends without a list of requirements beforehand. You let him leave the pack, but somehow, it's too dangerous for me. I feel like you guys don't trust me. You want me to be an adult, but you don't let me experience what adulthood is like," I shrugged. "It's just easier to do things my way and faces the consequences later."

Mom and Dad looked at each other, their eyes glazing over as they mindlinked. Garrett was looking at his plate, his brow furrowed. His red hair was messy from sleep. Even though we were twins, we honestly weren't that much alike. Our looks, obviously, but our attitudes as well. Garrett was adamant on following the rules. He always had been. He avoided trouble where he could, rarely ever getting into fights, and he studied hard at school. He was also introverted, preferring to keep to himself. I had no doubt he would make a great Alpha someday.

Not that I didn't try. I did well in school. I enjoyed a good book too. But unlike Garrett, who was content to stay in Blood Moon, I wanted to see everything I could. I had a wild side, an adventurous side. I was opinionated, probably a little too much at times. I didn't mind trouble, but I didn't go out of my way to find it. I had been suspended from school a few times for starting fights. For good reasons, I thought, like when Sarah was bullying a girl in my math class. Mom had laid into me, but I wasn't sorry.

Still, it seemed that I just didn't meet my family's expectations. Eventually, I stopped trying.

Dad cleared his throat, bringing me back to the conversation.

"We think you make a valid point, Violet." I raised my eyebrows. "So, here's what's going to happen."

"We're not grounding you," Mom said. "We're going to try a compromise."

"What kind of compromise?" I asked.

"You don't need to tell us where you're going or who you're with, as long as it's within pack borders. Also, you still need to take Aunt Clara's pendant with you wherever you go. And you need to be home by eleven if you go out."

"What if I want to leave the pack?"

"Then you need to take two warriors with you, and we will need to know where you're going and who you're with," Dad said.

It was the best I could probably hope for. I was excited at the prospect of finally having more freedom, even if it was supervised.

"I think. . . that's fair," I agreed. Mom exhaled, and Dad gave me a small smile.

"And," Mom said. I looked at her nervously. "We're sorry you've been feeling this way. From now on, let's just talk, okay?"

"Okay."

I gave her a hesitant smile, which she returned.

CHAPTER 3

DYLAN

Violet hadn't replied to any of my messages. Was she really that pissed at me? It wasn't entirely my fault; I wasn't expecting Sarah to pounce on me the way she did. Still, I had to admit she knew what she was doing. But I didn't think it called for Violet ditching me.

I pulled up to school, parked in my usual spot, and grabbed my bag from the passenger seat. I threw on my sunglasses and locked the car. As usual, there was a group of girls waiting inside the doors to swarm me. I smiled politely, pushing through. I needed to talk to Vie. I took the halls until I found her at her locker, gathering her books for the day. She glanced at me as I approached, but didn't acknowledge me in any other way.

"Hey," I greeted her.

"Hey."

I leaned against the metal, looking down at her face. "So, I missed you last night."

"Really? From what I remember, you seemed to be enjoying yourself." She closed her locker and turned to me.

"Come on, Vie. I didn't mean to."

She raised one eyebrow at me. "Seriously? What, did you slip and fall into her vagina?"

"She initiated it."

"Okay. Good for her."

I caught her hand. "Don't be mad, please. It won't happen again."

Violet shook her head. "I'm not mad, Dylan. At least, not for the reason you think I am."

"Then why are you?"

"Dylan, almost everyone in our grade was at that party. Your birthday is *tomorrow*. Your future mate could have seen what you were doing! It was so tasteless." She shook her head.

"Not this again. Not everyone waits for their mate, Vie."

"I know. But most people have enough class not to parade it in front of everyone. I know if I turned out to be your mate, I'd be pretty upset."

She patted me on the shoulder before turning and walking away.

"She's not wrong, you know."

Garrett appeared beside me, looking after his sister.

"You think?"

He nodded. "Violet can be a handful. But in this case, I have to agree with her."

A wave of shame engulfed me. I thought about all the girls I'd seen last night, making out with different guys. What if any of them turned out to be my mate? Looking at it from that perspective, I had to admit that I didn't like the feeling. I gazed after Violet's retreating form; I was so sure she was my mate. I'd been looking forward to it since I met her. Would she really be disgusted by me? Would she even accept me?

Garrett and I walked to class together. He told me about how Vie got caught last night and what happened this morning.

"It's about time, too. I told Dad ages ago to ease up on her," he said as we sat down. "I hate that she views me as being against her," he frowned.

"Awe, dude, she knows you love her. You're her brother."

"Yeah, I know."

Out of the corner of my eye, I saw Jasper Cole walk in. Jasper, attending class? That had to be a first. I saw Garrett give me a look, saying he was thinking the same thing. Almost as soon as he sat down, every girl in the class started eyeing him, giggling, and trying to get his attention. Goddess, what was with them? The guy was a douche. Yeah, he was okay looking, but his attitude sucked. I watched as a brunette leaned across the aisle, flipping her

21

hair and pushing her breasts together. Jasper barely looked in her direction, and eventually, she sat back, disappointed.

"If you catch more flies with honey with than vinegar, does that make Jasper the honey?" Garrett whispered to me.

"Nah," I whispered back. "You catch more flies with shit than anything."

"This shit isn't deaf," Jasper said loudly. He turned in his seat, eyeing the both of us. "You got a problem?"

"Nope," I replied. "Just wondering why every girl falls for an asshole like you."

He smirked. "Maybe they know what I can give them."

"What you've got isn't much to brag about," Garrett said. Jasper turned to him.

"Your sister seems to think otherwise."

I tried to stop him, truly. My hand grazed Garret's arm as he flew past me, hauled Jasper out of his seat, and pinned him against the wall.

"What the fuck did you say?" he growled.

"Oh, you didn't know I was with your sister last night?" Despite his situation, Jasper looked less than concerned.

"What did you do with her?!"

Jasper peeled Garret's fingers off his collar, giving him a shove back. "Chill, dude. I only walked her home. No goodnight kiss or anything."

My anger rose as he smirked at me. Everyone knew how I felt about Violet; it was no big secret.

"Stay the fuck away from my sister," Garrett snapped. Jasper simply widened his smirk.

The teacher then graced us with her presence, and Garrett returned to his seat angrily. The entire class, he eyed the back of Jasper's head murderously. I noticed a couple of girls passing notes back and forth behind the teacher's back. A few of the girls who'd already shifted were mindlinking.

When the bell rang, Garrett stalked out the door. I'd only seen him so angry a couple of times before, and always, it was about Violet. He really was protective over her. By lunchtime, he'd calmed down some, mostly, I thought, because he hadn't run into Jasper the douche again.

"You want to come over tonight, play some Halo or something?" he asked me. We were standing in line, waiting to get our food.

"Sure."

"I just got a new game; It's awesome."

"Sounds cool."

"You okay? You seem kind of-"

A loud gasp cut off Garrett's words. Actually, there was more than one; I think everyone in the cafeteria gasped simultaneously, creating one audible effect. My head turned in the direction of everyone else around me, almost as if I didn't have a choice. What I saw confused the shit out of me. Violet stood in the middle of the room, her chest heaving up and down, her face red, and an expression of pure fury I'd only ever seen on her mother's face.

In front of her, holding his right cheek, was Jasper. To my surprise, he was looking at the floor rather than at her. Had she *slapped* him? Why? As if on cue, she answered my question, speaking to Jasper.

"How *dare* you start such a vile rumor about me! I should kick your ass right here!" she seethed.

Rumor?

"What are you talking about?" Jasper asked.

Everyone leaned in, intent on the drama unfolding in front of us.

"You told my brother I slept with you!" she raged.

Jasper's eyes went wide. "No, I didn't!"

"Garrett!" Vie looked around until she spotted us. "Did he, or did he not, tell you this morning that something happened last night between us?"

I looked at my friend, along with everyone else. "I uh, made a joke about his, uh, size, and he said "that's not what your sister said last night" or something, and-"

Before he finished, Violet slapped Jasper again. Hard.

"Would you stop doing that? It was just a joke, I told him I was joking." Jasper grumbled.

"Well, clearly, someone didn't think it was a joke! Tell them, right now, Jasper. Tell everyone, or I swear-"

"Nothing happened. I walked you home, end of story." He looked around the cafeteria. "Who has been saying otherwise?"

A group of girls to my left ducked their heads. I eyed them, and Violet noticed. She stalked over to their table, slamming her hands down.

"Which one of you?"

They sat silently.

"Which one?!"

"I'm sorry." A small brunette spoke up, her voice barely above a whisper. I recognized her from our class this morning. "I didn't mean to. It's just, with his reputation-"

"You thought I'd fall onto his dick like every other girl at this school?" Violet finished for her. The girl just stared at her. "Keep my name out of your mouth from now on. Got it?"

She nodded vigorously, reminding me of the bobblehead I had in my car. Angrily, Vie swiped the girl's lunch tray onto the floor. It landed with a loud clang, food scattering. Then she looked at Garrett. "And you too."

With that, she stormed off, throwing the doors open and leaving. There was a collective release of breaths, the loudest from the brunette. Everyone started whispering, but I ignored it, turning back to Garett. He looked perplexed, a mix of guilt and annoyance on his face.

"You want me to talk to her?" I asked him.

"No. Let her cool off."

"Alright."

We got our food and sat down at a nearby table. Garrett ate silently, lost in his own thoughts. I looked around at the few teachers in the room, totally unsurprised they hadn't intervened. Everyone was more or less used to Violet's outbursts. They only got involved if it became physical. I looked down at my tray, picking at the mashed potatoes; I should have paid more attention this morning. Who knew those girls would take Jasper's words seriously? Even with his reputation?

Violet was proud, beyond proud, that she had waited this long for her mate. It was something her parents had instilled in them both: your mate was the greatest gift from the Goddess, your true other half. Growing up and learning about what her mother went through before she found our Alpha, I think that's what made Violet's resolve so strong. To her, her parents were her role models. They were iconic leaders, and the pack had never been better for it.

My eyes wandered up and landed on Jasper. He was sitting alone, his cheek stained red. His eyes were focused on the doors, the ones Violet had left through. *His* face was thoughtful. A tiny smile graced his lips, and a feeling of uneasy anger coursed through me. Just what was he playing at?

CHAPTER 4
DYLAN

I stayed at the packhouse that night, wanting to be near Violet when I turned eighteen. Garrett glanced at me every so often, probably wondering why I was so agitated. My legs were bouncing up and down like crazy, and my hands were shaking slightly. I was both nervous and excited. At quarter past eleven, Garrett was passed out sideways on his bed, the controller hanging limply in his hand. I took it and placed it on the floor, checking the time. Again.

What would it feel like? Mom and Dad told me there was nothing else like it, nothing in the world, to see your mate for the first time. I'll admit it: I was already in love with Violet. I had been for as long as I could remember. Would it feel more powerful than that, more powerful than the love I already carried for her? I was eager to find out. The problem was, would she accept me? I replayed her words over and over in my head from school; No, she will feel it too. The bond will help bring us together, help us move past my indiscretions.

I don't know how long I sat on the floor, staring into space and thinking about the girl down the hall, but when I checked the time again, it was five minutes to twelve. I jumped up, clutching my phone in my hand. I stared at it unblinkingly, watching the minutes tick down. Four minutes.

Three.

Two.

One.

I held my breath, waiting. When midnight hit, my head swung around to the door. My heart started beating faster with anticipation, and my hands felt clammy. I glanced back at my phone. Twelve oh one. Huh?

"Hello, Dylan."

"Whoa!" I jumped to my feet and looked around wildly. Laughter sounded, and it took me a stupid amount of time to figure out it was coming from in my head. It was my wolf!

"Hey. You're my wolf, right?" I thought to him.

"The one and only."

"Nice to finally meet you. What's your name?"

"Uhni."

"Uhni? That's odd."

"I did not choose my name, but I am proud to bear it."

"Oh. Well, it's nice to have you around. Finally. Hey, I have a question."

"What's that?"

"Why can't I feel the bond yet with Violet?"

"Have you considered the possibility that Violet is not our mate?"

No, that couldn't be right. Vie and I were perfect for each other. I looked at the door again, half expecting her to walk through. My eyes widened as I realized my mistake. I had to see her! Quietly crossing the room, I slipped out the door. She was only three doors down. My heart picked up with every step again, and Uhni was quiet in my head, waiting. I stood outside her door, my hand poised to knock. But something inside me held me back. Why couldn't I feel anything? I was close enough, for sure. Shouldn't I be able to scent her? According to my Mom, your mate's scent was the most attractive thing in the world to you. But all I could smell was the same scents I'd always associated with Violet.

Her favourite laundry detergent, a faint whiff of those damn incense she liked to burn, and the pizza we had earlier. Pepperoni, bacon, and extra cheese. These scents did not overwhelm me, though; they didn't make me want to break down the door and take her in my arms. I lowered my hand, suddenly unsure. As it swung down by my hip, the door opened.

"Hey. I've been waiting for you."

Violet stood in front of me, wearing blue silk pajama shorts and a matching top. Her hair was let loose, mussed from lying in bed. Her face was passive but nervous. She bit her lip, the little action that I loved so much. I looked into her unique, one-of-a-kind blue-green eyes, and I felt. . . nothing. Nothing like what was described to me. The disappointment that followed was crushing.

Violet wasn't my mate.

I reached out and caught the doorjamb to steady myself. I had been so sure. . .

"I'm sorry, Dylan," Vie reached out and patted my shoulder. The absence of sparks was another blow. "It just wasn't meant to be for us, I guess. But you *do* have a mate out there."

"I wanted it to be you," I said lowly.

"I know." She took a breath through her nose. "But that's not what the Goddess wants. She has someone else in mind for you."

I didn't know what to say. Vie smiled at me kindly.

"Did you meet your wolf?" she asked.

I nodded.

"What's his name?"

"Uhni."

"I can't wait to see what he looks like." She smiled again, her eyes wandering around the hall. "Well. . . I should go to bed. I'm sorry again. Maybe you'll meet your mate tomorrow at school."

"Yeah, maybe," I mumbled. "Night."

"Night."

She closed the door, and I dejectedly walked back to Garrett's room. To my dismay, he was awake when I entered.

"So?" he asked.

I shook my head. "It's not her."

His face mirrored my feelings. "Sorry, man."

"Thanks."

He rearranged his pillow. "But once you meet your true mate, you won't feel like this over my sister anymore."

"Yeah."

"It would have been cool though. Having you as a brother-in-law."

I gave a half chuckle. "I'm still your brother, man."

Garrett grinned at me as he lay back down. "I know. Get some sleep; we have school."

"'Kay."

I pulled out his day bed, not bothering to grab blankets or a pillow. Uhni talked to me until I fell asleep. It was nice having someone to talk to privately. And he had a wicked sense of humor, too. I guess it wasn't all bad; I got an awesome wolf. Before I knew it, Garrett was shaking me awake, ordering me to get moving. I rubbed my eyes and groaned.

"Come on, Dylan! We both slept in, and we're going to be late!" He was rushing around the room like a chicken with its head cut off. I briefly noticed he'd put on two different socks, and one side of his shirt was tucked in while the other hung loose. I shook my head.

"Dylan!"

"I'm up, relax!" Swinging my legs over the edge, I stood up, stretching. That wasn't the bed I'd hoped to stay in last night.

The thought made me remember, and with that came back my gloomy mood. I dressed quickly, borrowing some of Garrett's clothes. I let him pull me downstairs to the kitchen, where he rushed through a bowl of cereal, and I grabbed an apple. On our way out the door, we ran into Luna Lily. She looked at me expectantly, but she must have guessed rather quickly from my face because she placed her hand on my shoulder and gave me a sympathetic smile.

"Have a good day at school. I hope you find her." And she walked away.

"We have a great Luna," Uhni thought.

"Yeah, she's pretty amazing."

It felt like everyone was in attendance to witness my bad mood. We ran into Celia, one of the girls who worked in the pack house, who hugged me and told me not to worry about it. We ran into Isa in the driveway, who had already finished school a couple of years before. She kindly reminded me that if I *didn't* meet my mate, she was currently back on the market. *That* had me blushing and stuttering while Garrett laughed behind me. Awkwardly, I thanked her and got in the car. Thank Goddess Aunt Clara wasn't around to hear that!

Garrett yammered on the whole way to school. I didn't hear most of it. I was still trying to figure out why the Goddess would bless me with someone like Violet only to make her someone else's. Her face appeared in my mind, and I spent the rest of the drive thinking about the girl who would never be mine.

"Can I ask you something?" I interrupted Garrett.

"Sure."

"Would I even know? Doesn't Violet have to be eighteen, too?"

He sighed as he parked the car. Huh. When did we get to school?

"You know that's not how it works, Dylan." He side-eyed me. "She wouldn't feel as strong until she was eighteen, but she would know." He grabbed his backpack from the back seat. "So, you guys aren't mates. You can still be best friends."

"What if that's not enough? What if I don't meet my mate? Your parents are prime examples. Your Dad didn't meet your Mom when he was eighteen. . ."

"Our pack has grown a lot since then." He placed his hand on my shoulder. "I know how badly you wanted it to be Violet. But you have to let it go. She's going to end up with someone else, and so are you. Maybe not right now, but someday. That's just the way it is, Dylan."

"He's right. We cannot pine over someone who is not ours."

"I love her, though."

"I can see that. But the love you will have for our mate will be stronger."

I got out of the car, the wind blowing across my face. With it came an impossibly strong scent, one that nearly brought me to my knees: pineapples, strawberries, and a hint of lavender. Immediately, my feet started working while my nose tracked the smell. Garrett rushed to keep up with me, asking what was happening. Uhni was going absolutely insane in my head. The scent became stronger, and now I was running.

"Dylan!"

I left Garrett behind in my pursuit. Everything in me was trained on this one scent and my mission to find the source. Part of me, a huge part, hoped desperately that the Goddess had given me another chance. That the impossibly delicious smell was Violets, after all. Her face played in my mind as I ran. I turned left, right, and left again. Skidding around the corner of the building, I halted as my eyes found what my soul was searching for.

"Mate," I breathed.

CHAPTER 5
VIOLET

I felt awful. Terrible.

I could not get Dylan's face out of my head. His expression when he realized I wasn't his mate? Heartbreaking. All those times I'd secretly wished I wasn't. . . Last night had to be the first time I wished I had been. Yet, I was still relieved. Dylan and I were meant to be friends, best friends. But nothing more. And I was okay with that.

It just really sucked that he obviously wasn't.

I'd gotten up early, earlier than even Garrett, so as to avoid him. I'm sure I was the last person he needed to see right now. The last thing I wanted was to hurt him more. And it was clear as day that he was hurt. I'd stayed awake, lying in bed and nervously twisting the blankets, anxiously watching the clock on my bedside table. When the clock struck midnight, I half expected Dylan to come bursting through the door, and that would be it. But he didn't. As the minutes clicked by, and I realized that nothing in me had changed, I felt both relieved and sad.

And then he *had* come to my door, and what was I supposed to say? Better luck next time? Even if I didn't return his feelings, Dylan deserved happiness. That's all I wanted for him.

"What do you think, Vie?"

"Hmm?"

I looked up at Brianne. I hadn't heard a word she said. We were skipping first period, because neither of us wanted to do math today. Brianne and I had been friends since the start of high school. The girl I'd stuck up for and caused a fight? Yup, that's Brianne. She'd been so grateful, and we'd been buddies ever since. She was a cutie, with her medium-length golden blonde hair and freckles. She had a slender build, but with just the right amount of curves. Brianne was actually the niece of my Aunt Hazel, though I hadn't known that when I'd punched Sarah. Interestingly, she'd gotten the hazel eyes as well, complimenting her appearance.

"What's with you today?" She cracked open a bag of Doritos, offering them to me. I took a handful and popped one into my mouth.

"It's nothing. What were you saying?"

"I asked if you wanted to come to the party this weekend?"

"The party?"

"Yeah, Jasper's birthday party. He's turning eighteen."

My face clouded with anger at his name. Okay, so maybe the rumor wasn't his fault, not entirely, but did he really need to bring me into his spat with my brother? No, he didn't. So, yes, I partially blamed him. People at this school like to gossip- he should have left me out of it completely.

"Yeah, I'm good. I think I'd rather have a movie weekend," I said.

"Aww. That means I have to go alone!" Brianne pouted.

"Sorry chickie."

"Didn't you *just* get freedom? What better way to spend it than going to a party with your friend? One you don't have to sneak out for?" she argued.

Damn. She had a point.

"Plus, you know Isa is going to get wasted again. And that's always fun," she giggled.

"Fun, until it's your bathroom she's puking in the next day," I replied.

"Hmm, true. So, are you-"

Our conversation was interrupted by a figure rounding the corner. I jumped to my feet, which was the dumbest thing I could have done. The teachers knew our hiding spots though; If we were caught, we were caught. No sense in hiding. My insides clenched a little when I realized it wasn't a teacher though. It was *Dylan*. Oh, Goddess. Why was he here? I really didn't want to put him down again. . .

"Mate."

That one word coming from his mouth stopped my heart. I only started breathing again when I realized he wasn't looking at me. But that meant. . . I looked between him and Brianne. Her eyes were glued to his, both of them unmoving. Just starring at each other in awe. Gently, I gave her a little nudge forward. That's all it took. The next second, they were in each others' arms, trapped in a passionate kiss. I smiled hugely, beyond happy for my two friends.

"You smell like pineapples, but you taste like Doritos," Dylan told her. I laughed out loud as she blushed.

He looked at me, all traces of sadness gone. We grinned at each other, and I gave him a thumbs up.

"Looks like you have a partner for that party after all," I said.

"Looks like I do."

Of course, that happened to be the moment Mrs. Harris came around the corner, placing her hands on her hips. I smirked in her direction.

"Really girls? Again? And now you're dragging boys into your skipping!" She shook her head.

"Mrs. Harris, these two just found out their mates. Maybe give them the moment to bask in it a little?"

She looked between the two, her eyes growing.

"Oh. Congratulations." She sauntered off awkwardly back the way she came. I walked up to my friends, throwing my arms around them in a group hug.

"I'm happy for you guys." I looked at Dylan. "I told you so."

"Yeah, yeah." He brushed Brianne's hair back with his free hand.

"I'll leave you two alone. Have fun." I gave them one more squeeze and let go. "Just not too much fun. You're still at school."

"Vie!" Brianne hissed. Her cheeks were redder than a tomato.

"See ya!" I walked away as Dylan pulled her in for another kiss. Walking around the corner, I almost ran into Garrett.

"Did he find her?" he asked.

"Yup."

"Brianne?"

"Yup."

He grinned. "Didn't see that one coming."

"Me either."

We walked side by side back to the parking lot.

"Hey." Garrett turned to me. "I'm sorry about yesterday. About. . . you know. I get why you were pissed."

I shrugged. "Thanks."

"So. . ."

"So?"

"Our birthday is coming up."

"No shit?"

He gave me a look. "Are you excited?"

"I guess. You?"

"Yeah. I can't wait to find my mate." He looked back in the direction we left Dylan and Brianne. "I hope I get as lucky."

"You will." He looked at me, our eyes meeting. "Okay, so maybe I don't say this a lot. But you're a great guy, and I'm sure the girl who is my future sister-in-law is going to be just as great."

Garrett gave me his special smile, the one reserved for the people he loved best. I hadn't seen it in a long time. Not directed towards me anyway.

"Thanks, Vie." He punched my arm lightly. "Just don't *you* bring home an asshole," he laughed.

"No promises," I grinned.

We went our separate ways then, him to the little time of class he had left, and me to my locker. Skipping more than one class was sure to get me an earful from my parents if I wasn't in trouble already. I spun the lock, and it popped open. English, science, history; I grabbed everything I would need for the rest of the day. A shadow came to loom

35

over me. I glanced up to see Jasper smiling down at me. Ugh.

"Hey short stuff." He leaned against the metal next to me.

"Really? What happened to princess?" I asked casually.

He shrugged. "You said you didn't like it."

"So, you went with short stuff instead?" I rolled my eyes.

"Just trying out nicknames. You don't like that one either?"

I shook my head.

"I'll keep trying." His voice held a hint of a promise.

"Don't bother Jasper."

"Why not?"

"Why would you, I think is the better question." I shut my locker and looked up at him. Goddess, his eyes really were amazing.

"You coming to my birthday party this weekend?" He changed the subject. I narrowed my eyes at him.

"No."

His face clouded in disappointment. Though he could have been faking. "Why?"

"We're not friends Jasper. Truth be told, you kind of disgust me."

His hand flew to his heart is mock hurt. "Ouch! That's cold."

I shrugged. I wasn't going to take it back.

"You don't have to be someone's friend to come to their party," he continued.

"Actually, I think it's sort of a requirement." I started walking down the hall, and he fell into step beside me. Around us, other students stopped and stared.

"Why do you want me there anyway?" I asked quietly. I waited, but he didn't answer. "Well?"

I peeked up at him through my lashes, my stomach flipping a little at the look he was giving me. I'd seen him give that look to many girls before. Did he think his charm was going to work on me? Not likely. Yes, he was gorgeous, but I wasn't like the other girls here. I had respect for myself.

As if he could read my mind, he repeated my thoughts aloud. "You're not other girls. You respect yourself, and you're the only one not throwing herself at me any chance she gets."

I glanced at a group of seniors nearby. At Jaspers words, they looked away, but not before giving me icy glares.

"Thanks. But I have other plans," I told him.

"Alright. Well, if those plans change, here's my address." He slid a piece of paper into my hand; His skin was hot on mine, and my throat went dry at the touch. He gave me a dazzling smile, turned around and walked away. I stared after him for a second, trying to process.

Just what did Jasper Cole want with me?

CHAPTER 6
GARRETT

It was a Hell of a day. Dylan found his mate, I made basketball captain, and once again, my sister was the talk of the school. I'd been in the showers after gym class, minding my own, when I'd overheard the news.

"You think he likes her?" Jaden's voice echoed in the room.

"Nah. Not for real, anyway. Everyone knows Jasper only likes girls for one thing," Erik replied.

"I don't know man. Samantha said he was getting pretty cozy with her."

"Cozy?"

"Yeah, he was smiling at her shit. She said he never smiles like that."

"Huh. Maybe they're mates."

"Pfft!" Jaden laughed. "Jasper and Violet? No way! Everyone knows how the Purity Queen is. She'd reject him in a second! He's been with half the school!"

"Yeah, but half the school have been with other guys. Violets a virgin." There was silence for a minute. "A *hot* virgin. I'd do her."

"Same. Those tits. . ."

I'd ended my shower before they went any further. Their faces went pale as soon as they saw me, both muttering apologies. I got the Hell out of there after that. Now, sadly, I had nothing better to do than think as I drove home. Vie opted to go to Brianne's after school to get the details on her and Dylan. And Dylan himself went with them, unwilling to be away from his newfound mate. It was amazing, I thought, that only this morning he was heartbroken over my sister, and now he had eyes for nobody else but Brianne.

I frowned as I thought. Of course I was happy for Dylan. He was my best guy friend. But truthfully, I'd been hoping Vie was his mate. Goddess only knew who the guy was that's her other half.

"Maybe they're mates."

Eriks voice ran through my head again and my hands tightened on the steering wheel. Jasper couldn't be her mate, could he? I knew him, too well. He was a self-centered, selfish, egotistical asshole who didn't care about other people's feelings. Jasper Cole was the reason I, like my sister, was also waiting for my mate. Although I wasn't as 'pure' as she was. My heart clenched in my chest as the memories, never from far the front of my mind, came flooding in.

I'd had exactly one girlfriend my whole life. Sophia Chang. The love of my life. We met at the beginning of high school. She was so beautiful, with her long blond hair, kind brown eyes and a smile that lit up the whole room. When she talked, you just had to stop and listen. When she laughed, it was like a symphony of bells. Sophia was incredibly smart, too. When I hadn't been doing so well in science, she was the one to step up and offer to tutor me. A couple of sessions at her house, and the sweetest first kiss under the apple tree in her backyard, and we were a couple.

I thought she was super sweet, not wanting to broadcast our relationship to the public. She'd told me she didn't want to be seen as the girl who was dating me only because of my future title. And I'd been happy to oblige her. It was a reasonable request, after all. We'd spent the next eight months going for walks in the forest, swimming in the lake, going to the beach, having precious intimate moments under the stars. Sophia wanted to wait for her mate, though I never doubted it was me. We were perfect for each other, perfectly connected on every level. Our love of books, our shared passion for art. And she was always there to support me, to lift me up in my moments of doubt about my future. She made me believe I could become the Alpha my Dad wanted me to be.

And then, like waking up from a nightmare disguised as a dream, everything was gone. In the span of one night, one party, my life and my heart, were shattered.

I turned the car carefully around the corner, lost in the wave of memories.

The music blaring. The lights dimmed. Classmates and friends laughing and drinking and having fun. Somewhere in the chaos, I'd lost Sophia. It had been a while, hadn't it? Excusing myself from our friends, I'd gone to look for her. Room after room I searched. Checked all the bathrooms. I even checked outside. The one place I hadn't thought I'd find her though, was in the farthest room of the house. In bed. Naked.

With Jasper Cole.

I clutched the steering wheel tighter still as my heart shattered all over again. Tears brimmed my eyes, and I fought to keep them back; The last thing I needed was to hit a tree or something. But the sounds playing in my head, the sounds my Sophia was making under another man. . . it might as well have been happening beside me, it was so clear. She was getting pleasure from someone else. She was giving herself to someone who wasn't me. She was betraying everything we had. And she was *enjoying it.*

Her face played in my mind the second she realized I'd entered the room. Shock, embarrassment, sadness. I'd been frozen in place as she pushed Jasper off, stuttering over her words trying to give me excuse after excuse for this tragedy. Finally, she'd simply lowered her head, tears streaming down her face, and whispered "I'm sorry." Those words brought me to the reality of the situation. Jasper had left already, which was for the best. In those two minutes standing like a statue, I'd come up with approximately a hundred different ways to murder him.

"It's over."

I'd choked those words out, my heart impossibly breaking more, and ran. Sophia followed or tried to. I was out of the house and in my car probably before she was dressed again. I'd sped home, running lights and stop signs.

And immediately went to my sister's room. One look at my face, and Violet had understood. That night we curled up in her bed, huddled together, just like when we were kids. If one of us had a bad dream, we would simply crawl in with the other, comforted by our twin's presence. Mom and Dad use to give us shit, after a certain age, but they didn't understand. I had a familial connection with Violet that exceeded even Dad's connection with Aunt Thara. Violet had been with me since conception, she understood me better than anyone. We shared a womb, then a crib, then a room before we got our own. But the knowledge that she was always there if I needed her, just a couple doors down, made it easier.

I'd told her everything. Between breaking down multiple times, I'd managed to sob out the whole story. Everything except who Sophia cheated on me with; At the time, I couldn't bear to say his name. I thought I'd lose whatever control I had left. Vie had listened, soothing me, reassuring me. Letting me cry my heart out. I spent the week sleeping on Vies floor, waking her up more often than needed with my tears. And each time, she would sit beside me, and listen, get me water if I needed it, or simply rub my back as I sobbed.

Only once did she ask who the other guy was, but I never told her. Now I wish I had. As I pulled into the packhouse, and parked beside my mom's green mustang, I thought maybe I should. It had been almost a year since my break-up with Sophia. I avoided her like the plague at school. But I couldn't stand it if my sister's mate turned out to be Jasper. If Violet knew it was him, she would reject him on sight.

In the back of my mind, a little voice was calling me selfish. I paused with my hand on the door. No, this was different. Jasper was the reason for my despair.

But is he even her mate?

I groaned. My conscience just wouldn't shut up. Irritated, I opened the door, slamming it shut behind me. Swinging the keys around my finger as I walked, I tried to

41

really think it through. Was it worth starting up so much drama right now?

"Hello Garrett."

Looking up, I met Gamma Lukes eyes. I considered him my uncle, along with Ben, even though we weren't related by blood. His mate, Miguel, was standing beside him, smiling politely at me. I nodded at them.

"Hey. What are you doing here?"

"Had some business to go through with your Dad." He held up a stack of papers. "I'm telling you Garrett, I can't wait until you take over. I can finally retire." He sighed happily.

Beside him, Miguel laughed. "And what will you do in retirement? Admit it, you would be bored to death."

"You know me too well," Luke grumbled.

"Maybe I'll keep you on as my assistant or something. And give you plenty of paperwork to do," I joked.

"Ugh! No, I'd rather be bored to death, thanks."

"I'll keep the offer open, in case you changed your mind." I slapped his shoulder as I passed.

"Oh, your Dad is looking for you. He's in his office," Luke called after me.

"Thanks."

Starting up the stairs and wondering for the billionth time why Dad didn't put in an elevator, I tried to clear my mind of my own problems. It wasn't easy, reliving my worst memories only minutes ago. Mom and Dad still knew nothing about my relationship with Sophia, or how it ended. Not that I didn't trust them, but my humiliation wasn't something I wanted everyone to know. Violet, I knew, would never tell anyone. And there was something about my parents, the Alpha and Luna no less, knowing I'd been played for a fool that left my guts twisting in knots. As future Alpha, I should have known better.

Reaching our floor, I admired the art on the walls as always as I walked to my Dads office. Over the years, I'd helped him acquire new pieces from various artists that were now scattered around the packhouse. My particular favorite was an abstract piece hanging in the foyer, of bright yellows, blues, and reds smeared across the canvas in utter pandemonium. There was no rhyme or reason to the streaks of color, leaving the imagination open to run free.

I knocked on the door, three quick raps.

"Come in."

I pushed open the door and met my Dads tired eyes. His short black hair was messy, probably from him running his hands through it.

"Hey Dad."

"Garrett. Come sit." He gestured to one of the vacant chairs. I sat casually, setting my backpack down beside me.

"Luke said you wanted to see me?"

Dad leaned back in his chair, resting his hands on his desk.

"Yes. I wanted to talk to you about your birthday."

"Okay."

He met my eyes. "You'll be eighteen."

"No shit? You remember how old I am?" I feigned surprise. The corner of his mouth twitched in a smile.

"Don't be a smartass."

I chuckled in response. "Go on."

"With your birthday so close, I think it's time we talk about mates. Your future mate, specifically."

CHAPTER 7
GARRETT

"Alright."

Folding his hands together, Dad took a minute to think. I waited patiently, not sure where he was going with this. I thought we'd already had this talk? It was coupled with the incredibly awkward sex talk Vie and I had received a few years back. I hoped beyond hope that he remembered we'd had *that* talk, because I wasn't up for another round. It was bad enough the first time.

"You know that your Mom and I don't like to get involved in your personal lives, you and your sister," he paused. "Unless your sister gets in trouble," he added.

"Which is a lot," I said. He pursed his lips in agreement.

"Anyway, I called you in here. . . well, I wanted to tell you some things about me, my past."

I nodded. "Okay. . ."

"Before I met your Mom. . . well, I got around." His forehead furrowed. "And it caused problems in our relationship."

"I thought the biggest problem was that you were an asshole?" I interrupted.

Dad gave me a look which I returned.

"Okay, that didn't help," he conceded. "But you, Garrett, are not an asshole. I am beyond proud of the man you've become."

My face flushed with the compliment.

"My point is, I'm hoping that you have a better. . . reputation than I had. With girls, I mean."

Now my forehead furrowed. "What are you saying?"

Dads' cheeks reddened slightly. "To put it bluntly, I'm asking if you've had sex. With different girls."

I almost laughed just at the look on his face. "No Dad. I haven't uh, done that with anyone actually." Not that I was spotless on the subject, but he didn't need to know the other things I'd done. Still, he raised an eyebrow at me. When he did that, the resemblance between him and Vie was uncanny.

"Nobody?" he asked.

"Nope."

"Uh, alright." He laid his hands down. "Good. That's good."

"Was that really all you wanted to talk to me about?"

"Yes," he sighed. "The last thing the pack needs is a jealous ex-lover causing trouble for you when you meet your mate, whoever she is."

This time I did laugh. "I don't think the *entire* pack would be very effected if there was one."

He didn't laugh with me. In fact, his face grew serious. "Do not underestimate the power of a woman who feels betrayed son. As the saying goes, 'Hell hath no fury like a woman scorned.'"

My smile fell from my lips. In that second, the look in his eyes, I was positive there was something he wasn't telling me. The next second though, he was smiling.

"I'm glad you didn't take after me in this respect though. I'm also very happy that your Mother agreed to have this talk with Violet. It was bad enough she was away when Violet got her first period." He shuddered visibly. I knew he was trying to change the subject, so I went with it. I'd keep my questions aside for now.

"Yeah, that was pretty rough. For you."

He cringed at the memory. "You can go now. I'm sure you have homework."

"Yeah." Grabbing my bag, I stood. "Oh, by the way, I made captain."

"Did you? That's great Garrett! Give me a copy of the schedule so I don't miss any games."

"I will. See you at dinner."

He nodded, already focused on his laptop and reaching for his phone. I looked at him a second more, realizing I was looking into my own future, before I left the room. I walked to my room, remembering the times I'd sit in that office with him, begging him to give me something to do. Being Alpha wasn't just what I was born to do; It was what I always wanted to do. I couldn't imagine anything better than having the opportunity to help my pack, to give back to them. Mom worked as a doctor in the pack hospital, and I think she was always a little aggrieved that neither Violet nor I wanted to go down that path as a career.

Not that medicine didn't fascinate me. I read her medical books until I had them mostly memorized. But that was just another part of Alpha training for me. I wanted to know as much as possible, anything that would help me become a better leader. Dad was amazing- the best role model. But I had ideas and visions for Blood Moon. I wanted to take us further than ever. Hopefully, I would make him proud.

Shutting my door, I flopped onto my bed, pulling out my homework. I flew through the English and math, my most boring subjects. History and science were a bit trickier for me, but I liked the challenge, and still managed to pull off a low A grade. I was halfway done when my door opened, and Violet appeared.

"Hey."

"Hey." Her tone was tired.

"What's up?" I asked as I turned back to my work. "You're home early. I thought you'd be home after dinner."

"Had to come home." She face-planted onto my bean bag chair. "I couldn't be around them anymore," she groaned into the soft material.

"Brianne and Dylan?" I finished the last question in my history homework as we talked. "Were you starting to get jealous?" I smirked at her.

She turned her head and shot me a dirty look. "No, asshole. They're just so. . ." Her face scrunched up. "*Lovey.*"

"Lovey?" I chuckled.

"You know, like mushy and stuff." She flopped onto her back, staring at the ceiling. "I couldn't take it anymore."

I pulled out my science homework. "Just think, sis. In a week and a bit, you'll be the exact same way with your mate."

"Ew."

"Come on. I've seen you reading all those romance novels. You have a soft side."

"That stuff doesn't happen in real life, Garrett."

"Not according to Mom and Dad. Remember what Dad did for their anniversary?"

Violet grinned. "Yeah. The fancy candlelight dinner under the stars and moon. Mom loved it."

"See? Chivalry isn't dead."

"Maybe not. I guess it depends on who your mate is."

My pencil stopped, hovering over the page. I bit the inside of my cheek, wondering if I should tell her or not. I had planned to. . . But again, was it worth it right now? What if her mate turned out to be Bryan, from the basketball team? Or Erik? Hell, maybe he wasn't even in Blood Moon.

"What's wrong?"

I looked at my sister, who was watching me with curious eyes. She'd blow a gasket if I told her right now. Making up my mind, I determined not to say anything. Fow now.

"Nothing. Just thinking about this problem," I pointed to the page.

"Oh." She picked up the controller to my game station. "After your done, want to play? I have a feeling Brianne isn't coming over for a while."

"Sure. Dylan was supposed to come over, but obviously he's busy."

She made a face again. She played a couple rounds by herself while I finished up, and then I joined her on the floor. We played until Mom came to get us for dinner.

"You okay? You were really quiet at dinner," Violet asked me as we walked to our rooms.

"Yeah. Just thinking about the future."

"Like Alpha stuff?"

"Yeah."

She nodded. "Congrats on making captain by the way."

"Thanks. Night."

"Yup."

I carried on to my room. Not bothering to undress, I lay down in bed, staring at the wall. No, I wouldn't say anything. But if it so happened. . . if the world was cruel enough to give her Jasper as a mate, I would. That little voice piped up again, but I squashed it and went to sleep.

CHAPTER 8
VIOLET

I was, admittedly, extremely anxious. I couldn't quite recall a moment in my life when I was this nervous. My birthday was tomorrow! Tomorrow! Which meant I would find my mate. Maybe. Hopefully? Possibly.

"What if he's a monster?" I mumbled to myself as I walked through the woods.

I'd been taking these walks more often recently, having become restless the last week or so. I had barely eaten anything in the last three days, my appetite leveling off at zero. I knew this was normal; some people ate like they were eating for ten, and others were like me. Mom even ordered my favourite pizza last night, but I couldn't touch it. So, I went for a walk instead. Now here I was again, wandering aimlessly around the forest, talking to myself.

"I hope he's at least attentive," I sighed. "It would suck donkey balls if I had a mate who never listened to me."

That only made me think about my newly mated friends. Dylan and Brianne had been inseparable, going everywhere together, and pining vocally for each other when they couldn't be together, like in class. Me? I was the one who had to listen to it. As my birthday grew closer, I was getting more short-tempered. Wednesday, I'd snapped at Brianne in English, immediately feeling awful. She assured me it was okay, that she understood. But still.

Garrett wasn't much better than I was at the moment. The only difference is that he did have an appetite. Yet, he was as hot tempered as I was lately, which was unusual to see. I looked up at the sky, amazed that it was already darkening. I hadn't realized I'd been out here that long; I'd left around two. Then I realized where I was.

The clearing where Mom had her first shift.

A smile spread across my face as I looked around. Mom had brought me here years ago, and then a few times since, reliving the memory of her first shift, and how she thought she could avoid Dad because he'd upset her. And then how he'd found her, totally pissed off that she'd run away.

A laugh escaped me as I recalled the next part- dads face when he saw moms wolf for the first time, and her telling him off afterwards. Boy, I wish I had been alive then to see that.

"What's funny?"

I started at the voice behind me. Whirling around, I immediately took a fighting stance, my eyes narrowing as they landed on Jasper. He threw his hands up in surrender, taking a step back.

"Easy tiger. I'm not here to fight you."

Slowly, I straightened up. "What are you doing out here?" I asked him sharply.

"I was out for a walk, and I saw you. Thought I'd come say hi." He shrugged.

"You seem to be running into me a lot lately." I crossed my arms. "What's up with that?"

"Maybe I'm just lucky." He shot me a grin, and my stomach did a little flip. I pushed the feeling aside.

"Yeah, I don't think that's it."

"You missed my birthday."

I rolled my eyes. He'd asked me at least twenty times to go to his stupid birthday party. My answer was no every time. Instead, I'd stayed in and watched old horror movies and ate more junk food than I cared to admit. Still a better way to spend the night, though.

"Happy birthday," I told him nonchalantly.

He took a few steps, placing himself in front of me. "Don't I get a birthday kiss?"

"Nope."

"Ouch."

I rolled my eyes again, turning away from him.

"Are you excited for tomorrow?" he asked.

"What's tomorrow?" I played dumb. He gave me a look.

"*Your* birthday."

"Oh, yeah. How'd I forget that?"

He chuckled lowly beside me. "Think you'll find your mate?"

"I don't know," I replied honestly.

Jasper looked up into the sky. I took the chance to peek at him. The sky was clear, casting the last rays of light through the woods. Long shadows fell over the ground, ours and the trees and bushes. An orange hue played around him from the setting sun, lighting up his features. His hair shone, taking on an auburn colour, and his eyes reflected the light of the sky. In this light, he seemed even more muscular, his white t-shirt clinging to him. My mouth went completely dry as my eyes landed on his jeans, and the outline I saw there. Well, damn.

"It's rude to stare at people."

My eyes met his as I felt blood rush to my face. He smirked at me cockily.

"I wasn't staring at you," I lied.

"Sure."

I turned my face away, hoping my hair covered my blazing cheeks. Jasper sank to the ground, patting the spot next to him.

"Seriously?" I asked. "What makes you think I want to hang out with you?"

"I wouldn't call this 'hanging out'." He looked around. "I was out for a walk, you were out for a walk, and we both needed a break."

I almost smiled at his stupidity. Almost.

"Fine." I slumped to the ground next to him, keeping some distance between us. We sat in silence for a while. I stared at a tree with an odd shape in its trunk, listening to the sounds of the forest around me. After a while, Jasper spoke.

"I'm scared," he said.

I turned my head to look at him, but he was looking up at the sky still. It was slowly beginning to fill with stars, reflecting in his eyes.

"Why?" I asked.

"I'm scared of my first shift," he explained.

I thought about that for a minute. "But males have an easier time than females."

"I guess." He lifted one shoulder in a half shrug.

"If sure you'll be fine," I paused. "Honestly, I'm freaked out too." My voice wavered at the end, giving away just how freaked out I actually was.

"You?" He gave me a look of mock bewilderment. "But you're not scared of anything."

"Oh, shut up." I threw a twig at him. "Everyone is scared of something, you know."

"Yeah. That's true."

"You didn't meet your mate yet?" I asked.

"I'm out here with you, aren't I?" I shot him a wide-eyed look. He laughed. "What I mean is, I'm not holed up in my room with a mate right now."

"Oh." I looked away, another blush on my face. "Yeah."

"What about you?"

"Obviously not. Or I wouldn't be out here either."

"Fair enough." He leaned back on his hands. "Are you excited to meet him?"

I thought through my answer. "Maybe."

"Maybe?" His tone was confused.

"Well, I guess it depends on who it is," I said. "I know that some people don't get the best mates. And some people get rejected." I sighed. "I just hope whoever he is, he's good to me."

"I'm sure he will be. How could he not be, honestly?"

I met his eyes, and my breath hitched at the look in them. I'd never seen Jasper look at anyone so tenderly, so gently. Somehow, it made me feel better. Made me feel reassured.

"Thanks," I said quietly.

We lapsed back into silence, but it was less uncomfortable now. Actually, it was surprising me more and more how comfortable I did feel right now. Obviously, I wasn't his biggest fan, and given my mood recently, it was downright amazing I hadn't slugged him upon seeing him. What was even more odd, was a part of me wanted to keep talking to him.

"So, uh. . ." I cleared my throat, much to his amusement. "Are your parents coming tomorrow?"

His smile faltered, and I regretted asking.

"Yeah," he replied monotonously.

"You don't seem very happy about it," I pressed.

He let out a breath. "You don't know much about me, do you?"

His question took be my surprise. "Not really," I admitted.

He tugged his knees into his chest, resting his chin on them. "Did you know I wasn't born into Blood Moon?"

My eyes widened again. "No."

"My Mom was a rogue."

A rogue? "Did she bring you here?" I asked curiously.

He shook his head. "I wandered into Blood Moon territory when I was six. We were attacked one night and. . . she died protecting me."

"Oh." My eyes shifted to the ground. "I'm sorry."

"Don't be."

I lifted my gaze to his again.

"I loved my Mom. And she loved me. I know she would do the same thing again if she had another chance. There was nothing I could do, and I've accepted that."

As much as he tried to hide it, I still saw the pain on his face. Instinctively, I reached out and placed my hand on his shoulder, leaning over.

"I think that's a good way to look at it," I said.

"Yeah. I do wish she could be here tomorrow night, but my adoptive family will be, so I take that as a win."

"How did you. . . I don't mean to pry but. . ." I flopped around in my head, trying to find a way to ask my question. Jasper patted my hand that was still on his shoulder.

"Your Mom took me in actually," he smiled. "The Beta found me wandering around the woods and brought me to the packhouse. The same night, your Mom found an amazing family who were willing to take me in."

"The Coles."

"Yup."

"And your Dad?" I asked. "Was he a rogue too?"

His expression instantly hardened. The change was so fierce, my hand fell away from his shoulder. The air grew tense, and I knew I shouldn't have asked that particular question.

"My Dad-," He spit the word, "-was never around. Mom never mentioned him either. I don't even know if he knows I exist. He wasn't there to help protect us, to protect her. I'm better off without him, and I don't need to know who he is."

I stared at him, too stunned to reply. A sharp pang of sympathy, sympathy I knew he didn't want, hit me. I couldn't imagine my life without my Dad.

"I'm sorry. . ." I whispered.

Jasper took a deep breath. "No, I'm sorry. I shouldn't have snapped like that. I just don't like to talk about him."

"Understandable. I won't bring it up again."

"Thanks."

The silence was, once again, awkward.

CHAPTER 9
VIOLET

I looked at my phone, checking the time.

"I should get going. It's almost midnight, and I know my parents are waiting up so they can be the first to wish us a happy birthday." I rolled my eyes, but I was smiling. They've been doing that ever since I could remember.

"Sure. See you later Violet."

I paused as I got up. Even though this was better than any other time we talked, I didn't think I'd do it again. It wasn't like we were friends now; I just didn't feel the need to be quite as much of a bitch to him anymore. So instead of replying, I simply nodded and started walking away. I could feel his eyes on me as I headed in the direction of the packhouse.

I started running through the forest, jumping over logs and skirting bushes in order to make it back on time. My mind wandered as I ran. Tomorrow I would be running with four legs instead of two. I wondered what I would look like. Garrett had expressed his theory that one of us were Mother Wolves, like Mom, but I doubted it. Something like that happened once in a blue moon, and no blue moon was scheduled anytime soon.

A shiver of fear ran up my spine as I thought about my shift. Mom had described it to me many times, giving me advice on how to handle it in case I didn't have my mate there to help me. She made it sound horrifying, and it probably was. What if I did have to go through it alone? My parents promised they would be there in any case, but that didn't help me. Only a mate could take away the majority of the pain caused by the first shift. There was a lot of guys in our pack, and none had come to me claiming me as their mate. If they were eighteen or older, they would know before I would. I bit my lip worriedly as I exited the tree line and slowed to a jog.

What if my mate wasn't in this pack? Would he feel it when I started to shift? Would he come for me? I could only hope so. I rounded the side of the packhouse, my eyes finding Garrett walking up the steps.

"Hey," I said. "You were out too?"

"Yeah." He swept the sweat from his brow off. "I needed to go for a run."

"I know what you mean."

Together, we entered the packhouse, only to be greeted by our smiling parents, Uncle Ben and Uncle Luke, and their mates. Even Uncle Killian and Aunt Thara were here. Everyone except Grandpa Gideon and Grandma Rose, who were still on 'vacation.' They called it that, but really, they were travelling, enjoying being together again after so long a separation caused by Grandpa's adopted brother.

"Hi guys." Mom stepped forward, ushering us in. "We hoped you'd make it back on time."

"Sorry," Garrett and I said in unison. Mom waved her hand.

"Don't worry, we get it. I was the same way, restless before my shift."

Together, we walked to the cafeteria. My stomach growled as I took in the plates of food that had been laid out. Sandwiches, cheese and crackers, pickle trays, muffins, fruit bowls, meat trays, and different types of bread rolls. Garrett immediately sat down and started eating, while I nibbled on a cracker. I was hungry, but my stomach protested. Mom rubbed my shoulder as she sat beside me.

"Just eat as much you can," she said. I gave her a grateful smile.

The others sat down around us, chatting happily. I caught up with Aunt Thara, who I hadn't seen in a while. Being Luna didn't give her much time to come visit, even though she was so close.

"Where's Val?" I asked.

"We had to leave him at home. He's grounded." She shook her head.

"Uh-oh. What'd he do this time?" Luke asked.

Aunt Thara sighed. "We found out he was bullying at school."

"So, he's taking after you then?" Dad asked casually.

"Fuck you Dimitri," Aunt Thara snapped.

"Point in case." Dad smirked and she threw a muffin at him which he neatly dodged. I laughed at their antics.

"Hey, sorry we're late." Aunt Hazel and Uncle Clint entered the room, followed by their son, Damien. We smiled at each other. Aunt Hazel gave me a hug while Uncle Clint walked over to Garrett. "How are you, hun?"

"I'm good Aunt Hazel, thanks."

"You're not late- there's three minutes to go," Mom said.

My stomach twisted at her words. Everyone got quiet as we waited, eyes glued to the big clock above the doors. Garrett came to my side, and I could tell he was holding his breath just like I was. When the hands struck midnight, Mom jumped up and wrapped us in a tight hug.

"Happy Birthday!" Everyone cheered.

We were hugged by everyone there, being wished all the best and whatnot. My eyes met my brothers, and I could tell he was still just as nervous as I was. Mom left to get our gifts, but as soon as she opened the cafeteria doors, Garrett stiffened. I might have been the only one who noticed, as I was the only one still looking at him. His head whipped around faster than his body, and he nearly ran over Miguel on his way out the door.

"Garrett?" Aunt Thara called, but he was already gone.

I moved with everyone else, jogging after him as he ran down the hall and threw open the doors that led to the kitchen. His entire body went statue still, and I heard his breathing stop. We stopped behind him, crowding the doorway. Stepping around Uncle Ben, I looked into the room. My heart dropped into my stomach.

Standing by the sink was a pretty blonde, humming to herself. She was cutting up an apple, not paying any mind to the group of us staring at her. Then her face lifted, tilting to the side. Glancing behind her, her eyes went wide, and she dropped the knife she was holding. She turned around, facing us, and slowly removed a pair of headphones from her ears. Her eyes landed on each of our faces before finally settling on Garretts. Both of their faces went white as sheets.

"G-Garrett."

"Sophia?"

Anger coursed through me, hot and fiery. How cruel was this? This bitch had broken my brother's heart, and then it turns out she's his *mate*?! The Goddess had a sick sense of humor!

"You're. . . you're my mate," Sophia said. I heard Mom gasp quietly beside me.

A small smile played on Sophias face, but Garrett was shaking his head back and forth slowly.

"Why?" he asked. Sophia brows furrowed in confusion. "Why?!" he shouted, startling everyone but me.

"Garrett. . ." She took a step towards him, and he responded by taking a step back.

"Garrett, what is the matter with you?" Mom asked.

"What is going on?" Uncle Luke asked.

Before things got out of hand, I stepped into the room and faced everyone.

"I think Garrett and his mate need some time alone," I said.

Mom and Dad looked from me, to him, to Sophia. Everyone else just looked confused. I met my brothers' eyes, asking the silent question. He nodded.

"Stay," he said to me.

"Garrett, this is-" I cut my Dad off.

"Ten minutes guys. Please?"

Everyone looked at us before shuffling out the door.

"And no eavesdropping!" I called after them. When the door shut, I pressed my ear against it, listening to their retreating footsteps. Satisfied, I turned to Sophia.

She was staring at Garrett with tears in her eyes. Her bottom lip quivered, and I rolled my eyes heavily.

"Are you. . ." She sniffed. "Are you going to reject me?" she asked him.

I looked at him. He seemed to be struggling. "I don't know," he finally managed. Sophias face crumbled at his words.

"Please don't," she begged. "Please."

"Why shouldn't he?" I snapped. "You have no idea how much pain you caused him!"

She lowered her head. "I'm sorry. I know that's stupid to say, now, but I am. I never wanted to hurt you."

"Then why did you?!" he yelled.

"I-I don't know." A single tear left her eye, falling carelessly down her cheek.

"That's a bullshit answer," I retorted. She looked up at me. "You hurt him because you didn't care about him."

"That's not true!"

"Really? Then how did you end up in bed with another guy?"

She looked from me to Garrett. "You told her?"

He scoffed. "Of course I told her! She's my sister, my twin! I didn't have anyone else to go to! I was. . . I was destroyed by what you did." He leaned against one of the metal counters, covering his face with his hands. "Why should I accept you as my mate when you've already betrayed me once, in the worst way?"

She didn't answer right away, crossing her arms over her chest. Finally, she looked at him again.

"You shouldn't."

I raised my eyebrows, surprised by her answer. But she wasn't finished.

"What I did was horrible, and there is no excuse for it." She took a deep, shuddering breath. "All I can do is promise not to do anything so horrible again. And ask for a second chance. I loved you, Garrett. I still do. I never stopped and I don't think I ever will. But if you can't accept me as your mate, I understand. If that's the case, then please reject me now so we can both try to move on."

I watched my brothers face go from anger, to sadness, back to anger, to hope, confusion, and finally uncertainty. He opened his mouth, but nothing came out. He tried again, and again. After a few tense minutes, he simply shook his head and stormed out of the room. I turned back to Sophia, who was crying silently.

"What do I do?" she asked me.

I gave her a hard look. "I don't know what he's thinking," I told her. "But I'm here to tell you that if he does reject you, you better keep your word and move on."

She nodded sadly.

"And if by some miracle he actually accepts you, you better not hurt him again. Because if you do, not only will you be a disgrace to the word 'mate', but you will also be a disgrace to my family, and as the future Luna of this pack. And I'll make sure everyone knows it," I promised.

She met my eyes, understanding that I wasn't joking. Slowly, she nodded again. I turned to leave. Sophia called out to me as my hand touched the door.

"What?"

"How much did he tell you?" she whispered.

I looked at her over my shoulder. "Enough. Enough that you not only have to earn *his* trust again, but mine as well."

CHAPTER 10
GARRETT

I stormed past my parents and Uncles and Aunts. My vision was red, my mind hazy. Anger and confusion coursed through me at an alarming speed. The only thing that kept repeating in my mind was *why?* What had I done to deserve this? What kind of game was the Goddess playing with me?

"Garrett, what happened?" Aunt Thara called after me.

"I don't want to talk about it now," I replied gruffly.

"Son, if she's your mate-"

"I said, I don't want to talk about it!" I yelled at them. Every pair of eyes widened incredulously. Never in my life had I raised my voice to my parents, let alone my entire family. Violet joined the group, her face passive. Only she understood the turmoil going through me right now.

Mom stepped forward, reaching for me. "Okay. Just remember we are here if you want to."

Dad shot her a look. "Lily-"

"Don't," she turned to him. "This is something he wants to work out for himself. It's his mate, and his choice."

He didn't look very happy about it, but he didn't argue. Vie stepped around everyone, taking my arm.

"Come on."

I let her pull me away and into the foyer, starting up the stairs. Everything in my body was urging me to turn around, to go claim Sophia, to hold her. But I couldn't.

"So, what are you going to do?"

I gasped, looking around. Violet gave me a weird look, taking a step down towards me.

"Are you okay?" she asked, her face worried. Then her face lit up, a smile taking over. "Did you hear your wolf?"

Was that what that was? I reached out with my mind, calling.

"I'm here. Nice to meet you, Garrett."

61

Despite the wave of emotions in me, I grinned.

"I got my wolf!" I told my sister, and she laughed happily.

"What's his name?"

"Nice to meet you too. What's your name?" I asked him eagerly.

"Hugo."

I relayed the information to Violet. She opened her mouth to say something, but instead she gasped like I had. Her eyes became unfocused, staring into space. Then her face lit up with a huge grin of her own.

"My wolfs name is Hala!" she exclaimed.

"Spirit and Moonlight."

We turned to see Mom, Dad, Uncle Ben and Uncle Luke behind us. They were all smiling proudly.

"Is that what their names mean?" Violet asked.

Uncle Luke nodded. "Hugo is derived from German origin, meaning 'Bright of mind and spirit.' Hala is of Arabic origin, meaning 'Halo around the moon', or 'moonlight'. Both beautiful names."

I could feel Hugos pride swelling up at his words. He was obviously proud of his name as well.

"We're going to bed. Let us know if you need anything," Mom said. She kissed our cheeks as she went by, Dad following behind. Uncle Ben wished us a happy birthday again before departing but Uncle Luke leaned against the banister, staring between the two of us.

"Are you going to accept her?" he asked bluntly.

"I don't know," I told him. Hugo whined in my head.

"You know that she is more than just your mate. She is the future Luna of the pack."

"Yes."

His face grew serious. "I don't know what happened between the two of you, but you need to think carefully about your decision, Garrett. If you reject her, there is no guarantee of a second-chance mate. You know as well as I do how rare those are. You would have to take a chosen mate, for the sake of the pack. But heed my advice now;

Not every woman is meant to be a leader. The Goddess chose her for a reason."

I didn't reply, and he knew I wasn't going to. My sister was silent behind me as well. Uncle Luke pressed a hand to my shoulder before going to his floor. I thought over his words, not wanting to agree, but unable to deny that he was right.

"Are you going to be okay tonight?" Violet asked.

"Yeah. I just. . ."

"Need some time to think," she finished for me. I nodded. "Alright. I'm going to bed, too. Come get me if you need anything."

"Thanks."

She left me standing there, once again lost in a crazy mess of thoughts.

"You can talk to me," Hugo said.

"I know what you want. I can feel it."

"I know what she did Garrett. But you never did give her a chance to explain either."

I snorted. *"What is there to explain? She slept with another guy."*

"She did acknowledge that she was in the wrong. Let's go back and talk to her."

"No. Not tonight."

"You can't put it off forever. She's our mate."

"I know! But with my shift being so close, I don't want to say something I'll regret. Afterwards, okay?"

He pondered for a minute before agreeing.

"But we are going to talk to her," he pushed.

"Yes. I am the future Alpha, and I won't run away from my problems. I'm just. . . putting it off, until I have a clear head."

"Alright."

I started walking again, my brain in overdrive until I reached my room. I flopped onto my bed, rolling over and staring at the ceiling.

"So, what do you look like?" I asked curiously.

I could almost see his wolfish grin in my head. *"You'll have to wait and see."*

"You're not as big as my Mom, are you?"

"No." He barked a laugh. *"As awesome as it would be, there is only one Mother Wolf in this family."*

"Does. . .Can you sense Sophias wolf?"

"A little. She has a strong aura, because she was meant to be a Luna. But she has not turned eighteen yet, so I cannot talk to her." He sounded disappointed.

"Her birthday is-"

"Next month. I know."

"How did she know?" I wondered while I talking to him. *"She knew I was her mate, but she shouldn't have been able to sense it yet."*

"Like I said, she is meant to be a Luna. Our Luna. Her senses are stronger than regular she-wolves. She doesn't feel the full mate bond, like you do, but she felt enough to know."

I blinked. That was interesting. Then another thought came to me, and I groaned loudly. In my head, Hugo yipped happily. Sophia would have to be with me tonight, during my shift. Unless. . ..

"Trying to pull what your mother did?" Hugo scoffed. *"Remember how that worked out for her?"*

I shuddered, remembering how Mom told us about her first shift. Okay, so maybe having my mate there was better.

"Poor Violet. Unless she finds her mate by tonight, she'll have to do it alone."

Hugo was silent, and I frowned.

"What? Do you know who her mate is?" I asked.

"No. I can only sense our mate bond," he replied. But it felt like he wasn't telling me something, like he was holding something back. He sighed. *"Alright. I don't know who her mate is, but I know she has one. She just doesn't know yet."*

"How do you know?"

"Because like you and Violet, Hala and I are also twins."

I sat up, my mind whirring.

"But. . . that can't be right. Mom told us that the Goddess gave one of us a wolf who needed a second chance." She never told us who's wolf that was. Only that she was looking forward to seeing her again, making me think it was Violet, as the wolf was female.

"And that means the Goddess couldn't have blessed that wolf with a sibling?" Hugo challenged.

"Oh."

He laughed his barky laugh again. I rolled my eyes.

"Being twins, Hala and I have a stronger bond. I can sense that she has a mate, but I can't sense who it is."

"So, if Violet has a mate. . . and she doesn't know who it is yet. . ." I thought it through, my eyebrows scrunching together. *"That means that someone knows Violet is their mate, and hasn't told her? Why?"*

"I was wondering that, too. But I have no answers. You humans think very oddly at times."

I laughed, not even able to disagree. There were some pretty odd ducks in the world. We talked the rest of the night, getting to know each other. Rather, I learned about him. He was privy to all my memories already, having been with me throughout my life, just dormant until now. It was beyond nice having someone to talk to, someone I knew I could trust without a doubt in the world. Up until now, that person for me had been my sister, and even still, there were things she didn't know. Hugo knew everything about me, and I felt whole having him here with me, finally.

Light shone through my window as the sun peeked over the treetops. My body was full of energy, and I was also starving, despite everything I'd eaten hours before. I got up, going to the bathroom for a quick shower. Afterwards, I changed my clothes and went to meet my parents for breakfast. Violet was standing outside her door, waiting for me.

"Hey. Get any sleep?" I asked. She had light bruises under her eyes.

"None. You?"

"Same."

Our parents eyed us as we joined them, and I apologized for my outburst the night before, assuring them I was fine, but I still didn't want to talk. They respectfully agreed and we had breakfast. Thank the Goddess Mom made extra. I loaded my plate, barely fitting everything on, while Vie nibbled on a sole piece of toast and a glass of orange juice.

"Violet."

She looked up at our Dad as she chewed.

"I just want to remind you that we will be there tonight. Just in case."

She smiled at him, but even I could tell she was scared.

"Thanks Dad."

I almost told her. But somehow, I knew that would only increase her anxiety. I thought again about who her mate could be. Jasper's face came to mind. It would be just like him to not tell her they were mates. Hugo was silent in my head as I thought about this, and suddenly, I was just as anxious as my sister.

CHAPTER 11
JASPER

I stood on the dock, watching the fish swimming carelessly below the surface of the water. Their bodies twisted gracefully around each other, and I wondered what it would be like to live in their world. My eyes caught a streak of orange, and followed a huge Koi enter the swarm. Reaching into my pocket, I pulled out the fish food I always brought and tossed some in. Instantly, every fish swam to the surface, their little mouths gobbling the treat. I smiled.

This was my favourite place. Mainly because it was private, and nobody ever really came here. Years ago, I'd stumbled onto an abandoned cabin in the woods, only to learn later that it was just outside Blood Moon pack lines. It was rundown when I found it, the windows broken, the log siding overgrown with vines and the land with weeds and grass. The roof had holes, and the inside was a mess. The pond that was nestled to the side had a broken, unsteady dock that was half swallowed by the water.

It took me years to fix the place up. Sometimes my Dad would come and help after he followed me one day to see where I kept disappearing to. Now I had my own little getaway, one I no longer feared would come down on top of me. Sometimes I would come by and find a rogue or two, but I never kicked them out, and they never stayed anyway. Rogues had a habit of always being on the move, especially when they were close to a pack. Only once it turned into a fight, and thank the Goddess Dad was here that day, or it might have ended differently. In the end, we ran him off, the poor guy. We only ever lost our humanity that way after years and years of having no pack. Of having no one.

I sat on the edge of the wood, my bare feet dipping into the coolness below me. My eyes reflected in the water, and for the millionth time I thought about them. My mother had had brown eyes, chocolate brown. She always told me I had my Dads eyes- my real Dad. And that I should be proud of them. It was the only time she ever talked about him. But how could I be? The man didn't even acknowledge my existence. I wasn't proud to have anything of his, even his eye colour. Still, the silver in them was unusual. Like metal gleaming on a knife in the moonlight.

Mom, my adoptive Mom, said it was my eyes that drew the girls to me. Maybe that was true, but I didn't care. I had no interest in any of them, save for one.

Violet.

Her face flashed in my mind, and I watched the smile grow in my reflection. Now *her* eyes. . . a blind man could get lost in them. I know I did. Often. She was the definition of beauty, with her long black hair and her creamy skin. Her attitude turned people off from her, but not me. She was strong, opinionated. Not afraid to call you out on your bullshit. Yet, she was kind and caring. The kind of person who would take a bullet for those she loved without thinking twice. And the amount of respect she held for herself was incredible, and still she gave the same respect to those around her. I'd never met anyone like her.

I laid back, my face being warmed by the sun and thought about the first time we'd met. I had just started school, the new kid in class. Everyone else had been there since kindergarten, all part of the pack, so I was especially the odd duck. A boy had taken my drawing, making fun of it. Looking back, he might have had a point- I couldn't draw worth shit, even now. Still, Violet had calmly gotten out of her seat, walked up to us, ripped the paper out of his hands and given it back to me before punching the kid in the face.

I laughed as I remembered what she'd screamed at him afterwards.

"You're a bully and a cheesedick!"

To this day, I have no idea where she heard that, or if she just made it up. But it made me smile every time I thought about it. After that, we never really became friends, being the introverted kid that I was. But I was nice to her, and her to me. I greeted her everyday, always excited to see her. As we got older, I started seeing her in a different way. I started seeing every girl in a different way. The glories of puberty had me noticing all sorts of things about the opposite sex that I never paid attention to before. And apparently, they started noticing me too.

Too scared to ask out the girl I really liked, I started dating Melissa Smith, who turned out to my first kiss. Then Rebecca Lang, my first time getting to second base. Then Shelby Hughes, my first time. By that time, the rumors about me were notorious; I don't think she even realized I was still a virgin. But I never could stop myself from thinking about Violet. Even after the greetings stopped, and we were no longer nice to each other, she was still the most beautiful girl to me, a supernova in a field of stars.

I checked my phone. About four hours until the ceremony started. I'd been out here all day. Sitting up, I threw the rest of the fish food into the pond before getting to my feet and locating my shoes. My hands trembled slightly, the anxiety taking over again. I closed my eyes, focusing on my breathing.

"Everything is fine. It's going to be fine." I repeated it over and over until I was calm.

I could feel my body was getting ready for tonight. And once again, I felt a pang of longing. How I wished my Mother could be there tonight, encouraging me. But I assured myself she would be, from the Goddess's realm. It wasn't exactly the same, but it was enough. I ran all the way home, about forty-five minutes. I was pretty proud of that; I trained hard, and still held the record for being the fastest of my group. I slowed to a walk when I got to my street, seeing my little sister Elena playing in the front yard.

"Hey squirt."

"Jasper's home!" she yelled. I held out my arms, and she launched herself into them, giggling. "Where did you go?"

"Out for a run."

"Because you're shifting tonight!"

"Yup."

She squealed. "I can't wait!"

I set her down on her feet and she took my hand. Even though Elena was my adoptive sibling, I loved her like my own flesh and blood. She was an adorable five-year-old, with a sharp mind about her. She'd already skipped a grade and was reading at a sixth grade level. I was immensely proud of her.

"You know you can't come Elena. You'll be in bed, and the shift gets a little scary," I told her.

She gave me her most serious face. "I'm not scared. I'll be the toughest she-wolf ever when I shift. You won't hear me make a sound!"

I chuckled. "Wanna bet?"

"How much you got?"

"I'll bet a hundred bucks that you cry in the first ten minutes."

She stuck out her hand. "Deal. You better have my money."

We shook and I laughed.

"What have I told you about gambling Elena?" Mom came down the front steps shaking her head. "And *you* shouldn't be encouraging her," she said to me.

I held up my hands. "I promise I'll put her in rehab if she becomes addicted."

Mom sighed. "What are you betting on anyways?"

"Whether or not she'll scream during her first shift."

"I won't!" declared Elena. Mom looked at her with wide eyes before turning back to me. "Put me in for fifty," she said in a low voice. Elenas draw dropped and I laughed hard.

"Vicky is on her way," Dad said as he came out the door.

Elena pouted. "Do I have to stay with Aunt Vicky?"

"Yes," Dad said.

"But she smells like vinegar! All the time!" she complained.

"Elena. Don't be mean," Mom scolded.

I bent down and pulled her in for a hug. "I promise I'll shift for you tomorrow so you can meet my wolf. Okay?"

"Fine."

Aunt Vickys blue sedan pulled up, parking on the curb. The strong scent of vinegar hit my nostrils as she got out and Dad and I shared an amused look. Aunt Vicky cleaned houses for a living, and she always used homemade cleaning products. Sadly, most of them were vinegar based. Elena scrunched her nose up as Vicky gave her a big hug. Then she turned to me.

"Good luck tonight, Jasper. I'll be rooting for you."

"Thanks squirt."

"Alright guys, let's go." Mom clapped her hands together. "Vicky, I left some money on the counter for pizza. You know her schedule."

"Thanks Linda."

Elena gave us all a sour look as she led her into the house.

We didn't live that far from the packhouse, so we decided to walk, and I was grateful. I was coursing with adrenaline. Dad threw his arm over my shoulder, giving me a squeeze.

"You ready?" he asked.

I chuckled. "Nope."

"You'll do just fine," Mom said on the other side of me.

I stopped on the sidewalk, making them stop as well.

"Uhm, listen." I rubbed the back of my neck awkwardly. "I just wanted to say thanks to you guys. For everything. Taking me in, helping me with school. Giving me a family, you know? I know I'm not always easy to deal with but. . . I love you guys. And I'm really grateful that people like you are by my side tonight."

I looked at the ground, crossing my arms. It wasn't easy for me to say all that, but I wanted them to know.

Suddenly, a pair of arms went around me, and then another. We stood on the sidewalk in a mini group hug, and when Mom pulled back, she had tears in her eyes.

"You don't have to thank us, sweetheart. When Luna Lily brought you to us, we knew you would just bring more love into our house. And ever since Elenas been born, you've been the best big brother. You complete our family, and we couldn't imagine it without you."

"We love you too, son. So much," Dad added with a smile. I returned it.

"Come on."

Together, we walked down the street. If they thought my rare admission of feelings was surprising, they were going to be really surprised later.

CHAPTER 12
VIOLET

I stood in front of my mirror, finally finished getting ready. It was eleven already, and I couldn't be more disappointed or scared. All day I'd looked for my mate. I went to every store, every restaurant, every park. And nothing. I even went to the cemetery, only to find the old grounds keeper. That was probably the most productive part of my day; I went to say hi to my Grandma and Grandpa, Dads parents who had died before I was born. I stopped by Gretas grave, updating her on everything. I still missed her cookies- she made the best ones, always sneaking Garrett and I extras when our parents weren't looking.

As it neared nine though, I finally just accepted that I was going through this by myself. I tried to comfort myself with the knowledge that lots of people did. People who didn't find their mates before their first shift. And they made it through. I kept telling myself this, but the knot in my stomach only grew more intense as the time went by. Trying to ignore it, I grabbed the white dress from my bed and left my room. Garrett stood on the other side of the hall, leaning against the wall.

"Ready?"

"As I'll ever be," I muttered.

We walked down the stairs together, saying few words. I turned the fabric in my hands over and over again. Garrett held a white shirt and pants. Our clothes would be destroyed when we shifted, but we got pure white garments to put on after we shifted back. For this reason, I chose a plain black tank top, one of many I owned, and a pair of jean shorts that I didn't really care about. Garrett was dressed similar, in a plain blue t-shirt and old jeans, and both of us had bare feet.

At the bottom of the stairs were our parents and family, and to my surprise, Sophia. She gave Garrett a small smile, which he returned with a nod.

"Are you two ready?" Mom asked us.

We nodded.

"Alright. Let's go."

My brother and I walked behind everyone else out of the house and across the yard. My hands started to shake as we got closer and closer to the training yard, where the ceremony was being held.

"Hey," Garrett whispered.

"Yeah?"

"I'll be right there with you."

His words calmed me some. I gave a low laugh. "Thanks. But I think you'll be too busy with your own shift to worry about me."

His eyes landed on Sophia, and he nodded slowly.

"Hugo told me that our wolves are twins too," he said.

"I know. Hala told me as well."

"Pretty cool right?"

"Totally."

I knew he was trying to distract me. Unfortunately, it wasn't working. I kept looking around, hoping my mate would pop out of the night. I really, really, *really* didn't want to do this alone! My hope deflated when we reached the training yard, my face ashen. String lights had been set up, illuminating the area dimly. A low platform had been placed on the grass, and I watched as my parents stepped onto it along with Uncle Ben and Luke and their mates. Garret and I took our places in front of them, a good distance apart. To my right, Aunt Thara and Uncle Killian waved at me, both giving me sympathetic looks. I waved back shortly, looking around.

Groups of people, friends and family, were gathered around to support the shifters tonight. I saw a lot of proud faces, and a lot of nervous ones too. Everyone here knew what we go through tonight.

"Thank you all for coming." My Dads voice boomed out over us. I focused on him. "First, I would like to say how proud I am of my children. Violet and Garrett, you have both grown into incredible young adults, and it is a privilege to be here with you tonight." He smiled at us, and I forced a smile in return.

My skin started to tingle, and I looked at my Mom frantically. She checked the watch on her wrist and nodded at me.

"Hala?"

"I'm right here, Violet."

"Hala, I don't think I can do this."

"We don't have a choice."

"The time is upon us. Let me welcome the rest of Blood Moons shifters tonight," Dad said.

I felt a slow burning start somewhere inside me; It was hard to pinpoint exactly where it came from as it was moving steadily. The tingling turned into a painful itching sensation, and I dropped to my knees, trying to prepare.

"You'll help me?" I asked my wolf desperately.

"I will, I promise."

When the first bone snapped, I instantly started cussing my mate, whoever he was. All I had was my parents who watched over me worriedly, and my wolf to help guide me. But none of them could take away the pain. My stomach cramped; worse than any period I'd ever experienced. The cramp moved to every muscle in my being, and my vision blacked out for a second. Briefly, I glanced to my right. This might be the only time I was grateful for Sophia. Garrett was doing *much* better than I was, clinging onto his mate while his bones broke. Every so often he would twitch, while agonizing shrieks were coming from me. Our eyes met, his full of fear for me.

The pain then intensified, and I fell onto my side, screaming. Tears streamed down my face, and I begged and cried for someone, *anyone*, to make it stop. Through my blurry vision, I saw my Mom jump off the platform, coming for me. And then she stopped, a confused look coming over her face.

My leg snapped loudly, crunching and reforming. I opened my mouth to scream, only to realize it hadn't hurt. Raising my head, I saw a hand placed on my bare waist where my shirt had ridden up. My eyes followed it, down the toned arm, the broad shoulder and landed on Jaspers pained face.

"Mate," he breathed.

Distantly, I heard both of my parents' gasp, and a vicious snarl beside me. All of that was background noise though, as I stared into his eyes. The pull I felt for him and the way Hala was howling in my head, I couldn't deny it. Jasper Cole was my mate.

And right now, I didn't give a shit if he was a man-whore. I didn't care if he'd slept with ten million women! I clutched his hand for dear life, pulling him closer. He pulled me into a sitting position, my cheek resting against his chest. His bare chest.

"Mate," I sighed.

His arms held me tighter at the word, his lips connecting with my shoulder. Fur sprouted from my arms, my teeth growing and becoming sharper. Slowly, we repositioned ourselves, so we still had physical contact, but as to not hurt each other when we completed the shift.

"Let go of him, Violet," Hala spoke urgently in my mind.

"Let go?"

"Now!"

I did as she demanded, pushing Jasper away from me. The pain peaked, and once again I opened my mouth to scream. What came out was a howl instead. The pain disappeared, leaving me exhausted and honestly, thirsty as Hell.

But I'd shifted.

The first thing I saw when I opened my eyes was a long snout and a black nose. Jasper's wolf stood over me, whining quietly, and sniffing me. I stood on slightly shaky legs, letting him know I was fine. He rubbed his face against mine, and Hala purred happily.

"Violet?"

I turned to my Mom, shocked that I had to look down at her. I was at least a foot and a half taller than her in my wolf form. Was I as big as my Dad? Bigger?

Mom smiled up at me as if she could read my thoughts.

"You're bigger than your Dad. But still not as big as me," she laughed.

"Lily." We turned to the platform, where Dad and everyone else was gaping at me. Mom turned back, her eyes roaming over me until her hands covered her mouth.

"What on Earth?" she gasped.

"What? Are we missing a leg or something?"

"You're so silly." Hala shook her head at my stupidity.

"What does it mean?" Mom was looking at Uncle Luke, who was staring at me. He shook his head.

"I-I don't know."

"Violet?"

I yipped as Jasper's voice entered my head. I forgot I could mindlink now- nobody had tried yet. I turned my eyes on him. His wolf was beautiful. He was almost as big as I was, his fur black as night. His eyes glowed silver, even more in this form than when he was human.

"You're my mate? Why didn't you tell me?" I asked him.

"I'll explain later."

"But-"

"Vie, you need to look at yourself."

"Why? What's wrong with me?"

He shook his big head. *"Nothing. You're stunning. But you need to see this."*

Another wolf nudged my side. I looked into his eyes, shocked to see they were also silver. Unlike Jaspers though, they literally glowed. It was such an intense colour, they almost looked white. His fur was red- bright red. He stood at my height, eye to eye.

"Garrett?" I asked in disbelief.

"You okay?" he asked. He gave Jaspers wolf a look, and I wasn't sure in this form, but I thought it was a dirty one.

"I'm fine. You? Hugo is beautiful!"

"I'm good. And you should talk. Come on."

We looked at our parents, who nodded and shifted. Mom stood towering over us, her wolf Aya coming over to scent us. Hala yipped happily, trying to nip at her ear. Dad stood off to the side, obviously pouting. I gave a throaty wolf laugh as I realized he was indeed, the smallest one out of us. What a blow to his ego. Nonetheless, our wolves went over to greet him as well. Garrett tilted his head, and we headed off into the forest. The rest of the shifters joined us for their first run, and it was amazing. I was seeing the woods I loved so much through new eyes tonight. All of my senses were sharper. We stopped at the nearby lake, some of the wolves jumping in and starting to play.

"Come here Violet," Mom mindlinked me. I padded over to where her, Dad and my brother were standing by the waters edge. Jasper followed behind me. I looked into the water and started. I was completely black. That wasn't normal, not for a she-wolf. As a rule, only Alphas were all black, right? But then. . . I looked at my brother. Why was he red? He was taking over as Alpha, not me. Even weirder, why was Jasper's wolf black? Wasn't his mother a rogue?

"Look at your side. And your eyes," Dad said to me.

Inspecting my reflection again, I got my second shock. My left eye was blue, as blue as Grandma Rose's were. My right was green, the same colour as Moms. But the most shocking thing was the fur on my side. Standing out against the black was white fur, perfectly shaped into a crescent moon, a half moon, a full moon, another half moon and another crescent moon.

"What is it?" I asked Hala.

"A gift."

CHAPTER 13
VIOLET

"Why?" I asked.

"I am a wolf re-born. I was given to you, being given a second chance. The Goddess knows I will be treated right with you, Violet. This is her way of saying thank you for accepting me."

"But I didn't. Not that I wouldn't have, but my Mom made the decision."

"You don't think you are worthy of a gift from the Goddess?"

"I. . . not really," I admitted sadly.

"You're worth so much more than you give yourself credit for, Violet."

□ *"What about Garrett? He's the future Alpha. It should be him."*

"Our brothers have their own gift. Together, they will make a worthwhile Alpha."

I stared at my reflection, unable to grasp the truth staring back at me.

"What are we?" I asked.

"A Midnight Wolf. The first."

I blinked. *"The first? You mean ever?"*

"Yes."

"Holy shit!"

I was distracted from totally freaking out by a flash of sparks on my shoulder. I looked into my mate's eyes, trying to focus.

"Hello, mate."

That wasn't Jasper.

"Hello. Jaspers wolf?"

"My name is Ehno."

"Nice to meet you, Ehno. Your name. . . it means protector, right?"

"It does. Fitting, as I will always be here to protect you."
"Well, aren't you a charmer."

He gave me a lopsided grin, his tongue flopping out of his mouth. Hala was itching to run with her mate, practically bouncing on her feet. I still had questions for him, but I pushed them aside for now. Letting my parents know, Hala asked me to give her control, and then they were off. I sat back in my own mind, watching as they took off into the forest, jumping playfully at each other. I laughed, as they seemed like two pups, but I could feel how happy Hala was. That's what mattered the most to me. After a while, they found a spot to lie down, snuggling close and sharing wolfy kisses. I was going to count that as her first kiss, and not mine.

The sun was just starting to rise when we reached the training yard again. My dress was still in my spot, waiting for me. It seemed like we were the last ones back, and Jasper respectfully turned away as Hala helped me shift back. The morning air was cool as I donned the dress, turning my back now so Jasper could shift and get dressed. Once he was done, we stood on the grass, staring at each other.

"Why didn't you tell me?" I demanded. I was still exhausted, and hungry, but I wanted answers.

"Because I didn't want you to go through your first shift alone," he replied.

"But I wouldn't have!" I exclaimed. He shot me a look.

"If I had told you when I found out, would you have rejected me?"

I wanted to say no. But I couldn't. Because now I was in the same boat as Garrett. Jasper was the last person I expected to be my mate, and if I was being honest, I wasn't exactly jumping for joy.

"That's what I thought," he said. "Like you said, females have it harder than males when it comes to the first shift. I didn't want you to go through that alone. And you're so stubborn, I knew you wouldn't see it that way."

"I am not stubborn," I snapped. "So, you're saying you kept it from me, for me?"

"Yes."

I scoffed. "And did you consider the amount of anxiety I had to go through, believing I would have to do it alone?"

"I did. Still better than actually doing it."

I threw my hands up. "You're such an asshole!"

"Why?" He threw the question at me. "Because I was thinking about you? Your wellbeing? Geez, I'm sorry." His tone held heavy sarcasm.

I crossed my arms, thinking. The last thing I wanted to do was reject him, but seriously? First Sophia, now *Jasper?*

"I know what you're thinking." I met his eyes. They were suddenly cold, angry. "If you want to reject me, then just do it."

I raised an eyebrow. "You sound so sure that I will."

"I've kind of been expecting it."

"Wow. You think so much of me, don't you?"

He took two steps, planting himself in front of me. I craned my neck back to look into his eyes. I crossed my arms tighter, as the urge to be in his arms was almost overwhelming. How did he manage to stay away from me all this time? This was torture!

"You know what I think of you?" he asked lowly. He continued before I could reply. "I think your the most beautiful girl I've ever met. I think you're smart, and funny and strong. You're the most opinionated person I've ever met, and also the kindest. But I also know what you think of me. So, I'm not holding onto much hope for our bond."

I hadn't expected any of that. It was the nicest thing anyone had ever said to me.

"The number of women-" I began.

"Not as many as you think," he interrupted me roughly. "You know what you've *heard*. But not the *truth*."

I blinked. "What?"

"Three people, Violet. Three. That's the amount of people I've slept with in my whole life," he glared at me. "Anything else said is just a rumor."

"Then why not put a stop to them?" I challenged. I was having a hard time accepting this. How could I trust he wasn't lying for my benefit?

"Because I don't care what people think about me. Except you."

I shook my head, closing my eyes. "How do I know you're not lying Jasper?"

"Do you want to me gather all the girls in the pack? Get them to tell you?"

"That's ridiculous."

"How else am I supposed to convince you? Can't you just trust that I'm telling the truth?"

I searched his eyes, only finding sincerity. I bit my lip.

"It still bugs me that you've slept with other people," I said quietly. He sighed.

"I can't change my past Vie. I'm sorry I didn't wait for you, but it's only you from now on. If your parents could move past it, why can't we?"

I raised my eyebrows at him, but I shouldn't have been surprised. Everyone knew my Dad got around before he met my Mom. It wasn't exactly a secret. But now, Mom was the only one he looked at. And they were happy. The role model couple I'd looked up to my entire life. Looking at it that way, and regretting not looking at it like this before, I realized he had a point. It was beyond stupid of me to think my mate would wait for me. It was unfair of me to have that expectation, when in fact, there was plenty about me that wasn't exactly perfect. I realized how childish I'd been acting on this point; so much, that my own mate feared I would reject him.

I uncrossed my arms. Slowly, I wrapped them around his waist, giving him a small smile. Sparks erupted from our contact, and I couldn't get enough of the feeling.

"I'm sorry," I said.

Jasper stared down at me, his expression a mix between surprise and hope.

"You're not rejecting me?" he asked.

I shook my head. "Not today anyway," I teased.

His face lit up, taking my breath away. He looked so happy that I thought he would burst. His hands cupped my cheeks, hips facing coming down to mine. He stopped an inch from my lips.

"May I?"

"Yes," I breathed.

My eyes fluttered shut. His lips barely touched mine before a loud growl sounded beside us. I jumped, startled by the sudden intrusion, and Jasper straightened, keeping me in his arms. We both looked at Garrett, who was standing a few feet away. His hands were fists at his sides, and they were shaking. His face. . . I'd never seen him so angry, especially not towards me. He glared at us furiously.

"You accepted him?!" he spat at me. My mouth fell open at his tone.

"What is wrong with you?" I asked.

"You can't accept him, Violet!"

"Garrett!"

"What's your problem man?" Jasper glared at my brother.

"You wouldn't even look at him if you knew what he did."

I was getting irritated. "What are you talking about?!"

He pointed at Jasper, looking half crazy. "He's the one! He's the one who slept with Sophia that night!"

For the second time in so many days, my heart dropped into my stomach.

CHAPTER 14
JASPER

I felt Violet slipping out of my arms. I tightened my grip, not willing to let her go.

"What are you talking about?" I spat at Garrett.

I hadn't talked to Garrett much. Our confrontation a couple weeks ago was the most words spoken between the two of us probably ever. I never went out of my way to be his buddy, or even an acquaintance. But now he was trying to interfere between my mate and I? No.

"It was you?"

I looked down at Vie, who was staring at me with tears in her eyes. I couldn't tell if they were from anger or sadness- it looked like a mix of both.

"I don't know what he's talking about Vie," I said.

"Liar!" Garrett yelled. "I saw you! Have you slept with so many girls that you don't even remember all of them?"

"Jasper," Violet said lowly. "Did you sleep with Sophia? Sophia Chang?"

My face paled as memories flashed. The party. I'd been upstairs, wondering why I even bothered to attend the stupid thing, when Sophia had entered the room.

"Oops. This isn't the bathroom," she said.

I smirked. "Nope, sorry."

"Jasper Cole, right?"

"The one and only."

She giggled, dimples popping out on her cheeks. She was pretty, not Violet pretty, but passable. "What are you doing up here by yourself? The party is downstairs."

I shrugged. "I'm not really the social type."

"Oh, I know. I don't think I've ever heard you speak before now." She laughed again.

Taking a seat on the bed next to me, she sighed heavily. "Can I ask you something?" she said randomly.

"Sure."

"Well. . . it's more of a confidence."

"Whatever."

She started playing with a strand of her long hair. "I'm worried. . . is sex. . . hard?"

I almost spit my beer as I laughed. She glared at me, and I tried to sober.

"Sorry. The way you phrased that." I chuckled. "I don't really get what you're asking."

She looked down at her hands. "All of my friends have done it. And they talk about it. I can't imagine doing any of that. . . I'm scared I will disappoint my mate, when I find him."

"Oh." I thought about it. "I don't think that possible. According to my parents, the love you have with your mate is unlike anything else. One can assume physical love is the same." I took a swig of my drink.

Suddenly, her hand was on my arm, her body turned towards me. "Show me."

This time, I did spit my drink. "What?" I sputtered.

"It won't mean anything. And it doesn't have to be intimate. I just want to. . . learn something."

"Sophia-"

Her lips were on mine before I finished. I almost pushed her back. But I didn't. I don't know why, but the next thing I knew, we were under the covers of Goddess knows whose bed when the door swung open.

And Garrett walked in.

I stared at my mate, pleading with my eyes. But she knew. I'm positive my face gave it away. I swallowed and answered her anyway. "Yes."

Her face clouded in disappointment and hurt.

"But I didn't know she had a boyfriend. She never told me that," I continued frantically.

"Nobody knew we were dating," Garrett said. I turned to him.

"Then whose fault is it really? Look, I'm sorry for my actions, but it should have been up to *her* to tell *me* if she

85

was taken or not. Nothing would have happened if I'd known."

He scoffed but Violet looked back to me. She was biting her lip, the little quirk she had when she was thinking.

"I didn't know, Violet. I swear. You can ask Sophia; she came onto me."

A fist connected to my face, throwing me off guard and off balance. Instantly I released Violet so I wouldn't take her down with me. I hit the ground hard, my hand rubbing my jaw.

"Garrett!" Violet yelled at him.

"Sophia would *never*-" Garrett started screaming at me.

"But she did!" Violet screamed back. Both of us looked at her in shock. "Jasper's right, Garrett. It was her responsibility to tell him she was in a relationship."

"Are you serious right now? She probably did and he manipulated her into doing it anyway!"

Violets eyes sparked. "Excuse me? Are you accusing him of forcing her?"

He glanced at me, a nasty smirk on his face. "I wouldn't put it past him."

Two seconds later, Garrett was holding his cheek. He stared at his sister in complete and utter disbelief as she lowered her hand from the slap. Then she walked over to me, offering me the same hand. I took it and she pulled me up.

"You. . . you slapped me," Garrett gasped.

"You're fucking right I did," she hissed.

"For him? He's lying to you, Violet! You can't accept him; he can't be your mate!"

"He *is*. And I do." She looked at me. "We have stuff to work out, obviously. But I will not reject my mate just because my brother doesn't like him. In case you haven't noticed, I'm not *your* mate's biggest fan. But I'm also not telling you to reject her. I'm leaving that choice up to *you*. I just thought you had the same respect for me. Clearly, I was wrong," she said.

We walked away, leaving him standing in the training yard. I clicked my jaw; Garrett had a good punch, that was for sure. I focused on my mate, trying to figure out what she was thinking. Her grip on my hand was tight, and her face was like stone. Now, more than ever before, I regretted my past actions. I was making a mess of things, not just our bond, but her relationship with her family. I looked away, startled that she'd dragged me to the packhouse.

"Where are we going?" I asked.

"My Mom wants to meet you," she grumbled.

"Oh."

We earned a lot of stares as we walked through the foyer and to the stairs. I'm sure we looked comical, but my stomach was twisting in knots. Had Garrett already told his parents? Was I about to get beat up by none other than the Alpha of Blood Moon? Well, I had a good run. Though maybe I could still run. . .

"Stop fidgeting," Violet sighed. "They're not going to bite Jasper."

"Easy for you to say," I mumbled and she shot me an amused look.

I'd obviously never been to the Alphas floor. I looked around, admiring all the artwork as we walked. A particular piece caught my eye but Vie pulled me along. I'd have to take a closer look later. We stopped in front of a door, and she walked in without knocking. Slowly, I followed her, shutting the door behind me. Turning around, I was met with a smiling Luna and a passive Alpha. I gulped loudly, nodding my head respectfully.

"Alpha. Luna."

"Jasper," Luna Lily said. She came to stand in front of me, looking me over. "I haven't seen you up close in a while. You sure have grown."

"Only a little," I replied sheepishly and she laughed.

"Come, sit. I made an early lunch."

"Thank you," I said. I took a seat next to Violet at the round table in the center of the room. The Luna had prepared all kinds of sandwiches, crackers and meats, cheeses, tea and juice, and some delicious looking desserts. Feeling awkward, I took a sandwich and poured myself some orange juice. I could feel everyone's eyes on me.

"So," Alpha Dimitri began. "You're Violets mate."

"Yes, sir."

He looked at her. "And is this another case like Garretts?"

She shook her head. "No."

"So, you accept him then?"

She looked at me with a small teasing smile. "Most of him."

"Alright." He looked at his mate and she nodded.

"Violet, come help me in the other room for a minute."

"Uh, Mom-?"

"Your Dad would like to speak with Jasper."

Did my soul just leave my body? Standing, Violet shot her Dad a look, one I interpreted as 'don't kill him.' Or maybe that was just my wishful thinking. She glanced at me over her shoulder as her Mom ushered her through a door near the kitchen, shutting it behind them. I stared at the plates of meats and cheeses, already sweating.

"I've heard a lot about you Jasper," Alpha Dimitri said. "I hear you're very good with the ladies."

"Hardly, sir."

"No?"

Daring to look up, I met his eyes. "Most of what people hear about me is rumors. I'm not perfect, but I'm definitely better than the Jasper everyone hears about."

He raised one eyebrow, and I saw a lot of Violet in the action. "My daughter knows this?"

"I've explained it to her, Alpha. Honestly, I wasn't expecting her to accept me as her mate."

"Being Alpha, I hear a lot that goes on in the pack. Not much escapes me." He picked up a spoon, twirling it in his fingers. "But I am happy to hear that most of it isn't true. You're very lucky to have my daughter as a mate."

"I feel lucky."

"And I think she is also lucky. To have you."

I raised my eyebrows, surprised he would say that. A small smile played on his lips.

"I pride myself in being a pretty good judge of character, Jasper. And I know your Father well. I do not believe he would raise you to be the man I've heard so much about. As long as you treat my daughter with the respect and love she deserves, I am happy to accept you into my family."

Tears brimmed my eyes. Partly from being grateful that I was still alive right now. But mostly from the knowledge that I'd gained such a respected father-in-law. Alpha Dimitri was a great man, and I looked up to him.

"Thank you, Alpha," I replied lowly.

CHAPTER 15
VIOLET

I bit my lip worriedly. I wasn't hearing any sounds of a fight, so I guess that was a good sign. Still, Dad was the Alpha. I doubted he didn't know about my mate's reputation. And being Alpha, he could also be pretty scary when he wanted to be. It would make a lousy first impression if Jasper shit himself.

"Stop fretting," Mom said from across the room. "Your Dad just wants to talk to him."

"*Talk* to him, or interrogate him?" I asked.

She smiled. "Well, maybe a bit of both."

I groaned and she laughed.

"You have nothing to worry about, Violet. Jasper is a good man."

"He has a bit of a reputation," I told her.

"Oh, I know. But it's all rumors."

I narrowed my eyes at her. "You sound very confident about that, Mom." Her cheeks turned light pink, and my jaw dropped. "You didn't!"

"You're my daughter. Of course I wanted to make sure he was suitable for you," she said defensively.

I gaped at her, astonished she used her powers on my mate. How did he not feel it?! Mom did it to me once, when she thought I'd partaken in weed. It hadn't hurt, but I definitely felt her aura. Over the years, she'd gained tremendous control over her gifts, able to use them without physical contact.

"And you don't worry about your brother, either. He will come around eventually," she continued.

"Mom!" I gasped. "Just how much did you see exactly?"

"Only what I needed to. Jasper cares deeply about you Violet." Then she frowned. "As much as I hate to say it, he is telling the truth about Sophia. But that's something

Garrett and her need to work out, so don't feel guilty about it."

"He was telling the truth?" I asked hopefully.

She nodded. "People make mistakes. Goddess knows how many your Dad made with me. But I wasn't perfect either. I'm proud that you chose to try and work through it with your mate."

"Thanks Mom."

She smiled before her eyes glazed over. "They're done."

I spun around, yanking open the door, my eyes immediately finding him. Jasper's face was flushed, and he looked a little emotional. I quickly took my seat next to him, reaching for his hand. The sparks from our contact made me smile.

"Are you okay?" I asked.

Dad snorted. "You make it seem like I'm a monster."

"My monster." Mom leaned down and pecked him on the lips.

"I'm good. We just talked." Jasper squeezed my hand.

"And now I'd like to talk as a family," Dad said. He looked Jasper in the eye. "I'm very surprised about the colour of your wolf."

"I am, too," Jasper admitted.

"He won't tell you anything?"

"I've asked him. But I never met my Dad, and my Mom was a rogue."

"He wouldn't remember someone he's also never met," Mom said thoughtfully. "But we can recognize our kin. If you were to find you Dad, your biological father, your wolf would know him."

Jasper's hand tightened in mine, his jaw clenching. I knew exactly how he felt about his real Dad, and just how eager he was to find him. Not at all.

"You don't have to," I told him gently.

"Actually," Dad said, "I think you do. It's not just your colour that has me curious, but also your eyes."

"My eyes?"

"Only one family that I know of has your eye colour Jasper. It's uncommonly rare."

"Which family?" Mom asked.

Dad looked at Jasper as he spoke. "The Warrick's. Specifically Alpha Warrick and his son."

My eyes widened; Jasper's mouth fell open and Mom gasped.

"You. . . you think I have Alpha blood?" Jasper whispered.

"I think so," Dad nodded.

Jasper shook his head slowly. It wasn't hard to tell what he was thinking; you could almost see the words on his face.

"It would also explain why you're Violet's mate," Dad continued. "She is the daughter of an Alpha, and being mated to another Alpha, even with a diluted bloodline-"

"Dad!"

"No, he's right. My Mom was a rogue," Jasper said.

"Still." I gave Dad a dirty look. "You could word it a better way." By the look on Mom's face, I knew she agreed with me.

"We don't know the situation," Mom said, still frowning at her mate. "You're Mom may not have always been a rogue. Maybe she was forced to leave the pack."

Jaspers nodded mutely. "So, this means I have to. . . what? Get a hold of this Alpha?"

"Already done. I had my Beta get a hold of him this morning. He's on his way here and should be here by tomorrow."

"Dimitri!" Mom smacked his shoulder.

"What?"

"How could you do that? Without consulting Jasper first? It should be his choice!"

Dad looked between her and Jasper, his face reddening. "I. . . you're right. I'm sorry."

My heart squeezed. Jasper looked at me with wild eyes.

"I'll be right here with you. I promise," I mindlinked him.

"I don't know. I don't know if I can do this, Vie."
"You don't have to. Whatever you decide, I'm with you."
"Do you promise?"
"Absolutely."

He took a deep breath. Then he looked at my parents. "Okay. I'll meet him."

We still had things to work on, that was for sure. But if there was anyone I trusted, it was my Mom. If she said Jasper was a good guy, then I believed that heart and soul. He'd made mistakes. Mistakes that were causing drama between Garrett and I. But Mom was right about that too. Garrett needed to grow the fuck up and let me live my own life. Whatever problems he had with Sophia, he needed to work out. Just like I did with Jasper. Until then, I would be here for him, while we figured this out.

One step at a time.

"Can my parents be there?" Jasper looked at my Dad, who nodded.

"You can tell them. Be here tomorrow around noon. We'll meet in the cafeteria."

"We really need to set up a meeting place other than the cafeteria," Mom grumbled. "It's not very formal."

"Neither is the game room."

"Why don't we convert one of the free rooms?"

I tuned them out while they debated. Jasper rubbed slow circles on my hand on the table, his eyes searching mine.

"I'd like to meet your parents," I told him quietly.

"They'd love to meet you."

I smiled. "Shall we?"

He glanced at Mom and Dda. "Are we allowed to leave?"

I laughed and stood. "I'm going to meet Jasper's folks. I'll be back later."

"Alright." Mom barely dismissed me; she was too into her new renovation plans. I walked to the door, him trailing behind me, and saying an awkward thank you, to which Mom waved her hand at him. I snickered.

"Wow they really get in deep when they talk."

93

"Yeah. I think it's cute," I smiled. "You ready to introduce your new girlfriend to your parents?"

He chuckled. "Girlfriend?"

"Is that not what I am?"

His arms went around my waist. He had to bend slightly to place them there, he was so tall.

"I was under the impression you were something more, actually."

"Was that a roundabout proposal?"

"Would you say yes if it was?"

I smacked his chest lightly. "Too soon buddy. Try again in a year or so."

A smirk took over his face. "I'll remember that."

"I have no doubt."

We left the packhouse, and I looked towards the trees. He seemed to have the same urge, so hand in hand, we headed that way. Once we were deep enough, I went behind a bush and stripped. The second shift was a million times easier, considering only hours before I'd been in the most pain of my life. It was still a little tense, but it felt more natural. I shook out my fur, coming out to find Ehno sitting and waiting for me. Picking up my clothes with my teeth, I gave him the lead and took off after him.

I didn't think I'd ever get tired of running through the woods in this form. I felt so *free*. The feeling of the dirt beneath my paws, and the wind coursing through my fur was indescribable. We ran East, occasionally brushing against one another. I took the time to look at Ehno, really look at him. He was much bigger than a rogue, maybe even a few inches bigger than my Dad. Even if Jaspers Dad wasn't Alpha Warrick, he definitely didn't have a rogue for a father.

I came to a stop when he did, and he pointed with his nose in the direction I assumed his house was. Finding a wide tree, I shifted back and got dressed. I walked back to him with a huge smile.

"I love running in Hala's form!" I exclaimed.

"I know what you mean. We should go for a run, a real run, later. I know a place we can go."

"Okay."

He took my hand and started leading me. I was suddenly nervous, but probably not as nervous as he had been meeting my parents. I still wanted to make a good impression, though. We cut through the trees into a backyard. A playset was structured off to the side, complete with a swing set and a large apple tree nearby. A brick firepit was dug into the ground, a metal grill placed over top. Beyond that lay wide flower beds, dancing with colours. I picked out four different types of flowers and several rose bushes, and still more species that I didn't know.

"Your Mom likes to garden, huh?"

"Oh yeah. She has a green thumb."

"She's done a great job. These beds are beautiful!"

"Thank you very much."

I looked up to see a woman coming out the back door. She had medium length blond hair, gentle blue eyes and a kind smile. Her build was slender, but fit, and she had a graceful walk, almost bordering on dancing. She was lovely, and I liked her immediately.

"You must be Jaspers Mom." I held out my hand, but she ignored it, pulling me in for a hug instead.

"I'm so happy to meet you!" she gushed.

"Vie, this is my Mom, Linda," Jasper introduced her.

"You can call me Mrs. Cole for now, or Linda if you're comfortable with it, dear."

"I like Linda," I smiled shyly.

She grinned. "My husband is at work, but he will be home later this afternoon. You're welcome to come inside. Stay as long as you want."

She seemed so happy to meet me, I couldn't say no. I followed her inside and was instantly attacked.

"Hi!" A little girl who resembled Linda a lot was stuck to me, hugging my legs tightly. I looked at Jasper and he laughed.

"This is my little sister, Elena. She's a little eccentric."

Elena looked at me, and my heart melted. She was the most adorable girl ever, with her slightly chubby cheeks, dimples and big blues eyes. She was missing a top tooth, the gap showing as she grinned hugely at me.

"I'm the cool one!" she stated and I almost died.

"I can totally see that," I laughed. Jasper put a hand to his heart.

"You two wound me!"

"Are you Jasper's mate?" Elena asked me.

"Uh, yeah."

Her eyes lit up and she let go of me to hop around.

"I have a sister! A big sister!" she squealed happily.

Linda scooped her up and bopped her nose with her finger. "Come on. I'll put out some snacks and we can all get to know each other a bit better."

CHAPTER 16
DYLAN

"Babe, I'll be back later."

"Okay. Don't miss me too much."

"Impossible."

I gave Brianne a loving kiss, a tingle running down my spine. Who would have thought *I* would turn into such a mushy guy? This woman brought out the best in me, and apparently my best included this side.

"I love you," I told her.

"I love you, too. Have fun."

I kissed her cheek before finally making my way out the door. I was supposed to leave over an hour ago, but Brianne had other ideas. Fun ideas. Sexy ideas. Needless to say, I felt a whole lot lighter, and I was in one Hell of a good mood. Whistling a random tune while I drove, I made my way to the packhouse. I hadn't seen Garrett or Violet in a while, too caught up in Brianne. I felt kinda guilty, so I set aside some time to spend with them today while Brianne was spending time with her sister. After the shifting ceremony, both of them had taken off pretty quickly, and I hadn't had a chance to congratulate them.

I was ecstatic. Uhni was a great wolf, a deep brown. With my hopes of becoming a warrior someday soon, his colour would make for excellent camouflage. Brianne loved him, and he enjoyed being around her too. I couldn't wait until her birthday next week. Uhni was pretty eager to meet his other half, even if she wouldn't shift for another month. I pulled up to the packhouse, my whistling cutting off as I jogged up the front steps. Nodding hello to some of the maids, I made my way to the stairs.

"Hello Dylan!"

I looked up to see Luna Lily coming down. I smiled cheerily.

"Hey Luna. How are you?"

"I'm good. And you? How is your mate?"

I grinned and she smiled cheekily.

"She's amazing Luna. I've never been happier."

"I'm glad to hear it! Are you here to see Garrett?"

"And Violet."

"I think Violet went out for a bit. But Garrett should be in his room."

I nodded. "Thanks, Luna. Have a nice day."

She clucked her tongue at me. "No need for such formalities, Dylan. You practically live here, or you did. Call me Lily."

"And have the Alpha on my ass? No, thanks."

She continued to laugh as she passed by me. I took the steps two at a time, reaching his floor. I skipped along the hallway, tapping three times on the door. Nobody answered. Had he gone out too?

"Garrett?" I called.

"*What?*"

My smile faltered at his tone through the wood. Tentatively, I opened the door, peeking around and my eyes grew. The room looked like a tornado had passed through. The dresser against the wall had been taken apart, by force it looked like, the clothes strewn everywhere. The bed had deep gouge marks in it, the springs showing. Every game he owned was broken, the discs smashed into tiny pieces on the floor., mixed in with the clothes. Even the *walls* had holes in them. And sitting in the middle of the chaos was Garrett, glaring at me.

"What happened in here?" I asked as I shut the door.

"What does it look like?" He waved his arms around. "I got angry."

I pursed my lips. "And you thought destroying everything you own was going to make you feel better?"

"I kinda hoped, yeah."

I sat next to him, being careful of the broken disc shards. "What's wrong?"

"Violet." He said her name like it was a curse word. My heart stuttered and my jaw fell open. I had *never* heard either one of the twins use that tone regarding the other. Honestly, it scared the shit out of me.

"What happened?" I demanded.

"She found her mate," he snapped.

My face morphed into confusion. I remembered someone being with Violet when she shifted, but he'd had his back to me. And I was too focused on my own shift to pay close enough attention.

"Okay?"

Garrett slammed his fists down on the floor. "It's fucking *Jasper!*" he shouted.

He looked at me, and even though I was surprised, my face remained neutral. This aggravated him even more.

"Jasper? Jasper Cole?"

"Yeah, I know who you meant."

"Aren't you upset?!"

I sighed. "Not really, dude. I mean, I know I would have been a few weeks ago, if I hadn't found Brianne." I leaned against his bed. "I get why you're pissed, but it's Vie's choice. I'm assuming she didn't reject him, since you're this upset."

"You don't know the half of it."

"So, explain it to me then."

"Remember Sophia?"

My nose scrunched up as I thought. "That girl you use to hang out with and fawn over?"

He launched into the story, giving me every detail, right up to earlier when Violet smacked him. He grew more and more upset as he talked, and by the end, he was breathing hard, his chest heaving up and down.

"And now she's run off to spend the day with her precious mate," he sneered. "Can you believe that?!"

Oh man, he was going to hate me right now. "Actually, yeah I can."

"What?"

"Dude, I hate to say it, and you really don't want to hear it, but Vie's right." I shrugged. "Sophia should have told Jasper about you guys. And even though the guy is an ass, I doubt he would have forced her into anything. Don't give me that look, Garrett. If you guys were that close, and that in love, she would have come running to you if something like that had happened to her."

His shoulders dropped. He knew I was right. He knew Violet was right. He just didn't want to admit it.

"Look," I continued, "I'm sorry you're going through this. But honestly, I think you need to let it go. How does Sophia feel about everything?"

"I don't know. I haven't seen her since my shift."

I punched him in the arm. "Seriously?! You're giving Violet Hell about her mate, and you haven't talked to yours? Man, you need to grow up."

I stood, walking to the door.

"Where are you going?"

"Sorry, Garrett. But you need to figure shit out, and no offense, but you're not great company right now. Go find your mate, and stop being a baby."

And I left. If I was anyone else, he would have probably beat the shit out of me for talking to him that way. He was my future Alpha, after all. But even he did, he needed to hear it.

I ended up wandering aimlessly around town, window shopping. I saw a few things I thought Brianne would like for her birthday, making a mental note. I walked for a couple hours, hoping Garrett took my advice and he was with Sophia right now. I had always been suspicious of their relationship, assuming they were at least fooling around. She must be really special to have him so worked up; Garrett was the most level-headed person I knew.

"Dylan?"

I turned at the sound of my name, smiling when I saw Violet. She was sitting on someone's front yard with a kid, a blanket spread out under them. I crossed the street, waving.

"Hey. What are you doing?"

The kid she was with, a girl who was maybe five or six years old, looked over her shoulder at me.

"We're having a picnic. Duh." She rolled her eyes and Violet chuckled.

"What she said."

I looked around. "I don't see any food."

"It's an *imaginary* picnic!" the girl said. She looked at Vie as if to say, 'who is this guy?'

I pointed to her, a question on my face. Before she could answer, the front door opened and Jasper walked out, balancing three plates. He stopped when he saw me, his eyes narrowing a bit.

"Hey," I greeted him.

"Hey."

"Jasper, you know Dylan, right?" Violet said.

"Sort of."

"Well, come join us, Dylan. The more the merrier." She made room for me on the blanket, and Jasper sighed, but didn't argue. He joined us, setting down the plates with actual sandwiches on them.

"What do you say, Elena?"

"Thank you!"

He smiled at her. She must be his sister. Nobody spoke for several minutes. The tension was awkward.

"So. . ." Violet cleared her throat. "How's Brianne?"

"Good."

"That's good."

I glanced at Jasper, who was already eyeing me. I sighed, and so did Violet.

"Elena, do you have any sidewalk chalk?" she asked.

"I have lots!"

"Great! How about you get it and we can draw together?"

"Okay!" She ran off into the house, leaving the three of us alone.

"Okay," Violet said quickly. "I know you two don't necessarily like each other, but Dylan is my best guy friend.

And his mate is my best girl friend. So can we please, *please* try to get along?" she begged.

I looked at Jasper. "I've got no issues. I mean, I did. But I'm over it. I'm not here to cause problems man, I was just walking by when I saw Vie. And for the record, I'm sorry about the shit at school."

He put down his sandwich. "Yeah, same. I'm not looking for a fight if you're not."

"Not today." I grinned and he snorted.

Elena came running back out, dumping a ton of chalk onto the walkway. Vie got up and they started outlining a picture.

"You fish?" Jasper asked me randomly.

"Sometimes. Haven't been in a while."

He looked at Violet and his sister, giggling together. "I can tell she doesn't want anymore fighting. Especially with what happened with her brother. You heard?"

"Yeah, I saw him earlier. I told him to get over it."

"Did you?"

I shrugged one shoulder. "No point in being pissed off about the past."

He looked at me for a couple minutes, seeming to come to a decision. "I'm taking Violet to a place I know later, in the woods. You wanna come? I've got some poles there. Maybe if we catch something, we can make dinner."

"That sounds cool. But only if I can bring Brianne." I reached over, stealing Vie's sandwich. "The girls haven't seen each other in a while."

"Cool."

CHAPTER 17
VIOLET

It had been an amazing day with Jaspers family. His Mom was super nice, and super funny. We talked for hours, with Elena sitting on my lap the majority of the time. Linda liked to write short stories in her free time, and showed me some of her work. I had to admit, I was impressed. She told me she was working on a series of children's books, some already published and sitting on Elenas bookshelf. Around four, Jaspers Dad came home, and he was equally as excited to meet me as his wife was. I liked him as much as her, with his strong, yet kind personality and his endless array of Dad jokes that made Jasper groan.

I was in love with this family, and I felt so grateful that they had taken him in. When Linda asked Jasper to run to the store around the corner, I gathered the courage to ask her about it.

"There was no question," She'd said. "We were in the process of trying to adopt. We were told the chances of conceiving a pup of our own were very low, but we could keep trying. Your Mom was so nice throughout our struggle; she was my doctor. And then one night, we got a call from her, asking us if we could come to the packhouse. She said it was urgent, so we did. The last thing I expected was a little boy to be waiting there with her."

She'd smiled, lost in the memory. "He was covered in dirt, the poor thing, and he was exhausted. Your Mom made sure he had plenty to eat, and a nice bed to sleep in. Then she asked us if we would be willing to take him in. We said yes. Of course, we had wanted a baby, but how could I say no? I knew from the second I saw him that I loved him. And he's been our son ever since." She'd laughed, the noise tinkling in the air. "And then we got our miracle baby, Elena. At first, I was worried how Jasper would take it, having a sibling. But I never had anything to worry about; he's always been there for her, always protecting her and looking after her. Her first word was 'Haspa', until she learned to pronounce his name."

What made me love them more was the fact that they always encouraged Jasper to remember his birth mother. She'd told me they would sit down sometimes and ask him questions about her, and then always remind him to keep her memory close. They were truly rare people, and I felt lucky to be apart of their family now. It made me see a new side of Jasper, a side he kept hidden from people. The love and caring he showed his family was completely different than the sarcastic, sometimes asshole that I knew. And then Dylan had shown up, totally unexpectedly, and I feared there would be another spat like this morning with my brother.

Much to my surprise, Jasper had invited him and Brianne to wherever we were going today, and I was thrilled. The best part was there wasn't any awkwardness between Dylan and I. We chatted like friends as we walked through the woods, as it always should have been. He held hands with his mate, a small smile on his lips that never left.

"Thanks for coming along. I'm glad Jasper invited you," I told them.

"We missed you Vie," said Brianne. "Sorry I've been MIA that last little while."

"I understand. Don't worry."

She smiled. "We should make plans, just the two of us. We could go into the city and have a shopping day."

"That sounds awesome. How about Saturday?"

"Perfect."

"I hope Garrett smartens up by then," Dylan grumbled. "I'd hate to spend the day alone if you're out."

My heart squeezed and my guts twisted. I shook my head, pushing the negative feelings down. I didn't like fighting with my brother, but he was the only one stubbornly holding onto something that everyone else had let go of. If he didn't find a way to move on soon, I'd have to get our parents involved. This anger of his was eating him from the inside out. It wasn't healthy.

Dylan walked ahead of us, joining Jasper and they started talking. Brianne sidled up next to me, giving me a look.

"So, you and Jasper huh?"

"Yeah, it seems so."

"And you're okay with it? With his. . . you know, past?"

I looked at the back of my mate, catching him as he glanced back at me and smiled.

"I've learned recently that you shouldn't believe everything you hear. So, yes, I'm okay with it," I replied quietly.

"Have you guys done it yet?"

I almost tripped over a root at her words. "What?! No! We've only been mates for a day!"

She giggled. "Doesn't matter. As soon as you left, Dylan and I did."

"On school grounds?!"

"Yup!" she chirped. "Man, can he ever-"

I covered my ears. "Okay! I love you, but I do *not* need details about your sex life!"

She laughed, throwing her arm over my shoulder. "Just wait girl. Sex with your mate is unbelievable."

I nodded silently. After all, I didn't have anything to compare it to. Jasper would be my first, and my only. Even if he was terrible, I wouldn't know the difference. Which made me wonder, how would *I* be for *him*?

"Stop worrying, Vie."

"I'm not."

"You're biting your lip." She pulled my lip from between my teeth with her finger. "It'll be fine!"

I lowered my voice, slowing my steps even more so the guys wouldn't hear us. Hopefully.

"But what if it's not? What if I'm terrible at it?" I whispered to her anxiously.

"Just go with what feels right. And if anything makes you uncomfortable, tell him right away. Communication is key. But I'm sure he'll take it slow with you. The first time anyway," she smirked.

"How much. . . uhm. . . does it really hurt? Like, a lot?"

"Not as much as you think. And *definitely* not as much as your shift. And it's temporary, it only lasts a minute."

"Okay. And how do I-?"

"What are you guys whispering about back there?" Dylan called to us.

"Nothing!" I squealed. I could tell my face was bright red, and both the boys looked between us before shrugging. Though I thought Jasper was hiding a smile.

"Well, here we are," he said.

I looked around, my eyes finding the most adorable log cabin. The wood was red, with a black shingled roof. Two windows faced us on this side, reflecting the sunlight, and I could see a little dock hanging over a large pond. A barbeque sat off to the side, along with an old-fashioned barrel filled with fishing rods. It was the picture of comfort, a forest getaway. I loved it.

"Wow," I exhaled.

"I had no idea this was out here," Dylan added.

"I found it years ago. Dad helped me fix it up; it's actually just outside of pack borders, so be mindful of rogues," Jasper warned us.

Brianne looked around cautiously. "Do rogues come here often?"

"Not really."

"How far back is the border?" I asked.

"About ten minutes."

I nodded, reassured.

"I'll go set up the rods," Dylan said. Brianne went with him, and I stopped beside Jasper, looking up at him.

"You come here a lot?"

"Yeah. Mostly when I need to think, or I just want to be alone. It's nice, yeah?"

"It's beautiful," I replied.

"I think your beauty only enhances what's here."

I laughed, my cheeks turning pink. "That was cheesy."

"But it made you smile. I'll count it as a win."

I grinned up at him, shaking my head. Slowly, he took my hand, guiding me to the cabin. It was even bigger up close, and now I could see a small firepit, with some previously burned wood inside. A push mower was tucked around the back, along with a meat smoker. Looking into one of the windows as we passed, I saw a nice modern fridge and stove, as well as a long island. A living area was beyond it, and I wondered if the whole place was open concept.

"I don't have much here, yet. Just the essentials," Jasper explained.

"Well, I think it's amazing," I told him honestly.

"If you want, you can bring some stuff here." He rubbed the back of his neck. "I mean, you can come here whenever you want, but bringing some clothes might be a good idea."

"Thank you. I will, definitely." He smiled, my heart fluttering. Dylan walked over us to us, handing Jasper a rod before offering one to me. Brianne grabbed the sodas she'd bought for us out of her backpack, passing them out. Together, we sat on the dock, talking and laughing quietly as not to scare away the fish.

I was positive I wouldn't be home anytime soon. I was about to call my Mom when I realized I could mindlink now. It was easy to forget, as I hadn't been doing it my whole life, but it sure was convenient.

"Hey Mom?" I focused on her, reaching out with my mind.

"Violet? What's up?"

"I just wanted to let you know I won't be home for dinner. And probably not for a while after."

She was silent for a minute before answering. *"Okay. Where are you?"*

"I'm with Jasper, Dylan and Brianne. We're at a cabin in the woods. It is outside of the pack, but only ten minutes."

I could feel her anxiety rising. I really thought we were past her freaking out.

"Should I send some of the warriors?"

"No, Mom please."

"Violet-"

"I'm fine, Mom. Jaspers Dad knows exactly where we are, and if I really need to, the border is ten minutes away like I said. Can you just trust me? Please?"

I could almost hear her groan from here. *"Fine! But I am sending an extra group to patrol the border where you are. They won't bug you."*

I didn't argue, because I knew that's the best I was going to get. *"Thank you, Mom."*

"Are you spending the night?"

I raised my eyebrows at her question. *"Uh, I hadn't thought about it, but probably not. I thought you wanted me back by eleven?"*

"I would, but. . . since you're with Jasper I just thought you'd like to spend the night with him," she finished in a rush.

I decided to be honest with her. *"Mom, I'm not ready for that yet."*

"Okay. Well, if you come home, then alright. But if not, you'll be at the cabin? You won't go anywhere else without telling me?"

"Yes. I promise."

"Thank you. Have fun dear."

"Thanks. I will."

I ended the link, breathing out a sigh. I had expected her to demand me home by my curfew, and not a minute late. But it seemed like she was easing up on me, a little bit. Admittedly, I did feel a little better about extra patrols.

"I think we've caught enough," Jasper said then. "Well, Dylan and I have anyway."

I looked in the bucket behind me, filled with six big fish. I stuck out my tongue at Jasper and he laughed.

"Who wants to do the deed?" Dylan asked, nodding at the bucket. Brianne grimaced, and Jasper looked away. I sighed and stood. Dylan helped me move the bucket off the dock and onto the grass before turning and leaving me.

"Hey! Where are you going?"

"I catch em', I don't kill em'," he called over his shoulder.

"You all are a bunch of wusses!" I called back.

Jasper brought me a knife and one by one, I cut off the heads of the fish, letting the blood drain onto the ground. He watched me work with a disgusted face.

"How can you be disgusted by this, when you want to be a warrior? Killing rogues is a lot messier than *this*," I gestured to the blood-soaked ground.

"That's different. If I kill a rogue, or anyone, it'll be a life-or-death situation. These fish aren't trying to kill me."

"Then you should have thrown them back."

"Little late for that now."

"I'll say. You're silly, you know that?"

"Oh, am I?"

I nodded as I sliced through the last fish. "You will catch them, but not kill them, but then you'll cook and eat them? It makes no sense."

He shrugged nonchalantly. "I guess I am kind of silly."

I giggled. He helped me carry the fish into the cabin where I put them in the sink to clean them. After that, I left him to work, as he appeared to be in the zone. I took the time to explore the cabin. The living area was cozy, with a nice big fireplace, reading chair and sofa. I wandered down the little hallway, opening a door that led to a white tiled bathroom with a deep tub and a shower. I'd definitely have to make use of that tub later. It looked incredibly relaxing. There was a door that led to a room filled with some boxes of books and other various items. I assumed Jasper was using it as a storage room for now. The last room was the bedroom.

A giant king size bed sat in the middle of the room, with a deep red comforter pulled over. Four pillows were lined up at the headboard, and cute, home-made looking tables sat on either side with lamps on them. A long wooden dresser was placed to the side, and a bookshelf filled with books beside that. Standing in front of it, I examined the titles, recognizing some of my favourites. I picked one off the shelf, skimming through the pages, surprised at how worn the book was.

"You Like Elliot?"

I turned to see Jasper leaning against the door frame. He was studying me carefully.

"He's one of my favourite authors actually." I held up the book. "One of yours?"

He nodded. "He's one of my favourites, too. I've read that probably twenty times over."

"You know how to read?" I asked in mock surprise as I put it back in its place.

"Quite well actually," he responded anyway. He walked over, picking a book from over my head. "This is one of my favourites." He handed it to me.

The Philosophy of Aristotle by Renford Bambrough.

I gave him a skeptical look. "Seriously?"

He leaned over, placing one arm above me on the shelf. His eyes never left mine, and my heartbeat was starting to pick up.

"Want to know my favourite quote by him?"

"Sure."

"'Love is composed of a single soul inhabiting two bodies'," he recited, and my breathing nearly stopped. "Pretty accurate, don't you think?"

He took the book from me, tossing it onto the bed before placing his hand on my cheek. At this point, I didn't think I could answer him.

"Do you think. . . could we try this kiss thing again?" he asked softly. "Only if you want to, though."

I nodded mutely, excitement and nerves running through me. Jasper leaned in, and my eyes closed. When his lips touched mine, a single spark shot through me, running from my head to my toes. My stomach felt like it was full of butterflies, and my mind seemed to turn off. And then I was kissing him back, my hands running through his soft hair. I secured his face to mine, unable, and unwilling, to let him go. I pulled him closer, our bodies flushed together. Everything became heat and passion and sparks. A soft moan sounded from me, and he grinned against my lips before pulling back.

"Wow," I breathed. What a first kiss!

CHAPTER 18
JASPER

Our little group sat outside around the fire, laughing into the night. I hadn't been sure how this was going to go, with Dylan. But he seemed content to put whatever feud we had behind him, and so was I. If I was being honest, I actually liked the guy. He was pretty fucking funny, and just as sarcastic as I was. He also obviously cared about Violet, and that was a big thing for me. I wanted people around her I could trust, and I knew he would never let anything happen to her if I wasn't around. He'd been transparently honest with me too, telling me how he'd hoped Violet was his mate before he found Brianne. It didn't bug me. He looked happy as Hell with her.

Brianne, I knew I could also trust. She was sweet, kind of like a baby deer, but she also has a wild side, I was sure. They both seemed to warm up to me as the night went on, and we all got to know each other on a friendly level. Part of me hoped Dylan would talk to Garrett and get him to back off. The other part of me didn't really care, however. I was happy with Vie, and if the kiss we shared earlier said anything, she was happy, too.

All evening, she'd been sneaking peeks at me, holding my hand when she wasn't busy eating or talking. Another little quirk I loved about her, she used her hands to talk, some might say too much, but I thought it was cute. She was very expressive, animated. It took a lot of focus to pay attention to anything other than her. Finally, though, Dylan stood and stretched.

"We should get going. I have my first warrior training session tomorrow and I don't want to be late."

Brianne stood with him, but Violet stayed seated.

"I'll see you guys later. I'll text you tomorrow, Brianne, and we can decide where to go this weekend," she smiled.

"Sounds good. We'll see you guys later. Thanks, Jasper, for inviting us out. This was fun."

"No problem. You guys are welcome anytime."

They waved as they walked off.

"Should we walk with them to the border?" Violet asked me.

"Nah. We'd know if anyone was around. And didn't you say your Mom sent extra warriors?"

"Yeah. You're right."

"Shouldn't you be going home too?" I asked as evenly as I could. I didn't want her to go, and she surprised me by grinning hugely.

"Actually, Mom said I don't have a curfew tonight." She leaned back, staring into the fire. "I was thinking you and I could hang out some more. If you want."

I returned her grin. "I'd love that."

"Want to go for a run?" she asked eagerly. I nodded, just as excitedly. "Oh wait. I promised I'd tell Mom if we were going anywhere."

Her eyes glazed over for several minutes. I waited patiently. She blinked, her eyes going back to normal.

"My Mom would feel more comfortable if we ran within the borders."

"That's fine. We can shift here and head that way."

I walked inside, letting her shift in private. When I heard soft yipping outside, I knew she was done. I was barely out the door when Hala was in my face, licking me. I laughed heartily, putting my hand on her snout. Goddess, she really was beautiful.

"Hey Hala. You ready to run?"

She jumped back, crouching into a play position.

"You two have fun, okay?"

She snorted in response, and I took my shirt off. I had a few extra clothes here, so I didn't care about my pants, but I liked that shirt. I tossed it into the cabin before closing the door and shifting myself. Ehno stretched his legs before trotting over to his mate. They sniffed each other, giving little licks. I could feel my wolfs thought process and spoke up.

"Don't even think about it."

"But she's my mate too," he whined.

"You can wait until after Violet and I have mated. Keep it in your pants."

"I don't wear pants, though."

"Ehno!"

"Alright, alright! You're no fun at all," he growled lowly, making me snicker.

We took off, with me sitting comfortably at the back of my mind. I simply enjoyed the freedom of being in his form while he ran, played and hunted with Hala. We passed border patrol, who nodded at us. I was sure they weren't too far away, but they gave us space to be together, which I appreciated. Only once did I have to reprimand my wolf when Hala stretched, giving him a good view of her backside. He laid down, covering his eyes with his paw, grouching at me.

It was after midnight when we returned to the cabin. Violet went around the side of the cabin to shift while I shifted where I had before, quickly going into the house to find pants. She entered the bedroom as I was doing up the zipper, her eyes grazing over my bare chest until they met mine.

"That was fun," she said.

"Yeah." I leaned against the dresser. "What do you want to do?"

She pursed her lips, thinking. "You have a T.V. in the living room. Got any movies?"

"Tons."

She turned and I followed her out. Flopping down on the sofa, she curled her legs under her. I bent down in front of the T.V. stand, scanning the DVD's.

"What's your favourite genre?" I asked.

"Horror."

I looked at her. I had *more* than enough horror movies in here, including some old classics. "You're not into chick flicks?"

"Why? Do you want to watch one?" she teased.

"No, thanks. I've sat through my fair share with my Mom." I shuddered and she laughed.

I picked a DVD, holding up the case. She nodded enthusiastically, so I popped it in the player and joined her on the couch. Grabbing the blanket off the back, I threw it over us. I'd left the lights off, so the only light in the room came from the T.V. About half an hour into the movie, I felt Violet snickering beside me.

"What?"

"No matter how many times I watch this movie, this part always gets me." She gestured towards the screen. "This chick is the definition of stupid. Half of her friends are already dead, and her brilliant idea is to hide in a closet? Because that's not *obvious*," she giggled.

"There's always one dumb girl in a horror movie. And she always seems to fall down a lot, too."

"And why is she always thin and blond?"

I shrugged. "Sex appeal?"

"She's only sexy until her heads get chopped off!" she laughed. "I'm glad I'm smarter than that."

"Where would you hide?"

"Hide? Fuck that. If someone was killing my friends in a house, *I'd leave the house.*"

Now I laughed. She was something else. We settled back in, occasionally making fun of the idiocy of the people on screen and commenting on how fake the gore was. Violet picked the next movie, another classic horror, but this time, she snuggled into my side as we watched. I was still shirtless, and her cheek created tiny sparks and tingles where it touched my skin. I draped my arm over her, completely content.

We started talking, eventually forgetting the movie completely. It sounds corny, but I wanted to know everything about her, everything I didn't know already. Her

115

favourite colour was green, her favourite type of music was old rock n' roll. I asked her favourite foods and ice cream flavours, and where she liked to spend her time when she wasn't at home or with friends. After two hours of asking each other questions, teasing one another and laughing together, I felt closer to her than ever.

"So. . ."

"Yes?" She took a sip of her soda, looking at me sideways.

"Ehno says you're a Midnight Wolf."

Her eyes cast down and she nodded. "Yeah, I guess so."

"What is that, exactly?"

She tucked her hair behind her ears, suddenly looking self-conscious. "I'm not sure. Hala says I. . . *we're*. . . the first. Ever."

"Yeah, Ehno said that too."

She bit her lip, still not looking at me. Then she spoke. "I don't get it. Why me? Why not Garrett?"

"What do you mean?"

"Like I told Hala, it should have been my brother. I'm not the one who's taking over the pack; I'm nothing special. So why give me this gift?"

A little bit of anger spread through my chest. She thought she wasn't special? I vocalized my question, and she blinked at me, finally meeting my eyes.

"I'm the troublemaker. I sneak out, go to parties, get in fights. Goddess knows I'm always up to something behind my parents back, even if it's petty shit. *If* you have Alpha Blood, that will make me a Luna, but so what? I was never born to be the leader, any type of leader. Garrett was trained for that, not me."

I sat up, taking her face in my hands gently. I made sure she was looking into my eyes before I spoke, really wanting her to listen.

"Violet." Her name rolled off my tongue a bit harshly. "Don't say that about yourself."

"But it's-"

"No, it's *not* true. Yes, you get into trouble. Yes, you get into fights. But none of that makes you unworthy of what you were given. You know what I see? I see someone who stands up for what she believes in. You have never been in, or started, a fight that wasn't worth fighting. As for the rest, it's called being young. Nobody is going to look down on you because you climbed out your bedroom window a few times to go to a party," I smirked. "But most importantly, you're doubting yourself as a leader? Come on. I've seen you step in and take charge a million times while your brother sat on the sidelines. I'm not saying he won't make a good Alpha, I'm sure he will. But *you*. . ." I shook my head. "You never needed to be trained for something you have inside you. People look up to you, they admire you. They admire your strength, and your intelligence. So, no more putting yourself down. The Goddess knows what's she's doing. And I believe she chose you because of who you are on the inside; an amazing, special, intelligent, beautiful person with a good heart and an even better soul."

Her eyes were misty when I finished speaking, my thumbs caressing her cheeks lightly. She sniffed a little, opening her mouth, but no words came out. Never had I seen her speechless, but it was cute as fuck to watch. Finally, she nodded, a tiny smile forming.

"Thank you," she whispered.

I kissed her forehead. "Anytime."

She pulled my face down, connecting her lips to mine. And just like before, a jolt went through me, like a bolt of electricity. I never thought the mate bond could be so intense! Her hands were in my hair, pulling me closer to deepen the kiss, and I happily obliged. Somehow, we ended up with Violet lying on the couch and me hovering above her. The feel of her under me was driving me insane, and it wasn't as easy to hide my erection this way. It wasn't like I could help it, but I didn't want her to feel uncomfortable or think I was moving too fast. So, I gave her one more deep kiss before pulling away and sitting up. Her face dropped into a pout.

"Don't give me that look, missy. There's only so much I can handle when it comes to you." I pulled the blanket over my lap and her cheeks turned pink as she understood.

She looked at me for a minute before looking down, playing with her fingers. "Can we uh. . . talk about that?"

"That?"

"Well. . . Mom always told me that if you can't talk about sex, then you shouldn't be having it." She glanced up at me.

I raised a brow. "Fair enough."

She took a deep breath. "I'll be honest with you. I'm not. . . ready yet."

"That's okay."

"And it's because I'm. . . a little scared."

I leaned one arm on the back of the sofa, my cheek pressed against my palm. "What are you scared about?"

She blushed deeply now, her whole face turning red. It was amazing how well I could see in the dark now. Before my shift I probably wouldn't have noticed as much.

"You have. . . experience. I don't. I'm scared I'm not going to be good for you, that you won't like it with me." She rushed through the sentence, my mind replaying in slow motion to understand what she said. I almost laughed, but I was positive she would get angry if I did. Instead, I also took a deep breath, thinking through my words.

"I know you're expecting me to say this, but I'm going to say it anyway. You don't need to worry about that, now or ever, Vie. And if you think about it, this is kind of my first time too, because it's with you, my mate. Anyone else, they meant nothing to me. If you want the truth. . ." Now it was my turn to blush. "I uh. . . I only ever slept with anyone else because I couldn't have you." Good Goddess, that sounded bad.

To my surprise, she didn't get angry. "You. . . liked me? I mean, before you knew I was your mate?"

"Violet, I've liked you since you punched that kid for making fun of me in school."

Her eyes widened, her hands covering her mouth. "You remember that?!" she squeaked.

I laughed. "How could I forget? You were badass." I took her hand in mine, smiling. "Does that make you feel better?"

She nodded. "It does, actually."

"Good."

It wasn't like I didn't want her, obviously; I just wanted to move at her pace. I never expected she would jump into bed with me right away, regardless of the bond. When it happened, it be worth waiting for, because it was her.

CHAPTER 19
GARRETT

Hugo was relentless. He kept whining, nagging me to go to our mate and telling me to stop being such a brat. Even my wolf was against me! Finally, after hours and hours of his insistent complaining, I went to find her. She wasn't hard to find. Even when I wasn't following the pull of our bond, I knew the most likely spots she would be. And just like I thought, I found her sitting on her favourite bench in the park nearby, a book in her hands. I took a minute to just look at her. She was as beautiful as ever, even if seeing her stirred mixed emotions inside me.

As if she could feel my presence, her head lifted and turned, our eyes connecting. Hers with wide with surprise, but I kept mine neutral.

"Garrett."

Her voice drifted to me. I walked the remaining distance, sitting next to her the bench. Looking over the park, I noticed for the first time it was rather busy. Parents had brought their kids out to play in the nice weather, swinging and sliding and generally having a great time. The atmosphere of laughter and happiness contrasted hugely to the wave of angst inside of me.

"What are you doing here?" Sophia asked softly.

"I came to find you," I answered bluntly.

"Oh." She put a bookmark in her book, closed it and placed it on her lap.

"You know we need to talk," I continued.

"Yeah."

I sighed, pinching the bridge of my nose. So many things I wanted to say; I was afraid they would all come out at once, and honestly, some of them weren't nice. Sophia sat quietly, waiting. Finally, after I felt I had composed myself enough, I looked at her.

"Why?" I asked.

Her shoulders hunched a little, head bowing lower. "I don't know," she mumbled.

"Don't!" I snapped. She looked at me. "You had a reason. It's tortured me for a long time, the fact that you never told me why. I'm asking now, and I want an honest answer. Why did you cheat on me? Why did you destroy what we had?"

Tears brimmed her eyes, her long lashes fluttering as she tried not to cry openly.

"Because. . . I didn't want to disappoint you. I thought. . . I thought if I had some experience. . . you would be satisfied with me when finally. . ." She trailed off, her eyes once again on her book. I blinked at her, almost spastically.

"Are you telling me you slept with him because you didn't want to disappoint me in bed?" I whispered.

She nodded, her cheeks turning red, her hair falling over her shoulder to hide her face.

"That's. . ." I was stumbling. Stupid? Idiotic? Pathetic? "Dumb," I settled on.

"I know."

"Do you? We could have shared that experience together, Sophia. Wasn't that the point? To make love with the person you actually love?"

"I'm sorry. Looking back now, I don't know what I was thinking. It *was* stupid, and selfish. I should have opened up to you, told you how I was feeling."

"Yeah, you should have."

I got up, too angry to sit there anymore. In my head, Hugo begged to go back to her, but I pushed him aside. I didn't want to talk to her anymore. But Sophia came after me, grabbing my hand.

"Garrett, wait!" she pleaded. "Are you going to reject me?"

"I don't know," I said. Her hand slid out of mine.

"Stop that!"

I turned at the sound of her voice, incredulous to see her so angry. What right did she have to be angry?

121

"Excuse me?"

Sophia crossed her arms. "Stop doing this to me. I get that you want me to hurt, but this is wrong. You're not just hurting me, but you're hurting my wolf too. And yours."

I rolled my eyes. "I'm not vindictive like you Sophia. And you don't even have your wolf yet."

Pain flashed in her eyes, but she kept going. "You don't think I know that she feels what I feel? Even if she's still dormant? And really? I heard what you did to your sister."

"That's not your business," I bit back.

"Either reject me, or accept me, Garrett. I'm serious. This purgatory you're leaving me in is cruel! I haven't shifted yet, so our bond isn't so strong. But I won't let you string me along for days, weeks, months, only to reject me in the end. Just get it over with!"

I took a step back, shocked that she thought I would do that to her. Didn't she understand the effect this had on me? I needed time to think!

"But how long will you take? She's right, this is painful. For everyone," Hugo whined.

"I don't even know your wolfs name," she continued. "If you don't want me as a mate, I get it. I understand, I fucked up. But maybe we can both find chosen mates, or even a second-chance mate, and move on. And be happy. Please Garrett." She *was* crying now, silent tears running down her cheeks steadily.

"Is that what you want?" I rasped. "To be with someone else?"

Sophia scrunched her eyes tight, something she did when she was really upset. "No! Of course I want to be with you! But it's clear that you can't decide if you want to be with me, to move on from what happened in the past, and try to be happy."

"You expect me to forget about it so easily!" I hissed.

"I never said that! I know you won't forget, but you're not even trying to forgive, either. Look at what happened with Violet! The Garrett I know would *never* have tried to come between his sister and her mate! You're letting this hatred consume you!"

"Because of what *you* did Sophia! You expect me to be okay, to accept you, but do you even realize what you did? You took everything we had and threw it in my face!"

"I'm sorry!" she cried. "I know, I know what I did! And I know it hurt you! But I don't regret that as much as I regret what it did to you!"

"You have no idea what it did to me," I growled.

"This, -" She waved her hand at me, "isn't you Garrett. What I regret the most is taking someone so beautiful, and with my actions, turning him into *this*." She shook her head, tears falling on the ground. "Please, just reject me," she sobbed.

I flinched at the plea in her voice. She really wanted me to. She really wanted to end this, whatever it was. Heartbreak? It felt like it. I couldn't bring myself to answer, let alone form the words of rejection. Another sob broke from her chest and my heart hammered painfully in my chest. What was I doing?

She turned away, running back to the bench and scooping up her belongings. And then she left. I stood, rooted in place, for a very long time. By the time I came back to reality, it was getting dark, and everyone had already gone home. I reflected on the last couple of weeks, on how angry I'd been. Not just with her, but with everyone. The confrontation with Vie and Jasper played through my mind, and shame engulfed me.

Turning on my heel, I walked as fast as I could back to the packhouse. There was only one person I wanted to see right now; one person I knew wouldn't bullshit me. The trip back home was blurry, but I was more focused as I climbed the stairs, getting to our floor. I ran down the hall and knocked on his door roughly.

"Come in!"

Dad had barely spoken the words before I was inside his office, closing the door and turning to face him. He was on his feet instantly.

"Garrett? What's the matter? What happened?"

"Sophia. . ." My breath was coming hard, my mind whirling. Dads' expression turned to one of sympathy. He made me sit in the chair opposite his, getting me a glass of water. I chugged the whole thing, the cold burning my throat.

"You rejected her?" he asked quietly, taking the glass from me and setting it on his desk.

I shook my head. "No."

"Then what's wrong?"

"I. . ." I was on my feet then, pacing. "I don't know what to do!" I yelled.

"Okay, okay. Calm down. Breath son. Talk to me."

I told him everything. Everything including what I did to Violet. The words tore from my gut, and when I finished, I collapsed onto the sofa set against the wall. My face felt wet; when had I started crying? Dad stared at me for a while, his face expressionless. Part of me thought he was going to yell at me. The other part of me hoped he would just tell me what to do, because I still didn't fucking know.

Finally, Dad sighed. "Well, that's a mess."

I scrutinized his face again. He didn't look as surprised as one would expect. Which meant. . . "You already knew."

"Yes. Your Mom told me."

"Mom knows?!"

"You're surprised?"

I wasn't, not really. Mom knew more about the goings-ons in the pack than Dad did sometimes. Especially when it came to us. Dad pulled the chair up, sitting in front of me. He rested his elbows on his knees, regarding me with a thoughtful face.

"You still love her. Don't you?"

I clenched my jaw. "She cheated on me."

"That's not what I asked."

"I. . . Yes."

He nodded. "You want my advice?"

"Please."

"It's a tricky situation, because Jasper is your sisters'
mate. And whether you like it or not, she's accepted him.
Now, I won't claim to understand why Sophia did what she
did, or her reason for it. The one thing I will never claim to
understand is women," he smiled. "But it truly sounds like
she regrets it. And I don't think she ever meant to hurt you
the way she did, Garrett. Kids are stupid, they all do stupid
stuff. You guys did."

I opened my mouth, but he held up his hand, silencing
me.

"I know, not that bad. But still. Regardless of what she
did, she was still chosen to be your mate. And I'm sorry,
but she is right; you can't string her along like this, you
need to make a decision. However, I'm guessing that you've
already made your decision, and you just haven't accepted
it yet."

I looked at the ground, breathing deeply. "I want her,
Dad. I want her to be my mate, my wife. To have pups
someday. To have a family with her. But. . . I can't stand
the thought of her around him. And he's going to be
around."

"Jealousy is an ugly thing. Sometimes it takes control of
us, makes us do things we wouldn't do otherwise.
Sometimes, it turns us into monsters."

He leaned in, placing a hand on my shoulder.

"You are the next Alpha. You need to decide what kind
of Alpha you're going to be. I won't lie to you- I was a
monster myself once. It's not something I'd like to ever
return to, and it would break my heart to watch you go
down that path."

I blinked away a few more tears. "Are you saying this
because it's what's best for the pack?"

"I'm saying it because you're my son. This conversation
would be the same whether you were an Alpha, Beta, or a
rogue. You're my son, and I love you. I want what's best for
you, what's going to make *you* happy."

My guts untwisted, my breathing coming easier. It felt
like the hate I'd been clinging onto was physically leaving

my body. I felt lighter. Dad nodded at me, seeing on my face that I'd made my choice. I gave him a hug, mumbling a thank you. He shooed me out of his office after that, and once again, I was running. I flew down the stairs, and through the foyer. A maid dodged out of my way, shooting me a dirty look as she almost got knocked over. I didn't even bother to close the door as I ran out of the packhouse.

In the woods, I stripped and shifted quickly. Hugo was practically dancing on his feet, he was so excited. He took off, winding around trees and leaping over bushes. A herd of deer ran by, terrified of the monstrous wolf moving through the dark. But he paid no mind to them, racing towards the west side of the pack in record time. A few minutes later, we stopped, and I shifted back, getting dressed. Jogging to the edge of the forest, I looked up at Sophias house.

Memories flashed in my mind of when we use to hang out here. Her house was small, the siding painted a fading yellow. She always used to complain about it, saying how much she hated yellow. I smiled, looking at it now. Not giving myself time to turn back, or second-guess myself, I walked out of the trees and straight to the back door. Sophias parents worked nights, which was good tonight, as I didn't want an audience. Rapping on the door, I waited anxiously, bouncing from foot to foot. Was she home? Did she see me already? Was she not going to answer the door?

I looked up as the door swung open. Sophia stared at me, surprised. Then her face clouded over, her arms coming up to hug herself.

"What do you want Garrett?" she asked.

I answered by closing the distance between us. Cupping her face gently, the last thing I saw before I kissed her was her wide eyes. She didn't respond for a second, possibly too shocked. Then she was kissing me back, throwing her arms around me. Joy flooded through me. I wasn't letting her go, not again. We would get through this, somehow. For now, I was happy just to have her in my arms again. I pulled back, grinning at the dazed look on her face.

"My wolfs name is Hugo."

CHAPTER 20
VIOLET

We ended up sleeping together in the bed. Just sleeping.
But I did feel a lot better, thanks to Jasper. He also got me
thinking. What exactly was I? A Midnight Wolf, but what
did that mean? Hala wasn't giving me answers, but only
because she didn't know. It was frustrating. Why couldn't
the Goddess just call me up to her realm and explain
things? Or was that treatment only reserved for my Mom?
I'd always been fascinated when Mom recalled her visits
with the Goddess. Now all I felt was slightly annoyed.
Sometime later, I fell asleep, still grumbling to myself.

When I opened my eyes, I was in a meadow filled with
tall grass, blowing gently in a warm breeze. I shielded my
eyes against the glaring sun, too bright compared to the
cozy confines of the cabin. I blinked, suddenly anxious.
Wait, where was the cabin? How did I end up here?

"Jasper?" I called. My voice echoed around me, but
nobody replied.

Slowly, I stood, taking in my surroundings. There wasn't
much actually, just a lot of grass and an incredibly blue
sky, free of clouds. I looked down, noticing my feet were
bare. What shocked me more was the pure white dress I
had on. My breathing started to accelerate, and I started to
get dizzy.

Had I died?!

"You are far from dead, Violet."

I spun, searching for the voice. There was nobody.

"Who's there?" I tried to sound brave, but my voice
came out breathy.

Then I saw it. A small orb was floating towards me, just
above the tips of the grass. It was white, like a void, but
still had substance. It was beautiful, and scary. As it drifted
closer, it reformed, wiggling and stretching, taking shape. I

watched as the most beautiful woman I'd ever seen or imagined suddenly stood in front of me. Her hair was long, and black. So black, the complete opposite to the orb she just was. Her eyes were hypnotic, her skin creamy, yet ghostly white. She smiled a kind smile at me, and my brain stuttered over what I knew to be true yet couldn't accept.

"Goddess? You're the Moon Goddess," I whispered.

"Yes. You may call me Celeste."

Her voice washed over me, filling me with a sense of peace. I looked around again.

"Why am I here?" I asked her.

"Because you asked to come here."

"I did?"

She laughed, and I gaped. The sound was like music. "Not in so many words. But I got the hint."

She waved her hand, and a simple wood table and chairs appeared. Trying to be discreet, I pinched my arm. Twice. Celeste looked at me with amusement while I decided that perhaps, maybe, I wasn't actually dreaming.

"Would you like to sit? I believe we have some things to discuss," she said politely.

Dazed, I sat in one of the chairs, peering at her as she took the seat across from me. Everything she did was beyond graceful; I was in pure awe.

"I believe you have some questions for me?" Celeste asked.

I blinked. I was here because of *that*? Immediately, apologies started tumbling out of my mouth.

"I'm so sorry! I didn't mean. . . you didn't have to bring me here! I didn't mean to sound like a child, I was just curious. . ."

Celeste laughed her musical laugh, her head thrown back. My jaw opened and closed like a fish.

"You worry too much, Violet. I am more than happy to be here with you and talk. You are one of my children, after all."

Gulping, I sat back and tried to organize my thoughts. When I looked back, there were cups on the table, filled with tea. The smell of orange hit my nose, reminding me of Jaspers scent. Orange Pekoe tea was my favourite; I guess I shouldn't be surprised she knew that. Adding some sugar and cream, I stirred and then set my spoon down. I took a sip; It was better than any tea I'd ever had! I savoured the taste for a minute before placing my cup down. Celeste was sipping away at her own drink, waiting patiently.

"I guess I just want to know. . .why me? It's the one thing I keep asking myself," I said somewhat nervously. I was basically questioning her choices. Maybe that wasn't okay. Would she smite me?

"You are your Mothers daughter," she chuckled. "You need not be afraid of me, child. I would never do anything to hurt you."

My eyes widened. "Can you read my thoughts?!"

"I can, but I don't. And I didn't. They are clear as day on your face."

My face went tomato red.

"As to your question," Celeste set her cup down, "I do believe your mate explained it very well. You do not see yourself very clearly, dear. But I know that you are strong, capable, smart. You were the perfect choice for my gift."

"But why did you make a new wolf?" I asked, curious.

Her expression faltered, her smile slipping. "There is danger coming. To you, and your pack, but most specifically, your family. I am afraid your Mothers' wolf won't be able to handle it on her own," she sighed.

"What danger?" How serious was this threat that the Goddess herself felt the need to make a new breed of wolf?

"An old threat. Old, but it has grown strong. This is something you and your parents should speak about."

"Okay. . . How strong is this threat exactly? And what can I do about it?"

"Very strong. Guided by hate and jealousy, a true monster of rage. The time will come when you will know what to do. Hala will help you. She is special."

"She's a re-born wolf, right?"

"Yes. Her former life was tragic, and her human treated her without mercy or care. I know she will be happier with you."

"She. . . she can't remember that, can she?"

"No. I have also given her the gift of completely starting over. She knows she is re-born, but it is better she does not remember anything."

I nodded. At least there was that. I would hate for Hala to suffer in anyway.

"Can I ask you something?" I asked after a minute of silence.

"Of course."

"Why is Garrett red? Alphas are usually black. . ."

"Just like you, your brother is special to me. He is still an Alpha, as long as he continues down the right path. He is meant to do great things. He will see in time."

I nodded again, taking another sip of my tea. It was hard to look at her, with her celestial beauty.

"If this threat is so big, why don't you put a stop to it?"

"I will not interfere in the lives of my children. The greatest gift I've given to all of you is freewill. Even if some choose to use theirs distastefully."

My eyebrows scrunched. "But you made Hala. . . a new breed. Isn't that interfering?"

Celeste smiled an amused smile. "I will admit, it's a grey area. A tiny loophole if you will." She stood suddenly, smiling at me lovingly. "You are more special than you know Violet. You will flourish, I am positive. Try not to worry about mundane things so much, and don't doubt yourself. You will make me proud, daughter, as you always have."

Celeste walked to stand in front of me, cupping my cheeks lightly. Her skin was warm and cold, feathery light yet heavy. It was surreal, this feeling. When her lips touched my forehead, a jolt of light blinded me, before everything went dark. My eyes re-opened to the darkness of the bedroom in the cabin, taking me totally by surprise. I shot up, gasping hard, my heart accelerating so fast, I thought it might jump out of my chest. Jasper was awake instantly, his arms going around me.

"What? What's wrong?" he asked frantically.

I shook my head, trying to calm my dizzy thoughts. How could I even begin to explain to him what just happened?

"Violet? Vie!" He shook me a little. "You're scaring me! Tell me what's wrong, please!"

"N-nothing is wrong," I whispered. "I just. . . whoa. . . Just give me a minute."

He held me until my breathing slowed down and my heartbeat went back to normal. Pushing my hair away from my face, I looked at him and explained. His eyes grew wider every second I talked and when I finished, he looked almost as shaken as I had been a minute ago.

"So, your parents know what the Goddess is talking about? About this threat?"

"I guess so."

He nodded, still looking stunned. "At least we have a forewarning."

My stomach felt uncomfortable as I thought about what Celeste said. I had a bad feeling throughout my body. How far away was this threat? When would it come? And why my family? I definitely needed answers. Throwing the covers off, I got out of bed and looked for my shoes.

"What are you doing?" Jasper asked, but he got up as well.

"I can't just sit here, not knowing. I'm going to see my parents."

He handed me my shoes. I grabbed my phone, and together we left. It was still dark out, but I guessed it was close to morning. Maybe another hour. Even if Mom wasn't up, Dad would be. He still got up at crazy hours, due to all the work he did as Alpha. Jasper waited inside the door while I stripped and shifted, picking up my belongings in my mouth. Before he followed suit, he put our phones in a bag so he could carry them. I turned while he shifted and then we took off towards the packhouse.

I went over every single thing Celeste had told me in my head. Hala didn't have anything to add, and by the time we got to the packhouse, I was even more anxious. Nobody was around when we arrived. I shifted back outside the house, throwing my clothes on. Jasper came around the front, handing me my phone. Shoving it in my pocket, he took my hand, and we walked inside together.

"My Dad should be up, but I want Mom there too." I looked at him. "And Garrett."

His eyes darkened a bit, but he nodded. I went to Dad's office first, not bothering to knock. He was sitting behind his desk, still looking tired.

"Violet? Jasper?"

"We need to talk," I told him. He scrutinized my face.

"Something happened?"

"Yes."

"Talk."

I shook my head. "Mom needs to be here too. And Garrett."

He looked at me for a second. "Alright. Stay here." He stood and walked out. I pulled Jasper to the black sofa against the wall. I stared at the bookshelf on the other side of the room, waiting. It didn't take long; ten minutes later, Mom, Dad and Garrett came in. I was shocked to see Sophia enter behind my brother. Did she stay in the packhouse with him last night? Did that mean he'd accepted her?

Garretts eyes found my mate and he stiffened. Goddess knows why he thought I'd dragged them in here, but I didn't miss the anger that passed over his face. Without saying a word, he took Sophias hand, leading her to the opposite side of the room. Mom took the seat next to me, and Dad resumed his place behind his desk. Everyone looked at me.

"Sorry to wake you up," I said to Mom and Garrett. "But this is important."

"Don't worry, hun," Mom yawned. "Just tell us what's going on."

I looked her in the eye. "I had a visit from Celeste."

"*What?*"

"Celeste?"

"The Goddess?!"

Everyone talked at once, except Sophia and Jasper.
Though Sophia's eyes were wide as saucers.

"Well. . . more like she had me visit her. It's hard to
explain," I groaned.

Mom nodded. "I know. Don't worry about that, what did
she say?"

I told her everything. Her face grew paler by the second
until she looked sick.

"So, I told you. Now, can you please explain what this
threat is, and why it's coming for us?" I asked, looking at
her and Dad both. Dad hid his reaction better than Mom,
but I could tell he was worried. I could see it in his eyes.
Then his eyes glazed over, as well as Moms. Irritation grew
inside me until I couldn't take it anymore.

"Stop!" I practically shouted. Mom jumped, her eyes
clearing. "We're not kids anymore! Just tell us what is
going on!" I demanded.

Mom covered her face with her hands while Dad sighed.
I looked at Garrett, who was looking between them both.

"You're keeping something from us." He spoke matter of
factly.

"This threat. . ." Mom said quietly. "Is not a *what*, but a
who."

"Someone from our past," Dad added.

"Who? And why are they coming after us?" I asked.

"Her name in Jennine," Mom spat the word. "I was
hoping she was dead. After all this time. . ."

"You're not answering why, Mom."

She sighed hugely, finally looking up at me.

"Jennine was your fathers. . . fling. Mistress, girlfriend,
whatever you want to call it."

"She wasn't my girlfriend," Dad grumbled, but Mom
silenced him with a look.

"They were 'together,' up until I got here. But Jennine
didn't want to let go. She couldn't accept that your Dad

found his mate in someone who wasn't her. So, she tried to get rid of me. It didn't work out the way she expected. . ."

She told us the story, from start to finish. Only once, did she pause, stumbling over her words. My eyes narrowed; I knew she was hiding something else. An uneasy feeling spread through me as I listened. When she finished, I glared at her.

"You said she was turned into a witch? What happened to her wolf?" I asked.

Mom bit her lip. My jaw dropped and Garrett pushed away from the wall.

"She killed her wolf?!" he gasped.

They didn't confirm it, but I knew. My stomach twisted painfully, as I grabbed Mom's arm, forcing her to look at me.

"Was that her? The wolf you gave a second chance to? Is it Hala?"

". . .Yes."

Hala whined loudly in my head. It was so loud, it drowned out the sob that came from Sophia. She didn't remember, but now she knew. Her human had killed her, tossed her away like nothing. Tears filled my eyes as my wolf cried painfully inside me.

CHAPTER 21
VIOLET

Choking back a sob of my own, I leaned back against Jasper, who put his arms around me. This was. . . unreal. Pathetic, really. This girl, Jennine, was coming after us, all because Dad found his mate? How could one person hold onto so much hatred? Enough that they would kill their wolf! Hala was apart of me, I felt it. Not just in my mind, but apart of my soul. The thought of getting rid of her. . . it made my physically sick to my stomach.

"I'm sorry. I'm so sorry you went through that," I told her solemnly.

"Perhaps. . . perhaps it is better that I know. I am grateful I do not remember. But at least I know who to target."

She was getting angry now, I could feel it. My hands were shaking, my vision blurry from my tears. Hala's anger resonated through me, pulling me in. It was overwhelming.

CRACK

I jumped to my feet as Sophia shrieked. Garrett jumped in front of her in a protective stance. Jasper moved me behind him as well, and Mom and Dad were in immediate Alpha and Luna mode. I looked around for the sound of the noise, my eyes falling on the window behind Dad's desk and chair. My mouth fell open slightly.

The entire window was cracked, delicate webs of lines crossing from one end to the other. All eyes turned to look that direction, and as we watched, tiny pieces began to fall onto the floor. And then bigger pieces until there was nothing left but a hole where the glass use to be. Dad stepped over them, crunching the glass under his shoes. He glanced out the window, surveying the area.

"There's nobody out there," he frowned.

"Are you sure?" Mom asked.

"I'd hear them- smell them. What on Earth. . ." He looked at the glass shards again, completely confused.

"It could have been a sniper," Mom said worriedly. She glanced between Garrett and I.

But Dad shook his head, looking at the floor and the walls. "There's no bullet. And I doubt she would use guns."

"Magic."

Dad nodded.

Nobody said anything for a couple minutes. I opened my mouth, but Garrett spoke first.

"So, when were you going to tell us?" He looked angrily at our parents. "Didn't you think this was something I should have known about? I'm going to be Alpha! Were you just never planning on telling me there was a threat to the pack?"

"We didn't-" Mom started.

"Violet was out all night!" Garrett interrupted. "So was I! We didn't even know we had a target on our backs! How could you be so careless?!"

"You aren't the target!" Mom shouted. "We are!"

"How is that better, Mom?"

"You didn't need to know! *We* will handle Jennine," she said firmly.

"Like you did last time?" he scoffed. Moms' aura radiated around the room powerfully, thickening the air.

"Lily, calm down," Dad said. But Mom ignored him completely. She glared at Garrett a minute more before turning and walking out, slamming the door behind her.

I didn't like my brother talking to Mom like that, but I didn't say anything. I was angry as he was. They *should* have told us! Everything made more sense to me now- the intense training sessions, the strict curfews. Never being able to leave the pack. Having the warriors with us pretty much everywhere we went. I rounded on Dad, my own glare on my face.

"You should have told us. We didn't deserve to be kept in the dark!"

He sighed. "I wanted to tell you both. Many times. But your Mother. . ."

"Is totally overprotective! She needs to learn that we aren't helpless kids anymore!"

"It only makes sense that Jennine would go after Violet and Garrett, to hurt you, Alpha," Sophia said quietly.

"I never would have taken Vie out if I'd known some psycho was on the loose," Jasper agreed.

Dad observed all of us, one by one before looking at the floor covered in glass again. His expression transformed into one of anger and determination. Then he was walking past us, his hand on the doorknob.

"I will speak to your Mother." He looked at us over his shoulder. "I am sorry we didn't tell you. But I won't let that bitch hurt my family, not anymore." He opened the door, leaving to go after Mom.

I fell back onto the sofa, mentally drained. "What do we do now?" I looked up at Garrett.

"We keep our eyes open and watch our backs. And each others backs," he told me firmly. He turned to Jasper, his anger coming back in his tone. "I'm trusting you to watch over my sister."

"You don't need to worry about that. I'll always keep her safe," Jasper replied. Garrett nodded once, turning back to me. "You know they won't let us help. Mom especially will try to keep us out of it."

I smirked. "I'd like to see her try. She's not the only one who has people to protect, people she loves."

"So, who's going to talk to her?"

I pursed my lips. "Best two out of three?"

"Let's go."

Sophia and Jasper both chuckled as we rock, paper, scissored. Sadly, and with a big groan, I ended up losing. Wearing my best grumpy face, I left the room, praying hard that a fight didn't break out between the guys in my absence. When I reached my parents' door, I paused. Crying could be heard through the door, and my heart clenched. Mom was super strict; sometimes she went overboard. But I knew it came from a place of love, and her wanting to protect us. I admired my Mom more than anyone else. She was strong when she had to be, and she was one of the best fighters too thanks to training with my Dad for so many years.

But she was also kind-hearted, warm, and caring. Often, it was difficult to believe the Luna of Blood Moon was anything more than a loving mother and wife. Enemies had underestimated her before, all to their demise.

"Mom? Dad?" I pushed open the door quietly.

"What, Violet?"

Dad was sitting on their huge bed beside my Mom who was curled up on her side, her head on her pillow. Her face was tear-stained, her eyes puffy and red. I felt a rush of guilt, but not enough for me to let this go.

"Can I talk to you?" I looked at Mom.

"Fine." She huffed after a minute. Dad sighed, running his hands through his hair. Giving her a quick kiss, he patted my shoulder on his way out. I took his place next to Mom.

"Mom," I said firmly, but gently. "I know you want to protect us. I know. But do you really think Garrett and I are going to stand by while some bitch hunts down our parents?"

Her eyes narrowed a bit at my language, but she didn't say anything.

"You can't keep us out of it," I continued. "What was the point of training us then? Making sure we knew how to defend ourselves? There was no point if you're going to keep us locked up in the house."

She pursed her lips.

"I kind of understand why you didn't tell us." I sighed. "But at the same time, you also should have told us. And no matter what happens, we're doing this together, as a family. Or we can do this by ourselves. But one way or another, Garrett and I *will* step up to protect you, Dad, and Blood Moon."

Mom sat up, wiping her face. Then she took my hands in hers, our eyes meeting. Hers were filled with pain, anger, but most of all, fear. Mine, on the other hand, were full of determination. After a long silence, she squeezed my hands and softly smiled.

"You are so like your Father," she chuckled lowly. "Always ready to jump into action. Even Garrett, though he's more cautious. I just. . . I can't stand the thought of someone hurting you. Your Dad made me realize that keeping this from you might have been a mistake all this time. But I should have known that you would never be the ones to hide away while someone was threatening us. No, that's not you. Especially you, Violet. You give me such a headache sometimes, but you always stand up to protect others, and for that, I couldn't be prouder. We will do this together. Even if I'm hesitant about it."

She pulled me in for an unexpected hug, burying her face in my hair. Her words took me by surprise, but they warmed my heart too. I was just happy I wouldn't have to fight her on this. We pulled back, smiling at each other.

"Love you, Mom."

"I love you too, Vie. Come on, let's go back. Your Dad is getting Luke and Ben too."

I nodded, pulling her up with me. We made our way back to Dads office, both lost in our thoughts. Not surprisingly, Uncle Luke and Ben were already there, Ben crouching down near the broken window shards while Luke was glaring at the wall. Everyone looked up when we entered, and I went straight to Jasper. He wrapped his arm around my shoulder, and we resumed our seat on the sofa, Mom sitting next to me.

"So?" Garrett asked.

"We're good," I nodded.

"Garrett, I'm sorry," Mom said to him.

"Me too." They hugged briefly, Garrett bending down to wrap his arms around her.

"What's the plan?" Uncle Luke asked.

"I have the warriors already searching the area. Border patrol on every side said nobody got in but. . . I don't know. She could have slipped by with a spell or something. "Where's Clara?" Dad looked at Ben who stood up, shaking his head.

"Coming. Should be any minute now."

The door opened as his words ended, Aunt Clara walking in. She surveyed the room, taking in our serious faces before looking at her mate.

"What's going on?"

"Jennine."

Aunt Claras face darkened, her eyes sparking. Her fingers twitched, as if just the name of the enemy was making her want to blast something. "She's back?" she hissed.

"Looks like it." Uncle Ben glared at the glass. Aunt Clara walked over, frowning at the mess.

"Can you use a locator spell?" Dad asked.

Aunt Claras head suddenly cocked to the side. She examined the window closely, her heels crunching some of the pieces. "Ben, stand back."

He did as she asked, backing up to the wall. Aunt Clara stood back as well, muttering under breath and waving her hand over the glass. After a couple seconds, they started to float in the air; I watched in awe as one by one, each piece of glass flew back up to the window sill and re-assembled itself. Aunt Clara was watching too, her eyes following each shard, her frown becoming more and more pronounced. When the window was finally back in place, only the original spiderweb cracks were left, before it fell.

"It doesn't make any sense. . ." she muttered.

"What doesn't?" Uncle Luke asked.

"The window. . . it was broken from the inside."

"What?" Mom gasped.

"Are you sure?" Uncle Ben asked.

Aunt Clara nodded. "Positive. This was done from inside this room."

141

"Impossible. Jennine couldn't have gotten into the packhouse, let alone up here, without being seen," Uncle Luke said.

"I don't think Jennine did this." Aunt Clara looked around at us. "No, this was done by someone here. One of you."

CHAPTER 22
VIOLET

Everyone stared at her. Nobody said anything for a whole minute, but it was clear she was serious. Briefly, I glanced around. Could it have been Mom? She was the only one here who had any sort of magic to speak of. But Aunt Claras eyes landed on me and stayed there. I paled, holding my hands up.

"It can't be me!" I exclaimed. "I'm a werewolf, not a witch."

"But you're a new wolf. . . " Mom mused. "We haven't talked about that yet, but now seems like an appropriate time."

I shook my head in denial. "No, Hala would have said something. She would have known," I said firmly.

"Aya knew I was a Mother Wolf, but she never told me. Not until we shifted," Mom told me.

Everyone was staring at me, and I grew uncomfortable.

"Hala?" I called desperately for my wolf. *"Help me out here. Obviously, it wasn't us."*

She didn't answer me in words, but I felt her hesitation in my mind.

"No!" I denied internally.

"Calm down."

"You knew?! You knew and you didn't tell me!"

"I'm sorry."

"Why?!"

"There are things you need to discover for yourself first."

"That's such a bullshit answer! Why are you wolves so secretive?!"

"Perhaps it's in our nature."

Aunt Clara clicked her tongue, eyeing me.

"I think it's safe to say we have our answer, judging by the look on your face Violet."

"What did Hala say?" Mom asked beside me.

"Nothing helpful!" I groaned.

"Seriously calm down. So, you're a hybrid, that's not a bad thing."

"I'm. . . a. . . a. . . what?!"

"You are half wolf, half witch."

"That's not even possible!" I screamed in my mind.

In my frenzied state, I hadn't realized I'd also shouted the words aloud. Mom and Jasper both jumped beside me.

"What's not possible?" Uncle Luke asked.

"Hala says. . . she said. . ." I struggled to get the words out. "That I'm a hybrid. Half wolf and half witch."

Every pair of eyes in the room widened and every jaw dropped to the floor. I looked at each of my family's face, hoping someone would tell me my wolf was crazy. This had to be a joke, and it wasn't even a good one.

"Impossible. . ." Uncle Luke was the first one to break the silence. "Hybrids don't exist, not anymore. Everyone knows that."

"Pretty sure we exist!" Hala scoffed.

"Hang on." Jasper spoke for the first time in a while. "Can someone explain this to me?"

"Don't they teach this in school?" Aunt Clara asked.

"It's help when you actually pay attention in class." Garrett said. Jasper frowned at him.

Thankfully, Uncle Luke spoke before they could start bickering.

"A hybrid is pretty easy to explain. Half of one thing, half of another." Jasper nodded and he continued. "However, there hasn't been a hybrid in centuries. Actually, close to seven hundred years now. Before that though, they were quite common, or at least that's what all the books say."

"What happened to them?"

"They were executed," Aunt Clara took over. "Every story tells us that they grew too powerful; they got greedy, trying to exterminate other species, wipe them out. They thought of themselves as the dominant species. Utter chaos broke out, a complete bloodbath. A few species *were* wiped out, the fairies, the dragons. Humans found a way to survive, somehow. The wolves, witches, and vampires too. The stories say the four species left teamed up, working together to get rid of the hybrids once and for all. After the carnage, all species went their separate ways, for fear of more hybrids being born. It soon became forbidden to mate with other species because of that fear, even if you found your true mate. It seemed the Goddess herself agreed too; any child born of mixed blood would either take after the mother or father, but never both again."

"Until now," Uncle Ben muttered, but everyone heard him.

"So why create one now?" Jasper asked. "If hybrids were feared so much?"

Aunt Clara shrugged. "Who knows? Celeste also brought back the Mother Wolf in Lily."

They all started to speculate, talking hypotheticals and theories. I couldn't concentrate on that though, focusing on my mate beside me. His eyebrows were furrowed, a slight but poignant frown on his face. He wouldn't meet my eyes. My stomach twisted.

"Is this a problem?" I asked him bluntly. Around me, my family stopped talking.

Jasper finally looked at me. "It's unexpected," he replied slowly.

A hard, unamused laugh left my mouth. "No shit!"

"Violet. . ." Mom touched my shoulder, but I shook her off. I was filled with irrational waves of anger towards my mate; part of me knew it was just the shock, but I couldn't seem to stop it. I glared at him, moving away when he also tried to touch me.

"You think this is just a shock for you?" I nearly shouted at him. "Do you even care how I feel right now? Or are you trying to figure out the best way to reject me?"

Jasper seemed genuinely hurt by my words. Before he could answer, I was on my feet.

"Say it, Jasper! Say the words! You're mated to a. . .a. . . a *freak*!"

He stood up too, reaching for me, but I was too far gone. Tears were pouring down my face. I ran out of the room, sobbing.

"Violet! Vie, come back!"

"Violet!"

I heard them calling after me, possibly even following me, but I didn't care. I kept running.

"Violet! You need to calm down!" Hala shouted.

I barely heard her. The same scenario kept playing in my head, over and over. My family, turning away from me. My mate, rejecting me. The monster. I was a monster. . . people like me were exterminated, for good reason. I wasn't supposed to exist! How could anyone look at me the same way now? They wouldn't, I knew that.

My tears blinded me as I sprinted down the stairs with broken, strangled sobs vibrating in my chest. I was feeling too many things at once, and none of them were positive. I felt a pressure somewhere inside me, but I was too overwhelmed to focus. It was a foreign feeling, and I started to panic on top of everything else.

"Violet! Listen to me please!"

"No!"

"Please, stop! Go back to Jasper; let our mates calm you down!"

"He doesn't want me! Who could want me now? I'll be cast out of the pack! They'll want to kill me for what I am!"

"They won't! How can you think that? Don't- don't push me away!"

"You knew! You knew and you didn't tell me! I can't trust you!" I was so worked up that I had to say the words aloud. Every thought was jumbled; my head felt like it was full of wasps. I couldn't feel anything but the pressure, so heavy it was physically weighing me down now. My feet stumbled over the steps and I collapsed to the ground, desperate to get air but unable to move.

"Violet! Stop! Sto-!"

Halas desperate plea was silenced as the panic went into overdrive. I was on the verge of probably passing out when the pressure inside me suddenly came undone. An aura more powerful than I'd ever felt before surrounded me. It took a five full seconds to realize it was mine. It shot out, like it was its very own life force, invisible but strong.

And then it was gone. The sudden and complete absence left me winded.

One beat of silence- and then the stairs under me started creaking loudly. I watched in horror as they cracked and snapped, crumbling in on themselves like they were nothing more than paper instead of solid pine. I grabbed onto the railing, stunned to see the walls were shaking as well. *Everything* the stairs were attached to started to fall, including me. My body slid forward; instinct too over, and I rolled just in time. Going back up wasn't possible, but going down was a struggle, trying to place my feet on the least dangerous spots, racing against the destruction. Reaching the last flight, I risked it, jumping. I landed in the foyer, rolling to absorb the impact. I couldn't see anything in the thick cloud of dust that had materialized, but I could hear everything. Screams and shouts of panic echoed back to me over the sounds of the last bit of wood coming down. Had anyone been on the stairs aside from me? Was anyone hurt, or worse? Fresh tears started rolling down my cheeks at the thought.

What had I just done?

"By the Goddess!"

Dazed, I turned. A hazy group of people stood close by. Somebody had opened the front door, waving a towel or something in its direction, trying to get the dust cloud to clear. Others were doing the same at the windows.

Nancy, an older maid who worked in the kitchen, knelt in front of me. "Violet! Are you alright? Were you on the stairs?!"

147

"I-I'm f-fine," I managed to choke out.

"Half the house has come down!" I heard someone call.

"Was that an earthquake?"

"I hope the rest of the pack is alright!"

Shaking, I got to my feet. The room was clearing, but I winced. The entire foyer was destroyed. The decorative tables my Dad owned were broken, and various paintings on the walls were also now on the floor, some buried. Daylight was shining through a gigantic hole in the upper wall that had come down with the stairs. The more I looked around, the more damage I saw. Worse, I'd trapped everyone upstairs. How were they supposed to get down?

"Alpha? Luna!"

I jerked my head up. One of the maids was carefully picking her way across the rubble, looking up.

"Alpha, Luna, are you alright?" she called.

"We're here, we're fine!" Mom's voice came from above. I could hear someone coughing. "Is Violet there?! Is she okay?!"

The maid and I locked eyes for a second before she lifted her head again. "She's here, Luna! She's okay!"

"Get back! I'm going to shift and jump down!" Mom called.

I backed up to the door, grabbing the handle. If anyone could make that jump, it was my Moms wolf. Still, I didn't want to be here when she got down. I'd singlehandedly brought down a huge portion of the packhouse. Obviously, it wasn't safe for me to be around people right now. I slipped out the door while the group of maids and even some warriors who'd been in the cafeteria were making room for Aya, breaking into a run again.

I thought about going to the cabin, but I didn't exactly remember the way, and I didn't want to get lost either. I passed the first trees and immediately shifted, not even caring about my clothes.

"Are you okay?" Hala asked gently.

"Just run, Hala. Away- anywhere but here."

I gave her control, retreating to the back of my mind. I didn't care where she took us, as long as it was away from the packhouse.

"It wasn't your fault." My wolf tried again.

"Yes, it was."

"You are not the first witch to-"

"Hala, please!"

"Are you ashamed of what you are? Of what we are?"

"How can I not be? If I was just a witch or just a wolf, everything would be fine! I could have killed someone Hala! Do you not get that?"

She didn't answer me, for which I was glad. I didn't feel like arguing with her. She was just as stubborn as I was. Instead, she ran through the forest, taking us further from the people I was too scared to face.

CHAPTER 23
JASPER

I stood by the stairs, or what use to be the stairs, feeling like a complete jackass. Why had I said that to Violet? Could I possibly have said anything stupider? I didn't give a damn if she was a hybrid. Hell, I didn't give a damn if she turned out to be part witch, part wolf or part troll! As long as she was safe. . .

Glaring down at the mess below me, I had no idea if she *was* safe. I could feel her through our bond, thankfully, but she was already far away, far from the packhouse. Briefly, I stopped to wonder why I could feel her so strongly- we hadn't marked each other yet.

"Mom says we should be able to get down in a minute or so."

I was pulled out of my thoughts by Garrett behind me. He was visibly unhappy.

"Good. I need to find-"

"Haven't you done enough already?" he cut me off. I glared at him.

"Don't start, Garrett," I growled.

"Or what?" he scoffed. "You're the reason Vie got so upset."

"Enough, Garrett." Alpha Dimitri came up behind us, giving his son a stern look. "Violet was upset about a lot of things today. She just happened to lose her temper on the wrong person. Jasper didn't do anything wrong."

"Seriously?" Garrett argued.

"Perhaps it wasn't the best choice of words, but she was already overwhelmed by everything else. She's been dealing with a lot of stress since the shift." Alpha Dimitri eyed him meaningfully, and Garrett hung his head a bit.

"Are you guys ready?" Luna Lily called up to us.

I never really thought about how high the Alphas floor was; I'd never been here after all. I knew the packhouse itself was very large, but looking down at the Luna now, who looked like a child from this height, was rather unnerving.

"We're ready when you are," Alpha Dimitri called back.

"How exactly does she plan to get us down?" I asked curiously.

"And why can't Aunt Clara do this?" Garrett added.

"Because, -" Clara spoke up behind us, "-I have no idea how to judge the fall. In case you didn't notice Garrett, I'm not Harry Potter, and levitation spells aren't my speciality. I'd probably end up dropping you before you were halfway down."

"Good to know," he muttered.

They stopped bickering as a soft bark reached our ears. Suddenly, Alpha Dimitri stepped forward, walking off the edge of the hall that the stairs were once connected to.

"Alpha!"

"Dad!"

"Oh!"

Sophia, Garrett and I all rushed forward. We caught the last of his fall, all three of us wincing as he landed on his mate's wolf. She huffed at the impact but gave him a nuzzle after he slid off. She was laying down in the debris, so massive that there was no way we could miss her. Sophia went pale, her mate not looking much better.

"Next!" Dimitri called. Beta Ben stepped up.

He walked off the edge as casually as the Alpha before him had. Next went Clara, telling us not to be such babies before she fell. The three of us remaining looked at each other, unwilling. After a few minutes, and a couple barks from below, Garrett groaned.

"She better freaking catch me, or I swear. . ."

He closed his eyes tightly. His step wasn't as casual as the others. In fact, it seemed like he tried to step back at the last second, but he was already falling. Sophia and I looked over, making sure he made it. She let out a sigh of relief

151

beside me when his Mom caught him with ease. That relief didn't last long though.

"Oh Goddess. . . I can't do this. I can't. I'm terrified of heights! Oh Goddess, just leave me here!" Sophia rambled. Her face was going from white to green.

"Unless you sprout wings, this is the only way down," I pointed out.

"Why did it have to be the stairs? Why couldn't she have destroyed a tree or something?" She kept rambling.

"Sophia!" Garretts voice drifted up to us.

"Just focus on Garrett," I told her. I knew if I went first, she'd never jump. I had to get her down first.

"No, no, no, no!" she squealed as I led her to the drop.

"Close your eyes. Don't think about it, think about him."

"I don't even know where to aim!"

"Just. . . try to avoid landing on her head, alright?"

She was a sickly colour by now, but she took a deep breath, squeezing her eyes shut, nodding one jerky nod. The girl was shaking like a leaf and when she put her foot into open air, a terrified shriek left her lips. Regardless, she let herself drop. I watched her fall, my ears ringing at the scream she let out the whole way down. It cut off when the Luna caught her. When she looked back to me, I also took a few deep breaths. I wasn't a particular fan of heights either, but I could do this. Gathering myself, I stepped off.

The fall was rather short, until, with a grunt, I landed on the Luna. She turned her head, sniffing at me.

"I'm good. Thanks, Luna."

I slid off, joining the rest of our group. Well, most of them- Sophia and Garrett were just outside the door, Sophia getting sick into the bushes that lined the front steps. The Luna joined us, now back in human form and clothed.

"I'm going to find Vie," I announced, turning for the door.

"Hang on," Luna Lily put a hand on my shoulder, stopping me. "We need to talk about this."

"This?"

"Her being a. . ." She trailed off, eyeing the maids around us who were attempting to clean. "You know."

I shook my head. "I'm not talking behind her back. No offense, Luna."

"He's right, Lily," Alpha Dimitri said. "Let him bring her back first, then we can discuss the situation."

Still, she didn't let me go. Instead, she looked into my eyes, and a shiver ran down my spine at the fierceness I saw in hers. She looked every bit a Luna and Mother right now.

"Are you going to reject my daughter?" she half whispered.

"No," I deadpanned. "I'm sorry if that was the impression. I don't care what Violet is. She's my mate and I will accept her no matter what. I'm only worried about right now."

She held on to me a while longer, before nodding, believing I was serious.

"Go find her."

Nodding, I gave her and the Alpha a respectful nod before leaving. I ignored Garrett and his mate, going straight for the woods at the back of the packhouse. The only thing that caught my eye was the damage. Even on the outside, it was impressive. My heart clenched. Vie must have been really upset to cause this. I started stripping before I even hit the trees. Giving control over to Ehno, I shifted.

Her scent was easy enough to follow, even more so in this form. Her trail led mostly in a straight line. Obviously, she hadn't cared about where she went, as long as she could get away. Ehno whined.

"Don't worry, we'll find them," I assured him.

"I know. I hate that they are upset, though."

"Me too."

"You need to think before you speak!" he growled.

"I'll definitely work on it," I promised.

We ran for over an hour. Did Violet cross the border? I really hoped not; who knew where that psycho Jennine was? Not to mention rogues. However, to my relief, her trail turned left about twenty minutes from the border. Ehno pushed himself faster, jumping and twisting around trees. When he started to slow down, I took back control, much to his annoyance. Making my way at a fast jog, I looked around, until, finally, I caught sight of her.

She wasn't in wolf form anymore but sitting on the bank of one of the packs waterfalls. She was wearing a green dress- I guessed she found it in one of the many stashes of clothes hidden in the woods. Even from here, I could tell she was still upset, her knees drawn up with her chin resting on them. Her arms hugged her legs as she stared unblinking at the scenery. Quickly, I sniffed out the clothing stash and shifted back. All I could find was a pair of jeans in my size, but every shirt was too small. Whatever.

Tracing my steps, I stepped out of the shadows, hesitantly approaching her. She didn't even seem to notice I was here.

"What do you want, Jasper?" she asked. Her voice sounded a bit rough from the crying. So, she did know I was here.

"I came to find you."

The waterfall crashed into the water below, almost drowning out my reply. I'd never been to this spot before. Blood Moon had various waterfalls like this one. Usually, kids and teenagers flocked to the bigger ones for bonfires or parties. The biggest one was used for pack parties sometimes; I remembered the twins had their sixteenth birthday party there. Comparatively, this waterfall was significantly smaller, but somehow, I liked it better. It was more secluded, with no traces of past get togethers. As if it had been untouched, always. It was beautiful.

"I'll admit, it's a nice place to be rejected."

Violets words pulled my attention back to her. Silent tears ran down her cheeks. I sat in front of her on the ground, taking her face in my hands and wiping them away. I couldn't stand to see her in so much pain.

"I'm not rejecting you," I told her firmly.

Our eyes met. Neither of us spoke for a while, our breathing overshadowed by the noise of the water behind us. Eventually, she whispered one word, so low I had to read her lips to catch it.

"Why?"

I half smiled. "I'm sorry I upset you earlier. That wasn't what I wanted. Yes, I was shocked to discover what you were. But Vie, it doesn't matter to me what you are. To me, you will always be the girl who punched a kid over one of my shitty drawings. The girl who stuck up for her best friend when she was getting bullied. The girl who decided to look past my bullshit and accept me. You're a good person, inside and out. You're the girl I've watched for years, the girl I grew more attracted to every day. The girl with the attitude, and a temper, but who will also help anyone she can, simply just because she can. You're my girl, Violet, always. You could have a third arm and six eyes, and I would still want you."

Her bottom lip was quivering; I couldn't remember ever seeing Violet cry this much. Actually, I couldn't remember seeing her ever cry at all. It hurt worse that this was because of me, that I'd been the one to upset her. Gently, I pulled her onto my lap, wrapping my arms around her in a tight hug. She cried into my chest quietly, the tears dropping onto my skin and sliding down. I kissed the top of her head.

"To me, you will always be just Violet. Not Violet the hybrid; that's just another part of who you are. But that doesn't mean that's *all* you are," I told her.

The dam broke, a fresh torrent of tears and sobs erupting from her. I held her gently, but firmly, occasionally whispering reassurances in her ear, not even sure she was listening to me. Her cries echoed around us, mixing with the roar of the waterfall. Ehno was whining, pacing in my head, but I tried to focus on only her. After a long while, Vies tears ran dry, her sobs turning into little hiccups.

155

Resting her cheek against my chest, I waited until her breathing even out.

"Better?" I asked her.

"Yes," she sniffed. "Thank you. Thank you for coming to find me."

"Always."

I could feel her fidgeting with her fingers. When she looked up, she was biting her lip.

"Did you mean it? What you said?" she whispered.

I cupped her cheek, leaving one arm around her. "Every word."

"What if. . . what if I'm. . . dangerous? What if I can't control it?"

"Then we will deal with that. Together."

Something in her eyes changed; the worry dissipated almost completely. Taking my face in her small hands, Violet leaned in and kissed me. I answered her kiss eagerly, feeling an intense amount of relief. This time felt different than before. The sparks were definitely there, but there was more. A new level of mutual trust, of understanding. And a passion that wasn't there before, too. Violet kissed me like I was the air she needed to breath, and I was quickly getting lost in her. Her hands went to the back of my neck, playing with the hair there. I shivered under her touch. This was the first time I'd ever been so affected by a woman's touch.

I tugged her closer, our chests pressing against each other. My hand was splayed back into her hair, securing her to me. My other arm was holding her against me, unwilling to ever let go of her, of this moment. Too soon though, we both ran out of breath, forcing us to part. I rested my forehead against hers, our noses brushing.

"Home?" I whispered.

"Yeah. I need to talk to my parents."

Standing up, I set her on her feet, reaching down to take her hand.

"Let's go."

CHAPTER 24
JASPER

We got back to the packhouse later than expected, due to the fact that we hadn't shifted. I was fine with that, just enjoying being with her for a while. We didn't talk much on the way back, but I caught her biting her lip a lot. Clearly, she was still very worried about the revelation of her being a hybrid, and what her future would hold. I'd squeeze her hand, a reminder that I was here for her, and she'd gift me with a small smile. Now, her face fell into a grimace as she properly looked at the damage of the packhouse.

"Fuck. Mom and Dad must be so pissed," she groaned.

"I think they're more relieved that you weren't hurt."

"Nobody else got hurt, did they?" She looked up at me with worried eyes.

"No, everyone is fine."

"Thank the Goddess." Her gaze fell back on the broken wall, the sounds of people from inside reaching our ears. "I can't believe I did that. . ."

"Me either. Now I really have to be careful not to get on your bad side." I teased her. Thankfully, my lame joke had the effect I wanted. Vie punched my arm lightly, but she was smiling.

"Violet!"

We turned simultaneously at the Lunas voice. She was running in our direction and Violet let go of my hand, taking two steps back, looking afraid. Her Mom jumped, nearly tackling her to the ground in the process.

"Oh, my Goddess, I was so worried about you!" Luna Lily exclaimed.

"W-worried?" Violet repeated.

"Of course!" She checked her daughter all over, patting her cheeks, her arms. "Are you hurt anywhere?"

157

"I'm fine Mom." Violet's voice was just above a whisper, obviously stunned by this greeting.

"You sure? Alright. Come on, we have lots to talk about."

Taking my place next to her, the Luna led us inside. To my surprise, the people in the house had done a fast job at clearing away the damage. A third of it was gone already. Vie kept her eyes down as we passed through the foyer and down the hall leading to the cafeteria. The doors opened and once again, we were received with frantic activity. Everyone rushed to Violet, asking if she was okay. She gave me a look, and I smiled at her. No matter what, her family would always be there for her, just like me. Once it was relatively calm, and we were seated at one of the tables, Violet turned to her Dad.

"Dad I. . . I'm sorry. I know it'll cost a lot to repair the uh, damage."

"Don't worry about it. I already put in a request for new stairs to be bui-"

"No!" shouted the Luna. She was glaring at her mate across the table. "For the love of the Goddess Dimitri, just put in the fucking elevator! I swear, if you rebuild those stairs, I will be the next one to rip them down!"

"Hear, hear!" exclaimed Luke, and Ben nodded in agreement.

"Seriously, I'll help her," Clara added.

"Finally!" sighed Garrett. "Thanks sis!"

"Uh, no problem," Violet mumbled. However, even she had a tiny smile.

"I can't just put in one elevator," Alpha Dimitri said to his Luna. "It'll be too much for everyone here."

"Then put in two. Or three. I really don't care, but no more stairs," she replied.

Alpha Dimitri sighed heavily, rubbing his face. I got the feeling this wasn't the first conversation on this topic, but it seemed to be the last. He conceded with poor grace, looking like he lost a war. Everyone was visibly very happy about this decision.

"Fine. Moving on," he said. He turned to his daughter, who shrank a little into my side.

"I'm sorry. . ." she apologized again.

"Honey, nobody is mad. This wasn't your fault," Luna Lily said.

"Your Grandpa and I have agreed to work with you, to help you control your power," Clara spoke up.

"Really?" Violet sat up a bit. "Grandma and Grandpa are back?"

Clara nodded. "They are on their way now. Isa went through this too, Violet. So did I, and probably your Grandpa too. Your power is coming forth, and it's unstable right now. It will come out in waves when you get too emotional." She glanced towards the doors. "Though I can't say I've ever heard of a witch bringing down a house."

"It wasn't the whole house," Vie grumbled.

"Regardless, you're obviously very powerful. You just need to learn to control it."

Violet looked around, gazing at each of our faces.

"What if I can't?" she asked.

Her Dad took her hand, giving it a squeeze. "Then we figure it out. We will not turn our backs on you."

She looked like she was going to cry again, but held it in. Instead, she leaned in, hugging her Dad tightly.

"Thanks," she said, looking at everyone in turn.

"I'm afraid you'll have to stay home from school for a while. But you can do everything online, so you won't fall behind," her Mom added.

"Okay."

"Your Grandpa and I want to start training you as soon as possible. So be ready tomorrow and meet us in the training yard right after lunch. You can do online school until then," Clara said.

"Tomorrow?"

"We can't risk anymore, uh, incidents. I love renovating, but I'm not up for re-building the whole house." Her Mom chuckled and Violet blushed.

"Everyone will need to go to the second floor tonight, until the. . .elevators are put in." Alpha Dimitri announced. He pouted a little towards the Luna, but she studiously ignored him.

"And how do you suggest we get to the second floor?" Luke raised an eyebrow.

"Ever heard of a ladder?" Alpha Dimitri threw back.

". . .Asshole," Luke muttered while Ben laughed.

"Lastly, I want this to be kept under wraps for now. Nobody is to speak of this to anyone outside of this room. Understood?"

The Alpha looked around, all of us nodding.

"Good."

"Then we need a training spot other than the yard." Clara tapped her chin.

"How about the cabin?" I suggested.

"What cabin?"

"I have a cabin just outside the border. It's private enough."

"Jasper no." Violet shook her head. "I don't want to risk damaging that place, you worked so hard to restore it."

"It's fine Vie, I don't mind. Besides, it's the safer option, for you."

She frowned, but her aunt liked the idea. I agreed to take them there tomorrow, and it was settled. Despite her concerns, Violet fell into conversation with her aunt and Mom about her new training. The others broke off into different conversations as well, and I was left to just listen. The men were discussing how to locate Jennine, and I focused on that. But I felt uneasy, like I was being watched. My eyes cut down the table, and sure enough, Garrett was glaring at me. What was with him? Was he ever going to let go of his anger towards me? I wasn't the only one who noticed. Sophia touched his arm, making him focus on her. She spoke quietly to him for a minute, and they stood.

"We're going to bed," he said.

"Your room is the third on the left," the Alpha said, and Garrett nodded.

They said goodnight to everyone, but Garrett threw me one last look before they left. It was easy to ignore him though, when I had my mate to focus on. She was listening avidly to her Dad and uncles now.

"We've searched this whole area, many times. Killian expanded with his men, remember, but she's not here."

"Do you think she went back to Scotland?" Luke asked.

"Doubtful. She has to know we'd check there eventually."

"Violet. . ." Her Dad turned to her, surprised to see she was already involved in the topic at hand. "Did Celeste say anything else? About where Jennine was?"

"No. She just said danger was coming, but she didn't give any details. I didn't even know who she was talking about until you guys told us."

"Fuck." He ran his hands through his hair. "Okay. Well, we have a warning. So, she must be getting ready to make a move soon. Ben, send the search parties out again. She might be back in the area now."

"What about me?" Luke looked at him.

"You have another job. Gideon and Clara will be busy training Violet, Ben with the searches. I want you to see what you can find on hybrids. In the library, from our allies, anything."

I raised my eyebrows, but the Gamma just nodded. I got the impression he was very knowledgeable, and he didn't complain about his assignment either.

"Alright. I think everyone could use some rest now."

We stood, but I might have been the only one at a loss. Was I supposed to go home? Could I stay with Violet? As I was pondering this, Luna Lily came over to us.

"Your room is second on the right. I had some clothes delivered for you Jasper."

"Thank you, Luna."

"Please, call me Lily. You are my future son-in-law after all, no need for such formalities."

"Uh, okay. Lily." Both her and Violet chuckled at how awkward I sounded.

"Have a good night." She hugged her daughter again, kissing her on the cheek before she left side by side with her Alpha.

"I think Mom is already planning our wedding," Violet said.

"Seems like it," I agreed.

"Oh well. One less thing we have to do."

"Doesn't every girl want to plan their own wedding?"

"Most girls, I guess. I never really thought about it much." She shrugged.

"Yeah, that sounds like you." I smiled and she blushed lightly. "Do you want me to stay here tonight?"

"Yes."

I chuckled at how quickly she answered. I mindlinked my Mom, telling her where I was and then we left. It felt like morning was only minutes ago, but in reality, the chaos from earlier, finding and bringing back Vie, and this informal meeting had taken up the whole day. Where had the time gone? It was already dark outside, though I had no idea what time it actually was. Violet was clearly exhausted though. The foyer was almost completely cleared now, only a few spare wood chunks lying on the floor. As mentioned, a ladder was placed against the wall, leading up to the second floor. Violet climbed up first and I followed.

"I'm going to take a shower," she said once the door to the room closed. "Make yourself at home."

"Will do."

I plopped onto the bed, grateful that it was soft and comfy while she disappeared into the bathroom. A few minutes later, I heard the shower running. As if on cue, Ehno got excited, throwing out all sorts of images in our shared mind. I groaned.

"Can you not?"

"I want to mark our mate!" he growled.

"She's had a Hell of day man! Can't you be a normal, non-horny wolf for once?"

"Not really."

"You're impossible."

Of course, now my own imagination was running wild. Twice, I readjusted myself, to no real satisfaction. Violet's scent was drifting into the room, floating on the steam from the shower coming from under the door. I inhaled deeply, relaxing and getting more excited by her heavenly scent. I'd never smelled anything quite so intoxicating. It only made me wonder if she tasted just as good.

I was so lost in my own world, I didn't notice the shower had stopped running. I only shot up when the door opened, Violet shyly stepping into the room in nothing but a towel. I gulped loudly, my eyes following her as she walked to a large dresser, pulling out some pajamas. Neither of us said a word, and she avoided looking directly at me, but the air was thick around us. I released the breath I'd been holding when the bathroom door shut again. However, I nearly choked on it when she came back out.

She was wearing a purple set, the top showing off her cleavage beautifully, while the shorts were. . . well, short. I drank in the sight, wondering how the Hell I was going to make it through the night without going crazy. Meanwhile, Violet stood in front of a mirror on the wall above the dresser, brushing her wet hair. Her scent was stronger now, and it was a miracle of willpower I hadn't moved from the bed yet.

"Which side of the bed do you want?" her eyes found mine in the mirror.

"Doesn't matter." I hoped my voice was as casual as I wanted it to be.

Finally, she turned out the lights and joined me. Her expression said she was trying to act natural, maybe even pretend I wasn't here. But her nervousness was easy to spot. I pulled the covers back, then tucked them around her. I laid down, wondering if it would be okay, or too far, to be closer to her. Before I came up with an answer, Violet rolled over, facing me.

"Can I. . . ?" She gestured to the space between us. I nodded.

A big part of me wondered why this was such a big deal. We already slept in the same bed. So why did this feel different? We were both acting more cautious, obviously timid. Sparks danced across my skin as she laid down right beside me, her arm over my torso while my arms were behind my head.

"Goodnight," she whispered.

"Night." I kissed her hair.

In minutes, her breathing evened out. A soft snore came from the back of her throat; she really was just done today. I, on the other hand, lay wide awake. Lowering one arm, I started to play with her long hair, brushing it over her shoulder. The action calmed me a lot, and I sent a heartfelt thank you to the Goddess for giving me the girl beside me.

CHAPTER 25
VIOLET

When I woke up, I immediately had the sensation of being too hot. In those few seconds it took my brain to catch up to my memory, I panicked. Reacting on instinct, I rolled to my side, throwing the heavy thing on my torso off. At the same time, I aimed a sharp kick, propelling myself up and out of the bed.

"*Ow!* What the fuck?"

As fast as I had attacked, my hands flew up to cover my mouth, my eyes wide in horror.

"Oh shit! I'm so sorry!"

Jasper was sitting on the floor on the opposite side of the bed, rubbing his back, a confused and dazed look on his face.

"Damn Vie, what the Hell?" he grouched.

"I'm sorry! I'm not use to having someone sleep in bed with me and I-I panicked and. . ." I stared at his grumpy face, still half-asleep, and I started giggling uncontrollably.

"This is funny to you?"

"S-sorry. I-I can't h-help it!" I stuttered while giggling.

"Can't say I've ever been woken up quite like that."

Unable to talk, my giggles turned into laughter. He gave me a dirty look, only adding to my amusement. Standing up, Jasper crawled back into bed, face planting into the pillow.

"Awe. Don't be mad, please."

"No. You're mean." His voice was muffled.

I climbed in beside him, resting my head beside his. A goofy smile was still on my face.

"What would make you feel better?" I teased.

"Nothing. I am utterly heartbroken!" he said dramatically.

I giggled again but leaned my head over to kiss his shoulder. He didn't say anything, so I gave him another kiss further up. I kept going, planting light kisses over his shoulder, his neck, and his hair. Sparks danced across my lips, turning my previous fun into a more sensual atmosphere. I kissed his ear and below his short sideburn. Then I tapped his head.

"If you don't turn over, I can't give you a proper kiss."

Jasper didn't move, and I sighed.

"Fine then."

I flopped back onto my side of the bed. As soon as my head landed on my pillow, Jasper struck. In the blink of an eye, he was on top of me, his legs pinning my arms to my sides, a mischievous glint in his eyes.

"Payback time!" he exclaimed, and then he started tickling me. I squirmed, and writhed under him, breathless gasps and laughs coming from me.

"Stop! Please!" I half laughed. "Jasper, stop! I give, I give! You're going to make me pee!" I squealed.

"Say uncle!"

"Uncle! Uncle!"

Laughing with me, he finally released me from the tickle torture, though he didn't move from his position. I mock glared at him, pouting.

"Now who's the mean one?"

"Awe, don't be mad," he quoted me. "What would make you feel better?"

He leaned down, hovering over me before I answered. His silver-grey eyes were shining, I could easily get lost in them. Hala purred in my head. Slowly, I raised one hand from my side, brushing some of his hair off his forehead. Our surroundings melted away; I was only focused on my mate above me right now. Jasper's gaze dropped to my lips briefly, before meeting my eyes again. I could read the unspoken question, but it didn't feel like words needed to spoken at this moment.

Grabbing the back of his neck, I pulled him down to me, our lips meeting in a passionate kiss. Jasper was holding himself over me carefully, putting none of his weight on me, yet I could feel all of him. His scent was overpowering, drowning me, and I was happy to die like this if I had to. The sparks from our bond were stronger, radiating from my lips into my throat, down to my stomach and spreading throughout my body. The hand on his neck moved to his shoulder, down his arm, until he entwined our fingers on the bed. Out of breath, I pulled away, but Jaspers lips simply moved to my cheek, my neck, my collarbone and back up again.

He repeated the circuit over and over again, my breathing becoming more and more erratic with each pass. The next time, he went even lower, his lips grazing the top of my breast. A shive ran through me, an unfamiliar feeling starting in my lower abdomen. Just because I was a virgin, didn't mean I was a nun; I'd masturbated plenty of times before. However, this felt different. I wasn't simply horny, I felt like I *needed* him. It felt like I had an itch I couldn't scratch, and I wiggled my hips under him.

"You can tell me to stop," he whispered. His voice had changed, it was rougher than I'd ever heard it before. The sound only turned me on more.

"No. . . No, don't stop."

Contrary to my words, he paused, looking at me. I had no idea what my face portrayed right then, but whatever he saw there gave him the courage to keep going. Tentatively, he brought his free hand to my waist, softly tracing his fingers over the exposed skin there. I tried to focus on my breathing as he made his way up my torso, slipping under my top. I hadn't worn a bra to bed, and now his hand was inches away. . .

A small gasp escaped me as Jasper cupped my breast. His hand was warm, the skin rough from years of training so hard. Bringing his lips back to mine, he took my nipple in his grasp, pinching and tugging it lightly. It was such an odd feeling, someone else doing it. Odd, but so good. His hand slid over my skin to my other breast, finding the sweet spot. I could feel he was being careful, trying not to push me too far. But I wanted more.

Releasing his hand, I pulled away from our kiss. Instantly, his hand left my skin, a worried expression taking over his features. I kept our eye contact while I moved my hands to the hem of my shirt, pulling it up and over my head. Now, Jasper looked at me with a renewed heat in his eyes, his breath hitching.

"Vie. . ."

"I'm fine. I don't want you to stop, not yet."

"Well, if that's what my girl wants. . ."

He grinned, sitting up again. His eyes didn't leave mine as both his hands went to my breasts, starting to play, pinch, and arouse. Butterflies were crowding my stomach, but lower felt hot. Hotter than ever before. I didn't know how to express what I wanted, and I didn't know how to ask. Was it okay to just ask? I was new to all of this. . . would he think I was stupid?

"What's wrong?"

I hadn't realized I'd been biting my lip until he pulled it away from my teeth.

"Uh. . . How do I. . . Can I. . ." I blew out a frustrated breath. "I'm not sure how to. . ."

"Vie." He bent down to give me a kiss. "Is this making you uncomfortable?"

"No." Exactly the opposite, actually.

"Okay. Just tell me what you're thinking." He cupped my cheek.

"I. . . can I tell you what I want?" I asked quickly. I could feel my cheeks burning from embarrassment, but Jasper smiled.

"Of course. You can tell me what you like, and what you don't like, and if at any point you say stop, I will. That's how this works, by communicating with each other." He caressed my face softly. "Besides that, you won't know what you like unless you try new things. All you have to do is ask."

". . .Okay." I returned his smile.

"So, what do you want?"

"I want. . . you to use your mouth," I whispered the last part.

"As you wish, m'lady."

His words were playful, but his eyes sparked. He started out by kissing my mouth again, repeating his previous actions of slowly moving down. When he got to my breast, I closed my eyes. His tongue flicked out, licking my bud before taking it in his mouth. To my surprise, a soft moan came from my lips. This felt better than his hands. Now he was using his teeth to tug on me gently, his hot breath on my skin. Just as I was getting use to the feeling, he moved to my other breast, renewing the pleasure.

"Vie?"

"Yes?"

"Can I touch you?"

It took me a second to grasp his meaning, but not long to decide my answer. I wanted more of what he was making me feel.

"Yes," I breathed.

Jasper didn't let up with his mouth, just moved his hand to my shorts. His fingers slipped under the waist, and I was so grateful I'd shaved last night in the shower. When he gently ran over my clit, my hips bucked a little, my lips parting. He ran his fingers down my slit, already unbelievably wet, and I moaned again, louder than before.

"Feel good?" he mumbled against my chest.

"Yes. . ."

He repeated the action several times, until I spread my legs wider. It was a silent invitation to keep going, and he did. His lips had moved to my neck, kissing and sucking on a sensitive spot under my ear. My head fell to the side to give him better access. Finding my clit again, he began to rub in slow circles and my mind went hazy.

"Oh. . ."

His movements sped up a little, his mouth finding mine again. I continuously moaned into his mouth, his tongue slipping in and caressing mine. A small voice in my mind told me I was right to wait for this. I couldn't imagine this with anyone else. Jasper was making me come apart, slowly, but kindly, going at my speed. And I knew how excited he was, I could feel it. His excitement was rubbing against my hip through his pants.

"Can I go further?" he asked.

"Yes."

A second later, his finger slipped inside me. My lashes fluttered at the intrusion, my head tilting back. He started slow, picking up the pace in time with the sounds coming from me. He added a second finger, stretching me. It felt so good, if maybe a little awkward.

"Oh. . . Goddess. . ."

"Tell me if you want me to stop," he reminded me.

But I didn't want him to. This felt so amazing, so right. It may not have been how I imagined my first time, but did it matter? I'd promised myself to wait for my mate, for him. And I had. He was the only person in the world I wanted, the only one who could make me feel like this. And clearly, he wanted me too. So why wait any longer? I wanted to give him as much pleasure he was giving me. I was ready.

"Jasper."

He halted at the tone difference. I smiled up at him, assuring him I was fine.

"I want more," I told him.

His eyebrows furrowed. "Vie, this is already-"

I stopped him with a kiss. "I'm ready, Jasper."

"A-are you sure?"

"Yes. I want you."

Instead of eagerly jumping into it like I expected, he took several minutes searching my face, trying to find any hint that I didn't want this like I said. Finally, he leaned in to kiss my forehead.

"I'll take it slow. I promise."

"Okay."

I didn't want to get ahead of myself, but now that we were on the same page, I let him take the lead. His fingers started moving again, faster this time. Jaspers lips were at my ear, his breath tickling.

"I need to make sure you're ready, babe. This is the easiest way."

"Fine. . .by. . .me."

He chuckled, his movements increasing again. My hands gripped the bedsheets as I moaned, my hips beginning to move, trying to match his rhythm. Surprising me, Jasper moved his head down, kissing both of my breasts, down my torso, then settling between my legs. In one swift movement that had me impressed, he discarded my shorts, then resumed using his fingers. When he added his tongue, rolling it over my clit while he was inside me, I almost lost it. The combination drove me crazy, my knees bending off the bed while my head fell back. His mouth assaulted me in the best way possible, sending delicious tingles from my clit directly to my core.

"Oh. . .oh. . . Jasper. . . keep going. . ."

He groaned against me, the sound almost animalistic. My legs began to shake, my muscles tightening. I was lost in a wave of pleasure that I hoped never ended. I was completely at his mercy right now, and I loved it. I was so close. . . and then I did. It was better than anytime by myself before, so much more intense. It was great. . . and yet, I wasn't fully satisfied.

After coming down from my orgasm, I looked to see Jasper standing at the end of the bed. His shirt hit the floor. And then his pants. When he discarded his boxers, I gulped. Loudly.

"Oh."

I was sure my anxiety was clear on my face. Jasper only smiled at me, crawling back into bed.

"Still want to?" he asked.

I set my expression. I wanted him. I wanted this. Mom had prepared me a long time ago. My sex talk was more than where babies come from. She made sure I knew what to expect my first time; she gave me all the information on consent and respecting your body. Sexually transmitted

171

diseases weren't an issue for werewolves, they didn't effect us thanks to our incredible immune systems, but she still made sure I was educated on that, too. Still, I honestly never imagined my first time would be with someone so. . . *big*. Even though Jaspers size was intimidating, I pushed my worry aside and nodded. He wouldn't hurt me, not on purpose. I trusted him.

He carefully positioned himself over me, kissing me slowly. I felt him rubbing against my entrance. My chest moved up and down, our chests brushing against each other.

"It's going to hurt," he whispered apologetically. "I can't help that."

"I know."

"I'm not an expert, but I heard that breathing helps. Deep breaths."

"Okay."

"Ready?"

"Yes."

He began to push in. A second later, I winced. He stopped. It wasn't terrible, but it stung. Following his advice, I took a deep breath. It did help a little.

"I'm good," I whispered.

We repeated this several times. He would push, I would grimace, and he would stop. Eventually, I started to get frustrated. My insecurities were starting to get the better of me right now, and I felt angry tears brim my eyes.

"Vie?"

"I'm sorry," I groaned.

"Do you want to stop?"

"No. . . No. I just feel so. . . dumb right now. This is probably the worst for you."

His eyes softened. "This is far from the worst. I promised you I would go slow. I know it hurts. I wish it didn't hurt for you. But already, you feel amazing. I just want you to get past the pain, so I can show you the pleasure."

His words made me feel a thousand times better. "Okay.
. . you can keep going."

A few tries later, I felt him hit the resistance. He must
have felt it too, because he rested his forehead against
mine, his hand coming up to cup my cheek again.

"Remember to breath," he whispered. And then he
pushed through.

A short scream sounded, before I gulped in a breath,
holding it. My eyes were squeezed shut; my hands clenched
in fists above my head.

"*Fuck.*"

"Breath, Violet."

I did, taking deep breaths, letting them out against his
cheek.

"I'm going to start moving. It will help the pain, okay?"

"Kay," I grunted.

The stinging was worse as he moved, my insides
throbbing.

"Open your eyes, Vie."

I did as he asked. Jasper was moving slowly back and
forth, his hand now at the back of my neck. I whimpered
slightly, and he planted a kiss on the tip of my nose.

"Focus on me, babe. Just me. I'm here with you, right
here. . ."

Jasper continued to talk to me, kissing away my silent
tears. As he was talking, the pain changed. It dulled,
becoming easier to bear, with tingles of pleasure rising.

"Oh. . . oh, that's. . ."

"Better?"

"Mhmm. . ."

He grinned. The sight added to the increasing
enjoyment, my heart squeezing. The man above me was
dazzling. My eyes travelled down his torso, mesmerized by
the sight of our bodies connected as one. The sight made
me even more aroused and made it even easier for him. The
more he moved inside me, the more the pain dissipated,
until it was gone. All that was left was the euphoria I'd
heard so much about. Jasper felt incredible inside me,

filling me, even though I wasn't sure how. Part of me still thought he was too big, but our mixed breaths, quick kisses and bodies moving together were proof we fit together perfectly.

"I-it feels. . . good. . ." I whispered. "Faster. Please."

My hands clenched again as he willingly obliged my request. My body was shattering from the inside out, owned by my mate, and the way he claimed me. I gripped his shoulder, unintelligible sounds dripping from my lips. All I felt was pure bliss.

"Fuck. . ." Jasper groaned.

"J-jasper. . . *fuck*. . . hmm. . ."

"I love it when you say my name."

"I. . . I want. . ."

"What babe?"

"Faster. . ." Using my grip on his shoulder, I pulled myself up, my lips at his ear. "Faster, harder. I want to feel what you can give me."

My words triggered something in him. His silver eyes flashed with desire. Then he started to move, really move. I'd be sore, but who cared? This was worth it. My moans turned into screams, and I thanked the Goddess the walls were soundproofed.

"Oh fuck! . . . yes. . . yes. . . oh, Goddess. . ."

My core tightened, my toes curling. My voice was raspy, breathless. When my orgasm hit, spots danced in front of vision. It was unimaginable, out of this world.

"*Jasper!*"

His name echoed around the room a second before he found his own release, emptying inside me. The feeling prolonged my orgasm, producing a half moan, half scream out of me. We were both breathing heavily when he finally pulled out of me, the stain of my virginity on the sheets. Laying beside me, my mate pulled me into his arms.

"Wow," I mumbled.

"Yeah. No kidding."

"So that's what they call sex."

"No." Jasper tilted my chin up, kissing me heartily. "That's what they call making love."

CHAPTER 26
SOPHIA

Last night was awkward. It was very clear that Garrett wanted more than just sleep, but I said no. I wanted us to build a foundation of trust again, before anything physical happened. More so, I wanted *him* to trust *me* again.

Last night was the first time we'd slept in the same bed since we dated. It all felt familiar to me, yet strange and new. Garrett wasn't the same guy I knew before. He was much more closed off, less talkative. The guilt wouldn't leave, because I knew it was because of me. Because of what I did. If I had to, I'd spend the rest of my life trying to make it up to him. The bigger problem right now was dealing with his hatred for Jasper. Even I was surprised when he turned out to be Violet's mate. Who saw *that* coming? Not me. Certainly not Violet. However, they seemed to fit well together.

On the other hand, Garrett didn't seem to be able to get over it. He vented for over an hour before we finally went to bed about his sister's mate. I listened attentively, but not replying much. I feared he would twist my words, believing I had feelings for Jasper or something. It was a likely possibility, because most of his arguments were dull. In my opinion, he needed to accept this turn of events and move on. Everyone else had.

This morning, he was in a better mood, if still a bit grumpy. He'd gone for breakfast with his parents, in the cafeteria today as nobody could get up to the fourth floor, while I showered and got dressed. I picked out a navy-blue dress with sunflowers printed on it and white sandals. Grabbing my curler, I stood in front of the bathroom mirror, thinking. I didn't know how to explain it, but ever since the night of the party, I'd been feeling. . .off. I chalked it up to guilt, and shame mostly. But for over a year now, I never could shake the feeling, could never get that night out of my head.

I remembered dancing with Garrett, admiring him in his button-down black shirt, his hair wild and messy, in need of a cut soon. We'd laughed, chatted with our friends, drank a little. We'd even snuck off to catch a private, intimate moment outside. I remembered having to use the bathroom. And the next thing I knew, I was in bed with Jasper Cole, giving him my virginity.

I frowned deeply, trying for the millionth time to recall exactly what had happened. What had persuaded me to exit the bathroom and go in search of Jasper? Obviously, I remembered our conversation leading up to sleeping together. And I could remember the act too. But those memories felt hazy, dim, compared to the rest. The most vivid flashback was Garrett walking in on us and breaking up with me. Not that I blamed him; I'd have done a lot worse if the situation had been reversed.

I even thought about talking to Jasper about it. Did he have this fuzzy memory, too? Or had I just shoved my actions deep down? Nonetheless, asking Jasper directly was out of the question. If Violet didn't get pissed, Garrett definitely would.

"Ow! Awe, shit!" I groaned.

I chucked the strands of hair I'd accidentally burnt off with the curler. Thankfully, it wasn't a lot, but I'd have to hide the shorter strands somehow. I was way too distracted to do this. Unplugging the tool, I left the bathroom, throwing my hair into a ponytail instead. Garrett walked in as I picked up my jean jacket from the bed.

"Hey. How was breakfast?" I asked with a smile.

"Terrible!"

"Why?"

"Can you believe Jasper was there?" He sat heavily on the bed.

"Uh. . . well. . . yeah, Garrett. He is Violet's mate."

"Dad even called him 'son'." He continued as if he hadn't heard me. "And Violet was all red cheeks and smiles, too.

Ugh! I swear if he touched my sister. . . And I guess his maybe-bio Dad is here, so everyone was focused on *that* instead!"

"So?" He looked at me finally. "They *are* mates. It isn't really our business if they. . . are, er, intimate with each other." I shrugged, but Garrett narrowed his eyes at me. I knew what he was thinking.

"Why are you sticking up for him?" he demanded.

There it was.

"I'm not sticking up for him," I sighed. "I'm just saying that if they want to. . . do that. . . then it's their business, not anyone else's."

"You can say the word, Sophia. It's not like you're not familiar with it."

I took a step back, hurt washing through me. "What did you just say to me?"

"What? You *have* had sex."

I crossed my arms. "Did you consider that I just don't want to talk about your *sisters* sex life?"

"I don't get why nobody is worried about it! Next thing you know, they'll be having a pup and then he'll never fucking leave!"

"Violet seems to have accepted him, Garrett. Which means he isn't leaving. I think you should try to accept the situation as well."

"There you go again."

Anger sparked at his accusatory tone. "So, this is how it's going to be, Garrett? What happened to starting over?"

"We are starting over. Don't be dramatic."

"Dramatic! Do you have any idea how much you just insulted me right now?"

He scoffed. "Sophia, you can't be mad about the truth. And the truth is, you slept with Jasper, and now you're sticking up for him."

"No, the truth is-" I clenched my jaw against the words begging to come out. I didn't want to fight with him.

"What?"

"Nevermind." I put on my jacket, heading for the door.

"No, say it," he said behind me. His tone was unbelievably childish.

I whirled around, planting my feet. "Fine. The truth is that you never really planned to move on with me. The way you're acting right now, it only says that you're going to throw this in my face any chance you get! I'm not going to sit here and take that, Garrett! Grow the fuck up!"

His lips parted at my words, his eyes sparking with anger. Before this turned into a screaming match, I quickly left the room. The door slammed open behind me as I stomped down the hall.

"Sophia!"

I ignored Garrett. I wasn't going to fight with him anymore, it was too much. Why couldn't we just have a normal morning?

"Sophia, stop!"

"Go away, Garrett!"

His hand landed on my shoulder, twisting me around to face him. I shrugged him off, glaring.

"Just stop! I'm sorry, okay?"

I snorted, looking away.

"Look. I shouldn't have said all that. I just. . . I can't stand it. He's always around now, anywhere I go! And-"

"And what?" I snapped. "*You* are my mate, not Jasper! You have no reason to be jealous, Garrett! I don't want him!"

"But you did! You did Sophia, at one time. You wanted him more than me."

I grabbed my hair in frustration. "Oh, my Goddess! No, I didn't! I've never wanted anyone like I want you, okay? I don't know why I did what I did, but I'm so tired of my life revolving around it! I just want to move on! I am not fighting about this with you for the rest of my life!"

Tears of anger, frustration, and hurt sat on my lower lashes. I stared at him, trying to get him to understand that this was too much. I couldn't live like this, mate or not.

"What do you want me to do, Garrett? Stay inside the packhouse- the bedroom- forever? Just in case I happen to

179

run into him? Do you want me to say sorry every morning when you wake up, and every night before you go to sleep? How many times do I need to say sorry? What do you want me to do, to make you trust me again?"

"That's ridiculous, Sophia. I'm not going to cage you like an animal. But how do I know you won't go seeking him out? Or any other guy? How am I supposed to believe I'm enough for you, when I obviously wasn't before?"

Before I could answer, another voice sounded behind us.

"Enough."

I looked over my shoulder. Violet was standing, leaning against the wall with her arms crossed. To my surprise, she was glaring at her brother instead of me.

"This isn't the place to be doing this, Garrett," she said. "The whole lower floor can hear you guys."

"Don't you have a mate to get to?" Garrett replied sarcastically. Violet raised her eyebrows.

"He went home for now."

"Hallelujah."

"Stop being an asshole," she spat at him. "I understood before why you were upset, but this is getting fucking ridiculous!"

"Mind your own business, Violet."

"Why should I mind my business when my own fucking brother is treating a girl like shit?"

"She's my mate-"

"Exactly!"

To my utter dismay, Luna Lily and the Alpha, along with his Beta and Gamma, climbed up the ladder. The group stared between Violet and us, and my cheeks burned with embarrassment. This is what I had hoped to avoid.

"What is going on? Why are you two yelling at each other?" Luna Lily asked.

"Same as always, Mom. Violet can't keep her nose out of other peoples' business."

"Shut the fuck up."

"Violet!"

"No, Mom!" She pushed away from the wall, taking a few steps towards us. I'd seen her angry many times, at school, and I could only hope she wouldn't direct it at me. "You chose to accept Sophia as your mate! That doesn't mean you can belittle and degrade her whenever you feel like it!"

Every face turned to Garrett. His Dad seemed to be getting angry, while his Mom looked disappointed. Beta Ben and Gamma Luke just appeared to be shocked. My eyes refocused on Violet as she stood in front of me, taking my hand. I glanced at my mate as she dragged me away.

"V-Violet, it's fine! Really! I didn't help the situation so-"

"Stop that," she snapped at me. "I don't give a fuck what you two were arguing about, he doesn't have any right to speak to you the way he was. I heard what he said Sophia. If you think you deserve that then by all means run along back to him. I won't intervene again, though. You were right, he needs to grow the fuck up."

My eyebrows furrowed slightly as I listened to her. I knew I didn't deserve this. Yes, I'd fucked up. But how long was Garrett going to keep punishing me for my mistake? This man, the one seething in the middle of the corridor behind us, was not the man I loved once. This man was consumed by jealousy, and hate. When he showed up to my house, I really believed he was going to try and work things out with me. Was I stupid, or just naive? Regardless, I knew I was better than this. I wasn't the type of girl to sit down quietly and take this shit.

"I don't deserve this," I said more to myself than to Violet.

"No, you don't."

"Are you fucking kidding me?!" Garrett shouted behind us.

This time, his Dad stepped forward. His Alpha aura was strong, making me cringe.

"I thought we taught you better than to ever mistreat your mate, no matter who it is, or what happened in the past. You're living in the past Garrett, and it's not healthy."

"Who are you to talk to me about mistreating mates?"

I gasped, along with everyone else. Alpha Dimitris eyes widened, but that was the only part of his composure he lost. Violet was shaking behind me, looking five seconds away from attacking her brother. The other three were just staring at Garrett, various expressions of disbelief on their faces.

"Go to your room."

Alpha Dimitris voice was suddenly so soft, a sharp contrast to his previous tone that it threw me completely.

"Wha. . ..what?"

"I said, go to your room."

"Wha- No!"

The Alpha took a step in his sons' direction. "You want to act like a kid? I'll start treating you like a kid again. Only *boys* treat women this way, not *men*. Clearly, you are still just a boy."

"Fuck you!"

Moving faster than my eyes could see, Alpha Dimitri suddenly had Garrett by the back of his shirt, dragging him back to the bedroom. Garrett kicked and screamed the whole way, and I was ashamed at that moment to see how childlike he really was acting. A second later, Alpha Dimitri exited, slamming the door behind him so hard, I was surprised it didn't break. I glanced to my left. Luna Lily looked equal parts angry as well as sad.

"Are you alright?" Violet asked.

"Yes. Thank you."

"Sophia. . ." The Luna turned to me. "I don't know exactly what happened but. . . if you're thinking about rejecting-"

My jaw dropped, and I took a step back. That was the absolute last thing I ever expected to hear.

"No, no! I don't want to reject him, Luna!"

"I fucking would," Violet muttered.

I took a deep breath. "I know that Garrett was wrong. And believe me, I won't sit down and take it, ever. But that man, that's not Garrett. That's not your brother, or your son! He's just. . . lost. I was picked to be the future Luna of this pack, and part of that comes with helping the future Alpha of this pack. I want to help Garrett, even if I'm the reason for his torment. He is a good person. I won't give up on him so easily."

"Spoken like a true Luna." Gamma Luke smiled at me, and I blushed.

"Indeed. I remember someone else who was lost, once." Luna Lily glanced at her mate. "However, I don't suggest returning to your room just now."

"No, I've had enough fighting for one day."

"Come on." Violet grabbed my hand again, confusing me.

"Where are we going?"

She heaved a sigh. "If you manage to take my brothers head out of his ass, it's likely you're going to be my sister-in-law someday. So, let's go hang out and get to know each other and all that jazz."

"Uh, okay?"

I let her pull me out the packhouse and to her car. As I buckled my seatbelt, I glanced back at the house. Why did love have to be so damn complicated?

CHAPTER 27
JASPER

Mom and I were sitting at the kitchen table. She wouldn't look at me, just stared at the redwood finish with a profound frown. Twice, she'd opened her mouth to speak but closed it again. I didn't blame her; meeting my possible biological parent, even one of them, must be hard for her. These people took me in, raised me, fed me, clothed me. Loved me. I expected this to be harder for her than it was for me. I waited patiently, letting her gather her thoughts and feelings. Finally, she spoke.

"You want to do this?"

"Yes."

"Why?"

That was a tough one. But I couldn't be anything other than honest with her.

"I'm not sure. Partly to see if it's true. Another part of me just wants to look him in the eye and ask the questions I've been wondering about for years. Lots of reasons Mom, but none of them are solid, I guess."

"If he is your Dad. . . you're *biological* Dad. . . he might not accept you, Jasper." She finally met my eyes. "I know that's harsh, but I don't want you to have hopes of a reunion that might not happen."

I nodded. "I know, Mom. I'm prepared for any outcome."

"Are you? No offense son, but you're still just a kid. I don't want to see you get hurt."

Her voice choked up at the end. I stood, walking around the table, and wrapping her in my arms. This woman was worth a million in gold, yet she was priceless too. Once again, I found myself being eternally indebted to have been blessed with a Mom like her. I loved my bio Mom and missed her like crazy sometimes. But I was proud to be a Cole.

"You're allowed to come with me. Tell you what, if he turns out to be a complete asshole, you can have at him." I chuckled.

"Don't think I won't!" she retorted.

I pulled back. "So, you're coming with me then?"

"Of course! Your Dad too. When is this Alpha coming?"

"Well, he's actually already here. We were supposed to meet yesterday, but, uh. . . the incident at the packhouse delayed the meeting."

I rubbed the back of my neck, unsure if I was allowed to tell my parents about Vie. They would never say anything, but I wasn't sure about their feelings towards hybrids. Maybe I could sneak the topic in somewhere beforehand.

"Ah. So when?" Mom asked.

"Tomorrow morning. Alpha Dimitri wants us to be there by eleven. The Luna is making a brunch."

Mom clapped her hands. "Oh, yay! I love Lilys cooking!"

I laughed, silently agreeing. The breakfast the Luna prepared this morning was incredible. It was better than Moms, though I would never tell her that.

"How is Violet?"

"She's good."

"How are you and Violet?"

A smile crept onto my face, and I think I blushed, too. Mom smiled- a knowing smile. Parents. They knew everything, even if we didn't tell them.

"Did you mark her?" She leaned forward while I sat back down.

"No. I wanted to, but I didn't want to do it out of the blue. I wasn't sure how she'd feel about it."

"That was probably a good call. She is -or *was*- a virgin, right?"

I nearly choked on my saliva. "Mom!"

"What? Oh, please Jasper, it's not a big deal! We're adults, and if you're having sex, then you should be able to talk about it without being embarrassed!"

That was kind of what Vie had said to me at the cabin. Still, it *was* a bit weird talking about it with Mom.

"Yeah, she was," I mumbled.

"Well, I'm sure she will let you know her thoughts on it." She tapped her fingers on the table, grinning. "Besides, females get pregnant easier after being marked, and I want grandbabies soon."

This time I did choke. "Goddess Mom! It's way too soon to be thinking about that!"

She shrugged, totally serious. I simply shook my head. A knock on the front door saved me from more of this conversation. I practically ran from the kitchen, much to Mom's amusement. Whoever it was at the door, I owed them big time.

"Hey."

I pulled Violet to me, wrapping her in a tight hug.

"Thank you!"

"Uh. . . for?"

"Saving me."

My mate looked at me like I was insane. "Should I ask?"

"Oh, he's just all weirded out because I brought up sex." Mom came up behind me, giving Violet her own hug.

"You. . . he. . . what?"

"Oh, hello."

Mom was looking over Vie's shoulder. I raised one eyebrow; I hadn't even noticed Sophia. Why was she here? Did that mean Garrett was here too? Sophia glanced at me, looking nervous as Hell.

"Hello Mrs. Cole," she said politely.

"Friend of yours?" Mom asked Violet.

"My brothers mate."

"Ah. Is he here too?"

"He was being a jackass, so we left him at home." Violet shrugged and Mom shot me a look. "Anyway, we came to see if Jasper wanted to hang out?"

"Uh. . . sure."

My hesitation was sound. My past with Sophia hadn't been generally well received, which was fair. So, it was understandable that I was a little confused and surprised that Violet all of a sudden wanted us to all hang out together. Don't get me wrong, I was glad she didn't seem to have the same animosity towards me that Garrett had. But this situation was strange.

"Great. I thought we could go see a movie."

"Sounds good. I'll grab my wallet."

"We'll be in the car." She hugged my Mom again. "I'll see you later, Linda."

"You too, dear. Have fun."

Sophia and Vie waved as they walked back to her car. I went inside to locate my wallet, not wanting to keep her waiting. This would have been a great date, if Sophia wasn't here too. Oh well.

"Have fun. Are you coming home tonight?" Mom handed me my jacket as I passed.

"I'm not sure. I'll let you know though, okay?"

I kissed her cheek before running out the door. Sophia was in the backseat. Violet was driving, tapping her fingers on the steering wheel to the music playing. I slid in the passenger seat, smiling at her.

"What do you guys want to see?" she asked as she pulled away from the curb.

"The new Jurassic World movie is playing," I suggested.

Violet grinned happily. "I'm in. Sophia?"

"Yeah, sure."

I gave Vie a question mark look, which she ignored. "You mind if I pick up Dylan and Brianne?"

She looked at me, then Sophia in the rearview mirror. We both shook our heads, and ten minutes later, the car was full. Dylan and I got to talking about which Jurassic movie was the best, with Brianne and Violet chiming in now and again. Sophia sat in the back, gazing out the window, not saying a word. The theater was located in the center of the pack, about a half hour drive. The five of us got out after we managed to find a parking spot, and I held Violet's hand as we entered.

A couple kids from school lingered around the main area, either in line to get snacks or looking at the posters of the new releases playing. A lot of eyes turned our way as we passed, mostly on me and Vie. She ignored them, and I tried to, too. We bought our tickets, the guy behind the counter eyeing me almost rudely.

"Here." He shoved my ticket at me, and I grabbed it.

"What's his issue?" I grumbled as we walked away.

"Oh Tyler? Don't worry about him. He's just jealous," Brianne chirped beside me.

"Jealous?"

"Yeah. He's had a crush on Violet forever." She giggled.

I glanced back. Tyler was staring after our group, glaring at me. I shot him the finger and smirked. Too bad for him.

"Since when does Tyler have a crush on me?" Vie asked, peeking around my back to see her friend.

"Really? He stares at you constantly in math. You never noticed?"

"No."

Brianne shook her head, but I smiled, kissing the top of her head. We got in line for the room our movie was playing, chatting casually. I noticed a group of girls giving Violet the stink-eye. They quickly turned around when they caught me glaring at them. Who knew going to the movies would bring us so much attention? The doors opened and we moved entered the dark room and found our seats. I'd barely sat, when Violet pulled my arm.

"I'm going to get popcorn. You guys want anything?"

"Diet coke and extra butter for me," Brianne said.

"Same, except not diet," Dylan said.

"Sophia?"

"Nothing for me, thanks."

"Okay. Be right back."

We walked back out of the room, going to the snack bar. As soon as the line moved ahead enough, she leaned into me.

"I know you're just dying to ask me what she's doing here with us."

"Yeah, actually. What's the deal?"

She sighed. Then she launched into what happened earlier with her brother, Mom and Dad. My stomach knotted more and more as she spoke. Garrett really hated me that much, that he would treat his mate that way? Fuck.

"What can I do?" I asked.

Violet raised her eyebrows. "I didn't say you had to *do* anything."

"No, but this is obviously upsetting you. And your family. And it's because of me, I want to help. Should I talk to Garrett?"

Violet winced. "Please, don't. That might be the last thing any of us need. Besides, you've got enough to be worrying about, I'm sure."

Now I winced. "Good point. She doesn't seem to enjoy being out with us though."

"Oh, she was happy earlier. She only got all sullen when I told her I was going to pick you up. Understandably, she got a bit timid."

A question burned on the tip of my tongue, but I held it in. Honestly, I was afraid of what she would say if I did ask.

"I can almost see the wheels turning in your head Jasper." She grinned at me. "I know what you're thinking, and the answer is no. Is it weird you slept with her? Yeah, a little. She might be my future sister-in-law. But I'm not mad at you, or her. It's in the past, and that's where it can stay. But hey, way to keep it in the family dude."

Heat rushed to my face, colouring my cheeks. "Shut up."

Violet laughed as we made our way to the girl behind the concession stand. She was a tall brunette with big blue eyes that never left me. I rolled my eyes, but she didn't get the hint.

189

"That'll be. . . forty-two even. Cash or debit handsome?" She batted her fake lashes at me.

"Cash." Violet dropped a fifty on the counter. The girl unwillingly turned to her, taking the money in her fingers like it was carrying a disease. A few minutes later, I helped load up all the food and drinks.

"No tip?" The girl leaned over the counter; her blouse was way too undone to be appropriate for work.

"Yeah." Violet smiled at the girl sweetly. "Learn to keep your eyes off other girls' men. And do up your fucking shirt."

Brunette's jaw dropped, her cheeks instantly going crimson. I tried to cover my laugh, unsuccessfully. We left her standing there, hurriedly doing up her blouse and muttering to herself. We got back just in time for the previews to start, dispersing the snacks around. Violet handed Sophia a bag of gummy worms, earning a small smile in return. We whisper talked through the previews, commenting on a few movies that looked good, and then settling in for the main show.

"You like these kinds of movies?" I whispered a while later to Violet.

She nodded. "Almost as much as horror movies. I love dinosaurs."

Huh. That was something I never knew about her. Good to know though. True enough, she was invested from beginning to end, and I couldn't help but watch her more than the movie itself. She was too cute. When the movie ended, she was all smiles, talking excitedly with Dylan about it. I trailed behind as we left the theater, letting her have a moment with her friends.

"Jasper?"

I glanced at Sophia, now walking beside me.

"Yeah?"

"I need to talk to you," she said lowly.

I pursed my lips but nodded. "Go ahead."

I heard her take a breath. "About that night. . . the party. . ."

"Sophia-"

"No, I don't want to talk about it. Not really. I was just wondering. . . do you. . . remember it?"

I stopped, facing her. "What are you getting at?" I asked sharply.

She brushed her hair behind her ear, nervous. "I remember it, kind of. What we did. . . it's fuzzy for me." She frowned. "I know I wasn't drunk, so I'm not sure how but. . . I need to know if it's only me."

Unwillingly, the memory of that night came to mind.

"I don't know Sophia. Have you considered you just feel guilty about it?"

"Yes, actually."

"That's probably your answer then."

"Jasper. . . I'm sorry. None of this drama would be happening if it wasn't for me." She looked over at the rest of our group. "I can see how happy you two are. I'm sorry if my actions caused any problems for you."

I rubbed my forehead. "Thanks. But it wasn't just your actions. You know what they say, it takes two to tango. We're both at fault really."

"I guess."

"Was that all?"

"Yes."

"Alright."

We continued walking. Violet looked between the two of us as we approached, but she didn't look mad. Maybe she knew Sophia wanted to talk to me. I gave her a short kiss before looping around to get in the car, just happy that at least one of the Alphas twins knew how to be reasonable.

CHAPTER 28
VIOLET

I got back home around six after spending the day with our friends. Sophia had chosen to go home, not wanting another possible fight with her mate. I silently applauded her; let him reflect on his actions, maybe he'd learn. I already knew I was in for it, but I still grimaced when Jasper and I walked through the door.

"Hey Aunt Clara. Grandpa!"

Despite him trying to look stern, a smile cracked through as I ran to him.

"Good to see you Violet," he said.

"How was your trip?"

"Amazing. Your grandma had the best time."

I grinned. "I'm glad."

"You had training today," Aunt Clara growled at me.

"I know. I'm sorry. Didn't Mom tell you I was out?"

"She did. But you still should have shown up," Grandpa sighed. "This is important, Violet."

Usually, I'd have some smartass remark or comment. But not with Grandpa. I respected him too much to be snarky towards him. It had taken Mom a good amount of time to forgive him for leaving her at the Snow Moon pack. They had a steady, but not wonderful, relationship now. The choice he made was hard, and I wasn't sure I could ever do what he did. Hopefully, I'd never have to make that choice.

"Sorry," I told them sincerely.

"You're here now."

"So, let's go," Aunt Clara said.

"Wait, now?" I panicked a little.

"Yes, now. You need to learn this stuff Violet, as soon as possible. If not how to use your magic, at least how to control it. Luckily, that's the easy part."

I followed them back out of the house, Jasper trailing behind me. How was controlling this magic the easy part? We stopped behind the packhouse, Aunt Clara holding out her hand. I groaned.

"You don't even know where the cabin is!"

"I know where the border is."

Grumbling, I took her hand, while Grandpa took her other. Aunt Clara looked at my mate expectantly. He looked back, totally confused.

"Just put your hand on her shoulder and close your eyes," I told him.

"Kay. . ."

I squeezed my eyes shut, feeling the familiar sensation of being thrown into a tornado. It lasted all of two seconds, and then I was standing still.

"What the fuck. . ." Jasper had stumbled a few steps away, holding his stomach.

"I told you to close your eyes."

"I *did*." He groaned, bending at the waist.

"If you're going to be sick, be quick about it please. We don't have much daylight left," Aunt Clara sighed.

"Which way are we going?" Granpa asked him, and Jasper pointed vaguely.

The two left, leaving me to take care of my mate. After multiple deep, deep breaths and rubbing his back, we followed them slowly. I was a little pissed he hadn't gotten sick; I'd puked my guts out the first time Aunt Clara teleported me. The walk to the cabin seemed shorter this time. We stopped a good distance away from the log house. I eyed my teachers nervously as they surveyed the area.

"This seems good. At least, you won't damage too much out here."

"Nothing but trees anyway," Grandpa added.

"Good. Let's start."

They stared at me, and I stared back. Nobody said anything for a few minutes, and I wondered if they were waiting for me to do or say something. A minute later, Aunt Clara sighed again.

"Jasper," she snapped. "Unless you want Violet to accidentally hurt you, get your ass over here!"

"Oh. Sorry."

I giggled. Only Aunt Clara could bring out such a sheepish look on someone like Jasper. He strolled past them, sitting down against a tree, watching me intently.

"Okay." I focused on my Aunt. "We're going to do some exercises with you. Thankfully, I am prepared this time around."

"What she means, -" Grandpa said, "-is your Mom gave her a heart attack once when she tried to help her with her gifts."

"Really?" I asked.

"Ask her about it sometime. Now, close your eyes," Aunt Clara instructed. I did as she asked.

"Focus on your wolf. She is the other half to your soul; Listen to us and work together," Grandpa said.

"Hala."

"Let's do this!"

I smiled. She was as excited as a pup with a new toy.

"Tune out everything else Violet. Everything except us and your wolf."

That was trickier, especially with my accelerated senses, but I managed after a while.

"Good. . . now, look inside yourself. Communicate with your wolf, not in words, but in mind. You can work together without speaking. You know each other, inside and out. You are one, together."

At first, I wasn't sure how to do what she asked. Then I felt Hala's presence, slowly growing from inside my head and into the rest of my body. Then I understood. I felt like *me*, but I'd given part of the control over to my wolf without shifting. It was intense, and I'd never felt so close to her. She was everywhere within me, but I was still here too. We were, indeed, one. Together. It was incredible.

"Search further now. Find where your magic is hidden. Observe it, memorize it."

Together, Hala and I went inside ourselves. For a while, I struggled, trying to find any hint of the aura I'd felt in the packhouse, and coming up empty. Frustrated, I opened my eyes.

"It's not working."

Aunt Clara and Grandpa looked at each other.

"What's holding you back?" Grandpa asked me gently.

"Nothing!"

"Lying to yourself will only make this harder."

I bit my lip, averting my eyes. I hated that he was right. Suddenly, Jasper was by my side, taking my hand in his.

"Remember- it's part of you, but it's not all of you. You can do this, Vie." He smiled at me, and my heart skipped a beat. How did he know what I couldn't even admit out loud? That I was scared to find that power again? Obviously, the last time didn't work out so well. I didn't want to hurt anybody here.

"You don't have to be scared," Grandpa said. "We're here to make sure nothing happens to you."

"I'm here too. I won't let us loose control." Hala comforted me.

"Okay." I shook my head, trying to find my determination. "Okay, let's try again."

Jasper moved back to his spot under the tree, and I closed my eyes, blocking everything out. Once I felt that unique connection with Hala, I tried again. When I started to get frustrated, Hala replayed Jaspers words. It helped, a lot. After what felt like hours, I found what I was looking for. A smaller, considerably less powerful spark than before, hiding within my soul. I felt my head nod.

"Good Violet. Now. . . I want you to reach for that feeling, your magic. Take it and hold it close."

I shook my head vigorously. I found it; I didn't want to touch it.

"You don't need to be scared." Grandpa repeated. "That magic? It's yours. It's a part of you, Violet. It can't hurt you, and it can't hurt anyone else, because you won't let it. *You* control *it*□ , not the other way around."

Hesitantly, slowly, I reached for that part of myself. Hala was eager, but I was terrified. Beyond terrified. I tried to push the fear away, enough to do what needed to be done. I nodded again, waiting.

"I want you to imagine something. It could be a chest, a box, anything with a lid."

A vision of a treasure chest popped into my mind. I imagined it was gold, thick, with a heavy lid.

"Take that part of yourself, your magic, and put it inside. Close the lid. Lock it. Good. Open your eyes."

I blinked. Everyone was smiling at me, but I felt mentally drained.

"That's it?" I asked.

"For now. You did great."

"Anytime you feel yourself losing control, just imagine that enclosure, and keep it from opening. It takes some practice, but you'll get the hang of it."

"What do you imagine?" I couldn't help but ask.

"I keep mine in a white box, with pink flowers. It was my mother's jewellery box." Aunt Clara smiled fondly.

"I imagine my sock drawer," Grandpa chuckled.

"Really?" Jasper asked.

"It was the first thing that came to mind," Grandpa shrugged and I giggled.

"Thank you," I told them. Knowing what to do now, I didn't feel as scared. I felt like a was no longer a ticking-time bomb.

"Tomorrow, after your meeting, we will come back and walk you through some more of the steps, maybe even try a few simple spells."

I cringed and Aunt Clara noticed.

"What?"

"I. . . I don't want to. Can't I just keep it locked up?"

All three of them gave me sympathetic looks. Aunt Clara came to stand in front of me, putting her hands on my shoulders.

"Do you remember, when you five, there was a fire in the woods?"

I blinked at her, searching my memory. I did somewhat remember that. "We weren't allowed in that area for a while," I nodded.

"That was Isa."

My eyes widened hugely. "Huh?"

"She got angry at Ben. And she lost control. Whether or not you keep your magic locked up. . . It always finds a way to come forth eventually. So, it's better to learn when and how to use it. More so, you shouldn't hide it. It makes you who you are Violet. And it's nothing to be ashamed about."

"I-I'm not ashamed. . . I'm scared," I admitted lowly.

"We all were at times," Grandpa said. "Every witch you will ever meet has, at one point or another, lost control. It *is* a scary feeling, but we learn from it, grow from it. Magic can be scary."

"But it can also be beautiful," Aunt Clara smiled, releasing me.

She waved her hand, muttering a spell. I watched in amazement as the ground under me started growing new grass. Among the blades, little sprouting's popped up, reaching towards the sky, and opening into warm coloured tulips.

"That's amazing."

Jasper came to stand to the side, watching the little garden grow under our feet in awe. Aunt Clara looked back to me.

"The best lesson I can teach you is this: people say there is light in darkness. There is always some good in evil. But that's not always true, especially with our kind. When a witch turns to the darkness, there is no coming back. It eats at our soul, corrupts us irrevocably. Dark witches are not to be underestimated, and they deserve no mercy."

Her tone hinted at something, and I knew what she meant. Jennine would get no mercy from me. I nodded in acknowledgement.

"I'll remember that."

"Good."

"Let's go home," Grandpa said, walking to Clara. I stepped back.

"Uh, I think we'll run home," I said quickly. Jasper nodded firmly.

"Alright. I do plan to teach you how to teleport so you, -" She glanced at my mate, "-had better get use to it."

His face went pale, and I laughed. I gave them both a quick hug, and then they were gone. I turned to my mate, taken back when his lips suddenly connected with mine. Instantly, a whole new mood surrounded the air around us and I wrapped my arms around his neck.

"I knew you could do it. I'm proud of you," he whispered.

"Thanks. I feel better."

"I noticed something though."

"What's that?"

"Your magic didn't come out when we made love." He kissed the spot under my ear, making me shiver. "Do I not bring out intense feelings in you?"

His mouth was moving lower, his hands on my waist pulling me closer.

"I don't know," I teased. "Maybe we should try again and find out."

Our closed were soon strewn on the ground around us, our lips moving in sync as we lay together on the magical garden. I was feeling bold tonight. Bringing my leg over, I straddled Jasper, his erection pressing onto my backside. He gazed at me with such affection, I found myself blushing.

"I want to try something new."

"I'm not complaining."

Getting my position, I slowly lowered myself onto him. I was already very aroused, but it still stung a bit. I pushed past that until he was all the way inside me. From here, I wasn't really sure what to do. It felt different too, deeper. Pushing up with my knees, I slammed back on top of him, a deep moan falling from my lips. Jasper held my waist lightly as I found a steady rhythm, my cries echoing into the forest. I began to move faster, wanting to find that release. Jasper's name tumbled out of me over and over until, gasping and panting, I came around him. He followed not long after, sitting up and holding me against him. We took a few minutes to catch our breath. At this moment, I was utterly happy, maybe the happiest I'd ever been.

"I want to stay here tonight," I mumbled against him.

"Yeah?"

I raised my head to kiss his cheek. "I'm not quite done enjoying your company yet."

The silver in eyes shone at my words. Getting to his feet, he carried me all the way into the cabin, barely stopping to close the door. I briefly mindlinked Mom to let her know, and then my back hit the softness of the bed, my mate's body above mine and his lips claiming me again.

CHAPTER 29
JASPER

I woke up to the best sight. Violet was lying next to me, her expression completely peaceful, her black hair spread over the pillow. I took a few precious moments to just look at her. I was one lucky guy. I stroked her cheek gently, silently laughing when her nose scrunched a bit. Fuck, she was beautiful. I continued caressing her face until her eyes fluttered open.

"Morning," I said softly.

"Morning. What are you doing?"

"Just admiring the view."

The cheek under my fingers turned pink.

"You're corny," she mumbled.

"I know."

Suddenly, her eyes widened. "What time is it?"

I checked my phone. "Ten."

"Shit! We have to be at the packhouse!"

I nodded, but my stomach tightened. I would have been more than happy to spend the day in bed with her. Nonetheless, I rolled out of bed, going to the dresser. I tossed Violet a shirt, then grabbed clothes for myself.

"We can shift and get dressed later," I said mechanically.

"Okay."

If she noticed the difference in my tone, she didn't comment. Together, we left the cabin holding our clothes. I shifted first, Vie following my lead. Hala and Ehno jumped at each other, sniffing and licking. Quickly reigning him in- much to his disappointment- we set off for the packhouse. Even though everything in me wanted to turn around and run the opposite direction.

"Why are you so nervous now? We knew this was coming," Ehno commented.

"I know. I guess. . . It felt a little surreal, the idea of meeting my real Dad. Now it's going to happen, and I don't know what to expect."

"Our Alpha might be wrong. He might not be our father."

"Yeah. Maybe."

Deep down though, I knew I was about to meet my real dad. I would know immediately, and so would he- there was no need for a DNA test. Wolves could sense their kin, even if they'd never met them before. Hala bumped into me, whining quietly. Was my distress that noticeable?

I picked up the scents of the packhouse after a while, slowing down. This place was becoming more familiar to me. I dropped the clothes I'd brought from my mouth and shifted back. Once I was dressed, a now human Violet came to stand in front of me. She put her hand on my cheek, studying my face.

"Are you okay?"

"I'm good. Just nervous," I said quickly.

"I'm here with you, you know. No matter what happens."

I covered her hand with my own. "I know. Thanks."

She gave me a quick smile, reaching up on her toes to kiss me. "Come on. He should be here soon."

I let her pull me out of the shadows of the forest, and I suddenly felt too exposed. Vie chatted as we walked, an obvious attempt to distract me. For once, it didn't work. I felt too hot, and a little dizzy too. When we entered the house, I almost passed out in relief that nobody was there to greet us.

"I need to change," Violet said, her hand slipping out of mine.

"I'll wait here."

As soon as she was gone, I regretted not going with her. The last thing I wanted, or needed, was to have this Alpha Warrick come in and see me standing alone in the corner. My mind was busy, playing out every which way this meeting could possibly go.

"Jasper."

I jumped at a voice that was so close. Mom and dad were standing a foot away, looking at me with unreadable expressions. Only their eyes betrayed how worried they really were.

"Hey."

"Are we late?" Dad asked.

"Huh? Oh, no. I'm just waiting for Vie to change."

"Ah."

We stood awkwardly, nodding to the various maids who passed us by. Mom was tapping her foot and biting her nails, while dad stood stone-faced, giving nothing away. I imagined this was harder for him than anyone else. After all, he was the one I'd called dad since I was six. Even if this went well, in my mind he would always be my father, the man who raised me.

Violet walked back to us then, wearing a black t-shirt and jeans. She took my hand, leading me down the hall towards the kitchens. My parents followed closely.

"Dad says we're meeting in the old game room. I should warn you; Alpha Warrick is already there."

She glanced up at me, and I had no idea what expression was on my face. All I could do was focus on breathing normally.

"Jasper, it'll be okay." She squeezed my hand lightly.

"We're all here for you," Mom said behind me.

"And it's not formal at all. It's a game room," dad said.

"It was," Vie explained, "Before we were born, and Mom moved everything. It's basically a break room for the staff now."

They kept trying to reassure me, but I couldn't focus. We'd stopped in front of a double door, and I scented him. And I knew. On the other side of this door, was my father. The man who sired me, and then couldn't bother to make sure I lived or not. The man who abandoned my birth mother and me. My hands started shaking as a wave of anger engulfed me. Why did I want to meet him? No, I couldn't. I wouldn't do this.

Before I had the chance to walk away though, the door on the left opened, revealing a smiling Lily.

"Good, you're all here. Please, come in." She stood aside, gesturing for us to enter. Mom put her hand on my back, giving me a little nudge.

"Thank you, Luna."

"Just Lily, as always Linda."

They stopped to talk for a minute, while my feet unwillingly moved forward. The room itself was fairly impressive. I counted three refrigerators, and a couple mini fridges too. It was also large; I guessed every staff member could fit in here comfortably. Three long grey sofas sat on a blue rug, facing each other with only a low wooden table separating them. There were two more green sectionals and green armchairs to my left. A counter with a microwave and a few coffee makers was placed nearby. The walls were a nice, light peach, with a high ceiling and a skylight.

What was attracting my attention the most was the aura coming from the center of the room. Alpha Dimitri sat on one couch, facing us, with his Beta on the other end. The couch opposite them had one occupant. I stopped walking, unable to go any further. There was a tense silence as I held my breath, staring at the back of his head.

My eyes followed his movements as his head tilted to the right, scenting the air. And then he was standing, turning to us. I heard a low gasp, either my mom or Violet, I couldn't tell. I was too focused on the Alpha in front of me. His hair was the same shade as mine, but straight, and with hints of grey. It was cut shorter, too. I guessed we were close to the same height, though he was much broader than I was. I saw myself in him, his nose, his mouth. But most of all, his eyes. The silver in them matched mine perfectly, giving no more reason to doubt. This man was my father.

I was the son of an Alpha.

"Jasper, I presume?" Alpha Warrick's voice was low, deep, and held an edge to it.

I nodded once. We stared at each other a minute more before he sighed. He turned to Alpha Dimitri.

"Well, you were right. This boy is definitely mine."

"I figured."

Turning his back on me, he sat back down. "Well, come over. Let's talk a bit."

Reaching beside me, I grabbed Violet's hand. She held it tightly the whole way to the unoccupied sofa, sitting next to me. Mom and dad took the seats next to her, while Luna Lily sat beside her Alpha. Everyone stared between me and Alpha Warrick.

"Who is this?" He gestured to Violet.

"My mate," I answered shortly. My voice was shaky.

He gazed at her, sending another wave of anger through me. Anyone here could see the lust in his eyes, and I was thankful when Luna Lily cleared her throat, getting his attention.

"Violet is our daughter," she explained.

"Makes sense. She's a beauty."

"Thank you."

I felt Vie shiver beside me, obviously uncomfortable. I released her hand to my arm around her shoulder, drawing her closer to me.

The table between us had an assortment of snacks and drinks. My stomach was already full of knots, leaving no room for food. The whiskey was tempting though. Vie took a cracker and mom grabbed a few carrot sticks. Alpha Warrick poured himself a drink, sitting back. He looked at me over the glass.

"I suppose you have questions."

"One or two."

"Go ahead."

My brain stuttered, all the questions coming together too fast. I couldn't process fast enough to form a coherent one. Slightly panicking, I looked at my dad, something I did when I was unsure or stuck. Alpha Warrick noticed and misunderstood.

He scoffed loudly. "Come now boy. You need your mom to speak for you?"

Dad inhaled, his face turning a light shade of red. Mom's mouth opened, but I shook my head at her.

"Okay. I guess I'll start with the obvious one. Where were you all this time?"

He sipped his drink nonchalantly. "I have a pack to run."

I frowned. Was he dodging the question?

"Why didn't you ever come to me?" he asked.

"I didn't know who you were. My mom never told me who my dad was."

"Who was your mother?"

"Natalia Black."

He thought for a minute, his forehead creasing. "Ah. Yes, I remember her." He swallowed the rest of his drink in one go. "Didn't know she got pregnant though."

"How could you not know?" I snapped.

Alpha Warrick shrugged. "She was a maid in the packhouse. I didn't usually pay attention to the maids, unless it was to have some fun."

Beta Ben made a disgusted sound.

"What happened? Why did she go rogue?" Luna Lily asked.

"Another maid accused her of stealing. So, I banished her."

By now, my vision was red. So, he really didn't care about mom. Or me. He used her for his 'fun', and then kicked her out of the pack. He even had the audacity to insult her! If it wasn't for Violet holding my arm, I'd have punched him already.

"Didn't she have a family there?" Alpha Dimitri snapped.

"I don't know. Don't really care." He looked back to me. "Where is she anyway?"

"Dead," I said monotonously.

"Ah." He picked up a piece of fruit, as if he couldn't care less. He probably didn't.

"What is your pack like?" Luna Lily quickly interjected. I could tell she was trying to diffuse the tension.

"It runs smoothly. I have a unique system that keeps everything going the way I want."

"Unique system?" Mom frowned.

Alpha Warrick nodded. "There's me and my mate and son at the top. Below me is my Beta and Gamma, and their kids. Then we have a few honoured pack members who live close to the packhouse."

Son? He had a son. I had a brother. I wondered what he was like- if he was like the man sitting across from me, I doubted we would get along. It had been five minutes, and I already never wanted to lay eyes on him again.

"What about everyone else?" The Luna was asking.

"They exist as warriors."

I blinked, coming back to the conversation. "Everyone?"

"Everyone. We recruit at age ten, and they are sent out on the field by age twelve."

His tone said he was very proud of this. . . yet nobody seemed to know what to say. Me? I was vibrating next to Violet. This man was sending kids to fight, kids who weren't anywhere near shifting! Who hadn't even got their wolves yet! This was his 'unique system'?

"Does that include your son?" I snapped.

"Oh, no! He is too valuable to risk. The others. . . merely pack members who serve to pay us their taxes and fight on our behalf. This has been the way of Siver Moon for ages. We're prosperous, albeit, not as much as Blood Moon."

That did it. My self-control slipped, my rage coming to the surface. I was on my feet, nearly throwing Violet to the floor, but I would feel bad about that later. I was too pissed. This man was a pig, an asshole. How could I be related to someone like this?

"What is *wrong* with you?" I hissed furiously. "You think your pack members are only there to serve you? That they exist as maids you can fuck and throw away, or kids to be sent to their deaths? If it wasn't for those people, you wouldn't even have a pack! You're a sorry excuse for an Alpha!"

"Shut your mouth boy!" He jumped to his feet as well. "What have you got to complain about? Eh? You lost your mommy, boo-hoo. You're living in one of the wealthiest, most powerful packs this side of the world! To top it off, you got the Alphas daughter for a mate. I'd say you're doing pretty well for yourself."

"Don't you dare talk to my son that way!" Mom shouted.

"If he was truly your son, we wouldn't be here."

"Jasper *is* our son. *We* raised him," Dad defended her.

"You raised a weakling!" He pointed at me. "What did you expect to get out of me? A hug? Money? All you'll get from me is the acknowledgement that you are of my blood. But that doesn't mean shit to me."

"It should." Violet spoke for the first time, drawing everyone's attention to her.

"Excuse me?"

"Get out," she snapped.

"*Excuse me?*"

"I need to talk to my mate, and my family. You can come back in a few minutes."

"Like Hell I'm going to let some little bit-"

"Uncle Ben?"

"Yeah, you may not want to finish that sentence." Ben stood up, glancing at our Alpha. He was glaring at Alpha Warrick so coldly, even I took a step back.

"You heard my daughter. Get out." His voice was calm, making it somehow even more menacing. The only one not effected was his Luna, who was nibbling on a sandwich. Alpha Warrick glared around the room, but eventually gave in, stomping to the doors and slamming them behind him.

"What a fucking douche," Dad said.

"Should I stay with him?" Ben looked at Alpha Dimitri who nodded. When he was gone, everyone turned to Violet.

"What are you thinking?" I asked.

She pursed her lips. "Well, it's obvious he's your dad. Which means you have the same rights as Garrett does."

I furrowed my brows, not following her.

"By law, you have the right to challenge him for the title of Alpha."

Her words threw me completely. My parents started talking at the same time, totally against the idea.

"I'm not saying you should. But it might make him stop and think," Violet said.

I sat down. I hadn't even considered that being the son of an Alpha gave me the birthright to take over a pack. Maybe I would have thought about it more, if he hadn't turned out to be such a dick. Or if I'd been able to think about what came after meeting him, which I hadn't. However, knowing what he was like now, I couldn't help but think. I couldn't imagine the people of his pack were very happy; who would be, living under an Alpha like him?

"What about his other son?"

"He is only eleven years old," Alpha Dimitri explained.

"What is it like there?" I asked.

"I've only ever been to Silver Moon once, and my trip was short. Not even a full day. Though, from what I could see, it's a desolate place. Tiny houses, if you can call them that, but a grand packhouse. The few other nice places must belong to those 'honoured pack members' he mentioned."

I shook my head in disgust. Alpha Warrick was a tyrant for sure.

"Jasper." Mom's voice squeaked, her eyes glassy. "You're not actually considering this, are you?"

"What would you do Mom? Or you, Dad? I'm the only one who can challenge him."

"But you would have to leave! You would have to take over as Alpha!"

"Is that such a bad thing? If I win, I could liberate that pack. I could help them."

Her lower lip trembled, but Dad was looking at me with something like respect. He nodded, wrapping his arm around his mate.

"You do what you think is right son."

"What?!"

"He's right, Linda. Since when does Blood Moon turn away from those in need? It's in his blood- he'll make one Hell of an Alpha."

Mom pouted, visibly upset and grumbling.

"Bring him back in."

Alpha Warrick came in, just as pissed as before. He shot Violet a dirty look, to which she smirked. I looked at my Alpha.

"Alpha Dimitri, I request the challenge take place in Blood Moon."

He nodded. "Granted."

"What challenge?" Alpha Warrick snapped.

I stood up, looking him directly in the eye.

"I, Jasper Cole of Blood Moon, challenge you, Alpha Warrick for the title of Alpha of Silver Moon."

His jaw dropped. He stared at me dumbfounded for all of five seconds before he started laughing. It was a booming laugh that echoed off the walls.

"You know that's a challenge to the death, right boy?"

"I'm aware," I growled.

"You could make it easy on yourself, and just step down as Alpha," Violet suggested. "That way you don't have to risk anything."

"I'll eat a packs worth of wolfsbane before I step away from a challenge," Warrick snarled.

I shrugged. "Fine with me."

"Very well." He grinned, a hint of bloodlust in his eyes. "I Alpha Warrick of Silver Moon, accept the challenge for the title of Alpha of Silver Moon."

CHAPTER 30
GARRETT

Sophia hadn't come back. I'd texted her, called her, but all she said was we'd talk later, after I'd 'calmed down'. What the fuck? My Dad had dragged me into my room in front of everyone! I was obviously not going to be calm about that! I couldn't believe the way everyone ganged up on me. It wasn't like I hit Sophia or something. No, this was Violet sticking her nose where it didn't belong. As usual. Sophia and I could have worked something out, if she hadn't been eavesdropping.

"You really are a selfish brat sometimes," Hugo growled in my head.

"Wow. So even you're against me?"

"I am not against you, Garrett. But I do know that the way you treated our mate was wrong. I'm surprised you haven't acknowledged that yet."

"Okay, maybe I was a little harsh, but come on. You want to mark her as badly as I do."

"I do. But I do not want to force her either."

"I wasn't forcing her!"

"You lashed out because she would not mate with you. Your jealousy is getting the better of you, again."

"I'm not supposed to be upset about this? She gave herself to another guy, but she still won't sleep with me!"

"Perhaps she does not want to mate with you when the reason is solely based on your problems with Jasper Cole."

I growled at his words. Did it matter the reason? I wanted to be close to my mate; I didn't see a problem with that. I stared at the ceiling, bored as fuck. I couldn't be in here anymore. To Hell with this- I was leaving. I jumped off the bed, throwing on my shoes. I was shocked that nobody was guarding my door. After all, I was now the troublemaker in the family.

Making my way down the ladder, I nodded briefly to the workers who were putting in the elevator. It seemed Dad was putting in two large ones, side by side. Thank the Goddess. I couldn't wait until they were done.

"Garrett?"

I turned to see Aunt Hazel.

"Hey. Long time no see."

"Indeed."

Her facial expression said she knew exactly what had happened, and she wasn't impressed.

"I'm going out."

"Do your parents know?"

I scoffed. "I'm not a child anymore. I don't need their permission."

She didn't reply, only pursing her lips and eyeing me as I left. No doubt she was mindlinking Mom right now to tell her about my jailbreak. Whatever.

"Where are we going?" Ehno asked.

"I don't know. I just needed to get out."

"In other words, we're going to see our mate."

That was the direction my feet were heading. Thinking about it though, I really didn't want to see her. I didn't want to fight about Jasper anymore. I didn't want to fight period. It seemed inevitable though. Every time I looked at my mate, all I could see was her and Jasper in that bed. It wasn't getting any easier either.

"Perhaps there is someone else we can talk to."

"Like who?"

"Isn't your Grandpa knowledgeable on people hating him?"

I blinked. *"A long time ago. Mom doesn't hate him anymore. And that's different, Mom is his daughter."*

"Nonetheless, he may be able to give you some advice."

"Whatever."

I turned around, heading to Grandma and Grandpas. They lived fairly close to the packhouse, but never in it. After grandma had finally been rescued by mom and dad and grandpa, she couldn't live in a place with so many

211

people. I didn't really understand, but I never judged her or asked too many questions. Mom built them their own house, a true fresh start. It was cute, a small two bedroom, living room, kitchen and dining area. Vie and I use to use the spare bedroom when we stayed over. Now it was filled with books and a couple of reading chairs.

My feet crunched on the gravel as I walked up the short drive. Before I even made it to the porch, grandpa opened the door, smiling at me.

"Hey kid."

"Hi Grandpa. Welcome back. You busy?"

"Not at all. Come on in."

I took off my shoes outside, passing him on my way in. The house was quiet today. I also didn't smell any tea.

"Grandma not home?" I asked.

"She's grocery shopping."

"Oh."

He led me to the living room, gesturing for me to sit on the sofa opposite his recliner.

"Grandma hardly ever does the shopping," I commented.

He grinned at me. "She's becoming more comfortable going out. I'm proud of her."

"Me too. I'm glad she's getting out more often."

"So, what brings you here?" Grandpa asked.

I bit the inside of my cheek. "Well. . . can I ask you something?"

"Of course."

I blew out a breath. "How did you deal with. . . when Mom was angry at you?"

His expression didn't change, and he didn't answer. Instead, he waved one hand. A second later, a can of soda floated over to me. I mumbled a thanks as I snatched it out of the air.

"I could give you advice on that all day long, Garrett. But your mate being angry at you isn't really the problem."

I looked down at my soda, my shoulders hunching. This was the first I'd seen him since they got back from their trip, but somehow he always knew everything that was going on. Magic? Or just observant? Either way, he was right.

"I know."

"You need to work through this. It will ruin you, and any chance you have with Sophia. Is this the type of Alpha you want to be? An Alpha ruled by hate and jealousy and anger?"

"No."

"Then you need to figure something out."

I groaned, slamming my drink on the coffee table between us.

"I've tried, Grandpa! I keep thinking that soon it will get better. The memory will stop being so damn hard! But it never does. Every time I see him, I get so angry I want to murder him! And whenever I see Sophia. . . I'm just a mess." My head dropped into my hands. "I don't know. I don't know how to get past this!"

". . .I'm sorry." I raised my head to look at him. "I didn't know this was that painful for you. But I do understand- somewhat. The difference is, I actually got to kill the man who touched my mate." His eyes flashed with a cold anger.

"That's not an option for me."

"No." He leaned back, rubbing his goatee. "However. . ."

"However?" I prompted.

"There. . . might be another way. Mind you, it is the easy way out. Kind of a cop out."

My eyebrows furrowed. "Huh?"

"Perhaps we should discuss this with your mate."

Grandpa snapped his fingers. One minute it was just us, and the next, Sophia appeared in the living room. I jumped, and she shrieked, looking around wildly.

"Grandpa!"

"What the fuck?!"

Grandpa chuckled. "My apologies, dear. Sometimes that is rather amusing."

213

Sophias chest heaved, her hand on her heart. "W-what. . . did you just *magic* me here?"

"The word is teleport, but yes. I did."

"I don't care what the word is! Fucking warn me next time!" Looking a bit out of it, she stumbled to the other end of the sofa. "Goddess, I could have been in the shower!"

"Sorry." This time, I apologized. The man really had no patience. He couldn't have waited for me to contact her first?

"Now that everyone is here, let's talk. Garrett has explained to me that he is having a hard time getting over what happened between you two," Grandpa said.

Sophias face paled. She rounded on me. "You told him, too?! Goddess Garrett! Just how many people did you tell!"

"I didn't tell him!" I defended.

"He didn't. Actually, my daughter confided in me. As for how she found out, she got it from Jasper."

"Oh, my Goddess. . ." Sophia moaned, covering her face with her hands.

"Relax child. Only a handful of people know, and none of us are the judgemental type."

"I can't believe Mom told you," I scowled.

"She wanted our advice on how you would deal with it, and what to do if you reacted badly. Though I'm not sure why honestly. I wasn't there for her teenage years. Maybe it's just an instinct, to rely on your parents-"

"Grandpa." I pulled him out of his pondering.

"Right. Anyway, as I was telling Garrett, there is another way to work through this issue. Though, it's not so much working through it as just forgetting it completely."

Sophia and I looked at each other, then back at him. Neither of us knew what he was talking about.

"Care to elaborate?" I asked.

He turned to Sophia, leaning forward in his chair. "To put it simply, I can erase Garretts memory of that night, and all the memories up until now associated with it."

My mouth opened with an audible *pop*. He. . . was going to erase my memory?

Grandpa was right- it was definitely the easy way out. But he'd also made a good point earlier. What kind of Alpha would I be like this? More, what kind of mate? Replaying everything between us so far, I realized just how badly I'd hurt her. I treated her unfairly, because of a problem *I* had. I didn't want to do that anymore.

"Do mine too."

My head spun, and I stared at her wide eyed. "What?"

She was looking at her hands. "I want him to erase it from me, too. I. . . I hate what I did. It's selfish of me, but I don't want to remember it anymore. I just want to move on. I don't want to keep going like this."

"Me either. But. . ."

Sophia raised her face to me. "It's not the best way. It might not even be the *right* way. But I'd like to think it's a fresh start. Not many people get this kind of chance. If we can happier, with each other, then why not? I just want to be happy with you."

"I want to be happy with you, too."

"So, you're in agreement then?" Grandpa looked between us.

Sophia nodded, reaching over to take my hand.

"Yes," I confirmed.

"Alright. I can only do one of you at a time. It's better if you don't see each other until afterwards, too."

"I'll go first." Sophia stood. Maybe both of us were eager to forget this, literally.

"Alright. Come with me."

Grandpa led her out of the living room, I assumed, to the spare room. I leaned back on the sofa, waiting. I had no idea how long this would take.

"You're sure about this?" Hugo asked.

"Yes. She's right, it is selfish. But maybe this is the best way."

"Maybe it is. Though I don't believe it's selfish."

"No?"

"You are both agreeing to erase a painful memory that is still breaking you apart. It might be the easy way out, but

I think the selfish thing would be to keep it, and hold onto it, treating each other badly because of it. Now, you can move on."

There was truth in his words. I'd held onto this anger and hatred long enough. I was looking ahead, seeing a bright future with my mate. That's all I ever wanted.

I waited about twenty more minutes before Grandpa came back out. I stood up but he gestured for me to sit again.

"Well?"

"It's done. You should know that neither of you will remember finding out you're mates. So, when you see each other again, it will be like the first time."

I smiled. "That sounds good, actually."

"Alright. Lay down, get comfortable."

I did what he asked, looking up at him.

"Is it going to hurt?"

"No, I promise."

"Okay. And if you screw up, will my brain just be scrambled eggs?"

He put his hands on his hips, glaring down at me. "It's a fine thing when my own grandson thinks I'm a novice!"

I laughed. "I'm just teasing. Let's do this."

He rolled his eyes but knelt down by the sofa. "Close your eyes." He then placed his hands on my temples, and began to chant the spell.

"Til on dio. . .Til on pollah. . .Til on dio. . .. Gasven rew shen. . ."

He repeated the ancient language over and over. His fingertips on my head began to feel warmer. At the same time, I felt a sharp tugging sensation from inside my head and winced.

"Til on dio. . .. Try not to move, Garrett," he muttered.

"Sorry."

He continued, and I grew more uncomfortable. But, as he promised, it wasn't painful. My mind felt fuzzy, and also loud. It was as if grandpa was pulling different memories to the surface and discarding them just as fast. It left me disoriented. Every so often I would feel that sharp twinge, but I tried my best to stay still. After a while, I suddenly couldn't remember what I was doing. I'd come to grandma and grandpas, but why?

"Garrett."

Opening my eyes, I found grandpa kneeling next to me.

"What are you doing on the floor?" I asked curiously.

"Just checking you. You fell asleep."

"I did? Sorry about that, Grandpa."

"Don't worry about it. How do you feel?"

"I feel fine. . . why?"

He shrugged.

I looked around, a little confused. "Why did I come over again? Surely not just for a nap?"

He chuckled, placing his hand on my head. "You came over to bring some of your moms special tea. Too bad you forgot it at home."

Huh? Oh. . . right. How did I forget that?

"Oh. I'll bring it tomorrow for you guys."

"Thank you. I think you should get going home now though."

"Alright. See you later Grandpa."

"See you."

CHAPTER 31
JASPER

Alpha Warrick was staying in one of the unoccupied homes a little way from the pack. I didn't even bother to get the assholes first name. It didn't matter to me. That man was nothing but a sperm donor in my opinion.

"Jasper, how could you do this? He has years of experience on you!" Mom wailed.

I sighed. She'd been crying nonstop since Alpha Douche left. For the first time, she was very unhappy with Violet, and she made that clear.

"Linda-"

"Don't Linda me!" she snapped at Dad. "Our son is going to die!"

I scoffed. "Thanks for the vote of confidence Mom."

She glared at me. "This is a fight to the death Jasper. There is no yielding, no mercy. You're taking on an *Alpha*. Do you not understand how ridiculous this is? You've all but signed your own death notice!"

"Mom, I've been training since I was eight. I can handle any weapon put in my hand, and I'm the best shot around."

"He has a point," Alpha Dimitri added. "Jasper was already on his way to becoming the lead warrior. I'd even make him a Beta, if it was my decision. But he wasn't meant for those roles. He's an Alpha."

"This is different than training. You've never killed anyone before," Mom whimpered.

I got down on one knee in front of the couch, catching her eyes.

"That man is tearing families apart- sending children to the battlefield. The only thing he's fighting for is maintaining his lifestyle. I'm fighting for the freedom of the pack. I have way more motivation to win than he does. I will not lose this, Mom. I give you my word."

Silent tears ran down her cheeks, but she didn't argue again. Everyone else was already consigned to the fact that I was Hell bent on this challenge. We'd agreed it would take place as soon as possible, tomorrow evening. Enough time to clear the training yard and notify those who needed to be here. Namely, Alpha Warrick's mate and son and his Beta and Gamma. I gave mom a tight hug before I stood, but she caught my hand.

"If you die, I will kill you," she growled.

Low laughs sounded at her words. "I know," I chuckled.

I was ready for some alone time with my mate. However, just as I reached her, an unexpected figure appeared beside us. Literally, popped into the room out of thin air. I jumped about five feet back, pulling Violet with me.

"Hello everyone."

"Grandpa!"

"Good Goddess, Dad! I've told you to stop doing that!" shouted Luna Lily.

Gideon simply laughed, looking highly amused. "I seem to have a renewed interest in scaring people this way. I forgot how fun it was."

"Yeah, hilarious." I grumbled.

Gideon looked around. "Well, everyone is here. That's good, saves time from having to round you all up."

"What are you talking about?" Alpha Dimitri frowned.

Gideon took the seat next to my Mom, who was staring at him as if he was a demon that had appeared. He ignored her, focusing on his daughter.

"I reckon I beat Garrett home, as he just left my house. But I'll still have to make this short."

"Garrett went to your house?" Luna Lily asked.

Gideon nodded. "I could explain everything that happened, but the short version is he told me what was going on with him, his mate and Jasper here." He gestured to me. "I came up with a solution, and he agreed."

I was very confused, but the Alpha and Luna narrowed their eyes considerably.

219

"*What* solution did he agree to?"

"To take his memory of the conflict between him and his mate."

His words were followed by a tense, stunned silence. Every single pair of eyes were centered on him, and a lot of jaws had dropped to the floor as well. I personally had no idea what to think. Garrett had no memory of that night anymore? What about Sophia?

"What about Sophia?" Violet asked my unspoken thoughts.

"She was there. She also agreed. Well, she actually asked for me to do it."

"He. . . He agreed to let you take his memory?" Luna Lily whispered.

"Not all of them. Specifically the event that has caused so much torment, and anything resulting from it. Including finding out Sophia was his mate, and the resentment towards Jasper and Violet."

"Wait." Mom shook her head. "So. . . those two. . . don't know they are mates anymore? What about their wolves?"

"The spell works on them too. When they see each other again, it will be like the first time never happened." Gideon explained. Then he turned to the Alpha. "I would appreciate it if you refrained from punching me again. I'm not as young as I used to be."

That comment was lost on me, but everyone turned to Alpha Dimitri. To my surprise, he didn't look angry.

"Perhaps. . . it was for the best."

Gideon raised one eyebrow, but Luna Lily rounded on her mate.

"What?!" She shouted. "You're condoning this?!"

"Yes."

"Why?!"

"Because it was killing our son Lily. He wasn't himself, hasn't been himself. If there is one thing I don't want, it's for him to turn out like me. Like I was. If I'd had the option of erasing my pain, my anger, I'd have taken it too. Maybe. . . Maybe we would have had a different start if I had. I won't deny Garrett this opportunity to have that second chance."

The Lunas posture shrank, her chest deflating. "I can't argue with that, I guess."

"So, nobody is going to hit me?" Gideon asked.

"I still might!" His daughter hissed.

"In that case-," He stood, giving Violet a quick side hug as he passed us, "- I'll be going. Ta!"

He snapped his fingers, disappearing as easily as he had come. I really couldn't deny that I liked the guy. He was amusing, if nothing else.

"So. . ." Violet wrinkled her nose as she thought. "Does this mean that Garrett and Sophia. . . think they're still together? If neither of them remember that night. . . then they wouldn't remember breaking up, right?"

"I think so?" The Luna sounded uncertain.

"But they haven't been with each other in over a year. How are they going to-"

"Hey!"

Violet let out a high-pitched squeal at the sound of her brothers voice.

"Garrett!"

He looked around the room. I tensed, as usual, when his eyes landed on me. Instead of the anger and hatred I'd come to know, he simply nodded at me, no trace of his previous feelings in his eyes.

"Why is everyone in here?" He asked curiously.

"We were, uh, in a meeting." Luna Lily said.

"With another Alpha." Beta Ben added. He'd been so quiet, I'd almost forgotten he was here.

"Oh."

Violet cleared her throat. "So, uhm. What's going on? Did you need us for something?"

"Not really. I was just wondering where everyone was. Why are you guys acting so weird?"

Nobody seemed to know what to say; They were glancing at each other nervously. I stepped forward.

"They're just nervous. I'm challenging Alpha Warrick tomorrow night." I said.

Garrett stared at me. Again, there was no hint of anger. "Really? Why?"

"Partly because he's an asshole. It's a long story."

"Huh. Well, good luck."

"Thanks."

"I'll see you guys at dinner."

And he left. A collective sigh was released from everyone present. And then. . .

"Get. Back. Here. NOW!"

Everyone winced as the Lunas' voice sounded in our minds. Alpha Dimitri rubbed her shoulders, trying to calm her down. Clearly, she hadn't meant to mindlink all of us, her emotions taking over.

Gideon popped back into the room, a good distance away from his daughter, who was seething with fury.

"He doesn't remember anything!" She shouted at him.

"That is the point of the spell." Gideon told her.

"Violet says they've been apart for over a year! He's going to go crazy when he realizes he's skipped more than a year, with no memory of how or why!"

"Lily, relax. Do you take me for a novice?"

"A novice? More like a fuc-"

"What exactly did you do?" Alpha Dimitri interrupted. He had his arms around the Luna, rocking back and forth slightly. It didn't seem to be helping though.

"I replaced the memories he lost." Before he was yelled at again, he held up his hand. "Let me explain. There was one memory where he was in his room, doing homework. He started thinking about that party, and couldn't finish because he was so upset. I took the painful part of that. When Garrett looks back on that night, he will only remember being too tired to finish the homework and going to bed."

"But what about the break up?" Violet asked. "They haven't hung out, or been a couple in a long time. How are they going to explain that when they see each other again?"

"As far as they know, they did break up, but not the way it happened. It was a mutual break up, but they remained civil and friendly. They ended on good terms." Gideon explained.

"So, you took me out of the picture completely?" I asked.

"Yes."

I couldn't deny the relief that brought me. Yes, I had fucked up. Badly. What I had done was now the cause of so much grief and stress within this family. How could I not feel happy that the anger and tension was erased, allowing everyone to move on finally?

"Thank you." I told Gideon.

"I did not do it for your benefit." He replied. "I did it for my grandson."

"Understandable."

Luna Lily stepped forward. "You better know what you're doing." She scolded.

"I do. Trust me Lily, this will work out."

She rolled her eyes but it seemed the argument was over. It was already done, after all. I turned my attention to Violet again, rubbing my thumb over the back of her hand. I opened my mouth, but was once again interrupted.

"Jasper. Come here." Alpha Dimitri ordered. I released his daughters hand, walking to his side.

"Yes Alpha?"

"How do you feel about a little training? Refresh your techniques, loosen up a little before tomorrow?"

My jaw almost dropped. "Train? You mean, with *you*?"

He chuckled. "Yes."

I felt like jumping around like a little kid. Training with the Alpha? That was a privilege very, very few people got. I nodded enthusiastically.

"Absolutely Alpha!"

"Dad." Violet joined us, frowning. "Don't hurt him, okay?"

"Why do all you women not have any confidence in me?" I asked.

Violet hands went to her hips. "You forget who trained me? I know what he can do. I want you back in one, whole piece." She eyed Alpha Dimitri meaningfully.

"He will remain intact." He promised. Then he turned to me. "You good to start now?"

"Yes Alpha."

I turned to Vie, kissing her forehead.

"I wanted to spend time with you, but you can come and watch if you want."

"Actually, I want to talk to you, Violet." Luna Lily said behind me.

She frowned, until I gave her one more kiss.

"I'll see you tonight then. 'Kay?"

"Okay."

With one last smile, I turned and followed Alpha Dimitri out of the room. Beta Ben was accompanying us, and I hoped he would join in on the training too. I focused on why I was doing this, the will to win at any cost. By tomorrow night, I would either be dead, or I would be the new Alpha of Silver Moon.

CHAPTER 32
VIOLET

"Come for a walk with me." Mom gestured for me to follow her.

I was confused, but I did as she asked nonetheless. She nodded to all the maids on our way outside, stopping to talk to some of them about housework or asking how their families were. I, on the other hand, was growing a little impatient. Truth be told, I wanted to be with Jasper. Not even watching him and Dad train, I just wanted some alone time with him. I felt on edge today, and so much had happened. Garrett and Sophia getting their memories wiped, Jasper challenging Alpha Warrick. Two things, but it was a lot. My mind was still processing each one.

And, admittedly, I was terrified for my mate. I never thought he would actually challenge him; I just wanted that douche bag of an Alpha to shut up and realize that Jasper *could*, if he were so inclined. Turns out, he was so inclined. But what if he lost?

I shuddered, immediately blocking out the idea, even though it was a real possibility.

"You will have to learn patience, Violet. It is the one skill every Luna must have." Mom pulled me out of my thoughts as she continued walking.

I glanced at her sideways. "I'm not a Luna Mom."

"When Jasper wins the challenge, you will be."

"When?" I looked at her fully now.

"Yes, *when*. I have no doubt in my mind that your mate will succeed tomorrow. He is a clever boy."

I scoffed. "I don't think being clever is going to be much of an advantage."

"No?" She stopped to face me, her expression serious. "Alpha Warrick has years of fighting experience. He will rely on his favored fighting style, which is probably a little

225

outdated. I've seen Jasper train; He is quick on his feet, and uses others advantages against them. He analyzes his opponent carefully, learning their techniques and outdoing them."

My eyebrows pinched in the center. "Why are you telling me this?"

"To give you some hope that your mate will return tomorrow."

"Thanks Mom."

And then she dropped a bombshell on me.

"Violet, you won't be attending the challenge tomorrow."

I skidded to a halt, turning on her. "What?! I have to be there!" I objected.

But Mom simply shook her head. She took my arm, leading me out of the front door. Once we were out of earshot of anybody, she pulled me close to her.

"You cannot. We cannot risk you losing control."

I set my mouth firmly. "I won't lose control. I'm going."

"No, Violet. You have only just started to learn about your abilities. You may get too emotional; Jasper might get hurt. Our laws state that nobody can interfere with a challenge, *especially* an Alpha challenge. If you, by any chance, used your magic to protect Jasper, the fight would be considered null and void, and Alpha Warrick would have every legal right to execute Jasper for cheating."

"But I wouldn't do that!"

"Not intentionally, I know. I'm sorry, but this is how it has to be. And your father agrees."

I bit my lip, upset and angry. Though part of me accepted her words, and I knew she was right. It wasn't as if my magic was very subtle; my track record was against me there. A broken window, and then a great chunk of the house itself. Unwillingly, I nodded, and Mom pulled me in for a hug.

"Don't worry. He will be fine, and I will update you along the way."

"What am I suppose to do during the challenge?"

"You will be in the packhouse. Luke will stay with you."

"In other words, you're getting him to babysit me so I don't sneak off."

She smiled and nodded. I hated that she knew me so well.

"You better keep me in the loop." I demanded.

"I will, I promise."

Taking a step back, I walked around with Mom by my side. An uncomfortable cramping was starting in my lower abdomen, and the edgy feeling I'd had today was getting worse. I tried to shake it off, tried to listen as Mom talked. I found myself squinting at her. Why was the sun so damn harsh today? And why was it so *hot*? I was already breaking out in a sweat, constantly wiping my forehead.

"Violet?" Mom frowned. "Are you okay?"

"Yeah. I'm just. . . it's a little hot out here. . ."

Suddenly, the cramping got worse. It went from a dull ache to full on searing pain. I screamed, dropping to my knees. Mom echoed my cry, falling down to my level as well.

"Violet! What's wrong? Talk to me!" She pleaded.

"I-it hurts!" I gasped.

"What hurts? Where-" Her nostrils flared, and her eyes widened. "Shit."

"Mom?" Unshed tears were in my eyes. "What's happening to me?"

She rubbed my arms, a little too fast to be soothing. "You're in heat."

The pain in my stomach radiated down between my legs. That was all the confirmation of her words I needed. Mom looked worried as Hell. Her eyes were glazed over, and I knew she was mindlinking Dad. And then, a low growl sounded to my right. A man I recognized as one of the warriors was standing a few feet away, his eyes transfixed on me. I whimpered, tugging on Moms sleeve. This was bad.

"Mom! *Mom!*"

227

Her eyes came back to her regular blue, following my line of sight. When she noticed the man, she let out her own growl. Hers was fierce and threatening in comparison to his. She jumped to her feet, stepping in front of me.

"I suggest you keep walking Ian." She said.

He didn't even bother to acknowledge her. Another wave of pain hit me, and the man, Ian, took a step forward, his eyes turning black.

"I said *go!*" Mom shouted, her Luna voice echoing her words. Ian stopped, giving her an angry look. "Are you deaf? I said step away from my daughter, now!"

The realization of who I was seemed to clear his mind a little. Ian turned and walked away, looking back at me a few times with longing. When he was out of sight, Mom bent down and pulled me into her arms.

"I need to get you back to the packhouse. There are too many unmated wolves around."

Just as she was about to pick me up, Dads voice sounded. I barely noticed where they came from, only thankful to have them here at last. Jasper reached me first, and I nearly threw Mom to the ground as I jumped at him. His scent was so much stronger right now, the incredible aromas filling my nose. The pain was burning through me, and all I wanted was to touch him, taste him. I needed him like I needed air or water. Maybe more.

"Make it stop." I begged him. "Please!"

He smoothed my hair. "I will. Come on."

Scooping me up easily, I tried to adjust my position to wrap myself around him. I wanted him *now*.

"Vie, no." He held me tighter. "You're parents are right here!"

I really couldn't find it in myself to care much. They could leave, couldn't they? Nobody was making them stick around. But Jasper was already walking back to the packhouse. The pain had subsided a little from having my mate close, but it wasn't enough.

"Jasper!" I whined when another wave radiated through me.

"I know. We're almost there." He was panting a little, his eyes switching from silver to black and back again. At least he was hurrying.

"I'll make sure the maids know to give you privacy."

Was Mom still here? I lifted my head, finding that she, Dad and Uncle Ben were giving us an escort back home. Probably because of what had just happened with the warrior, Ian. She placed her hand on Jaspers shoulder, and a vicious snarl ripped up from my chest and out my mouth. Everyone jumped back, eyeing me warily. Their reaction cleared my head a little; Did I seriously just snap at my Mom?

"Sorry." I mumbled.

"It's fine." Mom gave me a reassuring smile. "I should have known better."

We left them at the front door. Somehow, Jasper managed to get me up the ladder without dropping me. He raced down the hall to our room, throwing the door open and kicking it shut behind us. He set me on my feet, his chest heaving.

I didn't waste a second more.

Wrapping my arms around his neck, I pulled him down into a kiss as hot as the fire inside me. His hands went to my waist, grabbing the hem of my shirt. We pulled back so he could lift it off. I wasn't as nice; grabbing the neckline of his shirt, I tore it top to bottom. He looked down at my handiwork before meeting my eyes again.

"I liked that shirt." He smirked.

I was already working on his belt, fumbling with it. He took my hands in his, guiding me backwards to the bed. He lay me down gently, using his arms to hover above me. I watched as he finished taking his belt off, followed by his pants and boxers. I was almost drooling at this point. The man was perfect, every line, every curve of him. The ache inside me intensified, and I grabbed his shoulder.

"Please." I gasped. "Please, take me."

Jaspers eyes flattened to pure black at my words. His mouth came down to mine, kissing me greedily. His hand slid down to undo the button on my jeans, and then he was pulling them off. When he started rubbing me over my underwear, I nearly lost my mind. I moaned loudly, wiggling my hips, wanting him to take this further, faster. Reaching between us, I grabbed his length, beginning to rub him up and down. He hissed at the contact, but it got my message across.

In one swift motion, my underwear was torn off, flung off the bed in shreds. I was absolutely soaked as he positioned himself at my entrance, thrusting into me hard. Something between a gasp and moan left me, and continued, as he moved inside me. *This* is what I needed. I found myself meeting him thrust for thrust, the feeling lifting me higher and higher. Jaspers mouth was everywhere; My lips, my neck, my collarbone, my breasts, my shoulders. Everywhere our skin made contact was pure, indescribable bliss. My nails racked across his back, earning low growls from him.

"Goddess. . .. Yes. . . Fuck me. . . Jasper. . .."

I found myself becoming more bold with him as the haze in my mind carried me. Things I never dreamt I would say in bed were leaving my mouth uncontrollably. And I liked it. I liked that I could illicit such reactions from him. The merciless way he took me, the way he held me tightly, the grunts and growls. The way he looked at me like I was the only woman in the world.

A few minutes later, we found our release together, his name like a prayer on my lips. But the relief I felt didn't last as long as I would have hoped; The pain came back only minutes later. And Jasper was once again ready to satisfy this need I had for him. It could have been hours, or days later when I finally cooled down and fell into an exhausted sleep, curled up in my mate's arms.

I couldn't have cared less.

CHAPTER 33
JASPER

I was in the training yard doing my best to focus on Alpha Dimitri and what he was telling me. Yet, my mind kept slipping back to the last two days with Violet. The challenge had been postponed for obvious reasons. Alpha Warrick wasn't happy, but I was sure his big problem was the reason for the delay. I'd briefly met his mate, Luna Anne. She was a bitter woman with a pinched face that always resembled someone who'd just sucked a lemon. I'd bet ten to one that he hadn't gotten any in a while.

I was exhausted, but happy. Vie hadn't let me rest for more than a couple hours at a time. I wasn't complaining though; The last couple days were the best of my life. I saw a whole new side of my girl, and I liked it. A lot. It wasn't just the sex either. She'd been so vulnerable, but bold too. If she needed water, I got it. If she wanted a cool shower, I sat in with her and washed her head to toe. And when she needed me, I was there to satisfy her. It made me feel needed, important, in ways I never had been before. It brought us closer.

Yet, I'd held off on marking her. That was something I didn't want to do while she was in heat. I wanted her to have a clear head, not driven by uncontrollable lust, when we marked each other. I thought maybe she was a little disappointed, but she said she agreed.

"Focus Jasper!"

My arm came up, almost a second too late, blocking Alpha Dimitris fist. I took a few steps back, holding up my hand.

"Sorry Alpha."

"You're head isn't where it should be." He frowned.

"I know."

He sighed. "I'm not going to even ask where your mind is, because I think I know. But you need to focus on this, not on. . ..*that*. You can't be daydreaming tonight."

"Sorry," I apologized again. "I think Alpha Warrick did this on purpose. He knew I'd be tired today."

He shifted uncomfortably, but nodded. "Probably. But I couldn't argue; Violets heat is over. There was no valid reason to postpone any longer. Unfortunately, being tired isn't a good enough excuse." He clicked his tongue, thinking. "I think we've done enough for today. Why don't you go back to the house and try to get a few hours of sleep? That's probably the best thing right now."

I stretched my arms. "Sleep sounds good. Thank you Alpha."

"Just Dimitri. We're family now, so we can drop the formalities."

I raised an eyebrow but didn't argue.

"Alright. . . Dimitri." I felt uncomfortable not using his title. Like I was disrespecting him. It would definitely take some getting use to.

We walked back to the packhouse together, the wind blowing wildly around us. A storm seemed to be on the way, though I had no idea when it would hit. The air was thicker today, humid.

"Are you nervous?" Dimitri suddenly asked.

I shrugged. "I think I'd be a fool not to be. This isn't a regular fight, after all."

"No, it's definitely not." He stopped walking, turning so we were face to face. "Have you ever seen a challenge before?"

I shook my head.

"They are rough. I need you to understand that. Your opponent won't go easy on you. And this is much different than fighting rogues. He will be looking to kill you." He met my eye. "No matter what Jasper, don't let him win. Not just for my daughters sake, but for the sake and future of Silver Moon. Warrick has no business holding the title of Alpha. Regardless, he will do anything and everything to hold onto his position. Be wary, and be careful. But don't forget that I, as well as everyone else, believes in you. Should you win tonight, I believe you will make a great Alpha, someone I would be lucky to have as an ally."

My face grew red with emotion. This man was treating me like an equal already, but I didn't feel like I'd done much to deserve that. So far, my only claim to this family was the fact that I was mated to his daughter. But I'd also been the cause of much discord among them, to the point that Garrett used magic to heal and move on. And he was saying he believed in me? That I'd be a great Alpha? I wasn't as positive on that as he was, but I would spend a lifetime trying my best if I got the chance.

"Thank you." I managed in response. "That means a lot."

Dimitri patted my shoulder. "However, if you hurt my daughter by dying, I'll wait the rest of my life and then kick your ass in the afterlife."

I laughed at that. "Understood."

"Good. You go on, I have some things to do. I'll see you tonight."

We went our separate ways, me dragging my feet back to the house. It was eleven in the morning, but Violet was still sleeping when I got back to our room. Typically, it took another full day for she-wolves to completely recover from their first heat. Quietly, I slid under the covers next to her, admiring her peaceful expression. My eyelids drooped as her scent wafted around me, and I was asleep within minutes.

***

"Jasper. Wake up."

My eyes opened. The first thing I saw was Violets face, no longer asleep, but hovering above me. She peered down at me with a strange expression. I forced myself to sit up, rubbing my eyes.

"What time is it?" I drawled out sleepily.

"Almost seven."

The remaining sleep in my brain fizzed away at her words. Our eyes met and I could almost feel the tension rolling off of her. Once again, she was worrying her lip with her teeth, while her whole body was fidgeting. I had exactly one hour before the fight started.

"I need to go." I said quietly.

"I know."

Neither of us moved. The words I wasn't sure if she was ready to hear sprang to my lips, but I held back. Although, what if this was the last time I ever saw her? Emotions crashed down on me; What had I been thinking, challenging Alpha Warrick? How could I chance losing Violet? No, she should know how I felt.

"I lo-"

She interrupted my declaration with a heartfelt kiss. The force of it took my breath away; I could feel the tears on her cheeks as they transferred to mine.

"Don't." She whispered. "Not now. When you come back, I want to hear it. Okay?"

I nodded mutely. Another reason to survive this. Vie gave me a small smile and another passionate kiss before she moved off the bed.

"Dad told you I have to stay here?"

"Yes. I'm sorry, but you know it's what's best."

"I know. I'll be down in the cafeteria."

"Okay."

Quicker than I would have liked, I got dressed in a tank top and loose-fitting shorts. I opted to remain barefoot, and I was ready. Vie was waiting by the door, and together, we left the room. It was silent between us as we walked down the hall and descended the ladder. Only when she started to part ways did I stop her, this time pulling her in for a breathless kiss.

"I *will* be back." I promised her.

"Go kick some ass." She smiled and I chuckled. Just then, Gamma Luke appeared, eyeing her meaningfully. "I'm coming." She told him.

We finally parted. The Alpha, Luna and Beta Ben met me outside the front door, and together we started making our way. I didn't feel at all as ready as I should. Too much was staked on this match; An entire packs wellbeing for one. And Violets wellbeing, if I didn't live.

"How do you feel?" Dimitri asked.

"Uh. . . Scared." I admitted.

He frowned. "You can't let him intimidate you so easily already."

I shook my head. "I'm not scared of *him*. I'm scared of what this will cost me if I lose. The damage my death will cause."

Dimitris face relaxed back into a neutral expression. "Ah. Then you are in a good frame of mind."

I stared at him, dumbfounded. "Excuse me?"

"You have legitimate reasons that will aid in you succeeding." Beta Ben spoke up. "You're scared of what you might lose, what will happen if you do. Warrick is only afraid of losing his title, his wealth, and position. You have something honest to fight for."

"Just think of everything you just said. All those people, including my daughter. That's who you're fighting for, not just yourself. Keep reminding yourself of that." Luna Lily said.

I nodded thoughtfully. They were right. I had people waiting for me, even if they didn't know me yet. People who were depending on me to free them from Warrick's brutal Alphaship.

We walked right across the training yard, heading to the forest. I would have preferred this fight take place in the training yard like so many other events; It was familiar ground for me. I knew every bump, every blade of grass. I'd been training there since I was eight years old, even though I hadn't technically been allowed to. After school, I would sit on the sidelines and watch the sessions, following along at my own speed. Until the head warrior, Ned, allowed me to train alongside the others, conditionally. I wasn't allowed to spar until I was thirteen. And that had been my routine for years, until I was old enough to train properly like everyone else.

Tonight however, the fight would be taking place in a more traditional setting, for werewolves anyway. As we neared our destination, the trees started to thin, and voices could be heard. They ran together, a low hum on the wind. About thirty feet ahead, I could see lights. My stomach started to twist, and sweat gathered on the back of my neck. I took a few deep breaths to try and calm myself, reminding myself why I was here again.

We stepped through the thicket. I was momentarily distracted by the view, my eyes wandering to take it all in. Torches had been placed in a large, wide circle, giving off more than enough light for everyone. And there was a lot of people. Obviously, the entire pack couldn't be here, but it sure looked like they tried. I scanned the crowd, recognizing some people from school. There were even people sitting in the trees, not able to find a spot on the ground. I received a lot of smiles and shouts for victory as I followed my escorts. The sounds of genuine support for me warmed me a little inside.

Looking ahead, I saw a low tent had been placed at the head of the circle. Inside sat Alpha Warrick, his Luna, and his son. I stared at the boy, a little shocked that he and I looked so much alike, given that we had different mothers. Aside from that, the only vibe I got from him was nervousness, and I felt a small pang that he might lose his Dad tonight. On the other hand, Luna Anne looked the same as always. Totally uncaring. Though when our eyes met, she shot me a smug smirk.

"Stand beside Ben, there." Luna Lily pointed and I dutifully walked to my place and waited. She took one of the seats inside the tent, while Dimitri stepped forward, addressing the crowd.

"Welcome, Blood Moon." His voice rang out, silencing the distinct chatter. "We are here for the official challenge between Alpha Warrick of Silver Moon, and Jasper Cole of Blood Moon. Elders?"

Three men I hadn't noticed before separated from the crowd, walking up to us. Each of them looked to be in their late fifties, or early sixties, and each one had an air of authority around them. They stopped in front of the Alpha, bowing their heads slightly.

"By whom was the challenge made?" One of them asked.

Beta Ben nudged me, and I cleared throat. "Me." I said.

"State your name."

"Jasper Cole."

"In front of the Goddess herself, do you swear this is a fair challenge, an honorable challenge, and have taken no part in anything that would aid you other than your skill, your mind, and your heart?"

"I swear."

"To whom is this challenge made for?"

Alpha Warrick stepped forward. "For me."

"State your name."

"Alpha Bryan Eugene Warrick."

"In front of the Goddess herself, do you swear this is a fair challenge, an honorable challenge, and have taken no part in anything that would aid you other than your skill, your mind, and your heart?"

"I swear."

"In front of your Alpha, your Luna and peers, and above all our Goddess, state why this challenge was made."

The seeming oldest Elder looked at me, and I fumbled for a second. Because Warrick was an asshole and a tyrant probably wouldn't go over well with them. Beta Ben nudged me again, and I shook my head slightly to clear it.

"I am the son of Alpha Warrick. By law, I have the right to challenge him for the title of Alpha. I believe he is no longer a suitable fit for that role."

I could see Warrick's jaw clench, but he had to abide by the same rules I did. He couldn't lash out in front of the Elders, even if he wanted to.

"Alpha Warrick of Silver Moon, you accept?"

"Yes."

All three bowed their heads again. "Let the challenge commence, and may the Goddess bless you both." With that, the three men walked off to the side, re-joining the crowd. Warrick gave his son a pat on the head, but barely glanced at his Luna. It was then that I noticed an actual circle had been painted on the dirt in blue. The ring.

"You coming boy?"

Alpha Warrick was already standing on the other side of the circle, a mocking smile on his face. Discarding my shirt, I stepped forward as well.

CHAPTER 34
JASPER

I took my spot across from Warrick, regarding him with careful eyes. Dimitris voice sounded behind me.

"The rules agreed by both parties are as follows! There will be no weapons. There will be no yielding. There will be no third-party interference. There will be no attacks on spectators. Shifting is permitted. And lastly, there will be only clean kills; No mutilation of any kind will be accepted as a victory. Begin!"

Warrick cracked his neck, the smugness never leaving his face. I had to admit, I was impressed by him. The man had a lot of muscle, and he was well toned. He was a big guy; But that only meant he would fall harder. We started circling each other, and the crowd was buzzing with anticipation. I tuned it out, totally focused on the man opposite me. I looked for anything I could use, any weaknesses. He had a long scar that ran from his left knee down to his ankle. An old battle wound?

"Not brave enough to make the first move boy?" My eyes snapped up to meet his. "What happened to all your confidence?"

"Sometimes too much confidence can lead to making stupid mistakes." I replied.

"And sometimes, it's called knowing what you're doing."

Suddenly, he lunged for me. I blocked his punch, sending a sharp right hook to his jaw. The impact had him flying back several feet, though he remained on his feet. Rubbing his jaw, Warrick eyed me with renewed interest, and a new anger.

"Not bad at all. But just because you landed the first hit, doesn't mean you'll be walking away from this."

He struck again, this time coming from the left. I dodged neatly, going on the defensive. Maybe it was a stupid plan, but it was my best shot right now. I had no idea what his fighting style was, but the more he attacked, the more I learned. It was becoming easier to tell where he would move, what he would do. And the more I picked up, the less I had to try. Meanwhile, Warrick was tiring himself out, exactly as I had hoped.

"His leg isn't as strong as the other. He's leaning more to the right." Ehno said.

"That's his weak point." I agreed.

I caught Warrick's wrist, twisting his arm. He cried out in anger, jerking back. I countered by pulling him closer, landing a solid kick just under his left knee. And down he went.

"You old fool! What are you doing!" Luna Anne screeched from the sidelines.

And that's when I made a terrible mistake. Taking my eyes off Warrick for just a second to glance at his screaming mate.

"Look out!" Ehno's voice shouted in my head, but it was too late.

Pain ripped through my torso and I gasped. I let go of him to clutch my side; It was wet, and warm. Blood ran down, pooling in my hands and dripping onto the dirt. I jumped back, nearly losing my footing. Warrick's claws were out, fury reigning on his face.

"Left!"

Acting on instinct, I rolled to the left, very narrowly avoiding another attack. He was back on his feet, and I was on my knees. It was at that moment that the realization of the situation struck me. Part of me had been hoping that if I could best him, get him down long enough, he *would* yield. But I knew now that wasn't going to happen. He was out for blood, aiming for the kill. And he would kill me without hesitation, without mercy. I'd been thinking like the boy he thought I was. But no more.

Warrick charged at me; I rolled again, this time landing on my feet. Channelling my wolf, I felt my own claws extend. I ducked around his assault, swiping my hand across his chest. Blood spurted immediately, though I knew I hadn't gone as deep as I wanted to. His foot connected with my chest, and I landed in a pile, the breath totally knocked out of me.

"Shit! Get up, we have to get up!"

"Oh no." Warrick stood above me, his foot pressed down on my chest. A wicked smile played on his face. He was breathing raggedly, while I was still having trouble breathing at all. "Stay down. If you give up right now, I might even make this a quick death."

"F-Fuck. . .you." I spat.

"You put up a good fight Jasper. I'm even a little proud, if I'm being honest. But this is where it ends."

His foot moved to my neck, pressing down and cutting off the little air I was getting anyway. I tried desperately to move it, to wiggle free, anything. But the position was against me.

"Ehno! Ehno, we have to shift!"

My bones started snapping, and Warrick frowned at me.

"Really? I'm an Alpha! Do you really want to take on my wolf?"

I glared at him as my face transformed. "You're not the only Alpha in this ring." I growled.

I gave control to my wolf, and then I was on four paws instead of two feet. Thankfully, my shifting had worked in throwing Warrick off. By the time I looked back at him, he had also shifted. It was obvious who was bigger; I stood at least two heads above him, easy. A loud, vicious snarl ripped out of me, and a lot of the crowd started backing away. I knew I had to be careful now; He might be smaller, but that only meant he had better access to go for the neck. We paced in a circle, snapping at each other, until he lunged, jumping at the still open wound on my side. I dodged, turning to grab his flank.

Blood filled my mouth as I tore a chunk of flesh away, throwing it to the ground. He yelped, jumping away, and I saw my opportunity. I ran at him, running my claws down his face. At the same time, I sunk my teeth into the fur on

241

his neck, shaking harshly. Warrick's yelps and whines echoed through the air, until, I let him go, throwing him across the dirt. He lay, bleeding and panting, his eyes on me and filled with fear.

"No! Get up! *Get up!* You idiot, you stupid fucking idiot!" Luna Anne was frantic.

I walked over, standing above the man that was my Father. Without hesitating, I grabbed him by the neck again, biting through fur and skin as hard as I could. He went limp, and I dropped him. Blood started to pool, his body reverting back to human.

Warrick was dead.

There was a moment of total, absolute silence. And then cheers erupted from the crowd. I turned to see everyone clapping, shouting, grinning. I caught sight of my parents; Mom was crying, the relief almost tangible even from where I was standing. Luna Lily walked to me, smiling hugely, and holding a pair of shorts. I shifted back, grateful that she brought extra clothes.

"The victory goes to Jasper Cole of Blood Moon!" Alpha Dimitri announced, and the cheers grew again.

"Come on. Let's get you cleaned up." Luna Lily took my arm.

"No!"

I looked up to see Luna Anne storming over to us, dragging her son.

"The challenge is over Luna Anne." Luna Lily said.

"Maybe for my mate!" She tossed the boy in front of us. He landed on his knees, and he looked terrified.

"What is this?" Dimitri demanded.

"He-" She pointed to her son, "-Is challenging him next!"

"What?!" I exclaimed.

"This boy isn't even old enough to rightfully take part in an official challenge!" Luna Lily yelled.

"That doesn't matter. He has Alpha blood, and as Luna, I have the right to offer him up as a challenger."

"Are you insane?!" I demanded. "I'm not fighting a kid!"

"You don't have a choice!" She spat back.

I looked down at the boy, my half-brother. He was shaking on the ground, looking between the three of us. Big, fat tears were running down his cheeks.

"P-please! I don't want to die!" He begged.

"Where are the Elders? This is legal, just ask them!" Luna Anne looked around for the three Elders, who unwillingly stepped forward.

"Unfortunately, the Luna is correct."

"The boy has been offered to fight, so he must as an Alpha heir." Another frowned.

"That's ridiculous! He doesn't even a wolf!" Luna Lily screamed at them.

"It is the law."

Luna Anne smiled viciously, but I felt like throwing up. There had to be a way out of this. No way was I going to lay a hand on that kid.

"If you refuse to fight, you yield your victory, and it goes to my son."

I glared at her, sickened she was using her own son this way. Was this her idea alone? Or had Warrick and her planned this together, in the event of him losing? It didn't really matter in the end, it was wrong. I wracked my brain, trying to come up with an answer.

"This 'law' of yours opposes my pack law of harming children." Alpha Dimitri told the Elders.

"The boy is not from your pack."

"Why does that matter?! He's on my land!"

"How can you do this?" I asked Luna Anne. "You know he will die. Why present him as a challenger? Do you not care about him at all?"

She shrugged. "My son has a duty to his pack. He knows that."

I looked down at him again, my guts twisting. Around us, the pack was shouting their disapproval along with insults at Luna Anne. And suddenly, thankfully, I thought I had the answer, the solution to this horrible scenario.

"What's your name?" I asked him.

"K-Kiren." He whimpered. I crouched down to his level, hoping my expression was reassuring.

"You're not going to fight today, Kiren." I told him.

"So you're conceding your victory then?" Luna Anne asked.

"No." I held out my hand. Hesitantly, Kiren took it and I pulled him to his feet. "He's going to renounce his claim as Alpha heir."

"What! Of course he's not!"

"Would he have to fight if he did this?" I looked at the Elders, who wore varying expressions of relief.

"No, he wouldn't."

"Kiren! Don't you dare!" His Mother screeched.

Alpha Dimitri stepped in between them. "Kiren, if you renounce your claim as Alpha, you can walk away. Otherwise, you have no choice but to fight Jasper. You know you can't win. This is the only way for you to live."

"He will *not*-!"

"I renounce my claim!" Kiren shouted. "I renounce it, I renounce it! I don't want to die! I don't want to be Alpha!" He wailed.

"You *brat*! You're as useless as your Father! Do you not care about the pack at all?!" Luna Anne screamed at him.

And then Luna Lily stepped forward, her hand whipping out and slapping the woman. The resounding *smack* echoed around the forest, audible gasps following it.

"How dare you stand here and talk about the wellbeing of your pack when you just offered their heir as if he were nothing! As if he was fodder for the livestock! You should be ashamed of yourself; You are no Luna! And you're certainly no Mother!"

"The victory of the fight is Jaspers. And your son has renounced his claim as Alpha. Therefore, you are no longer Luna of the Silver Moon pack." One of the Elders stepped announced.

She seemed stunned by the turn of events. Still holding her cheek, Luna Anne, or now just Anne, grabbed Kiren's arm and began to stalk away.

"Hold on!" I caught Kiren's other hand, stopping them from leaving. "You don't have to go back Kiren. You don't have to go with her."

"I'm his Mother!"

I ignored her. "You can stay here Kiren, and come back when I go to Silver Moon. You can stay in the packhouse with me." I got down on one knee. "I'm your brother, and I will take care of you."

"Enough!" Anne pulled Kiren out of my grasp. But he resisted.

"No! I want to stay with him! I want to stay with my brother!" He kicked at her shins. "I hate you! I don't want to go with you!"

"Kiren, I swear to the Goddess-!"

Abruptly, I was shoved to the side. Beta Ben landed on top of me, and I had a second of confusion before I looked up to see Luna Lilys wolf standing above us. A few screams echoed through the night at the sudden appearance of the Mother Wolf. I was just glad I'd been shoved out of the way of her shift.

Anne dropped Kiren's hand and stumbled back several feet, her mouth hanging open. He ran to me, launching himself into my arms where I held him tightly.

"Kiren stays at Blood Moon." The Lunas voice sounded in my head, as well as everyone else's. Anne whimpered in terror. *"You are hereby banished from ever stepping foot on our land again. Leave. NOW!"*

CHAPTER 35
VIOLET

"Would you calm down? We would hear if something happened," Uncle Luke said.

"Easy for you to say." I grumbled.

Mom had abruptly stopped mindlinking me and wasn't replying anymore either. My anxiety went from a little to over the top in seconds. I couldn't sit still, pacing the cafeteria while Uncle Luke sat and watched. I desperately wanted to reach out to Jasper, but I didn't want to distract him either. This was torture!

"Don't forget this was your idea." Luke said.

"*Why* would you remind me of that right now?"

He shrugged. "Just saying. Next time, keep your opinion to yourself."

I shot him the finger and he chuckled. "You're going to make one hot-tempered Luna."

"Only if Jasper lives. Which we don't know, because nobody is telling me what is going on!" I ran my hands through my hair in frustration.

"Kiren stays in Blood Moon."

Moms voice resonated in my head, causing me to jump at the sudden intrusion. I looked at Uncle Luke; He was on his feet, his light expression now serious.

"What was that? Who is Kiren?" I asked.

"You are hereby banished from ever stepping foot on our land again. Leave! NOW!"

I winced at the fury in her voice. I'd never heard my Mom so angry before, ever. Before I could stop, I found myself moving to the door, needing answers. Clearly, something had gone wrong, or Mom wouldn't have been intervening. But Uncle Luke beat me there, blocking the exit with his muscular frame.

"I'm sorry Violet, but you can't leave."

"What?! Come on Uncle Luke! I need to know what's happening!"

"Then wait until your Mom or someone else mind links you. I'm under Alpha orders to keep you here until they return. I can't disobey that."

I growled, turning away.

"Mom?" I held my breath. Hopefully she answered me this time.

"We are on our way back. Stay in the cafeteria; We need to talk."

My heart started thumping painfully. My lungs constricted, and I gasped at the air that suddenly seemed to thick.

"Why? Is it about Jasper? Is he okay?!"

"He's fine, don't worry. He won."

My legs nearly gave out at the news. I reached out to grab the nearest table, Uncle Luke coming up behind me and guiding me to sit.

"Is he. . . Did he get hurt?"

"Nothing that won't heal. See you soon."

I looked up at Uncle Luke, my eyes glassy.

"They're on their way back. Jasper won." I breathed.

He smiled at me. "I knew he would; You've got yourself one fuck of a fighter Violet. He alright?"

"Mom said he was. She said to stay here, that they need to talk to us."

He nodded, taking the seat beside me and rubbing my back. The action calmed the last of my nerves, and before I knew it, they doors opened and in walked a group of people.

Mom was first, her expression heated. Dad followed behind her, and he didn't look much different. Next came Uncle Ben, who nodded at me, and then, finally, Jasper. I jumped up, running towards him. Only to stop short when I noticed he had his hands full. He was carrying. . ..Was that a *child*?

"Uh. . ." I looked between the kid and him, my face a huge question mark.

"Sit down, and we'll explain." Mom said behind me. "Jasper, put him upstairs. There is an empty room three doors down from yours. He should be comfortable there."

He nodded, turning to leave again. I grabbed his arm before he could make it out the door, and he looked back at me with blank eyes.

"I'm really happy you're back." I told him.

The flatness in his eyes turned soft, and he smiled at me. "I promised I would be. Be right back."

As soon as he was gone, tears welled up and started running down my cheeks. I didn't even notice when Garrett walked in the door, only realizing he was there when he pulled me into a hug.

"Hey, don't cry. He's safe, he's here." He soothed me. It was so weird, my brother talking like this about my mate. Still, his words didn't calm the flood in me. They only made it increase. This time, my legs did give out, and I pulled Garrett down as I sank to the floor, all my strength leaving me as I sobbed.

All the anxiety and nerves and terror since he'd left were finally getting the better of me. Of course, I was overjoyed that he was safe, that he was alive. But the fact remained that he had risked his life because of me. Because of an idea I had, and stupidly put into his head. What would I have actually done if he hadn't come back?

"Oh my. Is she alright?" A new voice said above me.

"Poor thing is probably overwhelmed. Violet dear." I peeked through my hands to see Linda crouched in front of me. "What's all this now? Jasper is fine."

"B-but I-I made h-him g-go and f-f-fight. . .." I mumbled pathetically.

"You most certainly did not." She cupped my cheeks, making me look at her. "I'll admit I wasn't happy about the idea. But honestly, he would have done the same thing, eventually, once he figured out he could." She pulled me into a hug, rubbing slow circles over my back.

"Vie, if you'd seen him, you would be so proud." Garrett smiled at me. "He was amazing. There was never any reason to worry."

Everyone looked at him with mixed expressions, but I gave him a little smile.

"Really?"

"Really! He's going to be an incredible Alpha." He mock punched my shoulder. "But only if he doesn't have a snotty mess of a Luna by his side, so buck up girl!"

I laughed shakily, wiping my face.

"Thanks Garrett."

Just then Jasper walked back in, taking in the scene before him. His eyes landed on me and immediately clouded in worry.

"What happened? Violet?" He sank to the ground, and Linda released me. I threw myself at him, relishing in the feeling of being in his arms. I would never take this for granted.

"Sorry. I'm just *really* happy you're okay." I sighed. He laughed, kissing the top of my head. Then I remembered he hadn't come back alone. "Who was that kid?" I pulled back to look at his face.

"My brother."

His brother? Oh. . . Warrick's son?

"Why did you bring him here? Why didn't he leave with his Mom?"

"He didn't want to." Mom said. I looked at her. "I banished that bitch."

"Is that what we heard?" And she nodded. "Why? What did she do?"

Jasper picked me up, bringing me to one of the tables. Everyone sat down and, one by one, gave the replay of the fight from their perspectives. I almost choked when they told me about what Anne had done.

"*What?!* How could she do that?!" I practically yelled.

"I'll be talking to the Elders. And our allies. That law needs to be abolished." Dad sneered. "I've never seen anything so disgusting!"

249

"You already have my support in that." Jasper agreed.

"So, did Anne go back to Silver Moon?"

"If she did, she had better enjoy her time there. I'm banishing her from that pack as soon as possible." Jasper growled.

His words brought me to the reality that we would be leaving. We were now in charge of that pack now. The thought made me tense up; Was I good enough to be a Luna? I had every confidence in Jasper, but not so much confidence in myself. And how was I suppose to continue my lessons from Silver Moon? I couldn't ask Aunt Clara and Grandpa to just pack up and leave with me. Without my lessons, would I be a danger to the pack? Would I hurt someone?

"Hey." I looked up to see Jaspers staring at me intently. "Everything is going to work out. Okay?"

I released the breath I didn't know I was holding. "Okay." I whispered back.

"When are you leaving?" Dad asked.

"I'm not sure. Is there anything I need to do before we go?"

"Hmm. . . You may want to contact the packs Beta and Gamma first. Let them know the situation."

"Can I come to your office tomorrow to do that?"

"Sure thing."

They hammered out a few more details, and then people started to say goodnight. When Jaspers parents approached us, Linda looked determined.

"We're coming with you." She deadpanned.

"Mom." Jasper gave her a look but she held up her hand.

"Don't. We talked about this a lot, and we're okay with it. Besides, Silver Moon sounds like it could use a few extra helping hands. And Elena would miss you too much. We're coming."

He sighed. "I guess I can't stop you, if that's what you want."

"No you can't." I giggled and Jasper rolled his eyes. They gave us each a hug before departing.

"I have to admit, I was worried about leaving Elena." He admitted softly to me.

"Well, it seems that problem is solved." I said, squeezing his hand.

He gazed down at me, and I knew he wanted to be alone. I did too. So we quickly wished everyone a goodnight, and made our way to the doors. I had barely stepped into the corridor when Jasper scooped me into his arms, pressing his lips to mine in a hard, heated kiss. We stood like that, too absorbed in each other for several minutes. Eventually, I started to get dizzy from lack of oxygen and pulled away, breathing hard.

"I would say sorry, but I'm not." He sighed. "I've wanted to do that since the challenge ended."

"I'm not complaining."

He carried me all the way to our room, and someday I was going to ask him how he got so good at carrying people up ladders without dropping them. As soon as the door closed behind us, I pulled him back to me, the tension between us heavy. Part of me wanted to stop and assess if he had any injuries, but the majority of me just wanted him to be as close to me as possible, as soon as possible. Based on the way he was tugging my clothes off, I guessed if he was in any pain, he didn't mind.

"I want you." He growled lowly. "Right here. Right now."

His words made me shiver, his hands running down my sides, grasping under my butt. Then he lifted me, spinning so my back was against the door. I wrapped my legs around him, staring into his silver eyes.

"So take me." I panted.

He didn't waste any time. My panties ripped across my flesh as he tore them off, my bra torn off with his teeth. Adjusting our position slightly, he took one hand from underneath me and started rubbing between my legs. My head fell back, my mouth opening. I was already wet, and his fingers teased me relentlessly until I started to squirm. He pushed two fingers in and I bit my lip at the feeling. His eyes never left my face the whole time, as if he didn't want to miss a single expression that crossed it.

"Does it feel good?"

"Yes. . ." I moaned.

"Do you want more?"

"Yes."

Setting me on my feet, he removed his fingers. He got down on his knees, placing my left foot on his shoulder. I looked down at him confused, but he just smirked up at me. And then his tongue was on me, and I nearly lost my balance.

"Oh! Jasper.."

He licked, sucked, and bit gently, but mercilessly. I couldn't do anything but stand there and try to keep my legs from buckling underneath me. My head was swimming with pleasure as he sucked on my clit, my hands in his hair. The sparks from our bond felt electric, only sending me higher on this ride.

"O-Oh my. . . Jasper. . Jasper please. . ."

His speed increased and my words died on my lips. The only sounds I could make were moans at this point, getting louder and louder until I found my release. My legs shook violently, Jasper grabbing them to keep me standing. When he stood back up, he had the biggest smile on his face, though it looked kind of smug. Taking me by surprise, he lifted me again, placing me back against the door. I'd barely gotten my breath back when I felt him at my entrance, slowly sliding into me. My mouth formed an O, my nails digging into his shoulder.

"Fuck!" I hissed.

He kept going, stopping only when he was all the way in. The silver in his eyes was blazing, like icy fire. We were connected, one being, staring into each other eyes. The intimacy of the moment made my heart swell; What had I ever done to deserve this man? The man who put his life on the line to help a pack he wasn't even a part of. People he had never met. He could have died in his mission to liberate them, but now he would get the chance. I was so proud of him.

"Goddess, you're beautiful." He whispered. Blood rushed to my cheek at his words. He started moving, pumping in and out of me, eliciting moans from me. Damn, he felt good. . .

"I was thinking about you." He rasped. "The whole time. You kept me going, Violet. You helped me survive."

I wrapped my arms tighter around his neck, bringing my lips to his. He kissed me with a passion I'd never felt before, and it set me on fire.

"Jasper!" I whimpered. I could feel my core tightening, could feel myself tightening around him. He started going faster, harder, almost primal in his need for me. I saw when his eyes turned black, his canines elongating. He shook his head, but I stopped him.

"No. Do it. Mark me." I pleaded.

The only response I got was a fierce growl. He wrapped his arms around me, swinging us away from the door and practically throwing us onto the bed. Not once did he pull out of me, just positioned himself over me, his head at my neck. He continued ravaging my body, his wolf in control now. As soon as I orgasmed, I felt his teeth sink into me. The pain was very short-lived, followed immediately by the most pleasure I'd ever felt before in my life. I was positive I'd never feel like this again either. The feeling brought on another orgasm following the first, adding to the euphoria.

Something in my mind clicked, and I realized it was the chest. I'd lost control of it, setting my power free. However, a million other emotions kept me from panicking. My body acted on instinct, pure animal instinct, and my teeth came out. I gripped Jaspers' shoulder, finding the right spot, and bit him. He jerked a little at first, and then we were both riding this wave of ecstasy.

"I love you."

His voice flooded my mind. The fact that it was said this way, instead of verbally, at this moment, made it absolutely perfect. I could feel parts of him, his soul, as we bound ourselves together. I could feel the love flowing from him, his very essence. It was beautiful.

"I love you too."

A bright light shone in my eyes, blinding me. I closed my eyes, releasing my teeth as he did the same. When I opened them again, the room was as dark as before, and I wondered if I had imagined it. But as I went to lick his mark, closing the wound, I gasped, and knew I definitely hadn't imagined it. Because on his shoulder, right where my mark should be, was a tattoo. It was the same marking I had on my side in wolf form, now imprinted on his skin. It was a beautiful gold, almost shining even in the dark.

I felt his fingers touch my shoulder, and I knew before I even looked. Just as I thought, I had an identical mark.

"The mark of the Midnight Wolf." Hala said proudly in my head.

CHAPTER 36
GARRETT

Everyone had already gone to bed, but I wasn't tired. You'd think I would be, after that shit show of a challenge. But no, I was here wandering outside, lost in my thoughts.

Who would have thought that Jasper was such a skilled fighter? I mean, the guy trained like crazy, but I never expected *that*. Maybe it was the Alpha blood in him? Or maybe he just worked really hard at being the best. Part of me wondered if I could win against him; It would be fun to try anyway, us both having Alpha blood. At the very least, he'd be a good sparring partner.

I was starting to warm up to Jasper, even though I didn't think I would. His reputation had me uneasy at first, but he'd shown nothing so far except adoration towards my sister. Maybe even love. And she seemed happy, happier than I'd ever seen her actually, so who am I to complain? Maybe Jasper wasn't even that bad, not as bad as everyone made him out to be. These thoughts swirled in my head as I walked. I ended up in the park, completely deserted now as it was so late. My eyes caught something moving to my right and I turned that way.

Oh.

Not as deserted as I thought. A girl was sitting on the bench, her head bent down. Was she crying? She didn't look like it. My feet started moving towards her, and as I got closer, I actually recognized her. It was Sophia; We'd dated for a while, but decided being friends was better. We hadn't spoken much since then though. I wondered what she was doing out here, at this time of night, and alone?

"Hey So-"

She looked up when I spoke, and my words caught in my throat. Our eyes met and my wolf went absolutely insane. She gasped softly, her own eyes widening as we stared at each other.

"Mate." We said at the same time. I smiled softly at her as she put her book to the side. Her long hair cascaded down her back, her bright eyes even brighter than usual. She stood, coming to stand in front of me. Her scent hit me, delicious and mouthwatering. The moment was silent, yet so powerful. I raised my hand, stroking her cheek gently. Sparks jumped off her skin at the contact, and I inhaled deeply.

She was just as beautiful as always. Her honey blond hair complimented her skin perfectly, and her eyes had this way of capturing me, holding me. I can't believe we ever decided to break up. It almost felt surreal, knowing now that she was my mate. How did I get so lucky?

"Guess friendship isn't going to work for us." I chuckled.

"I guess not." She stepped closer. Close enough that I felt the warmth of her body. "I don't mind though."

"Me either."

My fingers strayed back into her hair and she tilted her chin up. When our lips met, I swear I saw stars. She was smart, funny, sweet and beautiful, inside and out. And I was more than happy to share this with her, just her, without a crowd. This was just us, together, exploring something new. Suddenly, Sophia pulled back harshly.

"What? What's wrong?" I asked her.

Her eyes scanned the area. "I don't know. . . I thought. . . I felt. . . Like someone was. . ." She trailed off.

"Was?" I prompted.

"Was watching us." She rubbed the back of her neck, her eyes still darting around. "Sorry."

I looked around, not seeing anything out of the ordinary. Though our senses were better than humans. If she had such a strong feeling someone was out there, I was inclined to believe her.

"Hang on." I said.

"Mom?"

"Yes?"

Even through mindlink, she sounded tired.

"Can you send a couple of warriors to the park?"

"The park? Why? Are you okay?"

"Yes. I uh. . . I found my mate. But she says she feels like someone is out here and I just want to make sure." I rushed through the explanation. On her end, Mom was silent. I waited, but she didn't reply.

"Mom?"

"Yes. I will send warriors to survey the area. So, who is your mate?"

"Her name is Sophia."

"That's a lovely name. We can't wait to meet her."

She didn't sound as excited as I thought she would have. Then again, she'd had a rough day, and she was exhausted.

"I'll bring her to breakfast tomorrow."

"Great. Stay in the park until the warriors get there. They are on their way."

"Thanks. Night."

I cut off the mindlink and took Sophia's hand in mine.

"My Mom is sending warriors to check the area out."

"Oh Garrett, you didn't need to do that. I'm probably just being silly."

"Better safe than sorry."

We waited exactly three minutes before six warriors showed up. Sophia explained awkwardly that she'd felt someone watching us, and they promised to look around. I wrapped my arm around her shoulder when they were gone, steering her away from the park.

"I feel so stupid. They shouldn't be wasting time with this." She mumbled.

"Don't worry about it. Maybe someone *is* out there- Maybe that wretched Anne came back."

She made a face. "Maybe. I hope not- If your Mom hadn't stepped in when she did, I would have." She growled.

I bit back a smile. My fierce little mate. I looked up at the moon as we walked. It was almost full.

"Hey- Wasn't your birthday recently?" I asked.

"Yes. You missed it."

"Sorry. I'll make it up to you." I kissed her cheek. "So, you'll be shifting soon?"

She fidgeted under my arm. "Yeah. . . I'm not really looking forward to it though." Then she glanced up at me. "Was it really bad? For you?"

My mind went back to that night. I remembered the pain, but I didn't want to scare her. Besides, I would be there to help her.

"I'm not going to lie, it was pretty brutal. But I'll be there with you." I smiled and she returned it.

"I can't believe it! I can't believe you're my mate!" She laughed. "I always hoped you would be, you know. . . "

"Dreams can come true." I sang and she giggled.

Hugo was jumping in my head, ecstatic that we'd finally found our other half. He was filling my head with wants of running through the forest together, hunting, and other, less innocent things.

"What's your wolves name?" I asked, trying to tune him out.

"You're no fun at all!" He whined at me.

"Skye. Yours?"

"Hugo."

"Can I. . . Can I meet him?"

"Really?"

"Yeah, why not?"

I couldn't see why not. I stepped away from her, but she took a few extra steps back. I took off the majority of my clothes, only leaving my boxers. And then I shifted. Sophia stared at me incredibly.

"You're red." She gasped.

I lowered my head a bit. I didn't know why I was red, instead of black, but I was a little embarrassed about it. However, Sophia seemed excited as she skipped right up to me, holding out her hand like I was a dog. I touched her palm with my nose, inhaling her scent. It was so much stronger through this nose.

"A red Alpha. Did you know there hasn't been a red Alpha in almost a thousand years?" She asked. I picked up on the tone, the one she used when she was excited. I shook my head, indicating a no.

"I was reading about Alphas a while ago. The book caught my eye in the library. Red Alphas are extremely rare Garrett. . . Hugo. Whoever." She giggled again, she her running through the fur on my face. It felt amazing.

"Did you know that?" I asked Hugo.

" I did actually."

"And you didn't mention it because. . .?"

"You never asked."

I scoffed, the sound coming out harsher in this form, and Sophia looked up at me. She smiled.

"You're beautiful." She complimented. Hugo swelled with pride. "And big. I almost wonder what it would be like to ride you."

That had Hugo practically bouncing up and down, filling our shared mind with all manner of dirty thoughts. I reeled him in quickly, not wanting to scare her away with my horny wolf. Instead, I kneeled, looking at her openly. Sophias eyes widened and she laughed.

"I wasn't serious Garrett! I'll shift soon, and we can run together."

I barked once, getting lower to the ground. Now that she'd brought it up, I wanted to try it. Maybe it would be fun.

"Are you sure? Really?"

I nodded once and she grinned happily. Without anymore hesitation, she climbed onto my back, gripping the fur on my neck tightly. I stood carefully and heard her sharp intake of breath. I may not have been as big as Violet, but I sure wasn't small either. I took off in a light jog and Sophia yelped on my back. Soon though, she got the hang of it, and I found the experience to be quite enjoyable myself. Her hands in my fur were soft, the sparks from our bond igniting. I made up my mind that we would do this even after she shifted.

Sophia leaned down, pressing her face against my neck. "This is amazing. I can't wait to run with you in wolf form." She sighed. "Skye can't wait either."

I gave a happy yip. I'd brought us on a detour back to the packhouse, taking extra time so she could enjoy herself. I stopped near some bushes, lowering myself so she could get off. She ran her hands through my coat once more before I walked behind the hedge to shift back.

"Behind that tree behind you, there's a stash of clothes. Could you grab me some pants?" I called.

"Oh, sure!"

A minute later, a pair of sweatpants were tossed at me. I threw them on and emerged.

"That was so fun!" Sohpia squealed, throwing her arms around me.

"Yeah." I agreed with a smile.

We stared at each other, and I didn't know where to go from here. Everything in me was screaming to take her hand and bring her to my room. But did she want that? Should I ask her? Should I-?

"So." Her hand ran up my bare chest, and I shivered under her touch. "Your place or mine?"

I glanced at the packhouse. "Uh. . . we're already at my place."

"Then we only have a little farther to go." She took my hand, pulling me in that direction, but I stopped her.

"Sophia. . . what are you doing? I mean, what do you want?" I shook my head. "I mean- what do you want to happen tonight?"

"What anyone in this pack wants. To spend the night with my mate."

"In what context though?"

She placed her hand on my cheek. "In the context of I want you. I've always wanted you."

"I want you too."

She smiled, leaning up to peck my lips. "Then show me."

My grip tightened around her. I pulled her closer, lowering my mouth to hers again. She accepted the kiss freely, her hands gliding around my body. I nibbled on her bottom lip, pulling it with my teeth.

"Come with me." I said when we pulled away.

We walked together to the house, and inside. She didn't question the missing stairs and I didn't want to explain. My whole focus was on her, and once we got to my room, she pretty much attacked me. Somehow we ended up on the bed, our lips fighting for dominance. Everything was heat, sparks, fire. I didn't even know she removed her shirt until my hands were skimming her smooth skin. I wanted to taste every inch of this girl, and I did just that. Starting at her forehead, my lips moved across her flesh, kissing and biting, licking and sucking. I spent some extra time on her breasts, my excitement growing at her moans.

I moved onto her stomach, her sides, down to her navel. Slowly, I removed her pants, leaving her in just a white lace thong. The sight alone nearly made me lose it, but I was determined not to lose my resolve. Continuing downwards, I kissed her thighs, legs and feet, up and down before settling between her legs. Her breathing was heavy as she looked down at me, her eyes half closed and full of lust. I slipped my fingers under the lace, pulling it down until she was revealed to me.

Teasing her, I let my tongue flick out once, fast, barely touching her slit. She groaned, wiggling her hips a bit. I repeated the action several times before finally giving her what her body was begging for. I pleasured her with my mouth, taking my time. The sound of my name falling from her lips was music to my ears, and it encouraged me to go further, inserting a finger into her. She jumped a little, but I held her in place with my arm while I ate her. Adding another finger, I focused on her sensitive bud, sucking and licking. Her legs began to shake on either side of my head, her breathing becoming deeper.

"Garrett. . . Oh my Goddess, yes!. . ."

When I felt she was close enough, I retracted my fingers, pulling away from her. The sound she made was almost scary, her eyes flashing. I chuckled while I removed my clothes.

"So impatient." I teased her.

She whimpered as I positioned myself above her. "Don't worry. I'll make sure you cum." I entered her slowly, watching her face. "Again. And again and again."

"You're. . .awfully. . . confident." She gasped.

I lowered onto my elbow, my lips at her ear. "Tell me how it feels Sophia. Tell me I don't have a reason to be cocky."

Her hand went into my hair, pulling it slightly. I grinned, glad I wasn't making an ass out of myself. This was my first time, but it was so amazing to be doing it with her. Truth be told, I'd fantasized about this moment more than once. Part of me really hoped this wasn't a dream, or I'd be pissed in the morning. I began to move inside her, afraid I might be hurting her. Wasn't she a virgin too? She did look a little uncomfortable.

"You okay?" I breathed.

"Yes. . ."

It came out as kind of a plea, which turned me on more. Increasing my speed, it wasn't long before she became a moaning, incoherent mess. My lips went to her cute, perky nipples as her hips starting moving, meeting my thrusts. She felt incredible, nothing else could compare. And when she finally found her release, she took me with her. We finished together, breathing raggedly and kissing lightly.

"Wow." She mumbled.

"And that was only round one." I smirked.

Time passed us by in a daze. By the time I became aware of anything but the girl in my bed, the sun was already up, shining in through the window and casting rays of light over us. Sophia was curled around me, fast asleep while I stroked her hair. At some point, I fell asleep too, a smile stuck on my face.

CHAPTER 37
VIOLET

The next morning, I woke up alone. For a second, I felt sad, until my fingers touched something smooth on Jaspers' pillow. Rolling over onto my elbow, I picked up the folded piece of paper and flipped it open.

Vie-
Gone to your Dad's office. Come join me when you wake up. You looked so worn out, I didn't want to wake you. See you soon. Love- Jasper. Xo

My lips curled into a smile. Could he get any cuter? This simple gesture-leaving me a morning note- warmed my heart and put me in a good mood. I tucked the paper under my pillow and then got out of bed, stretching minutely. And suddenly, a sharp pain hit my abdomen, making me wince. I doubled over, my face scrunching. The sensation hit again, and I streaked to the bathroom, making it just in time to empty last nights meek dinner into the toilet.

"What the Hell. . ." I muttered to myself.

"Are we sick?" I asked my wolf.

Unbelievably, she giggled in my head. *"Not in the technical sense of the word."*

I narrowed my eyes. *"What does that mean?"*

"It means you should probably get a check up."

I thought she might be right, but I stayed over the toilet bowl for another five minutes, just in case I had another bout of sickness. When I was sure I felt fine, I stumbled into the shower. I washed and dried quickly before trying to brush my teeth; I spit the toothpaste out immediately, my throat burning. Checking the tube, I frowned. Could toothpaste even expire? I mean, of course it could, everything had an expiration date, right? But it wasn't just

263

my throat; I had a weird taste in my mouth, and my chest burned as well as my throat. I put everything away, walking out to find clothes.

I opted for a white blouse and some low hanging jeans, and threw on my sneakers. Then I was off to find Jasper, heading towards my Dads temporary office at the end of the hall. I knocked once before letting myself in.

"Hey." I said.

Dad, Jasper, Uncle Ben and Uncle Luke looked up at me, giving me wide smiles.

"Morning." Dads eyes immediately went to my neck.

"Let's have a look at that." Uncle Luke was in my face in a second, brushing my hair back and peering at my mark. "Hmm. . . Incredible, just incredible. I've never seen anything like it!"

I pushed him away gently. "I'm glad you find it so interesting."

"It suits you. Both of you." Dad said. He looked between Jasper and I.

Jasper was looking at me with such tenderness, such love, that I felt a blush color my cheeks. Was I ever going to get use to this intense feeling I had when I was around him? I kind of hoped I didn't, if I was being honest with myself. Clearing my throat, I stepped away from Luke, taking my mates hand.

"Have you gotten a hold of the Silver Moon Beta and Gamma?" I asked.

"Yes. They're on their way here now. They want proof that Warrick is dead."

"Will he be buried at Silver Moon?"

"Yes. They will transport his body back."

"And where does that leave us?"

Dad leaned forward, crossing his arms. "You can leave anytime. Probably sooner rather than later is best; You shouldn't leave your pack unattended for too long."

'Your pack.' The words resonated through my head, seeming surreal to me. I always figured Garrett would be the Alpha of Blood Moon, and me? I hadn't really thought

about my future past meeting my mate. On the rare occasions I did, I assumed I would be mated to an Alpha, or even a Beta. Someone with blood to match mine. Still, I'd always brushed it off, thinking I'd cross that bridge when I came to it. Now that I was at it, I was more than a little nervous.

"I'll let you deal with them then. I need to go see Mom." I changed the subject.

"Why?" Dad asked.

"I'm not feeling too great. Probably just anxiety about everything." I shrugged, trying to seem like it wasn't a big deal.

But Jasper frowned, putting the back of his hand to my forehead. "You are a little pale. . . Do you want me to go with you?"

I shook my head. "No, you need to be here when the Beta and Gamma arrive. Silver Moon is only an hour or so away, right? They should be here soon."

"Alright. Let me know how it goes." He kissed my forehead, the more familiar sparks erupting.

"I will. See you later."

I waved to everyone as I left, opening a mindlink to Mom.

"What's up, Vie?"

I smiled internally. Mom rarely used my nickname; She must be in a good mood this morning.

"Are you busy?"

"Not really. Just doing some paperwork to discharge a patient."

"Can I come by the hospital?"

". . .Sure. Is anything wrong?"

"I just don't feel good. I was hoping you could give me a once over."

"Of course. Come to room three-ten when you get here. Tell Cal you're here to see me."

"Okay. See you in a minute."

I ended the mindlink, absorbed in my own thoughts as I made my way to the hospital. A few people stopped me on my way, politely exchanging morning greetings. I smiled at everyone, stopping to talk for a minute. Finally, I made it to my destination, hurrying up the front steps and through the doors. Cal sat behind the reception desk, clicking away on the computer, the screen reflecting in his glasses. He smiled when he looked up and saw me.

"Hello Violet. How are you this morning?"

"I'm good Cal. I'm here to see my Mom."

"No problem. She tell you where to go?"

"Yup."

"Then, by all means." He gestured down the white tiled corridor with a flourish and I laughed. Cal had been working for Mom for a few years now. Like herself before, he was training to become a pack doctor, under my Mom. He was a funny guy, with his light brown hair and Harry Potter glasses. He was a hit with the kids who had to come here; I'd never seen a child more at ease while getting a vaccination, not that we needed many due to our higher immune systems. In fact, werewolf children only ever got two vaccines, for diseases that effected our species exclusively. They were extremely rare, but it happened sometimes.

I gave him a salute as I passed the desk. My eyes scanned the numbers above the doors. I took a left, then a right, and then I opened the door to three-ten. Mom was already there, sitting on a chair and looking over a file.

"Just give me one second to read the rest of this. . ." She said. I took a seat on the bed next to her, swinging my legs. After a few minutes of silence, she placed the papers down, giving me her full attention. "Sorry about that."

"It's fine." I shrugged.

"So, what seems to be the problem? You said you aren't feeling well?" She stood up, grabbing her stethoscope off the desk.

"Not really. My chest hurts, and my throat, and I have a weird taste in my mouth. I also got sick this morning."

She frowned. "What kind of taste?"

"Kind of. . . acidic?"

"And on a scale of one to ten, one being the least, and ten being the worst pain you've ever felt, where is the pain at?"

I thought about it. "Probably a one. It doesn't really *hurt*, I guess. It just feels like a burning."

"Hmm. . ." She tapped her a chin with her finger. "What did you eat last night?"

"Uhm. . . Nothing really. I had half a sandwich. I was too nervous to eat."

"Okay. I'm going to ask you some basic questions."

"Okay."

"Did you take anything after you got sick?"

"No."

"Have you eaten this morning?"

"No."

She grabbed a pad and paper, jotting down my answers quickly before continuing.

"We already know when you went into heat. . ." She wrote it down. "Today is the first time you've been physically sick?"

"Yes."

"No pain anywhere else?"

"No."

"And how do you feel right now?"

Again, I stopped to analyze my body. "Actually. . . aside from the burn, I feel fine. Maybe a little tired."

She nodded, a small smile forming on her face. "And. . .. when was the last time you had sex?"

I shifted, but reminded myself there was nothing to be embarrassed about. This was my Mom after all, she'd given me the sex talk years ago. Besides, right now, she was a Doctor first and Mom second. I'd come to her, and she was doing her job.

"Last night."

"Okay. . ." She set her pad aside. "I want you to lie back on the bed. I'll be right back."

I did as she asked, getting comfortable. The burn was stronger in this position though, and I wondered over what it could be. Mom didn't seem overly concerned, and that was comforting. If I was in trouble, I'm sure she would be freaking out right now. She came back not two minutes later, pushing a weird looking machine with all sorts of cords and wires connected to it.

"What's that?" I asked.

"An ultrasound machine."

Our eyes met; She had a knowing look in hers and it took me a few seconds to catch up to where she was.

"No. . ." I breathed.

"I'm inclined to say yes, but let's make sure, alright?" She shut the door, giving us privacy.

"But. . . I. . . We. . ." The words wouldn't come out my mouth, so I closed it instead. Was I pregnant?

"Lift your shirt. I'm going to tuck this towel into your pants. . . There. Okay, just breath nice and steady, and relax." She touched my cheek gently, her eyes casting to the side. "Your Dad told me you and Jasper marked each other."

I blinked, unsure if I could respond right now.

"It's lovely. Unique, and magical. Just like you." She gave me her Mom smile. I hadn't seen it in a long time, and seeing it now, in this situation, almost brought tears to my eyes.

"Thanks." I managed.

"This is cold." She held up a tube before upending it and squirting the clear jelly onto my lower stomach. I watched as she started the monitor, grabbing the ultrasound wand. "We *might* need to do an internal ultrasound. But I'll try this first, okay?"

I nodded.

"Can. . . Can you. . ."

"She paused, the wand hovering above my stomach.

"Can you. . . turn it? So I can see too?" I whispered.

"Sure."

The monitor turned, a simple black screen. Mom adjusted her chair, then placed the wand over the jelly. The screen immediately lit up; It looked like static on a television, except it was blue and gray instead of white and black. My heart was almost beating out of my chest as she moved it around, turning it this way and that. I picked out every odd-shaped thing I saw, wondering if that was a baby. It was dead-silent in the room, only our breathing and my pounding heart made any ounce of noise. So it startled me when Mom stopped moving the tool and spoke.

"Ah."

She looked at me and I looked at her, then back to the monitor.

"Where?" I asked quietly.

She pointed. "Here." Then her finger moved to the left. "And here."

I squinted at the screen, not fully processing her words. And then I saw it.

I saw *them*.

Two little squiggles, side by side. Twins. I was having twins? Oh my Goddess, *I was pregnant with twins!*

"See, here,-" The screen enlarged, giving me a close up of my babies,"- you can see their heartbeats. It looks like you're only a few weeks along, you must have conceived even before your heat hit. And. . .Hmm. . ." She scooted her chair closer, enlarging even more. "I two sacs. . . so non-identical twins."

Surprisingly, her words hit me on impact. It was surprising, considered how shocked I was right now. Twins. . . would they be boys, or girls? What should we name them? Would they be healthy? A million thoughts ran through my head as I stared at the screen, watching two tiny hearts beating. Big, fat tears were running down my cheeks, but I didn't care. Love washed over me, more powerful than I thought possible. It was fierce, almost overwhelming. It was very similar to the mate bond I had with Jasper, but also very different. I knew I would do anything for those two little squiggles, protect them wherever I could, and love them unconditionally. My heart felt so full, I wasn't sure if it would burst or not.

"Violet." Unwillingly, I forced my eyes away from my babies to look at my Mom. "Can you please say something? I'm trying very hard to remain professional right now, given that I just found out I'm going to have grandbabies."

A slightly hysterical laugh burst forth from me. "I. . . I'm just so. . . happy!" I cried.

"I know. I am too. Here, let me print a couple of pictures of the darlings. . ." She clicked around on the keyboard a bit. I was sad when she removed the wand, the screen going dark, until she handed my the pictures. I couldn't stop staring at them.

"So, how are you going to tell Jasper?" Mom asked as she washed her hands at the nearby sink.

"Uhm. . ." I had no idea.

"You remember what I did when I found out I was pregnant with you?"

I laughed again. "Yes. Well, I remember the video. I'm not sure I want to do something like that though."

She came to sit beside me, giving me a side hug and a kiss on the temple.

"However you want."

Then I got an idea, and grinned. "I know how I want to do it. I'll need you there though, I want to take a video of his reaction too."

"I wouldn't miss that for the world."

CHAPTER 38
VIOLET

Mom and I hammered out the details. We decided to include Dad and Garrett too. And apparently Sophia, as they had re-discovered their mate bond last night. I wished we could plan a little more, but we would be leaving to Silver Moon soon, so it had to be done as soon as possible. Which meant today, of course. My mind was already wrapped around the fact that I was pregnant, that I was going to be a Mother. I wasn't sure why, but the shock didn't last long at all. Now I only felt excited and happy.

"I'll give you something for the burn; You likely just have some heartburn and a little acid reflux. It should go away soon, and if it doesn't, it will after the pregnancy."

"Did you have it with us?" I asked curiously.

"For a little bit. Drinking milk helped me, if you don't want to always take medication. They make you sleepy."

"Noted." I took the bottle from her, reading the label.

"And take these too." She handed me another bottle. This one was pink. "Those are prenatal vitamins. Take one a day, once a day. They won't make you tired, and they're packed full of good stuff for the babies."

"Thanks Mom."

She clapped her hands, her own excitement starting to show. "Alright! Let's go, I can't wait!" She squealed.

We left the room together, talking quietly until we reached the reception desk. Mom discarded her white coat, hanging it on a hook.

"I'm taking the rest of the day off Cal. Call me if there's an emergency, but *only* if there's an emergency. As in, life or death, but everything else can wait."

"Uh, sure. See you later Luna, Violet." Cal nodded at us, looking genuinely confused. He was probably wondering if there was something wrong with me, and if it was bad

271

enough that the Head Doctor would leave so early. I winked at him as I passed, reassuring him that everything was fine. His face relaxed into a more comfortable smile.

We walked to the packhouse, heading for Moms car. I jumped in the backseat, while Mom took the drivers seat. And then I mindlinked Jasper.

"Hey."

"Hey. How did it go with your Mom? Are you okay?"

Jasper instantly bombarded me with questions, the concern evident in his tone.

"I'm fine! But you need to come to my Moms car."

". . .. .Why?"

"Because we're going somewhere."

"We?"

"All of us. Just hurry up!"

I was practically bouncing on my butt.

"Okay. . .. "

I cut off the link, grinning.

"Your Dad is getting Garrett and Sophia. They're taking his car. And the Silver Moon guests have been told there is an emergency, so Luke and Ben are with them until we get back." Mom said.

"Perfect."

I wondered absentmindedly if Sophia knew I was hybrid still. It didn't seem likely, since that memory was attached to her previous mating with my brother. So, did we tell her or not? She would probably figure it out anyway; She was Garrett's mate after all. And she kept the secret the first time around. Either way, that conversation could be put off until a later time.

"Here they come."

I looked out the window to see four very confused faces walking towards us. Garrett and Sophia split to get into Dads car, while Jasper and Dad got in with us. Both of them gave us looks as they got in, but we just smiled at them.

"What is the big emergency?" Dad asked.

"You'll see." Mom replied. "Garrett will follow us?"

"I told him to. . ."

"Good!"

She put the car in reverse, and off we went. Jasper took my hand in the back seat, squeezing it gently.

"Are you really alright?" He asked. His brow was furrowed, his eyes scanning me head to toe.

I leaned over to kiss him. "Healthy as a horse." I assured him.

"Then where are we going?"

"It's a surprise."

"Vie. . ."

"This doesn't look very good, Violet. Jasper just met the ranked members as their new Alpha, and then had to leave. That's not a great first impression."

Mom scoffed. "Oh please! An Alpha gets called away all the time due to one thing or another! If they don't like it, it's too bad for them. I can recall *many* times you left meetings because of emergencies."

"But you haven't told us what the emergency *is*." Dad shot back.

"I told you, you'll see. Stop pestering me Dimitri."

Dad sat back, pouting and I giggled. We drove through the pack, right to the heart of town. When Mom parked in front of the mall, the guys stared at us. Not giving them time to voice their questions, we got out, Garrett pulling into the spot next to us. He looked just as confounded as he stepped out of the vehicle.

"Why on Earth are we at the mall?" He frowned.

"We have some shopping to do." I said. Everyone looked at me like I'd grown a third head. "Come on then!"

I started walking, leading our group. Jasper caught up to me, falling into step beside me.

"Violet-"

"This is important, Jasper. Trust me, you're not going to want to miss this shopping spree. Trust me, please?"

He pursed his lips, but nodded.

I didn't come to the mall very often; I mostly shopped online. But that seemed very impersonal for this experience, and I wanted it to be memorable. The place was buzzing with activity; Couples with their children, teenagers, and a few groups of girls who were eyeing my mate appreciatively from a distance. It sparked a tiny bit of petty anger in me, seeing them watch him with hungry eyes. But I was the one carrying his babies, not them, so I didn't let it bug me for long.

We weaved around people, passing various shops, until, finally, I stopped. I scanned the store, a store I'd never stepped foot in, and honestly, had never paid attention to. It was cute! The sign above read *"Little Wonders"* in happy red letters, the walls inside painted bright yellows and greens. Racks upon racks could be seen through the glass, filled with tiny outfits. I couldn't wait anymore, rushing into the store and grabbing a cart.

It was even bigger inside, a whole section hidden by the wall on the exterior. Bright pinks and blues jumped out at me, but for now, I would pick neutral colors since I didn't know the genders.

"Uh. . .. Violet. . ."

I turned to see Jasper slowly following me, his face contorted. Mom stood to the side of us, her phone in hand, recording.

"Yes?"

"Why are we in a baby store?" He looked around, touching an adorable outfit with dump trucks on it.

"To buy baby things, of course."

He frowned, and Dad gasped.

"Are you pregnant?!" He was looking at Mom with huge eyes.

"Nope." She grinned.

Everyone turned to look at Sophia, who was admiring a pair of pajamas. She caught their gazes and held up her hands. "Don't look at me!"

I watched in amusement as Garrett caught on first. Then Sophia. Then Dad. And at last, the lightbulb clicked on, and Jasper took a step towards me.

"Are you..?"

I nodded. I held my breath, waiting for his reaction. His expression was a mix of awe, nerves, shock, wonder. I watched as each emotion played across his face until it settled into a breathtaking grin. He moved so quickly, wrapping me in his arms and planting his lips on mine in a warm kiss. One of his hands went to my belly, caressing it gently.

"I can't believe it." He breathed after we pulled apart.

"Believe it."

"How far along are you?"

"A few weeks. They're just little squiggles right now."

His face went blank at my words. *"They?"*

I wrapped my arms around his torso. "We're having twins."

Because I was holding onto him, I felt when his knees went weak. Dad jumped in to steady him, and I bit my lip to keep from laughing. Yeah, it was rather shocking.

"Oh my Goddess! Congratulations!" Sophia shrieked. Her and Garrett nudged their way in, giving me a group hug. Mom ended the recording, coming to join. Jasper was possibly still absorbing the information, looking around the store with new eyes. And I looked at my Dad over everyone's shoulders.

"Dad?"

"I. . ." He cleared his throat. "I'm happy. Of course I'm happy for you. I guess. . . I'm just a little choked up." He chuckled, looking at the ground. "I guess I didn't realize how much you've grown up until now. But you'll be a good Mom, a great Mom. I'm so proud of you."

I smiled around new tears. Hearing that meant so much to me, more than he knew. I held out my arm, and he joined the group hug, kissing the top of my head.

"Uhm. . . is there anything I can help you find?" We broke apart at the voice behind us. A petite redhead was smiling at us, though she looked a little wary. I wiped my eyes, giving her a friendly smile in return.

275

"Yes, actually. We-," I pointed to Jasper, "-Just found out we're expecting. Twins. We're looking for all the necessities; toys, cribs, clothes. But neutral colors for now."

The girls face lit up. "Oh! Congratulations, that's so exciting! I can help you find everything you need. Follow me!"

I grabbed the cart, trailing behind her as she led us through the store. At some point, Garrett and Sophia broke off, admiring everything by themselves. Mom looked like she suddenly had baby fever, eyeing a pair of tiny shoes. Jasper simply followed me as I followed the employee, occasionally tossing stuff into the cart.

"You okay?" I asked him.

"Yes. Absolutely." He paused to add a cute green onesie to the heap. "You don't even know Vie. . . I don't think I could be happier than I am right now. Sorry about before, it was just. . . well I wasn't expecting twins. I guess I should have, since you're a twin. But I'm so excited. I can't wait to meet them!"

"Me either." I smiled, looking down at my stomach.

"Awe. You guys are sweet!" The girl said to us. "I want to show you this- We just got this in! It's a double crib, perfect for multiples! See, you can separate it like this-," She pointed to the picture on the box, "-Or, you can let them sleep together, if you prefer. It actually comes with its own mattress too. We sell them over there. It also comes in different colors; Gray, white, pink, blue, or green."

"It's perfect! We don't know the genders yet. . . so I think the white one is fine."

"Okay. Did you have an idea for a theme for the nursery or. . .?"

I looked at Jasper but he shrugged. "Whatever you want. I'll love it no matter what."

"Hmm. . ." I looked around. "I think I'll decide on that later, when we know if they are boys or girls."

"No problem! Let me show you the bedding section. . ."

We ended up staying in the store for over an hour. The girl, whose name I learned was Raven, was more than helpful. And extremely patient, and kind too. We talked a little, and it turned out she actually knew me from school, though we'd never talked before. By the time we were done, we'd filled three shopping carts instead of one. Dad pulled out his card at the register, the total being more than I thought it would. I thanked him profusely, but he waved me off.

"I may not have been able to spoil you two, but I'm definitely spoiling my grandkids."

"Same." Mom chimed in.

We each took a few bags to the cars, and for a while, it didn't look like Jasper and I were going to fit in the backseat anymore. We ended up piling mostly everything into Moms car, and riding home with Garrett and Sophia. Halfway home, my phone buzzed in my pocket. I rarely used it anymore; Mindlinking was so much easier. Brianne's name flashed the screen.

"Hey." I answered the call.

"Hey! I'm at your place, where are you?" She asked loudly.

"Oh shit! We were supposed to hang out today!" I gasped.

"Uh, yeah, we were!"

"I'm sorry dude, I totally forgot. Something. . . came up." I said lamely. "But I'm almost back home, can you wait for me?"

"Yeah. I'll be here."

"Thanks."

I hung up, feeling guilty. I'd been neglecting my friendship with Brianne lately. So much had gone on; I hadn't even spoken to Dylan either. Ten minutes later, we pulled up to the house. Brianne was waiting by a shrub, tapping her foot. I stepped out of the car, shamefaced.

"Hey. I'm really sorry." I apologized.

"It's fine. You still want to go shopping?"

"Uh. . ." I looked at the cars. "I kind of already did."

Her face clouded in disappointment.

"But here- help me bring this up. I have loads to tell you."

"Go inside. We'll bring everything up." Jasper said.

"You sure?"

"Just go." He chuckled. "We got it."

"Okay. Thanks." I took my friends arm, leading her into the house. We stopped as soon as we passed through the door. Two very large, very grumpy men stood in the foyer alongside my Uncles. They eyed us up and down, their eyes landing on my mark. To my astonishment, both dropped to one knee in front of us.

"Luna." They said in unison.

CHAPTER 39
JASPER

I rolled my eyes as I walked in behind Violet. These two were so *formal*. Sure, werewolf society was a little old-school, but this was next level.

"Beta King, Gamma Ashwell, you don't need to bow. I told you that already when we met; The same thing goes for Violet."

They both stood awkwardly. "Apologies Alpha. Force of habit."

Violet looked at me, but Brianne put her hands on her hips. "That's right, I almost forgot! You're a Luna now!" She smirked at her best friend.

"Uh. . . yeah, I guess I am." Vie looked in every direction that wasn't the two men. They shared a look that I didn't understand.

"You don't want to be our Luna?" Gamma Ashwell asked.

"Huh? Oh, no it's not that! I just. . . I never pictured myself as a Luna. But I'll do my best for your. . .our. . . *the* pack in any case!"

This time, the men gave her hesitant, soft smiles.

"You are different." Mused Beta King.

"Different?"

"From Luna Anne. From the time we were teenagers, she raved about becoming Luna, even if she wasn't the rightful one. It was a sad day when she turned out to be Warrick's mate. She never cared about the pack members, only about the packs money."

"Which there wasn't a lot of to begin with." Added Ashwell.

"She is the main cause behind the poverty that plagues Silver Moon members."

I frowned. "How can one woman spend so much? What does she spend it *on*?"

"Herself, and her concubines. She owns several proprieties abroad that she rarely uses, but mostly she buys clothes, jewellery, furniture, art. . . Expensive stuff."

"Meanwhile, upper ranked wolves, like us, are struggling from pay check to pay check, trying to make ends meet."

"Wait, wait, wait." Violet held up her hands. "Warrick said there were some nice houses that important pack members stayed in near the packhouse. He wasn't referring to you?"

Both men laughed. "I wish!" Snorted King. "I've got five pups at home and a mate, and we live in a tight three bedroom. No, those houses are for the Alphas 'friends'."

"By 'friends', he means his gambling buddies and men who like to have fun outside the mate bond." Ashwell sneered.

Both Violet and Brianne's' mouths were hanging open. I felt disgust on my face as well.

"That is. . . beyond what we were told. I had no idea things were that bad." Luna Lily put down her bags beside me, walking forward. "I'm Luna Lily. It's nice to meet you."

"You as well Luna." They all shook hands.

"I apologize for the delay in proceedings today."

"No problem. Though we are looking to getting back home as soon as possible. I trust your emergency was looked after?"

"Yes, thank you."

"Who's in charge of the pack right now? While you two are away?" I asked.

"Eh. . .." Beta King mumbled something, looking awkward.

"Pardon?" Violet asked.

"Luna Anne." He said louder and sighed. "She was the last resort, but the lesser of two evils. If not her, Warrick's friends were next in line, and no way in Hell I was leaving any of them in charge."

"Stop calling that woman 'Luna'," Violet snapped. "She is no longer your Luna, I am. I am Jaspers' mate, and he is the rightful Alpha of Silver Moon. And Anne won't be a member of Silver Moon for much longer anyway!"

King and Ashwell gaped at her, clearly not expecting such a strong response. "You are going to banish her?"

"For what she did to Kiren, yes."

"What happened to Kiren anyway?" Ashwell spoke up.

I stepped forward, explaining to them what had transpired after Warwick death. They listened, their faces growing more and more tense as I talked. When I finished, King swore under his breath.

"That stupid bitch. Kiren is just a boy!"

"I don't want Anne in charge for much longer. I think we should settle things up here, and head out." I said.

"Vie, can I have a word with you outside?" Brianne asked.

"Sure. Be right back." She said to me.

"Right." I turned to Dimitri. "So, as we were discussing before. . ."

He nodded. "Given the circumstances, I think we should do it now. Mind you, it will be a bit unpleasant."

"I understand. Go ahead."

He walked in front of me, looking me in the eye. His Alpha aura washed over me strongly. "I, Dimitri Varlos, Alpha of the Blood Moon Pack, hereby release you, Jasper Cole, as a member of this pack."

I tensed, waiting for the pain of being cut off from the pack. But it never came. I frowned, as well as everyone else.

"You have to use his biological surname Dad."

I turned to see Violet standing near the door, a few tears on her cheeks. She smiled at me.

"Don't worry. Just sad to say goodbye to Brianne." She explained.

"What were you saying?" King asked her.

"Jaspers adopted name is Cole, but his Dad. . . I think you have to use that name. That's why it's not working."

"I don't want to take his name." I growled.

"You don't have to. You just need to use it once, for this, and then when we accept you. You can keep your adopted name." Ashwell said to me. I nodded.

"Alright, let's try this again." Dimitri said. "I, Dimitri Varlos, Alpha of the Blood Moon pack, hereby release you, Jasper Warrick as a member of this pack."

Something in my chest snapped, and I gasped, clutching it. Dimitri winced, putting a hand on my shoulder to steady me. Tears burned behind my eyes, and my chest burned like someone had shoved me with hot-iron sword. That wasn't the worst though; I suddenly felt empty. Lonely, incredibly lonely. A wolf could not survive without a pack, and as of this moment, I had no pack. Even my mate bond felt lessened.

"You okay?" Dimitri asked.

"Y-yeah." I managed. I turned to Beta King, nodding my head. He stepped forward.

"Jasper Warrick." I winced at the name. "Do you promise from today onward to serve, protect, and honor the Silver Moon pack as it's new Alpha?"

"I promise."

"Do you promise to be fair, just, with no cruel or malicious intent towards our people?"

"I promise."

"And do you accept the title as Alpha of Silver Moon?"

"I do."

"Then I, Beta Lucias King, hereby accept you as my Alpha."

"I, Gamma Tyrone Ashwell hereby accept you as my Alpha."

The burn in my chest was washed away. My throat untightened, and I stood straight and tall again. A whole new sensation coursed through me from my head all the ways to the soles of my feet. A raw power, and new strength. My Alpha blood, finally coming forward. For a few seconds, my new aura ranged out around me, and King and Ashwell bowed their heads slightly in submission. I was officially Alpha of Silver Moon.

"Your turn Violet." Luna Lily called.

Vie walked over to her Dad, allowing him to release her from the pack. I felt her pain through the bond, and brought her close, hoping to ease some of it.

"Alright Jasper. Go ahead." Luna Lily nodded at me.

"Just repeat after me." King said.

I repeated the oath to Violet as quickly as I could. I wasn't sure if cutting her off from the pack would be good for the babies, but if it held any risk, I'm sure her Mom would have said something. Still, I wanted to make it end as soon as possible. And when it was, we both took a step back at the new feeling of our bond. The sparks were much stronger now where our skin touched, the bond itself already more intense.

"The bond between an Alpha and Luna is stronger than most." Gamma Luke explained. He walked over to us, pulling Violet in for a hug. "I'm going to miss you kiddo."

"I'm only an hour away, you can visit." Vie laughed.

Everyone took a turn hugging us, saying goodbye. When Garrett, who'd been very silent through this ordeal, stepped forward, I held out my hand.

"Take care of my sister, alright?" He said. His voice sounded rough, edgy.

"I will." I promised him.

Then he moved on to Vie. "I guess I'll uh. . . We'll come visit you sometime."

"Oh Garrett." She threw her arms around him. "You can be such a baby sometimes! Just admit you're sad to see me go!"

He scoffed. "Yeah, right!" But his body betrayed him by holding onto her tighter. I briefly wondered how he would get along from now on.

My thoughts were swirling, dizzy from the turn of events. In one day, I'd gone from being the mate of the Alphas daughter, to an Alpha myself. Not to mention becoming a dad-to-be! So much had happened, and it was barely afternoon. I hadn't even seen my parents yet! I suddenly felt a little lightheaded, everything coming down on me at once.

"Jasper?"

Violets soft voice pulled me out of my spell. I smiled at her, reaching out to pull her close and inhale her scent. Even that was stronger, more potent now. I loved it.

"I'm alright. Just. . . it's been a day, huh?"

She laughed. "It definitely has. I could really go for a chicken sandwich." She sighed.

"Cravings starting already?"

"I guess so."

"Cravings?" King looked at me, brows furrowed. Then his face lit up, and he gave a cheerful whoop. "You're pregnant?!" He looked at Violet who smiled and nodded.

"A new Alpha and an her already on the way." Ashwell smiled.

"Heirs." Violet corrected. Both men stopped celebrating the news to gape at us.

"Violet is a twin. Just like our babies." I rubbed her stomach gently while nodding to Garrett.

"Holy shit!" Ashwell exclaimed.

I noticed a few maids coming down the ladder with suitcases. Luna Lily nodded towards the door, and I gave her a questioning look.

"I've had some things packed for you; Clothes, toiletries, and your vitamins Violet. The baby stuff can go with you now, as much as you can fit, and we will send the rest in a few days, along with the rest of your stuff. Anything else you need just call me." The Luna said with tears shining in her eyes. Vie pulled away from me to hug her Mother fiercely, exchanging soft, but heartfelt farewells.

"Alpha."

Dimitri and I, both turned to the door, sharing a smirk. The maid bowed her head slightly at me.

"Everything is packed in the vehicle. Would you like me to take these bags?" She gestured to the baby stuff.

"Please." I nodded. She smiled, gathering what she could carry.

"We will be in the car. Come meet us when you're ready." King bowed again, a habit I was for sure going to break, before walking past me. Ashwell gave me a happy salute as he followed.

"Jasper dear." Luna Lily threw her arms around me, engulfing me in an unexpected hug. "I will miss you. Take care of my daughter."

"I will Luna. Er, Lily. Of course I will."

"Just Lily dear."

I cleared my throat. "Thank you. For everything. Without you. . . I wouldn't be Jasper Cole today. You saved my life."

She hugged me tighter. "You will do great things. I know it."

I pulled away before I started getting too emotional. Dimitri and I shook hands, Luke and Ben each giving me a hug as well. And then I was leading Violet out the door. Everything felt surreal right now, like I dream I wasn't sure I wanted to wake up from. Our group walked to a huge black SUV with King and Ashwell in the front seats. I helped Violet into the backseat, at least four feet from the ground.

"Geez, what kind of car is this?"

"A very expensive one. I took it from Warrick's garage." King answered.

"It's gigantic!" Vie gasped.

"He did like to lavish himself with gifts." Ashwell commented bitterly.

"This thing is like a tank." I muttered as I climbed in.

"I trust it will get you to Silver Moon safely then." Lily said with a smile.

I shut the door, rolling down the window.

"I love you guys!" Violet called around me.

"We love you too!" They chorused.

"You guys ready?" King said as he started the car. It gave quite a roar as the engine fired up.

285

I looked at my mate who nodded.
"Let's go." I said.

CHAPTER 40
JASPER

I tried hard to relax the further we got from Blood Moon. In an attempt to distract myself, I struck up conversation.

"Tell me about Silver Moon." I said into the silence. Ashwell looked at me over his seat.

"What do you want to know?"

"The truth." I looked him in the eye. "I get the feeling that Warrick's version of things was. . .off."

The Gamma scoffed. "Probably! Though I'm sure things were very nice from his position." He sneered.

"You really didn't like him, did you?" Violet asked beside me.

"We outgrew him." King answered. His eyes were on the road, but his expression was dark. "Tyrone and I grew up with Bryan. Thick as thieves, the three of us."

"What changed?" I asked.

"He did. Being the Alphas son. . . I think the power went to his head. No, I know it did. By the time we realized. . ." He trailed off.

"It was too late." Ashwell finished. He shook his head. "When Bryan took over as Alpha, the changes were slow. Small, undetectable. Until they weren't. The pack was falling apart, and all he cared about was doting on his friends and screwing the help. He made up laws, and ignored real ones. The pack was suffering, but he was too much in his own world to see it. Or maybe he did, and he just stopped caring."

"But you stayed on as Beta and Gamma?"

"Our families have held our titles for generations. It felt wrong to give them up now. We tried to fix things, but we're not Alphas, and we cannot go against our Alphas orders."

I leaned forward in my seat. "And now?"

"Now?"

"Are you willing to stay on as my Beta and Gamma now?"

They shared a brief look before King answered. "We would like to."

"Why do I hear a '*but*' at the end of that sentence?" Violet asked.

"We agreed. If you won the challenge, we would keep our titles. Unless you turned out to be exactly like Warrick." King said.

"We will not serve another tyrant Alpha." Ashwell nodded.

I smiled half heartedly. "Very well. All I ask is one favor."

"What's that?"

"If you two ever feel I'm going down the wrong path, you will speak up and set me straight. That's not a request either, it's an order." I used my Alpha voice for the very first time. I listened to it echoes through the vehicle, felt my aura radiate around me. Violet shivered beside me.

"Yes Alpha." King and Ashwell said together. I could hear the satisfaction in their voices.

The next half hour went by uneventfully. Violet and I chatted with our companions, getting a feel for our new relationship with them. I liked them both quite a lot, and couldn't help but feel that I'd lucked out a bit. Both King and Ashwell seemed like upstanding guys, willing to put the pack first. They would be detrimental to making the changes I knew had to come.

"What is *that*?"

My eyes followed Violets shocked gaze out the window. A small shack stood out amongst the trees, totally worn down. The grass was massively overgrown, with tall weeds clumped around. A few pictures I couldn't make out were painted on the wood side, but the most shocking thing about the scene was the woman and child hanging laundry on a poor clothesline to the side.

"We are at the edge of the border. There are a few houses here." King said.

"*House?!* That's not a house! Stop the car!" Violet ordered.

"We're almost-"

"Now!"

King braked, and Violet jumped out the door. I hurriedly undid my seatbelt before following her. King and Ashwell jumped out after me, trekking towards the so-called house. Vie approached the woman determinedly, but the woman looked fearful. She clutched her daughter to his side, eyes wide. Touching the girl's head, they both dropped to their knees.

"B-beta. Gamma." She whispered.

"Maybe you two should wait in the car." I said to them. King shrugged, turning back. Ashwell eyed the pair in front of us sadly.

"What is your name?" Violet asked.

The woman shook, her eyes never leaving the ground. I moved closer, noticing how thin and small they both looked. Neither seemed to have the intention of answering though. Violet must have realized it too, because she got on her knees in front of the woman, reaching out to take her hand.

"Please tell me your name."

"M-Ma-Marian."

"Is this your daughter Marian?"

She nodded quickly.

"It's nice to meet you two. My name is Violet. That is my mate, Jasper." She pointed to me. "Is this your. . .house?"

"Yes." Marian whispered.

"Can I ask why you're living so far from the pack?"

Hesitantly, Marian raised her eyes to meet Violets. There was still fear, but curiosity now too. She glanced at me, then at Ashwell and gulped loudly.

"Nevermind him. Gamma Ashwell brought us here, he won't hurt you." Violet assured her.

"A-Alpha Warrick. . . he put us here." Marian breathed.
"Why?"

"Because. . . Because I couldn't work anymore. My pregnancy. . . it was difficult."

I clamped down on the anger that was growing inside me. I could feel Violet doing the same.

"Are there others out here too?"

"A few. . ."

Violet gave her a tight smile before standing up. She rounded on Ashwell, fire in her eyes.

"Find every single person out here and round them up. I want them brought to the packhouse, today. I don't care how long it takes you."

He nodded. "Will do."

"N-no! Please!" Marian started to wail. "W-we will leave! I promise!"

Vie got back on the ground, taking the poor woman by the shoulders.

"Hush. I'm sorry. I'm not bringing you to the packhouse to punish you, I swear. I want to help you."

"T-the Alpha-"

"Is dead." Violet interrupted her. Marians words cut short with a choke.

"What?"

"Warrick is dead. My mate challenged him for the Alpha title and won. We are the new Alpha and Luna Marian." She smiled tenderly.

"The Alpha. . . You?" She looked at me properly for the first time. I nodded, hoping my face was reassuring. "Goddess. . . Oh, Goddess, thank you!" She clutched her daughter close, sobbing.

"Marian, we will give you a ride to the packhouse. Can you grab what you need?" Violet asked.

"We have little. . . maybe a few things. . ." She stood on shaking, weak legs, carrying her child inside their shack. I shook my head.

Violet stood, wiping the dirt from her pants. I could tell she was just as upset as I was, maybe more. We both looked into the forest; I spotted two more structures in the distance. I couldn't find the words to describe what I was feeling. The treatment of these poor folk was downright inhumane. Marian emerged carrying her daughter in one arm, and a dirty bag littered with holes in the other. I finally noticed how dirty the two were as well; Did they not even get the decency of clean water to bathe in? Or did they not get a bath at all? I doubted one would fit inside their 'home'.

"Come on." I motioned towards the SUV but stopped at her soft voice.

"No, we cannot. We must walk."

Walk? She could barely stand!

"I insist you ride with us Marian." I tried again.

She looked at Violet, who nodded and smiled. Slowly, we made our way to the car and I helped Marian inside. She sat far away from us, huddled against the door with her daughter in lap.

"Let's go." I told King. He acknowledged me by started the car and driving on. The entire rest of the way, I took a mental note on how many shacks I saw. By the time the trees started thinning, and more realistic looking homes came into view, I'd counted more than thirty. My heart sank in my chest at the cruelty of this place.

The further we went through Silver Moon, the more disgusted I became. We passed home after home that desperately needed care. Pack members dropped to the ground at the sight of our vehicle, trembling on the ground. Unknown to them was the fact that I, not Warrick, sat therein.

"How could he have enjoyed this?" Violet raged beside me. "It makes me feel sick."

"Me too." I agreed.

King said nothing, his eyes focused ahead.

We took a sharp right, and the difference in scenery was astounding. Grand houses were sat one after another, six in total. Everyone of them looked as though they could house a dozen families. The lawns were crisp, perfectly cut and cared for, with lush flowerbeds; One even had a fountain! I concluded these must be where Warrick's friends lived.

"We're here." King announced.

He came to a stop in front of the grandest house of all. Five stories, at least, a beautiful red brick mansion lay. Dozens of windows reflected light back to us, and vines crept up one side. Hundreds of flowers grew lazily around the base, some dotting off just outside the mulch barrier. The house was huge, easily as big as Blood Moons packhouse, if not a little bigger. A detached building sat to the right, I assumed the garage King had spoken of earlier.

Instead of standing in awe at our new home, I only felt unease. I was supposed to live here, in this luxurious space, while others lived in filth and poverty? How could I do that?

"Hey." Violet touched my shoulder. "Do you trust me?"

I nodded. "Of course I do."

"Come on." She took my hand, pulling me out of the car with her. Marian followed us quietly, staring at the ground. "Beta King!"

The sound of his door closing, and then he was standing beside us. Violet turned us in his direction.

"You're first order of business is to wait here until Gamma Ashwell returns. When he does, I want you both to find rooms in the packhouse for whomever he brings with him. Make sure everyone is fed, and has clean clothes."

"Yes Luna."

"After you're done that, you can also come back. With your family."

"Uh. . ."

"The Beta should be in the packhouse. Same with the Gamma. Understood?"

Relief flooded his eyes as he nodded. "Understood Luna. I will do as you wish."

"Good. While you're waiting here, I want you to send out a mindlink for everyone to meet here, tomorrow morning. And I do mean everyone."

"I don't think the entire pack will fit on the front lawn." He replied.

"Where should we meet then?"

"The Hall is used for pack meetings. It's about ten minutes that way." He pointed.

"Alright, that's where we'll meet. See you then."

Vie pulled me into the house. My first impression was one of excessive grandeur; costly furniture was arranged everywhere, with just as expensive art hanging on the walls. There was barely an open space anywhere.

"Good grief. . ." I sighed.

"May I help you?" A feminine voice floated to us. A maid had come from one of the entrances off the foyer, smiling at us politely, but her eyes were wary. She glanced at Marian who was hiding behind us with distaste. I stepped forward, hand extended.

"Hello. My name is Jasper Cole."

She was a tiny thing, with fair skin and highlighted blonde hair. Her blue eyes appraised me properly for the first time, and she gave me a smile I knew too well. Beside me, I felt Violet tense. The maid grasped my hand in hers, shaking firmly.

"Hello Jasper. My name is Stacy." She purred.

A low growl sounded from Violet and I stepped back.

"And I'm Violet, Jaspers mate." She said. Stacy's expression drifted to her unwillingly. Neither offered to shake hands.

"Alpha Warrick is away at the moment." Stacy told us. "But Luna Anne is here. Are you here on pack business?" She looked at Marian again.

I smirked. "Alpha Warrick will not be returning."

"Excuse me?"

"He's dead." Violet said. Stacy's eyes widened momentarily.

"Dead? How. . .?"

"I am his son. I challenged him for his title, and won."

"So. . . you're the new Alpha?" Her tone held way too much excitement.

"And Luna." I brought Vie to my side. Stacy bristled.

"I see. Well. I should inform Luna Anne-"

"Actually Stacy, I need you to gather everyone in the house. If Anne is here, that includes her. I want everyone down here in ten minutes." Violet ordered.

"Some of the maids are off duty." Stacy snapped.

"Then mind link them. I expect everyone here. Ten minutes."

The girls face went a shade darker, but she stomped off to do Violets bidding. I chuckled.

"You're so cute when you're jealous." I grinned.

Vie scoffed. "Jealous? No. I just don't like the way she was looking at you."

"That's called being jealous love."

She stuck her tongue out at me making me grin. I turned to Marian; Her daughter had nodded off in her arms.

"Marian, come here. Please, sit."

I pulled a wooden chair away from the wall, gesturing to her. She looked at Violet, who nodded before collapsing onto the seat.

"Thank you." She whispered.

"What is your daughters name?" I asked gently.

"Skye."

"That's a beautiful name."

She nodded, but didn't say anything more as voices began to drift down to us. Maids started appearing from the left and right, whispering as they entered the foyer. I looked them over, becoming uncomfortable at the common traits; All had blonde hair, blue or green eyes, and were fairly busty. It occurred to me that Warrick had held a preference for a certain type of woman, and had chosen to surround himself with girls who fit. I waited until everyone was gathered in a group, their blonde heads making a yellow and white sea in front of me.

"Is that everyone?"

"Yes." Stacy replied from the front.

"Alright. Vie?" She smiled at me. I had no idea what she was up to, but I trusted her completely. She stood in front of the girls, back straight and head held high.

"Hello everyone. I don't see Anne here?" She looked at Stacy who rolled her eyes.

"The Luna is in her office and doesn't wish to be disturbed."

"Anne is no longer Luna of Silver Moon." Violet snapped. "You will go and retrieve her, or I will get Beta King to do it."

"Fine!" Stacy huffed and left. Violet returned her attention to the group.

"I'll cut to the chase. Alpha Warrick is dead. My mate won his title, as his son. Kiren has given up his claim to the Alpha title as well. Going forward, we are the new Alpha and Luna of Silver Moon." Her words caused murmurs amongst the girls. It ceased when she continued. "If you could all do me a favor, can you arrange yourselves from youngest to oldest?"

The group moved, making a long line. I was stunned to see the girl at the very end couldn't be more than fifteen or sixteen years old. Violet frowned.

"Thank you. How many of you are under eighteen?"

Six girls raised their hands from the left end.

"Go home. You should be in school, not working."

"You're firing us?" One asked.

"Yes."

"You can't!" Another shouted. "We are the only stable source of income for our families!"

"What?" I gasped.

"Please don't worry about that. I promise you're families will be taken care of." Violet reassured them. The youngest started crying, being consoled by the girl next to her. She glared at us.

"You're sentencing us to become rogues! We need this job!"

"You *dare* enter my house?!"

Every head turned to see Anne storming in. I brought myself closer to my mate, ready to shield her from the unpredictable woman.

"What are you doing with my maids?! You have no right to be here! Leave!" She commanded.

CHAPTER 41
VIOLET

"Excuse me?" I sneered. *"We* have no right to be here? Wrong. *You* have no right to be here. You are no longer Luna."

Anne glared at me coldly. "Your mate cheated his way to winning!"

Whispers went through the crowd of girls around us. Behind us, Marion and Skye were silent.

"Cheated? How?"

"My mate had *years* of experience on him! He must have had outside help! Or he took something-"

I started laughing before she could finish. "Experience doesn't mean shit! I've personally bested some of the top warriors at Blood Moon. Know why? Because I had the Alpha and Luna as teachers! Those men were thrown on their asses by me, even though they had *'years of experience'* on me!"

Anne crossed her arms, smirking wickedly at me.

"You cannot be the official Luna unless I hand down the title. Which I'm not going to do!"

I sighed, shaking my head. She really was grinding on my patience. Jasper stepped forward, putting his hand on my shoulder, comforting me against this stubborn, annoying woman.

"You don't have to do anything. I've already been sworn in as Alpha. As Alpha, I can relinquish your title."

Her expression faltered, realizing he was right. Hatred shone in her eyes, and her thin lips curled in a snarl. Before she could say anything though, Jasper spoke again.

"I, Alpha Jasper Cole of Silver Moon, hereby banish you former Luna Anne Warrick from Silver Moon. As Alpha, I also strip you of your title." His aura washed over me, making my insides tingle. It was probably wrong to be aroused right now, but like I could help it?

Anne, on the other hand, clutched her chest, whimpering. Around us, the girls were wincing, shuffling uncomfortably. They should have been in a lot more pain, losing their Luna. My only conclusion was that Anne cared more about her title than the rest of them did, clinging to it. It was obvious that she wasn't well loved or even respected amongst the people in the pack, as losing her didn't affect them as much.

"It's done. You can leave now." Jasper said.

"No!" She cried. "How can you do this?! You've taken everything from me! My mate, my title! Even my own son!"

Her words attracted the most attention I'd seen so far.

"Kiren?" One said.

"What happened to him?"

"Where is the young Alpha?"

"Like I already said, Kiren has given up his claim to the Alpha title! He is perfectly safe at Blood Moon with my parents, the Alpha and Luna. He will come home when we've. . .cleaned up around here." I eyed Anne.

"This doesn't end here!" She hissed. She looked around. "How can you stand there and do nothing?! I've been your Luna for years, some of you your whole lives! How can you stand here and let them treat me like this? Where does your loyalty lie?!" She screeched.

The young woman who'd yelled at me earlier stepped forward. "Our loyalty lies with our pack. You are no longer apart of our pack."

"You may have been our Luna, but you were a terrible one." The youngest girl added.

"My family is starving and dressed in rags while you and the Alpha lived a life of luxury here! You don't deserve to be Luna!" Another shouted.

"Yeah!"

"Yeah!"

"I agree!"

I smiled, crossing my arms. "Seems like the majority has spoken. Would you like someone to escort you to the border?"

"Bitch! I'll fucking kill you!" And lunged at me, obviously very weak from her recent banishment. I dodged easily, simply stepping to the side. She landed behind me, growling.

Another, more vicious growl drowned hers out.

I looked at Jasper, shocked at the power coming off him. He almost looked taller, in complete Alpha mode. Or maybe it was complete mate mode? I wasn't sure. The only thing I was sure of was Anne had fucked up bad, and I needed to get better control of my hormones.

"You will *not* attack my mate! If you had any chance of remaining in Silver Moon, which were slim to none to begin with, you just lost it! I will not tolerate people attacking my pack! Get out! **Now!**"

His target cowered back fear, showing her neck. Then she ran from the building sobbing. I took a few deep breaths when she was gone, reminding myself that I was here to do a job, and had no time to worry about that infuriating woman. So I turned around, facing the girls.

"My order still stands. Those who should be in school, go home. Trust me when I say you're families will be taken of. The rest of you, I want you to split up and go through every single room in the house. Anything that is expensive, or belonged to the previous Alpha and Luna, I want down here. Try not break anything, please."

The girls scurried off through the two doors on the left and right of the entrance. The younger ones shuffled past me, but the youngest stopped, regarding me with new interest.

"Do you promise to look after us?" She asked.

I nodded. "With all my heart. Things are going to change around here, starting with the care and treatment of pack members."

Her gaze fell on Marian. She nodded, smiling a small smile before leaving. I opened my mouth to speak to

Jasper, taken aback when his lips claimed mine out of nowhere. He kissed me fervently, stealing my breath.

"Are you alright? She didn't hurt you?" He asked when he finally released me.

"She didn't even touch me. You worry too much."

"That's part of my job, as your mate."

"You know as well as I do I could have kicked her ass."

"I know. But no fighting with the twins."

"That's what I have you for. To protect us." I smiled. He placed his large hand on my stomach, returning the smile.

"You are pregnant?"

I looked over my shoulder at Marian, who was staring at us with an odd expression.

"Yes. Twins." I confirmed.

"By the Goddess. . ."

"Is everything okay?"

" The twins of the Silver Moon." She said that as if I was supposed to know what she meant. When I raised my eyebrows, she continued. "It is an old story my father used to tell me at night. He spoke of a time when a new Alpha and Luna would rise, and they would bless the pack with twins, the twins of the Silver Moon. He said they would be special."

"All babies are special Marian."

"Not like these."

"Why?" Jasper asked before I could.

"Because their Mother was a hybrid." She peered at me as if trying to look into my soul. I gulped loudly, and for the first time in a while, the chest in my mind rattled. Could she see through me? Did she know what I was?

Jaspers laugh shook me out of my thoughts. "That's a fun story, but hybrids don't exist anymore."

Marian didn't reply, simply giving me one more hard look before her eyes moved away. I let out the breath I'd been holding. Something told me Marian knew more about hybrids than she was willing to speak about. I'd have to get her alone, ask her my questions.

"Come on. I want to get to the Hall for the meeting." I tugged on my mates hand.

"Alright. Hey, excuse me?" He called to a girl carrying a very large painting. She placed it down, scowling at it.

"Tracy. My name is Tracy."

"Tracy. Can you find a clean, empty room for Marian and her daughter please? And can you get her some clothes and anything they want to eat?"

"Of course. I'd be happy to." She smiled at the woman in the chair.

"Thank you Tracy. We will be back soon."

"Okie dokie!" She chirped. She seemed like such a happy individual, a stark contrast to the majority of the girls here. I gave her a genuine smile as I turned for the door. I had a feeling Tracy and I could become good friends.

After making sure Marian and Skye were on their way, we stepped outside, coming face to face with Ashwell. He looked displeased and disturbed; Probably due to the large group of homeless looking people behind him. My heart throbbed brokenly in my chest as my eyes raked over them. Men, women, children. . . wearing nothing but dirty, holey rags and severely malnourished.

"Is this everyone?" I asked him. My voice cracked a bit.

"Yes. I made sure."

"How many altogether?"

"Forty two." He half turned. "Sixteen children, thirteen women and thirteen men."

"Mates?"

He nodded. My stomach dropped into my shoes.

"Bring them to the Hall. We're meeting King there. They need to be there too."

"On it."

The chest in my mind rattled again; I was admittedly overwhelmed with emotions. I wasn't sure if my hormones were playing into it or not, or if I was simply just appalled at the situation here. Both, more than likely. Ashwell gave the orders, and everyone started dragging their feet in the other direction. Jasper and I followed silently, sharing a look.

Part of me wondered why there were so many families, and Marian was the odd one out. Did she have a mate, somewhere in the pack? Or had she lost him somehow? I resolved to ask her later, when she was feeling better. As we walked, I took the chance to really look around; Silver Moon was very different than my own pack, and not in a good way. The town we'd driven through was small, and I'd noticed some shops had boards in their windows, out of business. The land was also different. Further out to the East, I could see poor looking fields that were ripe for crops. However, they were desolate, barren, in desperate need for some care.

The grand houses blocking the view of the fields were another problem. They weren't as awe inspiring or as big as the packhouse itself, but they were the type of homes that should have been used for the high rank pack members like King and Ashwell. And when we turned off the street leading to our new home, I was once again struck by the complete poverty of Silver Moon. The homes here were in seriously poor condition; Lawns overgrown, weak attempts flowerbeds to add some amount of color, roofs that needed repairing. One house had a large hole in the side! My mind couldn't conjure how that must have happened, but I made a mental note to address it as soon as possible.

Honestly, the entirety of Silver Moon was a mess. This was not a place I would want to raise my children in. But Jasper was right; I was excited to grateful that we were in a position to be able to put things right, and help where help was needed.

"It's just ahead. Should I go get everyone organized?"

"Please." Jasper replied.

Ashwell left us walking behind the group of cast out pack members. Thankfully, we only had to continue a little way more to the end of the street where a large domed building sat; It would definitely hold everyone. The building was concrete, the domed roof glass. I guessed this building was also used for parties, events, or any type of extravagant thing Anne and Warrick planned. The inside was even more surprising. A stage was built at the far end of the room, with a wooden podium and speaker. The walls were painted a lovely green, giving a kind of nature feeling. The last bits of daylight shone in through the roof, casting shadows; It was actually really beautiful, and would have been, if not for the circumstances. The rest of the Hall was packed with people, looking around anxiously.

I located Ashwell and King, picking my way around bodies until I reached them.

"Is everyone here?" I asked.

"Yes."

"Good. Please join us on stage." I tried to sound authoritative, but if I was being honest, I was nervous as fuck. Addressing the whole pack was much different than just the people who lived and worked in the packhouse! Jasper squeezed my hand as I focused on not tripping up the steps, and then we stood, facing the pack. I gulped loudly for the second time that day.

Jasper cleared his throat. "Thank you all for coming on such short notice. We really appreciate it."

Silence.

"I guess you're all wondering why we've brought you here tonight, and where Alpha Warrick and his Luna are. Well, I won't beat around the bush with a big speech so here it is. When Alpha Warrick visited the Blood Moon pack, it was in regards to determining whether or not he was my biological Father. The answer to that is, yes. However, after conversing with your Alpha for a while, I saw him as unfit to continue in his role. As was my right, I challenged him for his title, and won."

A few gasps echoed to us at his words.

"Alpha Warrick is dead. Luna Anne has been banished from the pack for several, and varying degrees questionable behaviors and decisions she made. Young Kiren, my half-brother, has denounced his claim to his title. As such, we stand before you as your new Alpha and Luna."

CHAPTER 42
VIOLET

I bit my lip as nobody said a word to Jasper's end. The tension in the air was high and thick, I could feel it. Ashwell and King, standing to the left of us, were tensed, ready for any opposition.

And then. . .

I jumped as a deafening uproar took over the crowd. People clapped and cheered. Grown men had tears running down their faces, and women were clutching their children tightly. A sudden harsh feeling of pity took over me. These people had held no love for their former leaders, people who were supposed to be their role models and care takers. They were actually celebrating their demise. I wondered if Warrick knew, or cared, how little love his pack had had for him.

"The Goddess has not abandoned us after all!" A woman cried in the front.

"The Devil is dead!"

"Can they lead us? They are so young!"

"What will happen to us?"

"We are going to be a mockery!"

"Our pack will be targeted! This is bullshit!"

Seeking out the owners of the loudest voices, I eyed a group of men and women in the front. They were standing away from anyone else, as if in their own bubble. And they were all very nicely dressed, far better than any other pack member. Even better than me. These must be Warrick's friends.

"You have something to say?" I directed to them.

The man in front stepped forward. He had to be at least my Dad's age, but with werewolves, it was hard to tell. He had shoulder-length black hair, dark blue eyes, and a chiselled face that might have been handsome if he weren't wearing a scowl on it. When he spoke, his deep voice drowned out the cheerfulness, full of mockery and criticism.

"You cannot possibly expect us to accept you as our new Alpha and Luna! What are you, sixteen? Have you even shifted yet?" He laughed, his buddies joining in.

"We've both shifted." Jasper replied evenly. "Very impressively, I might add."

The man scoffed. "Am I the only one who thinks this is some big joke?"

"Not at all." A woman in a red silk dress stepped forward. "My mate is right, this is ridiculous! We will not let children fill the roles us adults rightly deserve. We are far better suited in any case."

I placed my hands on my hips. "I suppose you mean yourself then, eh? News flash; If *anyone* other than us had the right to these titles, it would be Beta King and Gamma Ashwell, and their mates and families. Not any of you."

"You see how she speaks to me? Such a child!" Her voice carried over the crowd.

"Oh, I'm so sorry. I didn't realize you were a *ranked* member ma'am. What is your rank, again?" I asked.

"I was the Lunas dear friend." She said proudly.

"Oh, well. In that case. . . shut it!"

The woman gaped at me, her mouth hanging open. I held my head high. "Oh, yes we've heard about you." I waved my hand at them. "The group of Warrick's friends that he was so damn proud of. Tell me, where is your pride when you sleep in your great houses with real beds, and wear fancy clothes, while the rest of your pack if suffering? Where are your hearts when you see children completely malnourished from lack of food, while you go home or go to the packhouse and dine on fine foods? Don't bother answering, because I can tell you, you have no hearts! Any of you!"

"How dare you-"

"Tell the truth?" Jasper cut in. "Have you looked around lately? While you live in wealth, your own Beta and

Gamma are struggling daily. The people who protect you are living under you."

"That was Warrick's decision!" Another woman called.

"And that matters? I'm warning you, you had best prepare yourselves. Changes are coming, starting tonight." He turned back to the crowd. "Starting tonight, I want each and every family to go home and take a detailed inventory on everything they need. Whether that be home repairs, clothing, food, I don't care. Beta King, Gamma Ashwell, and myself will make rounds tomorrow to collect as many as possible. Once we've received everything, we will start the work. A fair warning though, this will take time! As for jobs, finances, and the like, I leave that in the capable hands of my Luna, Violet."

I blinked, taken aback. I hadn't expected that, but warmth flooded through my veins. Jasper winked at me, making me blush.

"Yes." I said. "Please don't hesitate to come to me."

"And one more important announcement before we leave you." Jasper met the eyes of many people, his face serious. "From this moment on, I am terminating the practice of training children against their wills, and sending them into the field. From this moment on, every child in Silver Moon will have the *choice* to train, until the required age. From this moment on, the children of Silver Moon are no longer to be used as pawns!"

Another deafening cheer roared from the pack. Many dropped to their knees, sobbing and hugging their loved ones. Children stared at Jasper like he was the Goddess herself, coming to save them from Hell on Earth. Right then, I loved my mate more than words could describe, and I knew our children would look up to him just as much as these children did.

"You would risk our warriors like this?!" The black haired man from earlier ranted.

Jasper turned steely, cold eyes on him. "*This* matter is not up for negotiation. Real warriors don't need to use kids as bait to win a fight."

The women in that group now looked more at ease. I saw several smiling down at their sons and daughters, giving them pats or squeezes. The men had no change however; Did they not care about their own children?

Jasper led me back across the stage and down the steps. Neither of us spoke to the unpleasant people, too caught up in others rushing us. I was pulled away by some men, who began bombarding me with questions and ideas for new jobs. Meanwhile, Jasper was discussing those in most need of home repairs and necessities. But I knew who really needed it most; Those like Marian. I was sure that would be his first focus.

"Luna Violet, the fields are still good for planting." An old man with a white beard pulled my attention to him.

"Yes, I noticed that too."

"We have no equipment though." Another said.

"If you make a list of everything you would need to start the fields back up, I will get started on it." I promised.

Their eyes lit up. "That would be amazing! I worked those fields most of my life. They were a reliable source of income for the pack once."

"Hmm. . . Perhaps you and I should discuss it more, in more detail. Can you come to packhouse tomorrow?"

"Sure!"

"Are you free for lunch? I will make us something while we talk."

"I will make the time for you Luna. Thank you so much." He gave me a toothy grin, him and his friends walking away with a little more bounce in their steps.

It took some time before we were able to make it out of the Hall. I promised everyone I would prioritize accordingly, and reminded them that the rebuild of Silver Moon would take time. They were nothing but grateful though, and seemed beyond happy at the sudden change in their fortunes. When the place was almost cleared, all those who were left were the outcast members. They too looked happier, but not nearly as much as everyone else I'd encountered. Cautiously, I approached them.

"If you could all follow us back to the packhouse, please?"

"Why?" A young girl asked.

I smiled. "Because that's where you're all going to be staying. For now, at least, until we can get you into homes of your own."

"W-what?" A man gasped.

"Of course." A hint of confusion laced my tone. "You didn't think we were going to help everyone but you, did you?"

They all looked at each other, wariness and hope in their faces.

"Uhm. . ." I cleared my throat, "Is there a reason you guys were living. . . well. . . kind of outside the main pack?"

"We were placed there by Luna. . . I mean, by Anne." A man frowned. "We used to work in the packhouse."

"I'm confused."

"Alpha Warrick had. . . a preferable taste in those who worked in his home." His mate, I assumed, spoke up. "None of us fit that profile, and their were no other jobs. When we couldn't afford our taxes anymore, Anne said we were no better than rogues. So she had us moved instead."

I clamped my lips together. Hearing more of Annes disgusting choices had me wanting to lash out, and I didn't want to aim my anger at the wrong people, the victims of her. Instead, I took a deep breath through my nose, glaring at the ceiling.

"That woman is a monster." I mumbled. Louder, I said, "I won't have pack members living like that, ever. Please come back with us."

"You don't have to ask us twice!"

"Thank you Luna!"

I smiled. "I'm sure there are rooms available. I haven't been through the house. . ."

"Trust me, there are rooms. That old man has more room than he ever needed."

"It's settled then. We will discuss getting your old jobs back later, if you want them. If not, we will find jobs for all of you who can work."

The wariness vanished, hope shining through. Despite how weak they all looked, they made their way from the building at a quick pace, beyond relieved to be going somewhere with food and warmth. I didn't know whether to feel happy or sad about that.

"Beta King. Gamma Ashwell." I called.

"Yes Luna?" They both smiled at me, the first sincere smiles I'd received so far. They stood together with Jasper, talking quietly.

"I've been told there are more rooms in the packhouse than are needed. If you can, find some for you and your families tonight. Tomorrow. . ."

"Tomorrow?"

"You'll be handing out some eviction notices."

King raised his brows. "To whom, exactly?"

"I'll let you know tomorrow." I smirked.

The three of them gave me knowing looks. I had a plan forming, and it was sure to get messy. But I wasn't going to single out anyone for special treatment, especially those who opposed what was best for the pack as a whole. My stomach rumbled loudly, and then Jasper was at my side.

"Let's get you home. You need to eat something, and rest." He told me.

"Food does sound pretty good right now." I admitted.

We bid goodnight to King and Ashwell, holding hands as we exited the Hall. The meeting had taken longer than I thought; The sky was dark when we got outside, a few early stars peeking through the clouds. The wind was light, blowing my hair lazily around my shoulders. My mind though, felt like a beehive, with a bunch of questions and ideas. One question in particular made its way to the tip of my tongue.

"You think I'll be able to handle this Jasper?"

"Being a Luna?"

"All of it. I'm grateful you included me in the reformation process, but. . .I'm scared I'll mess it up." I admitted softly.

"I have all the faith in the world for you Vie. Honestly, I thought we would do all of this together, but I don't want to put too much physical strain on you. We can handle the bigger, heavier stuff, like repairing homes. But that's still nothing, not compared to what you're going to do. You're going to be giving so many people jobs. Giving them a purpose again."

I frowned. "Be that as it may, you are the Alpha."

"And an Alpha is nothing without his Luna." He grinned at me.

"By that logic, how do explain Anne and Warrick?"

"Easy." He shrugged. "They were both selfish, greedy people. She contributed to his bad choices, and made countless ones of her own. They brought down this pack together."

I snorted. "I guess, looking at from that perspective."

"You and I are not selfish, or greedy. I'm assuming everything sitting in the foyer right now is being sold?"

"That was the plan. I'm going to put whatever money comes from it back into the pack, where it needs to go."

Jasper pulled me close on the sidewalk, leaning down an a couple inches from my face.

"I guessed as much. You can do this Vie. *We* can, together. I know it's going to be a bumpy road, but there's nobody I'd rather have by my side through it. Stop doubting yourself."

I decided to admit my biggest worry. "And. . .my. . .issue?"

His eyes softened even more. He sighed. "You want to tell everyone?"

I bit my lip. "No. . .Not right now. But I don't want to keep secrets from the pack."

"I know. I don't either. But maybe right now isn't the best time."

I relaxed against him. "Agreed."

"I love you, you know."
"I love you too."
Our lips met for a brief, but fiery kiss.

CHAPTER 43
JASPER

The next day was overwhelming. Vie and I crashed in the first room we found, after I'd located the kitchen and whipped up some food for us. As much as I would have loved to extend our morning cuddles, I had a job to do. And that job consisted of first meeting with my new Beta and Gamma for my first official pack business.

"What is this?" I pointed to a spot on a map of Silver Moon territory that King had dug up. He'd had to add some rough sketches around the edges to update it, but it worked for now. He peered over my shoulder.

"That area is for training. Theres a building here," He pointed, "With all our equipment."

I drew a circle around the area with a red marker. "I'll be wanting to check that out. How would you both say the warriors are?"

"Honestly? They could use some work." Ashwell said.

"What's the training schedule like?"

"Er. . . Well, there isn't really a *schedule*. . ." He rubbed the back of his neck. "Except for the kids, you know? Everyone else trains, kind of when they want?"

I rolled my eyes. "Okay, well that stops soon. I won't make a solid schedule yet, with everything else going on. But I'll draw one up. That'll be your area." I nodded at him.

"That works for me." Ashwell nodded.

"Excuse me Alpha?" Tracy appeared at the door, smiling brightly. "Another stack for you."

"Great. Thanks Tracy, just put them beside the others."

We were in Warrick's old office. The room had been full of things that I'd already sent down to be added to the 'To Be Sold' pile. After a thorough once over, all that remained was the desk with the two bookshelves, a few books, a lamp, and four comfortable chairs. I had no use for any sentimental items of his. Though King did suggest I keep a few of the books, pointing out which ones Kiren liked to read. And he was welcome to them, whenever he came home.

"The pack sure is making this easy on us." King picked up the new stack of papers.

"I'll say."

Instead of making rounds as I had promised, people had taken it upon themselves to instead bring their lists right to the packhouse. Clearly, everyone was eager for a change.

King whistled as his eyes scanned a page. "Damn. I had no idea the Roy's place was in such bad shape." He frowned.

"Let me see." I held my hand out for the parchment.

Roof collapsed in bathroom
Roof collapsed in kitchen- Appliances no longer work
Shingles torn off in storms
Floors rotted
In need of new clothes-Women's, kids female, men
In need of food

The list actually wasn't all that different from many others I'd read so far.

"How are we going to pay for all this? The amount of materials we'll need don't come cheap." Ashwell said.

"Violet is working on selling stuff from the house."

"That won't cover everything."

My frowned deepened. "I know." I sighed. "And the income we'll accumulate from farming again won't happen for a while either."

I sank into the chair behind the desk, rubbing my forehead. I'd been Alpha less than a week, and I already felt the stress of the job. I was running out of options. I couldn't just conger enough funds out of thin air. Sighing heavily, I reached for the phone.

"Who you calling?" Ashwell asked.

"The Alpha of Blood Moon." I dialed the number I'd memorized and put the phone to my ear.

"Hello?"

313

"Hey Dimitri."

"Jasper?"

"Yeah."

"How are you? How are things over there?"

I laughed once. "It's. . . Well, it's been interesting so far."

"How is Violet?"

"She's good."

"Good to hear. What can I do for you?"

"Uhm. . . Actually, I was calling for some advice."

"Oh?"

I lowered my head, embarrassed. "Yeah. Silver Moon is in worse shape than we thought. Almost everyone needs some type of repair on their homes, and nobody has enough food, except Warrick's buddies. We're working on that though."

"Go on."

"I. . . I just wanted to ask you how I should go about this. Where I should start, how I should organize." I flipped through the papers on the desk. "I really hate to admit it, but I'm pretty in over my head here, and-"

"Jasper, calm down son. I get it."

I swallowed. "You do?"

"Of course I do. Do you know how much help I had when I took over as Alpha? Violets Uncle Killian was a lifesaver. You sound embarrassed to be calling me, but you don't need to be. I told you I was here for you guys, when ever."

"I know. But I've been here all of one day." I sighed again.

Dimitri laughed into the receiver. "You're already doing better than me then. I reached out to Killian about two hours after my ceremony."

I chuckled. "I guess I'm ahead of the curve then. I just figured I'd know this stuff."

"I'll let you in on a little secret- No Alpha ever knows what he's doing, not at first. Hell, there are days I still get overwhelmed."

"Thanks Dimitri. That helps, actually."

"No problem. So what exactly is going on?"

I filled him in on everything since we arrived. He listened carefully, and I caught the distinct sound of a pen scraping across paper as I talked.

"Hmm. . . I'll tell you what," He said when I was finished, "There's not a lot going on here right now. Ben and I can come to Silver Moon for a while, help out. We can discuss further when I'm there."

I wanted to say no, that I could handle it without him. But really, who was I kidding?

"You sure?"

"Yes. We can be there by this afternoon."

"Alright. Thank you Dimitri."

"Anytime. I want you to know Jasper, that an Alpha who tries to everything by himself, is an Alpha who will ultimately fail. Nobody can do it all by themselves."

"Thanks Dimitri. I'll remember that. See you soon."

"Bye."

We hung up. Ashwell and King looked at me expectantly, having heard the conversation.

"Guess we better get some rooms cleared out." I said.

"He's right you know." Ashwell nodded at me. "Nobody can do this alone. You're not weak for reaching out for help."

"It's not like we can't use all the help we can get." King added.

"Thanks guys." I smiled at them. "Can you see to the rooms being prepared? I'll find Vie and let her know about our coming guests."

"Sure."

"No problem."

We left the office, going our separate ways. I found Tracy, who was humming cheerily to herself, and asked her to show me where Violet was. She agreed happily, skipping ahead of me. I shook my head; The girl had to have an extremely positive outlook on things, given the circumstances. Her home had been falling apart for

Goddess knew how long, yet she walked around with a smile on her face. I couldn't deny I admired that about her though.

She led me to a small room on the far side of the house where Violet was having lunch with an older pack member. She beamed up at me, dimples popping out.

"Another stack of lists should be coming soon. I'll put them on your desk Alpha."

"Thanks Tracy."

She danced away as I opened the door. Violet and her companion looked up at my entrance.

"Hey. What are you doing here?"

"I came to find you." I stood behind a chair. "May I join you?"

"Of course Alpha." The man replied.

I took a seat. The table was laid with finger sandwiches, a salad, juice, water, and vegetables. Also, a neater pile of papers in front of Violet than what I had upstairs.

"We're expecting guests this afternoon." I told her.

"Who?"

"Your Dad actually. And Beta Ben." I grabbed a sandwich.

Vie raised her eyebrows. "You called him?"

I nodded. "Originally, for advice. He offered to come."

"Alright." She gestured to the older man. "Jasper, this is Greg. He's my go-to guy for all things farming related."

We shook hands as he chuckled. "I'm just experienced dear."

"That's what I said."

"So the fields are useable?" I asked.

"Oh, yes. Not just the fields though." Greg said.

"I was going to find you soon. We've been discussing sources of income for the pack." Vie handed me a sheet. I looked it over.

"Fruit?" I looked at them.

Greg nodded. "The South of the pack. There is a great deal of apple trees."

"Opening a factory in the future would not only create a lot of jobs, but a great source of income for the pack." Vie smiled.

"A factory for. . .?" I inquired.

"That can be decided at a later date. I guess it depends on the skills of the people. You can make all sorts of things with apples."

"How did you plan to outsource it?"

"I was thinking of reaching out to human communities, as well as neighboring packs."

I raised a brow. "You want to sell to humans?"

"Why not?" She countered.

"I think that's a really great idea." I grinned at her. "Not a lot of packs sell to humans. Not a lot of competition. It's smart."

She returned my smile. "That was my thought process too."

"I think you two will do great things for Silver Moon." Greg said. "I'm glad an old fart like me is around to see it."

"Oh Greg. You're not that old!" Violet exclaimed.

"Keep saying that Luna, and I might come to believe it." He wiped his hands on a napkin, standing. "I should be off. You have the list?"

"Right here." Vie waved a paper.

"Great. Call me if you need me. Alpha." He nodded respectfully to me.

"Thank you Greg. I hope to see you soon." I said.

"Oh, you will. I plan to utilize his knowledge greatly." Vie said.

Once we were alone, I took the time to look over everything she'd done so far. I could feel her eyes on me as she ate, and I clicked my tongue.

"Staring is rude." I teased.

"Something is bothering you." She stated. "Tell me."

I set aside her work, meeting her eyes. "I'm a little embarrassed I had to call your Dad for help."

"You shouldn't be embarrassed about that."

"So he told me."

317

"Then listen to him. Dad didn't get to be where he is all alone."

I smirked. "You sound just like him, you know."

She grimaced. "Ugh."

I laughed. "Honestly, I don't even know where to start. This pack. . ."

"Is a mess. I know."

We were silent for a while. Violet picked at her food while I was lost in my own thoughts.

"I was thinking. . ." She pulled my attention back to her.

"Yeah?"

She looked at the door before continuing. She lowered her voice, "I was thinking that maybe I could help. With my. . .magic."

"My forehead creased. "How so?"

"I'm not sure. But like Aunt Clara said, I can't leave it locked away forever. I'm going to have to learn to use it sometime." She glanced up at me through her lashes. "Unless you think it's too dangerous. The last thing I want to do is hurt the pack more."

I thought about it. "I trust you. And I trust that you wouldn't do anything that would damage anyone or anything. If the time comes, you don't need my permission."

"I'm not asking permission." She flicked a cucumber from her salad at me. I popped it in my mouth. "But I wanted to let you know. In case. . . I can't control it."

"I'll be there to help you. I promise."

"Okay."

She relaxed in her chair. I stood, walking around to kiss the top of her head.

"I love you."

"I love you too." She grabbed another paper, sighing. "Here. This is a list of names of the people who work here. I want to give the jobs back to the people Warrick got rid of, but that means losing some of the blondes." She huffed.

"They should know we can't keep all of them." I said taking it from her.

"I feel like more people are going to yell at me."

For the next hour and a half, we worked on the list, agreeing together on who to keep and who to lose. Both of us agreed on keeping Tracy, if she wanted to stay. Likewise, neither of us were keen on keeping Stacey. The girl creeped me out.

"What about Marian?" I asked.

"I talked to one of the families earlier, they use to work in the kitchen." She pointed to two names. "They said Marian never worked in the packhouse. They weren't even sure how she ended up out there with them."

"I see." I circled Marians name, opting to decide about her later. Ultimately, it was her choice if she wanted a job here or not. "I'm demolishing those shacks."

"Good. They never needed to be there anyway."

"What needed to be where?" A voice came from behind us.

"Uncle Ben!" Violet jumped out of her seat, running around the table and launching herself into his arms.

"Hey kiddo!"

Ben stood in the doorway with Dimitri, and Tracy who for once looked rather intimidated.

"Do I get a hello?" Dimitri asked his daughter.

"Hi Dad."

He pouted, shaking his head. I made my way to them.

"Thanks for coming." I said as we shook hands.

"Where can we talk?" He got straight to business.

"I've been using Warrick's office. This way. Thanks Tracy, I got it from here."

She nodded, leaving us. Wrapping my arm around Vies shoulder, I led the way back to the office. The three of them looked around as we walked, until Ben snorted loudly.

"Why is there so much junk in here?"

"And her mate had. . .unique tastes." Violet explained.

"We're gathering everything that can be sold." I added.

Ben stopped in front of a painting, eyeing it for a minute. Then he lifted it off the wall and tucked it under his arm. Violet shook her head, while her Dad rolled his eyes.

319

"What? It's an original piece! Clara will love it!"

"You're paying us for that, you know." Vie threw over her shoulder.

"Seriously? I'm family."

"Which is why I'll give it to you at a lower price."

"Pfft. Fine."

Stopping at the door, I let Dimitri and Ben go in first. Violet sank into a chair, crossing her legs, while I took the seat behind the desk.

"Alright. Let's see what we're working with." Dimitri said. I handed him a few lists. He paced as he read them, handing them to Ben when he was done. "I'll be honest Jasper, I thought you were exaggerating. This. . ." He growled. "How could Warrick have let all this happen?"

"It's not all bad, Dad." Violet spoke up. "You should see his friends houses." She scoffed.

"Oh, I did." He looked at me. "What's the plan for that?"

"I'm leaving that up to Violet."

"Vie?"

She put her hands behind her head. "I plan to evict them."

Dimitri raised his brows. "And then?"

"All but two will be demolished. The two closest to packhouse will be remodeled into safe houses during attacks or emergencies."

Pride radiated from the Alpha. "That's my girl." He turned back to me. "There's a lot we need to talk about. The most important thing though, will require your Beta and Gamma to be here."

I sat up in my seat. "What's that?"

"An alliance. I'll need their signatures as well as yours."

CHAPTER 44
JASPER

"You want to make an official alliance with me?"

"It would have happened sooner or later. And this way, other packs in the area will know who you're friends with."

"I guess that couldn't hurt," I sighed.

"You don't seem thrilled about it." Ben commented.

I shrugged, a humorless laugh escaping me. "It sounds immature, I know. I just wanted to do this right. And myself. I talked so much about what I would do for this pack. . . and the first day I call my father-in-law for help." I laughed again, shaking my head. Violet walked over to me, taking my hand.

"You really need to let that go Jasper. I'm proud of you for reaching out to my Dad. This pack needs *a lot* of work. There's no way we could do it all by ourselves! Besides, how is this any different than being the son of an Alpha? Garrett has gone through years of training for when he takes the position. You stepped into this role, not only not knowing who you really were, but with no previous training." She squeezed my hand tightly. "And in one day, you've already given these people so much hope for the future! Don't think that doesn't count for anything."

"She's right son." Dimitri smiled. "You've done amazing so far. Let's call this a speed bump that we'll go over together. Now, how about we get your Beta and Gamma?"

I nodded. "Alright."

I reached out in the mindlink for the first time. *"King, Ashwell?"*

"Alpha."

"Yes Alpha?"

"Can you come up to my. . .er, the office?"

"On our way."

I looked around, uncertain. "You know, I think I might convert this into a storage space or something. I'm not comfortable using this as *my* office."

"I felt the same way." Vie said.

"Anne had an office?"

"Most Lunas do." Dimitri explained. "I converted an old bedroom for your Mother."

"Annes was very. . . tacky. I doubt she ever sat in that chair; It was an antique, old as dirt. I sent most of the contents of that room to be sold already."

"We'll look around later, see what we can find in the way of a bedroom and offices." I smiled at her.

"Sounds good." She looked at her Dad. "How is everyone at home?"

"You haven't been gone that long Violet." He smirked. "They are fine. Your Mom wanted me to tell you to charge your phone though. I guess she tried to call last night. . ."

They started chatting and I tuned out a little. Yes, I'd have to do a full sweep of the packhouse. I had the strong idea that neither Violet or I wanted to stay in Warrick's old room. Goddess knew what I do with it though. The more I thought about it, the more I was straying from the idea of living in the packhouse altogether. There were too many bad memories here, if not for me, then definitely for everyone else. This place hadn't exactly been the beacon of hope and leadership it was meant to be. Suddenly, I missed my little cottage in the woods.

"Alpha?"

"Jasper?"

My head snapped up, seeing everyone staring at me with mixed expressions, including King and Ashwell.

"Uh, sorry. I was lost in thought."

"No worries." King stretched his hand out to Dimitri. "Nice to see you again Alpha Varlos."

"You as well. I'm correct in assuming that you two will continue as Beta and Gamma here then?"

"Yes sir."

"Excellent."

"Dimitri wants us to join in an alliance." I announced. Both men raised their eyebrows, but relief flooded into their eyes. "I think we should get started right away, yes?"

"Let's do it." Ashwell pulled one of the chairs to the desk and sat.

For the next half an hour, the six of us went over the details of our alliance. I followed along, listening intently. It wasn't that much different than school, learning about different alliances in other packs.

"So, now the tricky part." Dimitri frowned slightly. "Legally, if Blood Moon were to help you out-supply necessities, food, materials- we would need a form of payment. At the moment though, Silver Moon is low on income."

Violet told him about her plans for the fields, and the orchards, and the possible factory.

"All great ideas, but all of that will take time. I'm willing to help out now, of course, but I don't want any issues down the road. The last thing any of us needs is the Elders stepping in and making something out of nothing. Or other smaller packs thinking I'm willing to give hand-outs. You understand where I'm coming from Jasper?"

"I do." I leaned on the desk, thinking it over. "What if we split profits?"

"What did you have in mind?"

"You provide Silver Moon with what we need, and in return, we cut you in. We can provide food from the fields, income from the trades with the humans, and maybe even some jobs at the factory."

He thought about it for a minute before turning to Ben.

"I think that's a pretty good deal. Though Blood Moon isn't lacking in jobs. I can't see anyone traveling here to work."

"What if you owned the factory?" Violet mused aloud. "Half the profit would then go to Blood Moon, but you would be in charge of paying the employees. We would have the factory here, in Silver Moon for easy access to

323

them. People could earn a living again, and you still get back what you put in?"

"I think that's a fair deal. Jasper?"

"I like it. But in that case, I'd like to lower your profit from whatever the factory sells."

"Fair. Everyone on board?"

Resounding yes's around the room. I took a deep breath and went for my next course of action.

"I'd like to talk about the warriors."

Dimitri raised an eyebrow at me.

"What about them?"

"I've been told they lack in training. I would like your permission to hire a few of your warriors. I will provide them with shelter, food, all the accommodations. And it would only be temporary."

Dimitri leaned against the wall, stroking his chin. "As part of this alliance?"

"It doesn't have to be."

He looked at King. "What shape are your fighters in?"

"Honestly Alpha, they need work. Their techniques, as well as their attitudes. I thank the Goddess we haven't had any serious attacks lately. But now, with Warrick dead and Anne gone, I do have a fear that rogues or even bigger packs will try to take us out."

"And you won't be able to defend yourselves properly." Dimitri nodded before turning back to me. "I will agree to this as your family. I want my daughter and my grandbabies to be safe. Go make some calls." He said to Ben, who nodded and left.

"Where are we going to put them?" King asked.

Violet smiled. "Haven't you handed out those eviction notices yet?"

"Not yet."

"Well, let's go get on that, shall we?"

"Right now?"

"No time like the present King."

Knowing I shouldn't let her do this alone, I followed her out of the office and down the Hall. King met us outside a few minutes later, papers in hand.

"Alright. Let's go. Who's first?"

He checked the names quickly. "Kettler."

"House?"

"First one." He pointed and we headed that way.

I was a little surprised to see Dimitri with us, but maybe he was just coming along out of curiosity. Or perhaps, like me, he didn't want anyone threatening his daughter. Either way, I was glad he was behind us, as an ally.

The first house was literally a minute's walk from the packhouse. It had white brick walls, beautifully laid out gardens that looked well kept. A few rose bushes grew under the large windows in the front, and I could see a swing set in the backyard. The roof was well done, the gutters clean. As we walked up the narrow walkway, I noticed not one stone had a crack in it, not one weed peaking up. Warrick really took care of his friends.

Violet bypassed all of us, walking right up to the door and knocking loudly. A few seconds later, an elderly woman answered, her small eyes roaming around each of our faces.

"Yes?" Her voice was rough and hoarse.

"Hello ma'am. May we speak with Mr. Kettler please?" Violet smiled.

"Mr. and Mrs. Kettler said not to let you in. . .Luna." She bowed her head, tacking the title on at the end.

"I'm not asking to come in ma'am. I would appreciate it if they would come out though."

"I. . .I'm not sure. . ."

"I can always have the Beta escort them out?"

They stared at each other for a second before the woman nodded. I thought I saw a ghost of a smile on her face as she turned away, but maybe I imagined it. Her eyes glazed over as we waited. And then heavy footsteps sounded from inside the house.

"What nonsense is this?!" A man, Kettler I assumed, threw the door the rest of the way open, nearly knocking the old woman off her feet. Violet reached out to catch her, just in time. I recognized Kettler as the black haired man who had spoken in the Hall. "Bertha! How dare you disobey me and allow them here! I should have you whipped!"

The old woman, Bertha, whimpered, backing away from him. I snarled.

"She told us you said not to let us in. We didn't come in." Violet snapped at him.

"I don't want you on my property at all!" He replied sharply.

"Your property is on Silver Moon land. Which means it actually belongs to the Alpha and Luna." Dimitri spoke up. He'd edged closer to Violet.

"Who the fuck are you?" Kettler challenged. Dimitris aura swept around us, although it wasn't so intimidating for me anymore. Kettler, on the other hand, took a step back.

"Alpha Dimitri Varlos of Blood Moon. Perhaps you've heard of me? Oh," He continued as Kettler gulped, "And that happens to be my daughter you're yelling at."

"A-Alpha Varlos. . . Y-yes. I'm sorry, so sorry Alpha. Please, come inside and have a drink."

"No, thank you." He declined.

"We're here on other business." Violet said.

Kettler focused on her again. "Such as?" His tone was neutral, but even I could tell he was trying very hard to remain polite.

"King?" She held out her hand and King gave her the paper. She gave it to Kettler. "This is what we're here for."

He scanned it, his face becoming a shade redder. "What is this?" He demanded.

"An eviction notice. We're giving you a month to get all of your belongings and relocate."

"Relocate?! To where?! This is my home!" His face was definitely red now.

"He's going to hurt our mate!"

I started. Ehno hadn't talked to me in a while. I wasn't sure why, but I'd been too distracted to really give it much thought.

"He won't hurt her. And we're right here to protect her."

"He better watch it." He grumbled. *"I don't trust him."*

"I know. I don't either."

"The upper ranks have decided that your home could be put to better use. Like housing visiting warriors, or Alphas and their company. You will relocate to the main part of the pack, like everyone else." Violet explained calmly.

"The fuck I will! Who do you think you are, you little bitch?!"

Dimitri and I growled at the same time. Violet stepped away, obviously realizing she pushed him too far. Ashwell pulled her behind his back.

"You will *not* insult your Luna." I snarled.

"She is not my Luna!"

"Then you are not a part of this pack." Dimitri stepped forward. "Everyone must look up to the Luna and Alpha, as leaders, role models, and care takers. If you can't accept her, then. . ."

"Then I will come join your pack." Kettler crossed his arms defiantly, but Dimitri laughed.

"I don't want you in my pack."

"Then you are sentencing us to become rogues!" This time he shouted at me. I shrugged.

"I never banished you. You can choose to remain here, if you want. But Alpha Varlos is right- You need to accept that Warrick is gone, and we will not give you special treatment any longer."

"You are doing this out of spite!"

"I'm not. But I will not stand here all day and argue with you. You've been served the notice, and I expect you to follow through with it. Plans will be made for your new home by the end of the month."

The realization finally sunk in, and he sputtered over his words. Finally, he managed a coherent sentence. "You can't do this."

"I can, and I have. I'll give you a choice though; You can choose to remain here in the pack, without special treatment, or you and your family can leave and start over somewhere new. If you're that opposed to us as your Alpha and Luna."

"I asked about you." Violet spoke up. "I'm told your mate graduated with a business degree in a human university. And you yourself are one of the top doctors around here. Don't me wrong, your attitude sucks, but it would be a shame to lose either of you."

That shocked me. "You're a doctor?"

"Yes." He huffed. "I work under the pack doctor."

"How in the fuck. . ." I heard Dimitri mumble.

"Why should we stay?" He looked between me and Vie. "Warrick took care of us. You obviously don't want to."

"Warrick coddled you." I argued. "I'm sorry that I won't, but everyone in the pack deserves to be treated equally. If one person is struggling, everyone helps out. If one person is getting ahead, everyone will have their back. But I expect those achievements to be *earned*, not given."

"I'm working on a plan for the pack hospital." Violet stepped around Ashwell. "I just got the report this morning. When things get better around here, I would love to look into updating things over there. For your benefit, and for the packs. I could really use your help, Kettler."

The offer seemed to shake him a bit. "You want to help the hospital?"

"Of course I do."

"Why would you do that? Warrick said things are fine, he never gave any money."

"You need to understand that we aren't your previous leaders. We want to help you." I stated. Violet nodded.

He leaned against the doorway, running his hands through his hair. Finally, after many tense minutes had passed, he looked at us again. "We'll stay. But I'm not happy about 'relocating'."

"I don't think anyone who lives on this street will be." Violet smirked.

"You're evicting everyone?"

"Like I said," I walked to stand beside my mate, "Everyone is equal."

CHAPTER 45
VIOLET

"How the hell is that guy a Doctor?" Dimitri asked. We were making our way to the next house, all visibly relieved things had sort of worked out.

"He also went to school in the human world. He graduated at the top of his class. When he came back to Silver Moon, he had to adjust a little to treating non-humans, but he is good at what he does." King answered.

"His bed manner isn't as good as his skills." Ashwell added.

"That, I can believe." Dimitri chuckled.

This time, I let Jasper take the lead in the eviction process. The whole ordeal with Kettler stressed me out. And I really wasn't keen on doing it again. As it was, the next people didn't put up as much of a fight, but it was clear they weren't thrilled about their impending move. It took us two hours to get the job done, and by the end of it, I was whipped. These were some colorful people, with some colorful choice of words.

"That was rough." I yawned.

"Thank Goddess it's done." Jasper agreed. "Are you hungry?"

"I could eat."

"I saw some chicken in one of the fridges."

"Could you make it for me? I really want to lie down."

"Of course." Jasper kissed the top of my head and I smiled. When we got back to the packhouse, the guys headed to the kitchen, presumably to further discuss the future of the pack. I steered myself towards bedroom we'd stayed in last night, collapsing on the bed. To be truthful, I really didn't like this room. The walls were an ugly, dark purple color, with weird black flowery designs. It felt kind of gothic, and dark. Not that I had anything against Goths, but it wasn't my style. However, it had a bed, and that's all I cared about right now.

"Only a few weeks in, and you two are already draining me." I patted my stomach.

"They can hear you."

I shot up so fast, I got a little dizzy. Marian stood just inside the room, looking around sadly. I hadn't even heard her come in.

"Hello Marian. Do you mean the babies?" I asked.

She nodded. "They hear their Mothers voice first. It soothes them."

"I guess that makes sense."

I really looked at her, noting how much better she looked already. She was still far too thin, but she was clean, free of dirt and rags, and in clean clothes. "How are you feeling? Are you and Skye settling in well?"

"It pains me to be back here." She said softly.

I bit my lip, unsure if I should ask. But I did anyways. "Why?"

"It reminds me of him."

"Him?"

"The old Alpha."

Our eyes met. Different scenarios started running through my head of why she would be upset about Warrick. Given his reputation with women, I guessed it was nothing positive.

"Did you use to work here?"

"No."

"Oh."

I already knew that, but I thought maybe with her quiet nature, the other former employees maybe just hadn't noticed her. Wishful thinking, on my part. Marian walked to the bed, sitting next to me. Her hands were crossed in her lap, her hair partially covering her face.

"Can I trust you?" She whispered.

"Of course you can Marian. I'm your Luna."

She shook her head. "Can I trust you. . . as a friend? Not just a Luna?"

Gently, I placed my hand on her shoulder. "Yes."

When she lifted her face to mine, there were unshed tears in her eyes. "Then I would like to tell you my story."

I didn't think saying no was really an option. I could tell she had thought hard about this decision, and I was ready to listen if she was willing to talk. I nodded, pulling my feet up under me. Marian nodded, taking a deep, shaky breath. Then she began to talk.

"I was not born in Silver Moon. I actually come from a pack far from here. When I was sixteen, we were attacked. Few made it out alive. We regrouped at a safe place, but the damage was done. My pack was destroyed."

She sniffled, remembering her past loved ones.

"Some stayed together, and moved to different packs. I chose to go a separate way, and I was on my own for a while. I didn't want to start over near the place my family had died. I went across the mountains, stayed in a few human cities for a while. But I started to miss the pack life, the feeling of being in that sort of community. I ended up coming out this way. I knew there were a few packs here." She looked at me. "I was headed for Blood Moon. A big pack, lots of security. A place I knew I would feel safe."

"You didn't make it." I said. Obviously, as she was here.

"I didn't. I was outside the border of Silver Moon when patrol spotted me. They thought I was a rogue. Soon, I was surrounded by wolves and men. I begged them to listen to me, I told them I wasn't a rogue. Although I guess I technically was." She shrugged. "They brought me here, to. . . him." She clasped her hands tighter in her lap. "I told him my story. I told him where I was headed. He offered me sanctuary in Silver Moon, but I was reluctant. It was nice, back then, but my hopes were pinned on Blood Moon. At first I declined, but the Alpha insisted. Eventually. . . I agreed."

"I told myself it was only temporary. I would rest here for a few weeks, recoup, and then be on my way. I wasn't an official pack member after all. The Alpha let me stay here, in the packhouse."

She stopped talking, seeming reluctant to continue. I waited, letting her gather her thoughts.

"One night," She continued in a hushed tone, "The Alpha came to see me. I was surprised, it was late. He asked if he could come in, and I even though I was unsure, I didn't want to be rude. So I invited him into my room. He asked how I was liking the pack, if I was doing alright here. I told him I still wanted to try Blood Moon, but I thanked his for taking me in in the meantime." Her bottom lip started to quiver. "He became angry. He asked me why his pack wasn't as good as Blood Moon, why I wanted to leave. He said all packs should have pretty young girls, and Blood Moon already had far too many. I didn't know what to say, so I told him I was tired, and asked him to leave. That only made him angrier. . . he. . . he grabbed me. Threw me on the bed. I was scared, confused. I didn't know what he was going to do. Not until. . . until he. . . ripped my nightgown off. . ."

Her unshed tears began to fall silently down her cheeks. Her breathing accelerated, a sob breaking from her lips.

"Marian it's okay. You don't need to tell me anymore." I soothed her. She laid her head on my shoulder, crying desperately. In that moment, I wished more than anything that Warrick had gone straight to Hell and was suffering the pain of a thousand deaths over and over. He deserved far worse.

"I-I do. Need t-to tell y-you." She sobbed. "S-Skye. . ."

My stomach dropped while bile rose in my throat. It was an uncomfortable sensation.

"Skye is Wa-His daughter, isn't she?" I asked her.

"Yes! A-Anne never knew! B-but he did."

"Is that why you were out there? Where we found you?"

She nodded. "He didn't want her to know." She whispered.

I wrapped my arm around her, hugging her tightly. "I am so sorry for what happened to you Marian." I wiped away a stray tear, not wanting to upset her more. "But he's gone now, forever. He can never hurt you again. And I would never let anyone hurt you either."

"I need to ask you something."

"Anything."

"I. . . I want to leave. I want to take my baby, and I want to leave."

My heart lurched but I nodded. I understood why she was asking me this. "I will talk to my Dad. You can leave with him, or he can have someone take you and Skye to Blood Moon. I won't tell him everything, though, okay?"

Marian hugged me even tighter. "Thank you! Thank you Luna!"

We sat like that until Jasper found me. He had a steaming chicken sandwich and some chips on a plate. His face grew worried and confused when he walked in, and he cleared his throat.

"Er, sorry. I'll leave this here." He set the plate on the bed next to me.

"No, I'm sorry Alpha. I should go." Marian stood, wiping her face.

"Are you sure?" I asked.

"I left Skye in our room. She should be waking up soon from her nap."

"Alright. Come find me if you need me." I pulled her down for a hug once more, and then she was gone.

"Is she okay?" Jasper took her place on the bed next to me.

"She will be." I grabbed my food, utterly starving.

"Anything I can do to help?"

"Yes, actually." I took a big bite, chewed, and swallowed. "You can release her from the pack, so she can go home with my Dad."

He searched my eyes briefly. Whatever he saw only made him nod and not ask anymore questions. Perhaps he guessed, or maybe he just trusted me that much. As long he was willing to do it, I didn't care. We were quiet for a while, each lost in our own thoughts.

"I don't want to live here." Jasper suddenly spoke.

I took in the room again. "Me either."

"Not just here, in this room. I mean the packhouse. I feel like it holds too much negativity."

I winced, Marian's story still fresh in my mind. "Yeah, I think it does."

He laid back, placing his hands behind his head. "I was thinking. My Dad has some connections in the human world. He could easily get us materials as a lower cost."

"You want to build a new packhouse?" I asked surprised.

"Yeah, I do. I think. . . I think it would be good. For us, for the pack. For the people who were here with Warrick, and suffered under him."

"A new start." I mused.

"Yeah." He propped himself on one elbow. "But we don't have to. I know there are tons of other, far important things to do right now. And it does sound selfish."

I looked at the door Marian had walked through. "No, I don't think it is. I think getting rid of this place would be good for a lot of people."

"Yeah?"

"Yeah."

"Alright. I'll call my Dad, see what he thinks. You sure you're okay?"

I nodded. "Just tired. I think I'm going to take a nap."

"Okay." Sitting back up, he pulled me in for a kiss. It wasn't exactly a peck on the lips, but I didn't mind. With everything else going on, I'd missed having these private moments with him. But it didn't feel right, right now. Not after knowing what I now knew about what had transpired behind these walls. I pulled back, giving him a soft smile.

"Wake me up in a little." I said.

"Will do." He left, closing the door behind him. And me? I finished my food, and curled up under the blankets, falling into an uneasy sleep.

CHAPTER 46
VIOLET

The next week went by with a slick tension in the air. I talked to Dad about Marian, and he'd agreed to get to Blood Moon as soon as possible. Within three hours, she was in the back of an SUV with a couple of his guys, thanking me tearfully, and profusely. I felt better seeing her leave the place that held memories of terror and horror for her. It was a kind of relief to know she would be safe from here on out. An even bigger relief to know the man responsible for her suffering was rotting.

Greg and I had drawn up several informed and detailed plans for the fields, and even a location for the future factory. We'd been informed that one field, at the South end of the pack, was now unusable due to heavy rain and flooding for so long. The area was big enough, and with some work, it would make the perfect spot. And it was easily accessible to the pack. We agreed to come back to the flooding issue when plans for construction were being made. Greg was gathering his old friends, their sons and daughters, and anyone else who wanted to work in the fields. Dad had special ordered all the machinery they would need; At this rate, they'd be back to work in a couple days.

The issue we were facing now was our ruling on the packhouse. After talking to the girls who worked here, and the pack members who used to work here, there wasn't a lot of positivity towards the place. The only one who seemed happy to be here still was Stacy, and I was starting to question her sanity. According to everyone else, the house was generally, and always had been, an unpleasant environment. Girls would be verbally and sometimes physically assaulted by Anne, while being harassed by Warrick when she wasn't around. A few of the girls had

had affairs with his 'friends', who were all mated men. Interestingly enough, Kettler wasn't one of them. Or at least, none of the girls had admitted to it. Either way, it made my outlook on him slightly brighter.

In fact, I was off to see him this morning for a follow up appointment about the twins. As much as I wished it was my Mom, I wasn't going to ask her to come all the way out here for one appointment.

"I'll come to the next one, I promise." Jasper was *still* apologizing.

"Jasper, I told you, it's fine. I know some women get worked up about this, but I'm not. As long as you're in the delivery room, that's all I care about."

"I know, you said. But I *want* to come. There's just so much I have to do today." He groaned.

"I know. And Dad is leaving today. You still have to officially sign the alliance contract, and then get down to the Masons place, and then over the Listowel's, and didn't you have another family?"

"The Piers. And after that, I have to go check on all the materials your Dad ordered for the rebuilds, sign off on them. . ."

I put my hand on his cheek. "It's a big job. I'm a little overwhelmed myself. But we'll fall into step soon. Like Dad and Uncle Ben said, usually an Alpha doesn't have this much chaos when he takes over. It's a unique situation."

"I keep telling myself that. We're making progress, little by little. I can't wait to see the end result. The new, and better Silver Moon."

"Me too. I have to go. I love you."

"I love you too. I want ultrasound pictures."

"I'll be sure to remind them."

We shared a kiss, and then I was out the door. As of right now, we were still in that horrid room downstairs, and I was always glad when I left it. I swung by the kitchen, grabbing a cream cheese bagel before I made my way out. King had instructed me earlier on the directions to the pack hospital, it wasn't far. However, it would be my first time

337

seeing it in person. It was the opposite direction from the Hall, perhaps I'd seen it when we'd first arrived and didn't notice. My mind wasn't focused on that though; I had a different agenda today, aside from the welfare of my babies.

"Two-twenty three. . ..two-twenty five. . ." I counted the address numbers as I walked until I was standing in front the hospital. I blinked, confused. This couldn't be it.

The building in front of me looked like any run down house on the street. Old red-brick, with vines growing carelessly and lazily up the sides and front. The lawn was slightly overgrown, and one window had a hole in the bottom corner, reminding me of the time I'd accidentally thrown a baseball through the window of our packhouse. The roof was in bad shape, desperately in need of repair, and the stone porch and steps were absurdly cracked and chipped. It was a wonder nobody had an injury just trying to walk up to the door.

Mindful of this, I tread carefully, knocking on a worn brown door that had the paint peeling away. Everything about the place was falling apart!

"Oh."

Looking up, I was face to face with Kettler. Today, his hair was tied back into a ponytail, and he wore the standard white coat of a Doctor. He also didn't look particularly happy to see me.

"I'm here for my appointment. . ." I said.

"Come on." He replied gruffly.

I stepped inside awkwardly, looking around. The inside wasn't much better than the outside; Faded yellow walls, a narrow hallway with a dirty rug, and some plants that gave an weak impression that someone was trying to keep the place up. I frowned.

"In here." Kettler stood beside an open door. I nodded as I passed him. The room seemed generally clean enough, but nowhere near where it should be. I took off my jacket, hanging on the back of the patient chair.

"I'll need to open a new file for you." He sat down at a desk, starting to click around on the computer there. "You can take a seat."

"Alright."

"I'll need your full name, birthday, rank. And I would appreciate a phone number to your old hospital so they can send me your medical history."

I gave him all the generic details about myself, noting that Ashwell had been correct in his assessment of Kettler attitude. The whole time he typed away on the keyboard, he never looked at me. Anytime he asked me something, it was quick, to the point, but not friendly.

"Anything I should know about your past? Any substantial injuries?"

"Uhm. . . I fell out of a tree when I was four?"

His lip twitched slightly. "How bad was the fall?"

"I broke my arm." I shrugged.

He entered the information, sliding his chair back. "We can begin now."

I tried very hard not to roll my eyes as I stood and walked around him to the bed. I laid down, placing my hands at my sides. Kettler stared at me, visibly hesitating.

"Is there a problem?" I asked.

"No." He snapped. I watched him walk to a small sink that was, like everything else here, rather unhygienic looking. Even after he'd put the gloves on, I wasn't sure how clean his hands really were. Wheeling the machine he needed out from the head of the bed, he finally looked me in the face. "Any idea how far along you are?"

"My Mom said a few weeks before we came here."

"Your Mom?"

"She's the head Doc at Blood Moon."

"Figures." He muttered. Louder he said, "So you don't know the genders yet?"

I shook my head.

"Alright. Can you lift your shirt, and place this towel down?" He hadn't me what was essentially a rag. With holes. I raised my eyebrows at him and he scoffed. "I know it's not as fancy as you're used to-"

"I'll pass on the towel." I interrupted him.

"Fine."

I lifted my shirt to reveal my abdomen and he applied the gel. It was ice-cold, making me jump a little. However, when he put the ultrasound wand on my stomach, I focused on my gut feeling, my instincts. Mom and Dad always told us to trust our instincts, especially when it came to people. And to trust our wolves.

"What do you think?" I asked Hala.

"I don't like him."

"Really?"

"His attitude sucks, and he's an asshole." She huffed. *"But I don't feel the need to rip his head off. Yet, anyways."*

"I get it. I'm not uncomfortable, not really."

"As long as his focus his on our pups."

"Ahem!"

Turning my head, Kettler was frowning deeply at me.

"What?"

"I asked you a question."

"Oh. I was talking to my wolf, sorry."

"Was it important?"

I shrugged. "She called you an asshole."

He paused. "Is that so?"

"Yup. What did you ask me?"

His lips pressed into a line. "I asked if you wanted to know the genders today."

"You can tell that?"

"Obviously, or I wouldn't be asking."

"Yes, please. But first I want to know how they look. Are they healthy?"

He looked back at the screen. "Appears so. Baby B is very active."

"Can. . .Can I see?"

He turned the monitor without answering. My mouth fell slack. They were so different! Last time I saw them, they were little dots, barely resembling anything. Now, I could make out limbs, heads, even a tiny little foot! Kettler pointed to the screen in two spots.

"These are the heartbeats. Both look good, normal."

The twin on the right started moving, appearing to be jumping around. I laughed, watching my babies play in the womb. How amazing they were already!

"The genders?"

He adjusted the wand on my skin. "Baby A. . . is a boy." He stated.

My heart flipped. I was having a boy.

"And Baby B. . ." He moved the wand to other side of my stomach. Adjusted it. And then again. "Stop moving little one. . ."

I was amazed to hear Kettler's voice so soft, almost kind when he said that. After a few minutes, he sighed.

"Try turning on your side. Sometimes that settles them down enough."

I did as he instructed.

"Ah. Baby B. . . is also a boy."

I gasped. Identical boys!

"Oh Goddess."

"Not what you wanted?"

I shook my head. "I don't care what they are, as long as they're healthy. Just. . .. boys. Wow. Mom said boys were easier than girls though."

"I wouldn't know, I only have girls."

"Can you print off a couple pictures for me? For Jasper?"

"Sure."

This time I took the towel to clean off the gel while he went through the stills he'd taken and printed some out. He handed them to me, leaning back while I looked them over, smiling widely.

"These are adorable. Thank you."

"We'll need to schedule another appointment, in two weeks."

"Okay."

He stood, but I called out to him. "Kettler, wait."

341

He half turned back. "I prefer *Dr.* Kettler in the hospital."

"Right, sure. I think we should talk."

"About?"

"The hospital." I said, as if it should be obvious.

He let out a breath. "I thought about what you said, about new equipment. It's a generous offer, but honestly, I'll have to decline. We don't have the room."

He sounded so defeated, so angry. Given the state of the place, I could understand why.

"That offer still stands." I said.

"Didn't you hear? We don't have the room."

"Well, not here, no."

He swung around, fully facing me. "What does that mean? You expect me store it somewhere else?"

"Yeah. Like at a new hospital." I crossed my arms.

He blinked slowly. Opened his mouth. Closed it. Finally, he shook his head, running his hand down his face.

"What am I supposed to say to that?"

"You're supposed to say yes."

"What are you even talking about? Are you saying. . .what? You want to move the hospital?"

"More like I want to build a new one."

He laughed. Hard, enough that he doubled over.

"You and that mate of yours. . ." He gasped. "Absolutely crazy!" Kettler straightened, a new glint in his eyes. Like someone who wanted to hope, but was too afraid to.

"What is so crazy about it? This place is obviously in no shape anymore for a medical practice. How rusted is that sink?" I jerked my chin towards it.

"Almost to the point of falling apart at the touch." He smirked. "The roof has holes that open into two of the rooms, so they are unusable. The Head Doctor barely comes in because the state of things here is so poor. The floors are garbage, the walls probably have mold behind them, and yesterday, I chased a rat out with a broom."

"If that's the case, then why are you so against the idea of a new building?" I asked curiously.

"Do you know how many times I talked to Warrick?" He sneered. "How many times I told him about the roof before it finally gave way? That we needed updated equipment, a new paint job, new computers? I begged him to do something. At one point I begged him to relocate us to a more suitable place." He took a step in my direction. "Nothing ever happened. I stayed loyal to that mutt for *years* on the promise that something would get done! And then he dies, and *you* walk in, wanting , not to relocate, but you *build* a new hospital."

"I don't see what's so unbelievable about that. My Dad-"

"That's right. Your Dad is going to pay for it." He sank into his chair, glaring at me. "And what's the plan for that huh? You know it has to be paid back. You know a cost like that will carry over well into your children's lives. Maybe even your grandchildren. You and your mate want to rebuild Silver Moon on someone else's dime. You think you're helping us, but you're only putting us into debt with a pack that could wipe us off the planet in an instant if we fail to repay!"

Pursing my lips, I thought his words over. It was understandable he would worry about that, and I wondered how many others thought the same. But they didn't know Blood Moon, didn't know my family. How could they know they didn't have anything to worry about if they'd never met them? Moreso, how could I address that issue with pack members, and reassure them? I supposed I'd have to try with Kettler first.

"My family wouldn't do that to you." I said.

"Yes, I'm sure the Heartless Alpha is just pining to help out a poor pack without any hidden agenda!"

"He isn't like that anymore." I argued calmly. "Not for a long time. Not since he accepted my Mom. He would never put so much into helping someone only to take it away like that. If a problem occurred, his first thought would be to find a solution, not to wipe out Silver Moon." I walked back to my seat, plopping down.

343

"I can only apologize for the way you were treated before. I can't change the past. But I can help you now, and in the future. This place. . . this isn't suitable for anyone. My Mom would definitely agree, being the Head Doctor at Blood Moon. And I know for a fact that she would murder my Dad if he ever even thought about taking a hospital away from a pack. And believe me, if you should fear anyone, it's her."

"Really?" He mocked.

"Ever heard of a Mother Wolf?" His eyes widened.

"Wait. . . So that's *true*? The Luna of Blood Moon really is a Mother Wolf?"

I smirked. "You can ask Anne if you don't believe me. I heard Mom shifted when she wouldn't leave after the challenge."

His eyes were now the size of dinner plates. "Are you. . .?"

"No. Though I am quite large. Or Hala is, rather."

I swear he exhaled in relief, and I chuckled. Then I leaned forward in my seat.

"We don't have to be enemies Kettler. *I* don't make empty promises. If you're willing to work with me, I really can help you."

He stared at me for a while. I never budged, showing him I was totally serious. Eventually, he made a decision.

"Alright." He agreed. "On one condition."

"Name it."

"I want the hospital to be top priority. You don't know. . . I've had to turn away so many pack members because I don't have the room to put them here. Elderly, and even some children."

I nodded. "I'll talk to Jasper. Later we can address the pack as a whole, but I agree with you."

I stood, grabbing my jacket. I turned back at the door, amused to see Kettler still looking kind of stunned. "I have a condition of my own." I said.

"What?"

"You work with me on this. I can tell you really care about what you do, and I need someone like that, with that dedication, to help me see it through."

Unbelievably, a slow smile spread across his face. "Deal."

I returned his smile, leaving the room.

"Violet?"

I paused with my hand on the doorknob of the front door, looking over my shoulder.

"Yes?"

". . ..Thank you."

"That's what a Luna is for."

CHAPTER 47
JASPER

"Vie, I have to focus on the homes."

We were outside, having a private picnic away from the packhouse. I'd set it up for Vie, knowing how much she hated eating the kitchen. I couldn't blame her. It should have been one of the biggest rooms in the house, but it was actually one of the smallest. Neither of us liked the room we were in either.

"I know, but this is important Jasper. Have you seen that place? It's disgusting! I don't want to give birth there." She took a bite of her sandwich. Chicken, as was her craving.

I sighed. "Even if I agreed, a whole new hospital wouldn't be ready by the time you give birth anyways."

"It would be, if we had available hands. I was thinking of asking Dad. . ."

"He's done a lot already."

"I know." She rested her chin on her knees. "But this is important. Blame it on me growing up around a Doctor Mom, but *this* should be the priority right now. Imagine if we got attacked? That building can only hold two patients, *maybe*. How would we be helping the pack then? We need this hospital!"

I let my head fall back, staring at the sky. I knew she was right. There was just much else to do!

"How do we tell people we're putting the rebuild on their homes off?"

"We just tell them. They'll understand." She sounded so confident in that answer.

"And you really want to work with Kettler on this?" I looked at her. "The guy who called you a bitch? The guy who yelled at you on his doorstep?"

"He's. . ..not a pleasant person." She admitted. "But he was better at the end. I feel that he really cares about his job."

"Remember you said that." I teased. "Alright. The hospital comes first."

Her eyes lit up. She crawled over the blanket, kissing me heartily. "You're the best mate in the world."

I grinned. "Remember that too, when Kettler gets on your nerves."

She laughed.

I focused, reaching out to the pack. As an Alpha, I could now mindlink everyone at once, helpful in emergencies.

"Attention Silver Moon." I felt tension rise within me, a reaction to everyone receiving the min-link. I thought about how to word the next part. *"Something has been brought to my attention, something that concerns everyone. Today I received a report on the condition of the pack hospital, and have concluded that it is not suitable for safely treating patients. I hope you all understand that the health of pack members is vital. As such, we have decided to not to re-locate, but to build a new hospital. Unfortunately, this means the rebuilding of houses will be put on temporary hold. As your Alpha and Luna, we apologize sincerely, but we must think of the most necessary improvements to make first."*

I cut off the link, hoping the news would be generally well received. Violet squeezed my hand.

"I'll call Mom when we get back. She has all sorts of contacts that can help us with equipment and stuff."

"Sounds good."

We spent another half hour outside, enjoying each others company. Of course, I was stressed about having to put plans on hold, but I didn't let that ruin my time with my mate. Besides, even if the population of Silver Moon was angry with me, I still had good reason to celebrate. Running my hands over Vies skin, I leaned down to kiss her stomach.

"I still can't believe it. Twin boys!" I exclaimed.

347

I'd jumped like a kid when she'd told me. Like her, I didn't really care about the genders, but now I couldn't stop thinking about them. Would they take after me, or Violet? I kind of hoped they would take more after her, except in attitude maybe. It would have been great to have a daddy's girl, but it's not like this was our only shot. If Vie wanted to, we could always have more kids.

"Little Jaspers." She giggled now. "I can't wait to meet them."

"Me too." I smiled softly at her. "You're going to be an amazing Mother."

Her cheeks coloured red. "And I know you'll be a great Dad."

"I really hope so." I could hear the doubt in my voice, something she picked up on. I felt her hand on my cheek, making me look at her.

"What's wrong?" She searched my face, and I knew I couldn't lie to her.

"Well. . . My Dad is great, you know? A great role model. But. . . he's not my Dad. And where I came from. . . who I came from. . ." I laughed bitterly. "I'm just scared."

"Listen to me." She got on her knees, eye level with me. She placed her hand on my shoulders firmly. "You are *not* that man. You are kind, caring, sweet, considerate. You care about others, not just yourself. You've done more for this pack since you've been here than he did in his lifetime. You saved them Jasper. You are not him."

"You really believe in me that much?" I whispered.

"Of course I do. I was wrong about you. And all the nay-sayers will see it too- You're a wonderful person, with a big heart. You're going to be a great Alpha, and a great Dad. You're already a great mate."

I pulled her in for a hug, kissing her forehead. "Thank you."

"Anytime."

We sat, embracing, until a noise sounded behind us. I peeked over my shoulder, seeing Tracy running towards us. Her face looked panicked.

"Alpha! Luna!" She hollered.

Violet pulled out of my arms. "Tracy? What's wrong?"

She came to a stop a few feet away, panting hard.

"You need. . . to come. . .. the pack. . . man, I need to start working out." She rasped.

I jumped to my feet. "What happened? What about the pack?" I demanded.

"They. . . everyone is outside the packhouse. You need to come back."

"Everyone?" Violet stood too.

"Mostly everyone, yeah."

Immediately, the three of us starting jogging back. As out of breath as she was, Tracy kept pace, her face worried. I was as well; I could only come up with the conclusion that people were angry about the temporary hold on home repairs. I tried to come up with ways to calm a potentially angry mob, but I was coming up blank. My only saving grace was hoping Dimitri was there to help me, and once again, I felt like an incompetent Alpha. However, when we reached the house, I didn't hear any protests or shouting.

"Did they say why they're here?" I asked Tracy.

She shook her head quickly. "They only demanded to see you."

We strode to the front lawn, but I kept the girls behind me, just in case. I looked over the crowd, peering at each face, gauging reactions. King and Ashwell stood on the bottom steps, waiting for us. Dimitri and Ben stood further back, at the doors.

"What is going on?" I asked when we reached them.

King clapped me on the shoulder. "Ask them." He nodded to the crowd.

"Okay?" I stepped down. "How can I help you?" I called out.

A woman stepped out of the throng of people. She had to be in her thirties, with a kind face that only got softer as she smiled at me.

"Is it true? What you said about the hospital?" She asked.

"Uh, yeah. Look, I'm sorry about that, but-"

"We don't want your apologies!" Someone shouted.

"We will get everything done, but it's going to take time." I tried again.

"We don't care!" A teenage boy stepped forward beside the woman. "We just want it done."

Violet took a place by my side, holding up her hands. "We're very sorry about the inconvenience, but a new, safer hospital takes precedence right now. The pack needs a place to treat people, and the current hospital just isn't good for that."

"Oh, we know dear." The woman laughed.

Violet blinked at her. "Uh, good."

"I don't think we're on the same page." She said. "We're not here to complain. We're here to help."

"Help?"

"We want to help build the hospital."

"What?" Violet and I spoke at the same time.

"My name is Patty." She introduced herself. "This here is my son. A year ago, he was injured by a rogue. Dr. Kettler did what he could for him, but it wasn't enough."

The boy lifted up his pant leg, revealing a prosthetic from the knee down. I gasped, shocked. Never had I seen a wolf that badly injured. We healed wicked fast.

"How. . .?" I couldn't help but ask.

"It shouldn't have happened." Patty shook her head. "It was only a cut, but it got infected. Bad. We didn't have the supplies or medicine we should have, and Nikkie had to get it amputated. He was lucky he didn't die from the surgery." She stroked his hair.

"I'm okay with it now though." Her son, Nikkie said. "I'm the only wolf in the pack with three legs." He grinned.

"And this," Patty pointed, "Is Tara, and her daughter, Yelena. She gave birth at home a few months ago, because the hospital was full."

"There was only one room." The girl said. She was a slim brunette, holding her daughter on her hip.

"We told the Alpha we needed a better hospital, but he didn't listen!" Someone called.

"He never listened!"

"We've lost good men because of his ignorance!"

"We want to help!"

"Let us help!"

I looked at everyone, committing their faces to memory. Men, women, teenagers, kids, even babies. They weren't angry. They weren't even upset. Not for the reason I thought they'd be. Instead, they'd gathered together in a cry for help, willing to do the work themselves. At the edge of the crowd, I saw Kettler, who was looking around as well. Judging by his expression, I guessed this was overwhelming him as much as it was me. I cleared my throat, holding up a hand to get everyone's attention.

"I am. . .awestruck. You know what I see right now?" I shouted. "I see a group of people, who choose to come together and offer to spend hours helping with something that will benefit everyone. I see selfless, amazing people, who have suffered, starved, and been neglected. You could have come here with complaints, but instead you're here, willing to work together for the betterment of your pack. And I am so proud to be standing here with you."

I reached down to take Vie's hand.

"Your Luna realized the importance of this project and came to me. She has agreed to work with Dr. Kettler to bring Silver Moon the hospital and health care it deserves."

Cheers went up in the crowd, and Violet looked down, blushing.

"Anybody who wants to work, can. Thank you, so much, for coming out today. Let us meet, and we will inform you with our plans."

More cheers, and excited chatter. I found Kettler again, motioning for him to join us. We headed inside, King and Ashwell right behind us.

"That went better than expected." Dimitri commented.

"The pack has been requesting updated healthcare for years." King said.

"We've lost too many and too many others have paid the price for Warrick's poor choices." Ashwell agreed.

"I treated that boy myself." Kettler spoke up. He was staring at the floor. "He never should have lost that leg. I was close to sending him to a human hospital, or going myself for medicine, but Warrick wouldn't allow it."

Violet touched his shoulder. "That will never happen again. At least he's alive."

He nodded, but he was still visibly upset. I wondered if that was the reason for his attitude, or of it was the situation itself. Either way, we had a starting point for the pack now.

"I want you to go make a list of everything you need. Materials, equipment, everything. Call your Mom too. King, I want you with me upstairs. I want to find the best and most accessible place to build."

"On it."

"Ashwell, I want you to do an updated population check on the pack. I need to know how many rooms we need. I also want a list of all the expecting mothers in the pack, and people with injuries."

"Yes, Alpha."

"What about us?" Ben asked.

"I don't really need you guys, unless you want to help with the construction."

"I need to make some calls actually. A hospital isn't cheap."

Kettler shuffled beside us. Violet glanced at him, wary.

"How much?" Kettler asked.

"In this case. . ..no charge."

His head snapped up. "What?"

"I said it wasn't cheap, not that I wouldn't do it. I want my grandbabies born in a safe place. I also want you to have everything you need so people get the treatment they deserve."

Kettler gaped at him. "W-why would you do that for us? We're not your pack."

Dimitri walked to him, placing a hand on his shoulder. "Maybe not. But my daughter is your Luna, and even if she wasn't, I would do this. Why should I stand back and let people suffer when I know I can help?"

Kettler's mouth flapped, resembling a fish. Violet giggled, nudging him. "Told you so." She said.

"You people are all nuts."

"Are you saying you don't want the help?"

"Help!" He scoffed. "I'm not one to look a gift horse in the mouth. Let's go start on that list. I really want that new computer, mine is crap. It keeps freezing, and the junk folder is crammed. . ." He pulled Violet away, talking animatedly. I had a feeling she was regretting asking him to help her right now.

"Thank you." I said to her Dad.

He waved me off. "Jasper, do you have any idea how much money I have?"

I shook my head. "Never thought about it."

"Too much. Building a hospital won't even make a dent. The alliance we have is only for legality reasons." He shoved his hands in his pockets. "I could build Blood Moon three times over, and still be well off."

"I guess you need a new name then. Can't say you're heartless after all."

"I vote for marshmallow." Ben said. I laughed.

"Try it, I dare you." Dimitri grumbled.

"We'll see what Lily thinks about it." Ben replied, uncaring. The Alpha groaned.

"There is something else I would like to discuss." I glanced at the door Vie had disappeared through.

"I changed my mind." Ben said. "You're more of a s'more. Hard on the outside, but soft in and gooey in the middle."

"Shut up Ben."

"Whatever S'more."

"What Jasper?" He turned away from his Beta.

"I was wondering if you could help me find a jewellery store?"

CHAPTER 48
JASPER

It had been exactly one month now since the construction on the hospital started. After Dimitri made some calls, and Luna Lily as well, I was extremely happy to be standing in front of a brand new building. It was definitely the most modern of anything in Silver Moon, but not for long. Construction on the homes had started a few days ago, and was going fast paced, but efficient. The pay-off of both projects was huge.

Everyday, more and more people would come to help, and so, new bonds were formed. Working side-by-side the people of my pack, I started to make friends. I even looked forward to waking up to a hard days work, using my bare hands to create something so necessary. Violet put in her share by setting up tents and distributing food and drinks, as well as making sure any and all deliveries were delivered, signed for, and stocked accordingly. Her right hand man was Kettler, of course, and I was shocked and amazed at how close they'd grown over the course of thirty days.

He was still rough around the edges, and it was safe to say his former friend group had abandoned him. But he was much kinder to those around him, even helping by taking heavy items from the elders, or helping setting up the tents for the day. Mostly, he helped Violet, making sure everything was the way it should be. The Head Doctor had formally put in his request to retire, making Kettler the new Head as well.

Another big, and very welcome, surprise was my parents and sister finally coming to Silver Moon. They'd expressed so much pleasure in what we were doing already, and Dad came everyday to help while Mom worked the tents when Vie wasn't around. Elena was perfectly content helping our

Mom, never once complaining. Kiren was due to arrive back home too, soon enough.

"Ladies and gentlemen." I took Violets hand, smiling hugely. "I am so pleased to announce to you that the pack hospital of Silver Moon is officially open!"

A deafening roar went up. People hugged, and many expecting mothers were in tears. Vie rubbed her now swelling belly, her own eyes misty.

"This is amazing." She said.

"I know." I pulled her to me. To the crowd, "The tents are set up over there. Food and drinks have been laid out. This is a great cause for celebration, so please, help yourselves and celebrate."

People started moving towards the designated area. Music was playing from a table inside, the tables making a wide horse shoe. The center was for mingling, as many were already doing, while others took the seats spaced around. Kettler jogged up to us on our way.

"I'm going to do one more full sweep." He said to Violet.

"Oh, Kettler. We've done five already, *and* we've been cleared through the proper channels to be open and running. Come on, eat something, talk to people."

"Not really mt thing, you know."

"Your mate and children are here." She pointed. "Just go pretend you're enjoying yourself then."

He smirked. "Perhaps, for a little while." He waved before taking off.

"I don't see any of Kettler's former acquaintances here." I noted, looking around.

"I'm not surprised. None of them helped with the build either. It seems some people just don't want to mature."

"It's a bit more than that." I smiled at Greg and his buddies as we passed. "I'm not sure what to do about them. I meant what I said about having each others backs; They don't look out for anybody but themselves."

Vie pulled me to a stop. "I get it. But maybe, for just right now, you can turn off being Alpha? Just come and enjoy this with me."

My eyes raked over her face, down to her chest and legs. She looked downright stunning. in a long flowy black dress, her stomach round at the middle. She wore minimal make-up for the event, but she didn't need it. She was glowing. Slowly, I ran my hand up her arm, over her shoulder and to her cheek.

"I am very tempted to enjoy you." I said lowly.

She bit her lip. "That's not what I said."

"It's what I'm thinking."

Lust sparked in her eyes. I leant down until our lips touched, taken aback by the force of her kiss. Sparks electrocuted between us, and I almost forgot we were surrounded by people.

"Ahem!"

We pulled apart, finding Dimitri standing next us. He looked awkward. Vie giggled.

"Dimitri." I nodded. "Enjoying the celebration?"

"Yes, thank you. I just came to tell you that we're leaving in a little while."

"Oh?"

"I've stayed longer than I expected, not that I minded helping. But it's time to home. Ben won't shut up about Clara, and I really can't listen to their phone calls anymore."

"Awe, Uncle Ben knows what phone sex is?" Violet asked calmly.

"Goddess Violet! No. . .Well, maybe. But I haven't been around for that. Just. . . Ugh, come give me a hug before I go."

I laughed as they embraced. I felt a little sad to see him go, but I was more able mentally now. I felt ready to take on this job without him now, he'd taught me a lot in the short time he'd been here. I held out my hand when Violet stepped back. Dimitri took it firmly, smiling.

"Thank you Dimitri. For everything. I'll make sure Silver Moon remembers what you did for them."

"I didn't do anything but throw some money away. You and Violet did it all son. You inspired hope in these people, gave them anew start. A few new buildings don't mean much compared to that."

"Come back when the babies are born." I said.

"Wouldn't miss it. We'll keep in touch."

"Bye Dad. Love you."

"Love you too kid."

"Tell Garrett I said hi, okay?"

"Will do."

Ben strode over to us. "C'mon s'more, the cars are packed."

"I told you to stop calling me that!"

"Never."

Dimitri rolled his eyes at his Beta. With one last wave, they sauntered out of the tents together.

"Do you want anything?" I asked my mate.

"Is there any chicken?"

I chuckled. "Of course there is. I made sure it was on the menu."

"Then you know what I want." She grinned.

"Be right back."

I made my way through the party, stopping briefly to talk to some people. When I reached the table with the meats, I started loading up a plate with chicken, mashed potatoes, peas and carrots, cheese and pickles. Violets appetite had grown considerably, and I knew I'd be filling another plate within the hour, even with this one piled so high.

"My, someone has an appetite."

The smooth feminine voice was at my ear. Head turning right, I found Stacy smiling up at me. Her blonde hair was done in loose waves that fell to her waist, and she was wearing a very low-cut red dress that hugged her skin. She was also standing extremely close to me, one hand on her hip, the other on the table. I took a step away from her.

"Hello Stacy." I greeted her politely.

"Are you enjoying yourself Alpha?"

"Yes, I am. You?"

"I'm enjoying myself very much." She flashed me a wide smile.

"Good."

"I can't believe we have a hospital." She continued. "So much work, am I right?"

I almost snorted at her remark. Work? *She* hadn't done any work. I'd seen her plenty of times over the past month hanging around the site, but she never lifted so much as a hammer and nails. Mostly her and her friends would sit around, giggling and trying to chat up the men who were working. Twice, I asked if she was able to help out in the tents, and twice, she denied me, saying she was happy where she was. After that, I'd stopped bothering.

"It's a big accomplishment." I agreed with her. I poured some gravy onto the mashed potatoes. "Excuse me, I have to get this to Violet."

She wrinkled her nose a little. "Aren't you sweet, bringing her food?"

"Yeah, I guess."

She sighed dramatically. "I wish I had a mate to take care of me like that."

"You will someday."

"I doubt it." She pouted. "I didn't find him on my eighteenth."

"Well, maybe he's not in this pack. Sorry, but I have to go."

"Bye Alpha."

I walked away, relieved to end the conversation. The girl was weird, and it was obvious she didn't like Violet. Girls were way too jealous sometimes. I found Vie at a table, chatting with some other girls. They nodded respectfully to me as I approached, taking their leave. I set the plate down in front of her, pulling up my own chair.

"Extra gravy, just the way you like." I smiled.

"Thank you." Her eyes cast to the side, narrowing a bit. "Were you talking to Stacy?"

I nodded. "Briefly. She came up to me while I was getting your food."

Vie took a big bite of the chicken. "About?"

I shrugged. "Nothing, really. Whining about not having a mate to take care of her."

The fork froze halfway to her mouth, her eyes immediately finding mine. "What?"

"It's not a big deal, I didn't even really pay attention."

"You know she was flirting with you, right?"

"I kind of figured that." I reached across the table, taking her hand. "I have no interest in Stacy. Or any other girl for that matter."

"I know that. But it still bugs me that she would try." Her eyes grazed sideways again. I followed her line, finding Stacy, now talking with her usual group. She saw us looking and gave waved. Violet gave a tight smile in return, looking away. She stabbed her chicken.

"Calm down Vie."

"I'm calm." She snapped.

I scooted my chair closer to her. "You never have to worry about her, or anyone else. I love *you*, and I always will."

"Good. Because I'm kind of the coolest chick there is." She smirked.

I laughed. "Yes, you are." Leaning over the table, our lips almost touched before a loud, terrorized shriek filled the air. Jerking away from each other, I jumped to my feet, trying to locate the source of the sound.

"Rogues!"

As soon as I heard the word, I gently, but firmly pulled Violet up.

"Go! Get the women, children, and elders to the packhouse!" I said.

She shook her head. "Too far! I'll get them into the hospital."

"Alright, go!"

359

I walked away quickly, pushing my way through panicked pack members. Growls were erupting now, and the sounds of a fight. I exited the tents, finding an already full force battle going on not thirty feet away. At least a dozen wolves were charging forward, trying to get through the warriors. I snarled, ripping my jacket off and kicking off my shoes. And then I was on all fours, teeth bared as I jumped into the fray. I went for the closest wolf, his scent a dead giveaway of his rogue status, and sunk my teeth into his shoulder. He yelped, jumping around. My claws came up, and then back down his side, fat and blood pouring out. Leaving him on the ground, I moved onto the next.

"Leave one alive!" I commanded through the mindlink.

I spotted two rogues on top of one of the warriors, biting away. The brown wolf on the ground was clawing, kicking, and biting in an attempt to escape. Sprinting their way, I collided with one, sending him flying. The other let out a surprised whine, jumping back. The brown wolf jumped at him, immediately sinking his teeth into the neck. We worked chaotically until the ground was littered with bodies.

"Got one over here. Knocked him out." Ashwell said. His gray wolf was circling a now naked man lying in the grass.

"Good job. Take him. . . Where do you usually take them?"

"We have cells. They aren't too reliable."

I growled. *"Of course they're not. Just take him there, and post guards. Inside and out. If he makes it outside before I question him, he's dead."*

"Yes Alpha."

I shifted back, looking for pants, and grateful when someone handed me a pair of sweats. Then I looked around, wincing. The once green grass was stained with red. Deceased shifted men lay all around. I counted fourteen in total, including our prisoner. What a mess.

"Vie?"

"Jasper! Are you okay?"

"I'm good. It wasn't much of a fight."

"It's over?"

"Yeah."

"Alright. I'll move everyone out, away from here. See you at the house?"

"I'll be there soon."

Cutting off the link, I made my way to the warriors huddled together.

"Anybody injured?" I asked.

"A few scratches. Nothing that won't heal within the hour." One of them answered.

"Alright. Can we clean this up?"

"What should we do with the bodies?"

I paused. "What do you mean?"

They exchanged looks. "How should we uh. . .dispose of them?"

I frowned. "The same we always do?"

"Burn them?"

I swung around, rounding on them. "What?! No! Where the fuck did you get that from?" I eyed each of them, the lightbulb going off. "Have you never been properly trained in how to deal with rogue corpses?"

They all shook their heads.

"*What?!* Do you *usually* burn the bodies?!" I demanded.

"Sometimes, if there isn't a lot. . ."

"Other times, we just toss them in the woods." Another replied quietly.

Disgust and anger were evident on my face, I could tell. "We *don't* burn bodies! *Or* toss them! We *bury* them for Goddess sakes! Even rogues have the right to be buried like you or I!" I shouted. Some men flinched at my words.

"Yes Alpha. Where?"

"Find a spot away from the housing and away from here. I don't care if it's in the woods. And dig *deep*, no shallow graves."

"Yes Alpha." They chorused. I stormed away from them, appalled. King hurried up to me.

"I want every body that was tossed in the woods found, and buried where ever those men are burying these guys." I ordered gruffly.

"Of course."

"You ever seen them before?" I nodded to a rogue on the ground as we passed.

"Never. We don't get random attacks here much. Last time was a couple years ago, I think it's because we're close enough to Blood Moon."

"Well, let's hope the guy Ashwell took down talks. I want to know why they attacked."

He glanced at me. "Their rogues. They attack for food, or money, or just because their dumb."

I stopped in my tracks, facing him. "Did you see the way they moved together? How they were trying to get around us? If they wanted food or money, they could have gone straight for the packhouse, or for town. But they came here instead."

He thought about it. "You're right. It is odd, for rogues."

"Exactly. Go find your mate, and then I want you posted at the cells, outside."

"Can do." He bowed his head before running off.

I quickened my pace as well, anxious to see my own mate.

CHAPTER 49
VIOLET

"Didn't think we'd have to the hospital this soon," I said.

"Neither did I. But let's be thankful it was today and not a month ago." Kettler replied.

Both of us jumped as the woman on the bed, Natalia, screamed, again. It'd been a little shocking when, in the midst of getting everyone out of here and back to their homes, her water had suddenly broke. I'd mindlinked Kettler immediately, asking what I should do. Yes, my Mom was Head Doctor, but that didn't make *me* a medical expert. I could stitch someone up though, and I had knowledge on emergency situations in the field, but delivering a baby? Not within my capacity. The best I could do was get her to maternity ward and wait for Kettler.

"Where the fuck is my mate?!" She screamed.

"He said he was on his way." Kettler reassured her. I could tell he was trying to remain polite. It was nice to see him working on his attitude with patients at least.

"He's always late! For *everything!* Last week, he was thirty minutes late to dinner with my parents! Oh, Goddess, here comes another one." She winced, shutting her eyes tightly. Her low moan turned into another scream.

"Would you like me to go try and find him Natalia?" I offered.

"No! No, stay. Please. If that moron doesn't make it, I want someone here." She panted. "And then you can kick his ass for me afterwards."

I giggled. "Whatever you want."

The door burst open, and in ran a dishevelled looking young man with black hair and blue eyes. His eyes found Natalia immediately. Relief crossed his features, but she glared at him murderously.

"Kain! Where the *fuck* have you been?!" She screamed at him.

"Nat, I am so sorry! I got lost trying to find your room." He walked to stand beside her. "I'm here now baby. How you doing?"

I took a step back, knowing from my Mom how stupid that question was. As expected, Natalia exploded.

"How am I doing?! *How am I doing?!* Well, I don't know Kain! I feel like I want to puke and shit at the same time, my insides feel like they're being lit on fire and drenched in acid with every contraction, and soon, I'll be pushing out a fucking watermelon from my vagina! How the fuck do you think I'm doing?!" She shrieked. Kains eyes were wide and frightened as he gulped.

"I-I'm sorry baby. What can I do to help?"

"You can never touch me or come near me again." She hissed.

"Oh. Okay."

Kain started to walk away.

"Where are you going?! Come back here and hold my hand!" Natalia shouted. Her poor mate looked all kinds of confused and I had to turn away to hide my laughter. Even Kettler had his head ducked.

"You got it from here?" I asked him.

He nodded. "Shiela should be here soon too. You're good to go."

"Thank You, Luna, for staying with Natalia. We really appreciate it." Kain smiled at me, then winced when Natalia caught his hand in a death grip.

"No problem." I replied and backed out of the room. On my way out of the hospital, I ran into Shiela, a woman in her mid-thirties who had recently come back to Silver Moon from University. Her parents had told her everything that had gone on in recent months, and as soon as she came back, she handed Kettler her resume to be a nurse. We were glad, but also still looking for more, obviously. A hospital couldn't be run by two people.

"Hello Luna. Can you point me to the room of the patient?"

"Just down there. Room seven oh nine."

"Thank you." She hurried off.

Exiting the hospital, I almost missed King standing outside. In fact I might have, had he not fallen into step beside me.

"Were you waiting for me?"

"Yes. I need you to come with me. The Alpha wants you to meet him in the cells."

My brow furrowed. "The cells? Why?"

"The prisoner we captured isn't cooperating."

"Okay. . . And he wants me to talk to him?" I asked confused.

"No, he doesn't. But the man, he won't even give us his name, said he will only talk to you."

"He asked for the Luna?"

King glanced at me. His expression was neutral, but his eyes were filled with mixed emotion.

"He asked for you. By name."

I stared at him. What rogue could possibly know me? I'd never had any interactions with rogues, never talked to anyone of them. My whole life, there had been two rogue attacks at Blood Moon, and each time I was sent down to the basement with the other women and children. And as sheltered as I had been growing up, never leaving the pack until recently, it wasn't likely my name got around easily. Or maybe it had, and I just didn't know. I was thinking of many possibilities, sorting through them in my mind as we walked to the cells. It was a small building, dirty on the outside with what used to be white brick.

King nodded to the guards at the door as we walked in. I followed him down a concrete corridor with a metal door at the end. He opened it, cautioning me to watch my step as we then descended down a flight of concrete steps. The air had a chill to it the further down we went, and a pungent odor floated into my nostrils. We ended up at another metal door and I shook my head. Two doors and a flight of stairs?

Yeah, great security. The smell was a lot stronger when we stepped through the door, making me gag.

"Sorry. Alpha ordered or the place to be cleaned ASAP."

"Good. I know this is where prisoners go, but that stench is unreal." I grimaced as a rat ran across my foot.

I counted twelve cells as we walked, all no bigger than a closet. Each one had two rusty buckets, and I didn't ask for what they were for. I could guess. Standing at the end of the room was Jasper, Ashwell, and a few warriors I didn't know the name of. Jasper looked angry, more angry than I'd ever seen him. His expression relaxed only a fraction when he saw me.

"What's going on?" I asked when I reached him. He was blocking my view of the cell behind him.

"That mutt won't talk. Not to us." He growled.

"I know. King said he asked for me."

"Yeah. But you don't have to talk to him Vie."

Two of the warriors glanced between him and I, their faces suspicious. I tried to ignore it; It *was* unusual for a rogue to ask for the Luna by name. And we hadn't been Alpha and Luna for very long. Considering their old leaders, I could see why they'd be wary.

"No, it's okay. I'll talk to him." I said. "We need some answers."

Jasper sighed. "Alright. But not alone." He half turned, glaring into the cell. "You hear that? She's here, but we're not leaving."

"Fine." The voice that answered back was rough, deep. It was not one I recognized.

Jasper stepped aside, keeping close to me. I took two small steps, peering into the dark space. It was the same as all the others, two buckets, small and dirty. Unlike the others, this one held the man who claimed to know me. He was leaning against the back wall, arms crossed. Someone had given him clothes, gray sweatpants and a black tee. He was a tall guy, at least six foot, with tattoos covering his arms. His hair was short, maybe dark brown or black, I couldn't tell for sure. He wasn't thin like I'd heard rogues were. This guy was built, healthy looking. My eyes roamed up to his face. He had penetrating green eyes, very unnerving. He might have been classically handsome, if not for the scar that ran from his left temple down to his chin.

I had no idea who he was.

"You asked for me?" I questioned him.

"You are Violet?" He replied in that rough tone.

I nodded. "Yes. How do you know my name?"

"A lot of rogues know your name sweetheart."

Jasper growled behind me. I crossed my arms, leaning against the wall next to the bars of the cell.

"Is that so?"

"You're becoming quite famous."

I raised an eyebrow. "How is that? I have no dealings with rogues."

He laughed. The sound was humorless. "Nobody said you did."

"I don't understand."

"You've got quite the bounty on you Luna. A hefty price to take you in alive."

My insides turned cold. "Explain."

"You want me to dumb it down? Alright." He leaned away form the wall, holding my stare. "Someone wants you. Said they pay my buddies and I if we brought you in, alive. Obviously I don't trust that, so I got half the money up front."

"Who wants me?" I asked numbly. "And why?"

"Now, why should I give up that information?"

"Because it might help save your ass."

He laughed again. "You think I'm stupid, don't you? I'm a rogue. I attacked a pack. Either I'll spend the rest of my miserable life down here, or your boy there will do me in." He nodded at Jasper. "Why not leave you with a mystery?"

"Because," I snarled, "If you don't tell me what I want to know, you'll be putting my unborn children at risk. If anything happens to them, you won't need to worry about my mate. It'll be *me* you deal with."

"You going to rough me up buttercup?" He smirked. "I'd love to see you try."

"Would you like to know who my father is?"

"Do I care?"

"Alpha Dimitri Varlos, of Blood Moon." His eyes flicked up to meet mine, surprise playing in them. "I've been trained my entire life on how to deal with rogues. And not just interrogation wise. You can trust every word I saw when I tell you if my children are hurt because of the information you refuse to give me, the rest of your life will indeed, be miserable."

"You're lying." He whispered.

I turned to Jasper. "Do you have your phone? I want to call my Dad."

"Right here."

Surprisingly, the reception down here was decent. I pulled up Dads contact and hit send. The rogue waited, obviously trying to call my bluff.

"Hello?"

"Hi Dad."

"Violet?"

"Who else? I'm calling because we have a situation here."

"What kind of situation?"

"The pack was attacked shortly after you left. Rogues. We have one alive. I'm talking to him now."

"What?! Why are you talking to him?"

I filled him in quickly. He snarled so fiercely, the man behind bars flinched.

"This doesn't prove anything! You could be talking to anyone." He said.

I pressed the video invitation. Dads face appeared on screen, looking every inch the Heartless Alpha he was known to be. I turned the phone around, watching as the mans face paled considerably.

"Do I need to come back to Silver Moon?" Dad growled. The man gulped.

"Does he?" I asked.

He looked at each of in turn, his bravado vanishing. "No. I'll tell you."

"Violet?"

"Yeah?" I flipped the phone back to myself.

"Remember Vincent?"

I glanced at our prisoner. "I do. I think that punishment is a little too light for this guy though."

"I'll leave that up to you. Keep me informed."

"We will. Bye Dad." I ended the call, tossing Jasper his phone.

"Who's Vincent?" The man asked.

I shrugged. "Some rogue we caught at Blood Moon. He was sneaking in and 'playing' with underage girls. So my Dad decided to rid him of his appendages. *All* of them."

He went even paler than before.

"If I were you, I'd start talking." Jasper ordered.

"Alright, alright!" He held up his hands. "I don't know who wants you, but I do know it's a chick. And she was adamant you were brought in alive. Alright?"

"Not alright. Who is she?"

"I don't know! She never told us her name."

"What did she look like?"

"Blond, white. Scary as Hell."

I scoffed. "Really? Two minutes ago you were saying I couldn't do shit to you, but this girl freaked you out?"

"Don't witch's freak you out?"

I stepped away from the wall, staring at him to see if he was joking.

"She was a witch?" I demanded. "How do you know?"

"At first I told her to get lost. She set one of my guys on fire, right in front of me. There was nothing left but ashes. Never touched him, only waved her hand, mumbling some shit."

"Did she tell you why she wanted me?"

"She only said you were important, that you'd help get what she wanted. I agreed and she demanded half the money. She paid up, told us where to find you, and left.

369

Actually, she vanished into thin air. Haven't heard from her since."

My hands moved to my belly protectively. "Did she know about my babies?" I whispered.

"I don't know. She never said you were pregnant."

Suddenly, the stench down here was overwhelming. I doubled over, my insides numb with a fear I'd never felt before. Fear for my children. Vomit spewed from me, controlled by that fear.

"That's enough." Jasper rubbed my back, helping me to stand straight when it was over. "You need to go rest."

"No. I have one more question." I said weakly. "You said I was becoming famous. What did you mean by that?"

"We came across two other groups on our way here. Both were coming for you, so we took them out. I'm just assuming she got to more people, in any case any of us failed."

"Well, you did fail." Jasper snapped. "Your buddies are dead, and you're in here. Where you'll be until I decide what to do with you."

"I helped you!"

"After we threatened you!" He shouted. The sound echoed off the walls. "We're leaving. Enjoy your stay." He spat.

CHAPTER 50
VIOLET

I called my Mom as soon as we left the cells. She confirmed me theory; Jennine was back. Hearing it out loud, I was more determined than before to catch the bitch who'd been terrorizing my family. But Jasper wasn't having it, demanding I go home and rest. I only accepted because I knew I'd need a shower after being down there in that hole. And I did feel better afterwards. And apparently more exhausted than I thought. As soon as my head hit the pillow, I was out.

I woke up to find Jasper sitting on the bed, combing his fingers through my hair and trailing along my neck.

"Hey. Did I wake you?" He asked softly.

"No."

We were silent for a while, just looking at each other. Eventually, I couldn't hold it in anymore.

"I'm scared." I whimpered.

"I am too." He settled in next to me, sitting with his back against the headboard, and pulling me into his arms. "I won't let anything happen to you. Or the babies."

"What about the pack?" I whispered. "We are not equipped to deal with multiple rogue attacks."

"I've been discussing that with King and Ashwell. The warriors your Dad left here are going to start rigorous and thorough training, starting tomorrow. I'll be joining in too. I've also doubled the border patrols."

"She could just teleport herself in here, if she really wanted to." I reminded him. His arms tightened around me.

"I'll think of something." He promised. "I won't let that bitch come anywhere near you."

A knock on the door made us look up. It cracked open and Tracys face peeked inside.

"Sorry, I know you said you didn't want to be disturbed. But there is a man here wanting to see you."

"A man?"

"He says your Grandpa?"

Jasper and I looked at each other. And then we were both scrambling to get out of bed, and rushing to the door.

"Where is he?" I asked.

"Outside." Tracy ran after us.

I raced down the hall, as fast as I was able to go, and into the foyer. Throwing the door open, I gaped for a second, as there indeed, stood my Grandfather. He was casually looking around, dressed in blue jeans and white shirt. When he saw me, he smiled widely.

"Hey kiddo."

"Grandpa!" I hurried down the steps and practically threw myself into his arms.

"Easy there! You're carrying a precious load." He laughed.

"I'm so glad to see you!" I looked over his shoulder. "Is grandma with you?"

"No. You know how she doesn't like to travel." He replied sadly. I nodded.

"Hello Gideon." Jasper came up to us. "It's nice to see you again."

"And you. I heard you've had quite a lot of your plate since leaving."

"It's been rough at times. But we're doing alright."

"Why are you here?" I asked.

"Your Mom told me." He gave me a knowing look. "I came here as. . . how I should I put it? Your backup?"

"Let's go inside. We can talk more openly there." Jasper suggested. I nodded, taking Grandpas hand.

He whistled lowly as we walked up the stairs to the office. "No offense you two, but this place is pretty. . ."

"We know." I interrupted. "We want to build a new packhouse. But more important things came up first."

"I can help with that."

I walked into the office first, taking a seat. "How?"

"It's pretty basic magic actually." He caught my eye. "Have you been practicing?"

"No. I didn't want to without you or Aunt Clara."

"Fair enough. I was coming to visit soon anyways, for that reason. We'll start tomorrow." He walked to the wall, placing both palms against it. "Until then, I'll work alone fixing this place up."

He whispered something under his breath, the sounds and syllables mixing together. I jumped when the room started to transform before my eyes. The dull looking walls rippled, becoming brighter and cleaner, as if a fresh coat of paint had been applied. The carpet under my feet changed from a dark blue to a lovely golden brown. Grandpa leaned away from the wall, flicking his fingers separately at three of the chairs. They flew against the wall, one lined up beside the next. Waving his hand, they appeared to melt together, resulting into a soft looking white sofa.

"Anything else?" Grandpa asked, grinning.

"I'd ask you to do something with the desk, but I already ordered a new one." Jasper laughed.

"It doesn't look like there's anything wrong with it."

"It was Warrick's. I don't need anything of his."

"Ah. In that case. . ." I watched as the center piece of the room started to shrink. It didn't stop until it was the size of a kitten. Jasper walked over and picked it up.

"You can just toss it. I promise it won't unshrink."

"Thanks." Jasper tossed it in the trash can near the door.

I sank onto the sofa. It was as comfortable as it looked. "You're doing this for our room next." I said cheekily.

"I can do the whole house if you want."

"I'm holding you to that."

"Now," He crossed his arms, "Tell me what's been happening."

We told him everything, from the time we left Blood Moon. I let Jasper do most of the talking, only filling in the gaps when needed. I was seriously happy to see my Grandpa. It was an extra hand in this fight, a hand we needed. Being a Dark witch, Jennine wasn't bound by the same rules as regular witches. Grandpas knowledge and skill was in short supply around here, and undoubtedly useful.

"I think I can help at the border. I can make it so nobody can cross without being invited in." He told Jasper.

His shoulders sagged in relief. "You have no idea how much that would help."

"Do they know?" He looked at me. "About you?"

I shifted in my seat. "We're going to tell them." I evaded the question.

"So, that's a no. When are you telling them?"

"Soon. . ."

"Violet." He came to kneel in front of me. "You cannot keep this from the pack. You've done so much good here, but if they find out you've been lying to them? All that good won't matter much anymore. You'll just be another Luna who kept stuff from them."

"This is pretty complicated Gideon." Jasper spoke up. "How do we just announce that?"

"Simple. You just announce it." Grandpa looked at him. "It's going to come out sometime. And it should come from you two."

"He's right." I sighed. "We both know I can't keep my magic bottled up inside; I'll have to use it at some point. I'd rather not try to explain to the pack after another incident like the stairs."

"I think the sooner the better." He patted my knee.

I groaned. "Fine! Jasper, call a meeting. We'll gather everyone in the Hall."

"When for?"

"Tonight."

He raised a brow at me. "You sure?"

"Yeah." I looked between them. "You'll help me, right?"

"Of course."

"Always."

I smiled at them, even though my stomach was churning in knots. Telling the pack I was a Hybrid was very low on my priority list. I'd been putting it off for a while, too long.

But if I was being honest, the chest in my mind had been rattling more frequently, and I was restless at times. Often lately, I thought about going out to the woods and unlocking it. But I was scared of what I could do, scared that I wouldn't be able to control it. My magic should be a bigger part of my life, but I was keeping it locked away, trying to forget about it. Pretty much doing exactly what Grandpa and Aunt Clara had told me not to do.

However, now that Jennine was back, I felt a new fondness for what I was. If I could learn anything, it might just help us win against her, bring her down. For good this time.

"Done." Jasper sat next to me. "I'm not worried, really. Except for Warrick's old pals."

"We'll deal with it. I'm more worried about Jennine."

"We should head to the border." Grandpa said. "I want to get that shield up as soon as possible."

"Good idea."

"What about me?"

"I don't mean to sound. . ..controlling. . ." Jasper trailed off, looking uncomfortable.

"You want me to stay here?" I guessed.

"Yeah. Just until your grandpa puts up that shield." His eyes pleaded with me to not be angry.

"Alright. I'm getting hungry anyway." I stood and stretched.

And someone stretched back.

"Ah!" I gasped. My hands flew to my stomach.

"What?! What's wrong?!" Jasper was on his knees in an instant, his hands fluttering around my torso anxiously.

Gently, I guided his hands to my stomach, breathing deeply. Waiting.

"They moved. I swear they did." I grumbled.

Without answering, Jasper rolled my shirt up. Sparks flickered when he laid his hands back down, and just like before, I felt a nudge from inside. And then another. And another! Jasper looked up at me, his eyes lit up with wonder and love.

375

"Hello boys." He said softly. "You're quite energetic, huh?" He kissed my skin softly.

"May I?" Grandpa stood in front of me, his hand outstretched. I nodded. The grin on his face as he felt what we felt made him look younger than he was, totally carefree. "Amazing."

Jasper stood. "I'd love to do this all day, but we should get going. I'm glad I was around for the first time they kicked though." He tilted my chin, kissing me deeply. "I love you. All three of you."

"We love you too."

He kissed me again and then they were gone. I sat on the couch for a little while longer, just enjoying the feeling of my babies nudging and rolling around, until my stomach grumbled. Shuffling to my feet, I began to make my way to the kitchen. Halfway there, I ran into Tracy.

"Hello Luna!" She greeted me.

"Hey Tracy."

"Can I help you get anywhere?"

"Thanks, but I'm still able to walk on my own for now." I laughed. Regardless, she skipped along beside me.

"For now. I remember when my Mama had twins. She could barely move by the end."

"You're a twin?" I asked curiously as we took a corner.

"Oh, no, not me. My brothers. They're three years younger than me."

I smiled. "I'm having boys too."

"Really?! Awesome! Have you decided on names yet?"

"I've come up with some, but I wanted to run it by Jasper." I shrugged.

She skipped ahead, holding the kitchen door open for me. I thanked her, looking around and trying to decide what I wanted. Of course, I already knew.

"Is there-"

"In the fridge, top shelf." Tracy smirked. "I made some fresh yesterday for you." She pulled down a container full of chicken.

I blinked at her. "Thank you Tracy."

"No problem! I'm always happy to help."

She began humming to herself as she flitted around the kitchen, almost dancing. I rested against the wall, watching her work. Tracy really was the happiest person I'd ever met; Nothing seemed to bother her. Her attitude was so different from everyone else's at Silver Moon. There was nice people, yeah, but even they had their fair share of problems.

"So, Tracy." I interrupted her humming. "Have you always been at Silver Moon?"

"Oh, yeah. Born and raised."

"Did you work in the packhouse before?"

She glanced up, smiling softly. "I can see where you're going with this. Yes, I worked for the old Alpha and Luna. Lucky for me, I was assigned to look after the Luna."

"You count that as luck?"

"I was in charge of her day to day; Making her breakfast, making the bed, doing her laundry, etc. Which meant I hardly ever saw the Alpha. Sure, Anne was a bitch, but I think I got the lesser of two evils, you know?"

It was the first time I'd heard her ever insult someone. And even as she did so, she did it with a smile. Her words and attitude were so different, it made me laugh.

"I'm not sure about that, but I'm glad you weren't around him much."

"Actually, none of us were, a whole lot, except Stacy. The only times we were gathered together was at one his parties, or pack events." She must have caught my look, because she continued. "Stacy was the Alphas maid. Everything I did for Anne, she did for him."

I thought maybe she did a little more for the Alpha as well, but I didn't vocalize my thoughts.

"Do you miss your old job?" I inquired.

Tracy shrugged. "I guess. The pay helped my family a lot, but we don't need to worry about that now. Most of us are just grateful you let us remain in the packhouse."

She danced over to me, holding out a plate with a delicious looking chicken salad and macaroni on the side. I thanked her, my mind forming an idea.

Around a big bite of sandwich, which was as good as it looked, I asked, "How would you like your old job back?"

She froze in place, regarding me with bright eyes. "What?"

I swallowed. "Why don't you work for me? If you want. I can pay you the same as Anne did, but I'd actually think you deserve a raise just for tolerating her that long." I giggled.

"A-are you serious? You would let me work for you?"

"I don't see why not. You already have the knowledge of the job. Who better than you?"

Suddenly, her arms were around me in a tight hug. I moved the plate of food barely in the nick of time.

"Thank you! Thank you!" She cried. Then she gasped, pulling away. "Does this mean I'm the official nanny too?!"

"Of course! I can't think of anyone else I'd want." I grinned.

She leaned down, pointing a finger at my stomach. "You hear that you two? I'm going to help your Mama look after you! I'm so excited to meet you both!"

The twins kicked in my stomach, further cementing the theory that Tracy was a good, if not the best, choice for this job.

CHAPTER 51
JASPER

The shield was up, and I was exceedingly grateful. I felt like I could sleep tonight knowing my family, and the pack, was that much safer.

"Thank you." I said again.

"No need to thank me."

"You think you'll be staying for a while?" I asked.

"For a little while. I don't like to be away from Rose too long."

Vie had told me her grandparents story. It was heartbreaking, to say the least.

"I understand."

We stepped onto the sidewalk. Violet was waiting for me, standing under a tree with Tracy. They were chatting happily and I smiled for the fact that she'd made a friend here. A few times she'd expressed how much she was missing Brianne, even though they talked on the phone.

"Hey." I greeted them.

"Evening Alpha!" Tracy grinned at me. She seemed more bubbly than usual.

"Tracy, you remember my Grandpa?" Violet gestured at him.

"Oh, yes! Hello again, Mr. Gideon!" She shook his hand firmly.

"Hello Tracy." Gideon smiled.

"Well? Let's get this over with." Vie sighed.

We started walking together, Tracy supplying most of the conversation. I glanced at my mate when she mentioned she was our new nanny, but Vie wasn't looking at me. Or Tracy. She was staring at the sidewalk, breathing deeply and steadily. I stepped closer to her, wrapping one arm around her shoulders.

"Hey. It'll be okay." I whispered.

"What if it's not?" She looked up at me with fearful eyes.

"Then we deal with it, just like we've dealt with everything else so far."

"Together?"

"Together." I nodded.

As we came up to the Hall, she clutched my hand tightly. I rubbed her back slowly, hoping the mate bond would help ease her nerves. When we got inside, we were greeted with cheerful hellos and hand shakes. A few women stopped us to inquire how Violet was feeling, and congratulated us on twin baby boys. She thanked them politely before moving on. Mom and Dad were also in the crowd, and Elena. I gave her and Mom and hug. Tracy got lost somewhere in the crowd, but Gideon joined us on the stage where King and Ashwell were already in their respective spots. I went to them first.

"Is everyone here?" I whispered.

"Everyone except four guards at the cells."

"No problem. I'll fill them in later."

We stepped apart, and I went to the podium, raising my hand. The noise of the pack quieted.

"Thanks everyone, for coming tonight." Violet whimpered quietly behind me. "We've gathered you all here tonight because we have an announcement to make. Violet?"

She made her way robotically to the podium, staring out at the pack. They looked back expectantly.

"I-I'm not sure. . .what to say. . ." She whispered in a low aside to me.

"It doesn't have to be a long speech. Just do your best." I assured her.

She looked back at the crowd, clearing her throat.

"So, uhm, as many of you know. . .Jasper and I care about this pack very much." She took a deep breath. "Even though we've been here for. . .such a short time already, we've grown to want the best for each and every one of you. And part of that is, we believe, not withholding important information from you. That said, I'd like to tell you what we've uncovered from the rogue who was captured earlier. He was working for a woman, set upon this pack to kidnap me."

Gasps echoed around the room.

"We learned there were more rogue groups with the same mission, and we don't doubt there are more out there now."

"What can we do?" Someone called up to us.

"Tomorrow, training by the Blood Moon warriors will begin for those who want to join. We've also taken some safety precautions as well." She looked over her shoulder, motioning to Gideon, who stepped up beside us. "This is my Grandfather, Gideon. He is a witch."

Every pair of eyes in the Hall went to Gideon. A few people standing near the stage took several steps back. I internally sighed, hoping the reaction to Violet was better.

"You don't need to be afraid of him. He came here to help us. A short while ago, he created a protective shield around all of Silver Moon. Now nobody can cross our borders without being invited in by either myself or my mate."

People started whispering, looking at Gideon a little less warily, while others still clearly didn't trust him.

"But why are they after you?" Tracy shouted from her spot. She might have been the only one here who was looking on with a face full of concern.

"Because. . . because of what I. . .am." Violet replied lowly. She closed her eyes briefly, then said the words I knew she was terrified to speak. "We believe this woman is after me because I am a Hybrid."

It wasn't exactly the truth, but it could have been. We'd not discussed whether Jennine knew or didn't know about Violet being a Hybrid. Though that was a far easier explanation than retelling her parents' whole history. It was also safe to say Jennine would figure it out, if she hadn't already. However, it was very clear nobody at Silver Moon had suspected. Violets words were met with a dead silence.

Everywhere I looked, I saw that people just didn't know how to react. Some looked at her like she was telling a not so funny joke. Others were shocked, and some were just dumbfounded. It was silent for so long that I started counting in my head. Two minutes went by, and nobody had come up with anything. They were all frozen, resembling an odd painting.

I leaned over the podium. "Uh, we're going to need someone to say something."

"I knew it!" A voice shrieked from the far wall. Everyone turned that way, almost in perfect formation. Of course, it was a woman from Warrick's old friends, pointing an accusing finger at us. "I knew you would wreck this pack! You come here, pretending to be so sweet and innocent and wanting to help us, but really, you've just been biding your time!"

"That girl is a monster! She will kill us all!" Her mate yelled. Violet winced, flinching back.

"She would never hurt anyone!" Mom screamed back. Once again, I was glad they had relocated here with us.

"Isn't that your son?" The woman snapped. "Of course you would defend him and his mate!"

"Now, hang on just a minute." Kettler, of all people, shouted back across the room. "They *did* come here and help us. They just built us a new fucking hospital for Goddess sake!"

His argument sent the pack whispering again.

"Not to mention all the work of getting the fields back again. And the Orchard. Didn't I see you out there today Greg?" Kettler looked around.

"Sure did." Greg spoke not far away. "Our new tractors run like a dream. Wouldn't have happened without these two." He nodded at us.

"Violet is a sweet girl, she wouldn't do anything to hurt the pack. She only wants to help." Dad said firmly.

"They brought a witch to our pack!" The woman yelled again. "They've been hiding things from us! We can't trust them!"

"I came here to help protect you." Gideon shot at her. "I didn't have to. And nobody asked me either. But if you wish, I can take down the shield, and you can go up against the rogues yourself?"

The woman backed down, nudging her mate. I finally remembered him as Ricardo Perez; He had fought us tooth and nail when we evicted him. Obviously he would hate us, no matter what.

"We apologize for keeping this from you." I said. "Our intent was never to lie. You have to understand, Violet is the first Hybrid in a *very* long time, and that name already has a poor reputation. We wanted to gain some ground with this pack first, show you that we have the best intentions for you at heart. And now we're hoping you can forgive us for our mistake."

"How can we trust you?" An elderly woman stepped forward, placing her hand on the stage. "How can we trust that she isn't dangerous? We all know the stories. Hybrids tried to take over, get rid of us all!"

Violet stepped around me, her arm brushing my back. She strode to the forefront of the stage, looking down at the woman.

"I am not like them." She stated firmly. "I know what they did. The Hybrids of the past looked down on regular werewolves, thinking they were better than them. Tried to wipe them out."

She jumped, leading neatly in front of the elder. They came face to face as she straightened.

"I am not them." She said again. "I am not higher than anyone else. I am the daughter of an Alpha, the mate of one, and a Luna. And a werewolf. But I am also part witch. And even though I am all these things, they don't justify *who* I am. Because at the end of the day, I'm just a girl who is trying to help this pack, and loses sleep wondering how in the Hell I can do it. At the end of the day, I'm a mother-to-be who has no idea what motherhood will be like, but is really looking forward to it. I'm just a girl, just like you." She looked around. "And like you. And you. And you. I did not grow up as a Hybrid. I grew up as a wolf, only discovering what I was after my first shift."

She climbed back up onto the stage, further away than before.

"You may call me a Hybrid, but my wolf and I? The Goddess has another name for us. We are a Midnight Wolf, the first of our kind. This leads me to believe that my ancestors were not the monsters who committed such horrendous crimes."

And then she shifted.

The planks under her feet creaked from the new weight. But the loudest sound of all was the gasps and murmurs of awe as Violet turned, showing everyone the marking on her side. Her aura, so much stronger now as Luna, wrapped around those of us standing closest to her. Her large head found the elder again, her eyes piercing.

"I believe that is the correct answer, young one." She smiled. "You are no danger."

A low whine came out through Hala's teeth.

"Thank you." I said to her. "If anyone has anything else they'd like to say, any questions or concerns, please feel free now."

"I'm not concerned at all!" Greg scoffed. Around him, others agreed.

"I'm a bit surprised, but I don't believe we have anything to fear." Kettler added.

Sounds of agreement sounded all over the Hall. My eyes briefly landed on Stacy, who unlike everyone else, was staring at me instead of Violet. Her gaze was cold, and maybe calculating even. I looked away.

"Alright. If that concludes tonight's business, you can all go home. Thank you again for coming out." I turned away from the podium, coming to face my Beta and Gamma.

Ashwell's lips were in a thin line, and King looked equally as pleased.

"Yes?" I asked them.

"You should have told us." Ashwell whined.

"We would have kept it to ourselves." King added sourly.

"We weren't keeping it from you specifically." I apologized.

They both pouted and I chuckled. "So, you two can work under a Hybrid?"

"We work for you."

I laughed harder. "Don't kid yourselves. We all know who the boss is." I looked at Hala, who rolled her eyes.

"I suppose every Luna is the true boss." Ashwell eyed her as well.

"I want to go for a run." Halas voice sounded in my mind.

"Sounds good."

"I'll see you guys later." I clapped them on the shoulders as I left, following Hala. We waited until everyone had left, then she shifted back.

"Come on. Let's go outside." I took her hand, leading her out to the side of the building. This time we both shifted, shaking out our fur.

"Where to?"

"Anywhere."

We took off at a nice pace, heading for the woods. We hadn't found the time to run together since we left Blood Moon. I felt overjoyed at having her next to me again, racing through the woods, our bodies brushing against one another every so often. Eventually, I let my conscious drift the back of my mind, letting Ehno take over. The two yipped, playing with each others tails, jumping at each other and nipping ears. They hunted for a while, bringing down two large deer and sharing their spoils. After a while, Hala lay down, panting. We lay next to her, nudging her belly with our nose, whining softly.

Part of me wondered if it was safe for Violet to shift, but I knew I was being paranoid. Lots of she-wolves shifted during pregnancy, unless otherwise instructed not to be a Doctor. Some even said it was good for the pups. Ehno stood, whining again. Hala got to her feet, and they retraced their steps, stopping at a stream for a drink. Ehno gave me back control when we came up to the edge of the woods, and I shifted back.

"I think there's a stash of clothes around here." I said as Violet shifted as well. I sniffed the air, following the scent of familiar fabric. A wooden chest lay at the base of a tree, full of clothes for men and women. I grabbed shirts and pants, tossing a pair to Vie.

"Thanks." We dressed quickly.

"So. . . That went better than expected." I said, referring to the meeting.

"Yeah. But people are still going to be wary of me for a while."

"They'll get over it. Once they see you really aren't a danger."

She smiled softly, reaching out to take my hand. "I hope you're right."

A scream echoed through the dark towards us. Instantly, we were both running, Vie holding her belly as she went. We'd come out pretty close to the packhouse, and I judged that's where the sound came from. But when we got there, I couldn't do anything but gape.

"Dear Goddess." I gasped. "Gideon, what did you *do*?"

CHAPTER 52
JASPER

I stared at the house in equal amounts awe and confusion. Everyone who lived here was gathered outside, with clear mixed emotions as well. Gideon, on the other hand, seemed very pleased with himself.

"You said you were going to tear it down, build a new one. I just saved you a lot of money."

A strange noise came from the back of my throat. I had no idea what to do right now. Be angry? Be happy?

The house that stood before me now was brilliant. The walls were a lovely, almost glowing white brick now instead of red. The vines that had previously been caressing them were now healthy, vibrant, with yellow flowers complimenting their green stems. The flowerbeds had grown twice in size, with as many plants. I picked out rose bushes, daffodils, lilies, and many more. The roof looked brand new too, and the windows seemed as if they'd always looked so clear. I was stunned.

"He told us to go outside, and then bibbity-bobbity-boo!" Tracy reported.

"It's beautiful.." Vie whispered.

"It sure is." Tracy agreed. "Can we go back inside now?"

"You absolutely can." Gideon grinned and I groaned.

Everyone rushed to the front door, and their gasps of amazement told me the inside had changed just as much. I knew I was right when I stepped through the door.

"Holy shit." Vie said.

What once was the foyer was now an open room. The walls and doors that had separated the rooms on the sides were no longer there, making the area feel much more spacious. The walls themselves were a bright white, accentuated by the dark wooden beams framing them. The floor was now a medium brown wood floor, but the most

387

impressive thing of all was the grand staircase that led up to the second floor. It was set a good ten feet from the front door, with intricate railings and polished steps. I couldn't wrap my head around it.

"Did you change everything in the house?" I asked.

"Yep. You should see the kitchen." He clapped his hands.

"Oh, I'm definitely going to see the kitchen!" Vie squealed. She ran off with Tracy, leaving me to shake my head.

"You don't like it?"

"No, I do. I just can't believe it. But maybe you should have started with something smaller, you know? Some people here are already unsure of you."

He scoffed. "Give me one reason this isn't beneficial for the pack?"

I looked around again, conceding he had a point. "Maybe the people who live here. But I see where you're coming from."

"You should know the Alphas old bedroom no longer exists. I essentially buried it behind a wall. I made you two a new bedroom."

"You *made* a bedroom?"

"Well, not out of thin air, no. Whatever I took from other places, I put into that room. It's one of four on the fourth floor."

"I really don't know what to say." I laughed. "Thank you. So much, Gideon."

"Anytime. Now, I'm going to find my room, because that just about sapped my energy. Goodnight Alpha."

"Just Jasper. Goodnight." I waved as he walked away, whistling.

After he was gone, girls rushed back into the room, talking excitedly. They all seemed very happy with the new house, and I was glad. Deciding to see what other improvements Gideon had made, I went in search of Violet. And each step I took, I was more and more in awe. Finally, I reached the kitchen, which now had shiny metal double doors. Pushing them open, I found some of the old staff, some of the girls, and my mate and Tracy. In an *extra* large kitchen.

"Oh, wow." I looked around at the new floors, new counters. New appliances? Had he ordered those? Or teleported them here?

"Jasper, I could live here!" Vie giggled.

"Did he at least get you chicken?" I smirked.

"Yes! A whole fridge full!" She pointed to one of the six refrigerators.

"Wow." I repeated.

"I had some doubts Luna, but your Grandpa is one outstanding fellow." Nicholas, the old cook, said.

"He's pretty special." She agreed.

"Doing all this for us, and just because he could? He's definitely a good witch. No, he's the *best* witch!" Tracy said.

"Well," I rubbed my hands together, "Who's up for a snack?"

Everyone raised their hand, so I got to work. Nicholas helped me put on some spaghetti, and together we cooked meat and cut vegetables for the sauce. I found a cupboard full of spices, and made garlic butter. Nicholas found the bread, and in no time at all, we had a huge platter of garlic bread and spaghetti to serve. I copped an extra big helping for my mate, setting it down in front of her with a grin.

"Mmm, what smells so good?"

Stacy entered the kitchen, her nose lifted in the air.

"Spaghetti and garlic bread." Nicholas held out a plate to her.

"Thanks." She took a seat at the end of the new island. "Who made it?"

"Nicholas and I." I replied.

"Oh." Her eyes appraised me, never looking away she scooped up a forkful and slowly lifted it to her mouth. Her tongue flicked out to lick the sauce off her lips. "It's *delicious.*"

Ignoring her, I turned to my mate. "Gideon said we have a new room. Want to go see?"

She gave me a grateful look. "Sure. Dinner in bed?"

"Sounds good."

I grabbed my own plate, bidding everyone goodnight, and wishing them luck on finding their rooms. Stacy pouted, her eyes drilling a hole in my back all the way out of the kitchen.

"She's lucky I didn't dump this plate over her head." Violet growled.

"That would have been a waste of good food, you know."

"True."

I helped her up the staircase, taking her plate for her. When we got to the top, we both stopped. And then laughed together until my stomach hurt.

"I guess he learned that nobody likes stairs." I chuckled as we got into the elevator. I hit the button to the fourth floor, the door sliding closed smoothly. When it opened again, we were in a long hallway, with soft, plushy brown carpet and beige walls. I counted four doors, like Gideon had said. Crossing over to the first, I opened it, and frowned. It was empty.

"I think this is supposed to be the nursery." Violet smiled beside me. "He didn't put anything in so we could decorate it ourselves."

I shut the door, moving onto the next. It was an office, and sitting in the middle was the desk I had ordered. I shook my head again, closing the door. The door on the other side of the nursery revealed our bedroom. We stepped in together, softly shutting the door. Violets hand went to her mouth as she looked around. I stood by the doorway, completely and totally speechless.

It was the cabin.

Somehow, Gideon had managed to bring the interior of my cabin into this room. Everything looked exactly the same, from the windows, to the floors, down to the bed. Even the old brick fireplace had a roaring fire already lit and dancing. I was tempted to ask him if he took the furniture and moved it here, but I didn't want to move. The only difference, was there were no walls to separate the bedroom and living room and kitchen. It was an open concept, but the same. My throat felt clogged with emotion. That guy was just too sweet a guy.

"This is. . .amazing. Unreal." She went to the bed, her fingertips stroking the blankets. "I can't believe he did this."

The way she looked right now, healthy and round with our children, black hair flowing down her back, skin glowing. . . She was the most beautiful woman I'd ever seen. Her eyes flicked up to meet mine, the blueish green popping out against the colors of the room. Vie looked at me sheepishly.

"What?"

For an answer, I turned and locked the door. Then I strode to her, catching her face in my hands and capturing her lips with my own. We hadn't been intimate much since coming to Silver Moon. With everything we'd had to take on, and the fact that neither of really wanted to in this house. But this room didn't belong to the old house. This room never existed until now, and that made this so much better. Warrick had never stepped foot here, had never conducted dirty work here. This was our room, and ours alone.

I knew Violet felt the same way when she pulled me down on the bed. I hovered above her, careful not to put too much of my weight on her. My lips moved from hers, down, along her jaw, her ear, down to her neck. I inhaled her scent. And then we were kissing again, clothes being ripped off; Literally, I was going to have to replace her shirt at least, as it was now shredded on the floor. My skin was set aflame wherever she touched, my breath coming faster and deeper.

My fingers found the sweet spot between her legs, rubbing and teasing. She moaned under me, driving me further to insanity. I needed this girl like I needed air to breath. Bringing my mouth down to her mark, I nibbled at the spot, letting my canniness extend.

"Jasper. . . I need you.." Violet whimpered. I was too happy to give in.

Lining up with her entrance, I entered her slowly, enjoying every miniscule expression that crossed her face. For a minute, we simply lay together, connected without words. She nodded, and I started to move.

"Oh. . .. Goddess, I missed this!" She breathed.

"Me too." I panted.

We moved together, finding our rhythm. Every stroke was pure heaven, utter bliss. Violets moans filled the room, urging me on. When she shifted, I leaned back, gently pulling her with me until she was straddling me. Hooking her arms around my neck, she began to lift herself, coming down hard and deep.

"Easy love." I cautioned.

"Silly. Sex doesn't hurt the babies." She came down even harder, causing me to groan.

"Fuck Vie." I buried my face in her neck, going back to her mark. This time my teeth came out on their own, piercing her skin. My hands lowered, running down her back and grabbing her ass. My name on her tongue was music to my ears, and soon I couldn't hold back anymore. My teeth sank into her marking spot, her blood filling my mouth. As I knew she would, I felt her teeth pierce me as well and together we rode the high of our orgasms.

She fell slack against me, her tongue running over her puncture marks. I returned the favour. Gently, I lifted her off me, bringing her with me to the head of the bed.

"I love you." She whispered, her eyes already closed.

"I love you too. Sleep tight love." I kissed her nose.

Wrapping the blankets around her, I left her in the bed. If I was right, and Gideon was accurate. . . I grinned as I found the bottle of whiskey in the top cabinet of the kitchen. Grabbing a glass, I poured myself a drink, glancing at Violets sleeping form. Not wanting to disturb her, I sat on the sofa, taking a sip and letting the liquid run down my throat. It burned as it went down, but I liked the feeling. My mind drifted to the little box in my jacket pocket.

Dimitri had given his blessing, even came with me to find the ring. We'd traveled back to Blood Moon, to a well known jeweler Ben had suggested. Nobody but us three knew we'd even gone, our cover story being we were out getting materials for the houses. I just needed the perfect time to do it, because that's what Violet deserved. And there was no doubt in my mind she was the girl I wanted to marry, mate or not. I'd loved her since I was a kid. So, I sat there and thought up the perfect way to propose to her, without her catching on.

"Don't be cliche, and do at a restaurant or something." Ehno said.

"I didn't think you were still here, Ehno. You've been quiet the last few weeks." I took another sip of my drink.

"I've had a lot on my mind."

"We share the same mind."

"Alright, I've had a lot going on then."

"Such as?"

"I've been talking to Celeste."

My forehead creased. *"The Moon Goddess?"*

"Do you know another Celeste?"

I rolled my eyes. *"What have you been talking about?"*

"This and that. You'll know, when the time comes."

"Gee, you're so helpful." And then I had a sickening thought. *"It's not about the babies, is it? Everything is okay with them?"*

"Yes, the babies are fine. It's not about that."

"Thank the Goddess."

"Yes, we can all thank the Goddess. Now, about Hala."

"What about her?"

"Am I allowed to mark her now?"

I choked back a laugh, covering my mouth so I didn't wake Vie. *"You're silent for weeks, and the first thing you come back with is getting it on with your mate."*

"Whatever. You can't talk, you just had sex!"

"And it was great." I grinned and he growled. *"Go for it. You don't need my permission."*

"You told me I couldn't!"

"Not before I marked Violet!"

"You humans. . .." He trailed off, and I could feel his frustration. I chuckled lowly, finishing the rest of my drink.

CHAPTER 53
VIOLET

I woke up the next morning feeling better than I had in weeks. Stretching out, my arms landed on Jaspers side of the bed. But it was empty, my fingers trailing along the silk sheets. Lazily, I opened my eyes, spotting a folded piece of paper.

'Vie,

I went with Ashwell to help with the training today. I made you breakfast though; It's in the microwave. I love you. XOXO.'

The thought of food had me getting out of bed quickly, the babies nudging me impatiently. I smiled, rubbing my stomach, which seemed to grow more and more each day. Now that I knew what their kicks felt like, I was eager to feel them, and overjoyed when I did.

My first order of business was to use the bathroom, which I found myself frequently using nowadays anyway. Then I went to the kitchen, pulling out a plate of eggs, bacon, hashbrowns, and blueberry waffles. A small fruit bowl had been left on the top shelf of the fridge, along with a glass of orange juice. How did I not smell him cooking this morning? My mouth was watering already! Taking my food and glass, I took it over to the sofa, digging in greedily, and savoring each bite.

I nearly choked when Grandpa popped into the room, standing three feet away.

"Goddess! Now I see why Mom hates it when you do that!" I chastised him.

"Sorry." He smirked, looking not sorry at all. "That looks good." He eyed my food.

"It is. What are you doing here?" I forked another bite of waffle.

"Just wondering how you like the room." He flopped on the cushion beside me, looking around.

"It's wonderful Grandpa. Really. We love it." I smiled at him.

"Good."

"Just curious though. . . How did you do it? Is this the furniture from the cabin?" I patted the sofa, raising an eyebrow.

"Yes. But I was going to replace it at the actual cabin."

I laughed. "Good, do that."

He let me finish my breakfast in silence. When I was done, I took the dishes to the sink, then I looked at the closet. Jasper and I had never unpacked our clothes, we'd been living out of suitcases. The old room downstairs was never a permanent room; As for the babies' belongings, we'd put them in the closet there, resolving to unpack them when we chose as room we liked, or had a new house.

"You didn't happen to bring my clothes up here, did you?" I turned to Grandpa.

"They should all be there." He replied easily.

I shook my head, opening the double doors to a huge walk-in closet. As promised, all my clothes were hung up, Jaspers on the other side. A long dresser was set against the back wall. Opening the first drawer, I found my socks and underwear. The one under it had my old favorite t-shirts. I settled on a red AC/DC tee and faded blue jeans. However, getting the jeans on was a different story; They were too tight.

"Shit." I mumbled.

"Everything okay?" Granda called.

"My pants are too tight." I groaned.

"Ah."

Taking them off, I shuffled through the drawers until I came upon a pair of sweats. Good enough. Satisfied, I walked out, heading to the bathroom.

"What did you want to do today?" I asked casually as I brushed my hair.

"We should start on your training."

I bit my lip. "Alright. After I'm done, we can go find a spot."

He came to stand in the doorway. "I already found a spot, actually."

"Away from the houses? And the fields?"

"Yes."

Throwing my hair into a low ponytail, I nodded. "Let's go."

He raised an eyebrow at me. "You're in a good mood today."

"Is that a crime?"

He laughed. "Not at all." He held out his hand, but I shook my head.

"We're walking. I just got over the morning sickness, no need to revisit it."

"You've done this a hundred times."

"Not pregnant."

"Fine." I huffed.

I giggled as we headed out. But when I opened the door to the room, a piece of paper caught my attention. It was taped to the outside, folded in half. I frowned, wondering why Jasper had left me another note like this. But when I unfolded it, I quickly realized it wasn't from Jasper. My throat tightened as I read the words, printed in an elegant script.

'Silver Moon does not need a MONSTER as our Luna. Get lost, freak!'

The sheet was ripped from my hand, and then it was incinerated in front of my eyes. I looked at my Grandpa, who was glaring at the ashes.

"They don't know what they're talking about Violet." He said.

"Yeah." My eyes cast downward.

"You're not a monster, or a freak. You're a first, the first of your kind. That only makes you different, and different doesn't necessarily mean 'bad'."

397

"Clearly not everyone believes that." I mumbled.

"To Hell with what others think. The Violet I know has never cared either."

"But I'm a Luna now." I sighed. "I kind of have to care what others think of me. I'm in a position of respect, and trust."

"You only have to care up to a certain point. Don't let one persons immaturity ruin your whole day."

He was right. I was going to start training today, officially, and it was long overdue. Soon, I would be able to show the pack as a whole that I wasn't a danger. Or a monster. As we got into the elevator, I had to wonder who would be brazen enough to come up here with such petty intent. They had to have come up the elevator, but there were so many scents in here from people going to different floors, it was impossible to tell. I should have paid more attention to the scent by our door.

The door slid open, and I took Grandpas hand as we descended the stairs. Tracy waited at the bottom, practically bouncing on her feet.

"Good morning Tracy." I greeted her as we reached the bottom. "What's up?"

"I'm so excited for your training!" She clapped her hands.

"Uh. . ." I looked at grandpa questioningly.

"Tracy has happily agreed to sit in on your training, even join in when the need arises."

"Why?"

"Several reasons."

"But what if I-" I swallowed, unable to finish the sentence.

Tracy took my hand. "Oh, Luna, you don't need to be scared of hurting me! Mr. Gideon will be there the whole time to make sure nothing happens, he said so! And I *want* to help you! You hired me as your personal attendant, remember?"

"Yeah, but like, to do laundry and help me with paperwork, Tracy. Not put yourself in the line of fire."

Her eyes widened excitedly. "You'd let me help with pack paperwork?!"

"You're missing the point Tracy."

Her face got weirdly serious. "I'm willing to put myself in the line of fire if it helps you. That's what a pack does for their Luna and Alpha."

Her words threw me off. I floundered around in my head for an argument, but when I couldn't find one, I conceded.

"Fine." I grumbled.

"Perfect. Let's be on our way, shall we?" Grandpa ushered us to the door. Tracy bounced along happily while I dragged my feet.

A few people were out and about this morning. Some stopped to say hello, while others simply nodded. At least, nobody was giving me dirty looks or whispering about me. Tracy and Grandpa chatted while I followed just behind them. We walked past the field closest to the packhouse; Greg and his co-workers were already out, planting. I waved to them as we passed, unsure if they noticed.

"What's going here?" I pointed to the field.

"Corn, I think. We haven't had fresh grown corn in so long! I can't wait until it's done, Mama makes the best corn on the cob!" Tracy said.

"I'll have to try it sometime." I replied.

Another twenty minutes passed of easy topics until Grandpa and Tracy stopped. I looked at my surroundings curiously. We were well away from the packhouse and the town. The forest lay ahead, but this area was desolate, covered in patchy grass. I could hear the tractors in the distance, but we were quite alone. I wondered what, if anything, used to be here.

"What was this place?" I looked at Tracy.

"Originally, it was another orchard. The old Alpha uprooted it though, saying he was going to build more houses. He never did though, so it's been like this for a few years now."

"Huh. Well, I guess this works then."

"Do you remember the techniques Clara and I went over with you?" Grandpa asked.

I nodded.

"Good. Let's start with that then. Tracy, why don't you go take a seat over there?"

"Okie dokey!"

I waited until she was safely sitting on the ground a good distance away. Then I closed my eyes, focusing on blocking everything out. Grandpa walked me through it, just like before. It seemed a little easier this time around, even though it had been a while.

"Now. I want you to unlock the chest, open it. Let your magic out."

I hesitated. The fear of hurting him or Tracy was strong in my mind.

"Don't be afraid Violet. I'm here, I won't let anything happen. Nothing is going to happen."

Taking a breath, I imagined the lock on the chest. Conjuring up a key, I unlocked it, slowly letting the lid open. A rush of energy through my body took me by surprise. My eyes flew open, my feet staggering back a few steps. It wasn't unpleasant per se; It felt warm, almost like being cuddled in a blanket by the fire, or being embraced. Grandpa watched my every move like a hawk, but he didn't seem unnerved, as if my reaction was expected.

"You good?" He asked. I nodded once. "Okay. Here's what I want you to do. Close your eyes again, and this time, I want you to take a step away from Hala. Try to block her out, like you did everything else."

I tried, but Hala whined loudly, fighting me.

"What's wrong?"

"It hurts." She whimpered. I immediately stopped, opening my eyes.

"Hala says it hurts her."

His forehead furrowed. "It shouldn't."

"She says it does. She was fighting against me."

He scratched his chin. "But all the books say. . . Can she describe it?"

"It feels like you're pulling away from me, from our bond. It feels wrong." She said.

I relayed her words.

"But that's what a Hybrid is. Someone who can tap into the two sides of themselves."

I shrugged. "I don't know Grandpa. But I'm not willing to hurt Hala."

"No, no of course not. I don't want to either. Hmm. . . Okay, let's try another way. This time, focus on Hala *and* your magic, together."

For the third time, I closed my eyes, reaching for that bond I had with my wolf. She embraced it readily. At the same time, I tried to tap into the energy inside me, the warmth. And then something I wasn't expecting happened; I gasped as my mind and my wolf's seemed to merge. It wasn't anything like having her in my head, a feeling I was very familiar with now. And it wasn't like when we shifted, essentially trading spots of control. This was a surreal feeling, an experience of seeing what *she* saw in wolf form, but in my human body. We thought *together*, felt *together*. But on top of that, or maybe mixed in, was my other side, my magic. It was the glue holding us together, bringing us together, as one being that was neither wolf nor human nor witch, but all three.

"Violet?"

I opened my eyes. Grandpas eyes widened considerably. "Hala?"

"Both." I replied. My voice mixed with my hers, coming out a little rougher.

"Whoa." Tracy said from her spot on the ground.

"How do you feel right now?" Grandpa inquired.

"I feel. . ..In control."

He nodded slowly. "Alright. . . If you're up for it, I'd like to try a simple spell."

I nodded.

He took a step closer. "I'm going to make a rose grow. Watch, and then repeat after me."

He said the words clearly, waving his hand over the ground. A single rose sprout peeked through the grass, blossoming into a brilliant red flower. I smiled.

"Now you."

Lifting my hand, I opened my mouth to repeat the spell. In my head, I imagined another rose growing. The warm energy inside me zoomed through my arm, pooling in my palm. The temperature grew, almost to the point of hot. Before I'd uttered a single syllable, grass started to grow under my feet. Not just grass, but tons of sprouts as well, popping out and reaching towards the sky. In the blink of an eye, we were surrounded by fresh grass and all types of roses ranging from red to white to yellow. In front of them all was a tiny tree, the only one in the clearing. I stood there, bewildered.

"I. . .I'm sorry."

"No, I am." Grandpa stared around us. Further out, Tracy was approaching, looking in awe at the new plants.

"I don't know what happened," I admitted. "I was going to say the spell, but-"

"But you didn't need to."

"What does that mean, Grandpa?"

He met my eyes calmly. "It means we were wrong. You are not a Hybrid."

CHAPTER 54
VIOLET

"What do you mean she's not a hybrid?"

Grandpa, Jasper, Tracy, King, Ashwell and I were sitting in one of the common areas. As soon as Grandpa realized something was off kilter with me, he'd told me to mindlink the boys right away for an emergency meeting. I'd invited Tracy along; I wasn't entirely sure why, but her never-ending positivity made me feel better.

Grandpa paced back and forth, occasionally wringing his hands together. Like me biting my lip, that was his nervous habit.

"I suppose the technical term could still be 'Hybrid', but. . . She doesn't use her abilities like one." He said.

"*She* is sitting right here." I said from my seat on the sofa. "Why don't you think I'm a Hybrid anymore?"

"Ever since we discovered what you were, I've been reading non-stop. I even went to visit an old friend, Alistaire. He was always intrigued by Hybrids, always wanting to learn more. Naturally, he had tons of books and journals I could read. He even had an old scroll, dating back to who knows when!" He threw his hands up. "Most of what I read I already knew; Knowledge passed down from the time of their extinction. What I *didn't* know is how they used their abilities."

"But I'm assuming you found out?" King inquired.

Grandpa nodded. "The one piece of Hybrid history that was the same in everything I read. To access one side of themselves, they had to pull away from the other side."

"I don't understand." Ashwell said.

"For example, imagine a wolf and a vampire Hybrid. Vampires have vast abilities that are actually similar to our own. However, they are far stronger, faster, and they need blood to survive. Unlike us. So in order to tap into that extra strength or speed, the Hybrid would have to mentally and emotionally pull away from the bond with their wolf, giving themselves over to their vampire side. The same goes for a witch Hybrid." He stopped and looked at me. "It should not have hurt Hala when you tried to tap into your magic. You were not severing your bond with her, simply pushing it to one side temporarily. And you should *not* have been able to use magic without any incantation."

"But you do?" Jasper asked confused.

Grandpa shook his head vehemently. "It's not possible. I've all but mastered saying spells in my head. Same with Clara. You don't need to vocalize the spell for it to work." He tipped his head to the side. "Is that what you did?"

"I. . .I don't think so." I replied carefully. "I remember the words. But I wasn't thinking about them, not really. I was imagining a rose growing, like you did. And then lots of them grew."

"And you felt the sparks?"

"Sparks?" My brows came down on confusion.

"When you used your magic."

"It doesn't feel like sparks."

He sat down across from me, leaning in. "What does your magic feel like Violet?"

I thought about it for a second before answering. "It feels like. . . an energy. And it's warm. Like stepping into a warm bath, I guess. It's not. . .spark-like. . .it's more of a . . .buzzing? Like adrenaline." I looked at Tracy, Goddess knew why, but she smiled and patted my shoulder.

Grandpa didn't say anything, and I began to worry. My whole life, I'd never gotten anything truly *right*. I was the trouble-maker, the odd one out. I did alright in most things, but I always felt kind of off. Then I learned I was a Hybrid, the most *off* anyone could be in this day and age. Now, here I was, debating whether or not that's what I truly was in the first place. Could I be defective? Was something wrong with me? Could I not even be a good Hybrid?

Finally, Grandpa spoke, his voice very low. "You have different magic than I do."

My heart sank. "What does that mean?"

"It means that I *was* wrong. I really don't think you are a Hybrid Violet. You have magic, that much is obvious. But it's different than a witches magic."

"Remember what you said the other night?" Ashwell leaned over the back of the sofa. "You said that you're the first of your kind, that your ancestors maybe weren't Hybrids. Maybe that's true."

I sighed. "I don't know why I said that. For all we know, every witch Hybrid had different magic than regular witches."

"Not according to Alistaires books."

"Well, maybe those are wrong. It's been centuries since a there was a living Hybrid. Information gets scrambled."

"Violet-"

"I don't want to talk about this anymore right now." I interrupted whatever Jasper was going to say. "I was just learning to accept that I was a Hybrid. Now I might not be one. I announced to the whole pack what I was Jasper!" My head sank into my hands. "I just want to know who I am." I mumbled.

Tracy rubbed my back in soothing circles. "Well, that's easy. You're Violet, silly."

I raised my head slowly to look at her. As usual, she was smiling.

"That's not what I meant." I told her.

"I know. But does it really matter *what* you are? Look at everything you've done. You're a good person Violet. You're loving and attentive and you care about others above yourself. You're a great mate as far as I can see, and you're going to be a great Mother too! You could be a dragon mixed with a fox, and I wouldn't care! As long as you were the same person you are now on the inside."

A soft smile touched my lips at her little rant. "Thanks Tracy." I whispered.

"She's right." King stepped forward. "It doesn't matter to any of us what you are."

"Damn straight." Ashwell added.

Grandpa and Jasper both nodded as well. I already felt better, knowing I had their support and love. As long as I had that, I was good.

"I think I know who to ask for some answers." I said, getting to my feet. "I'll see you all in a little while, I'm going to bed."

Everyone looked at me with varied expressions. "Vie, it's only quarter to twelve." Jasper said.

"I know. But I think I have to be sleeping for this to work."

I gave a half wave, leaving them all in a state of total bewilderment. I maiden a quick detour to the kitchen, grabbing a sandwich out of the fridge, and eating it on my way upstairs. The elevator door opened to our floor as I was brushing the crumbs from my fingers. Going straight to our bedroom, I made a beeline for the toilet; I'd never fall asleep if I had to pee. I did my business, washing my hands quickly. Then I was under the covers, my eyes closed, and calling out with my mind.

"Celeste? If you're there, I would really like to talk to you. I don't know how I did this last time, but I'm hoping this works."

I focused on calming my breathing while calling out to the Goddess. My advancing pregnancy actually helped the process too; I'd been taking at least one nap a day lately, becoming tired more easily. Soon, my breathing evened out and I drifted easily off to sleep. At first, it was just blank. And then I was thrown into an extremely vivid dream. Large, mossy trees surrounded me, with equally mossy rocks spread on the ground between them. The air was crisp, the smells of the forest floating to me on the light breeze. Unlike most dreams, I wasn't watching from a third persons point of view; This time I was in my own body, experiencing things first hand.

I realized I was standing in the middle of a dirt path. Shrugging, I started walking deeper into the thicket. The further I went, the darker the forest became, the trees growing closer together. Shadows fell over the path, but I passed them over casually, feeling calm and carefree. My thoughts drifted as lazily as the wind in my hair, a soft melody humming from my throat. It was when the black wolf ran into my field of vision that I stopped. It looked oddly familiar. . .And then it clicked.

"Hala!" I called. Her head turned at the sound of her name, her brilliant eyes watching me.

"She is quite beautiful, isn't she?"

I screamed, spinning around so fast my vision blurred. "What the *fuck?!*"

The words fell from my lips involuntarily, my face paling considerably at the sight of the Moon Goddess standing before me. She stood like a Queen amongst mortals, gazing at me with those mesmerizing violet eyes of hers. Her skin matched the white of her dress, her raven hair standing out against both magnificently. However, her expression was amused.

"I-I'm sorry!" I squeaked.

Her laugh was like the most endearing music.

"No harm done child. I have heard worse."

I suddenly remembered why I was here, but I was too shy to start asking my questions after my inappropriate outburst. Celeste, ignorant to my inner embarrassment, raised her hand, crooking her finger to Hala. My wolf jumped and leaped over rocks and bushes, stopping in front of her Mother and rolling playfully in the path.

"You've been having quite an adventure at Silver Moon." She said the words as easily as if we were discussing the weather.

"Uh, yeah. It's been interesting."

"How do you like being a Luna?"

I rocked back on my heels, unsure if I should tell her the whole truth. "I like it."

Her eyes met mine knowingly. I bit my lip.

"It is not an easy task, taking on the role of a leader." She stated.

"Not really, no." Looking away into the trees, I decided to ask an easy question first. "Why did you choose me?"

"Because I know you will succeed."

"You sound very certain of that."

"I am certain of the person you are."

I swallowed hard. "And who am I?"

Celeste smiled softly at me, love and adoration in her expression. "You are a Midnight Wolf."

I almost groaned aloud. Instead, I asked, "But what does that mean? Am I not a Hybrid?"

"No, you are not a Hybrid."

So, Grandpa was wrong about me after all. I thought I might feel relieved at this news, but instead I felt even more downcast. Didn't I fit in anywhere?

"Do you know what this place is Violet?"

I shook my head. Nothing about this place was familiar to me.

"I brought your Mother here once." She drifted backwards, sitting on a large rock at the edge of the path. I followed, listening closely. "At the time, she was very unsure of herself. Of her position in the pack, her role as Luna. As a mate. She got through it all though. A strong woman."

"She is that." I agreed.

"Back then, Hala had a different name. Nia. I brought your Mother here to ask if Nia could get a second chance."

I gasped, my gaze going to my wolf. She was laying peacefully at Celestes feet, her eyes closing sleepily.

"This is where Hala was reborn?" I asked.

"It is. This is where your fate was decided too. I gave Hala to you as a gift, but I knew together you two would do wonderful things. You were made for each other."

"But she was made for Jennine first."

A sharp growl echoed out of Halas mouth at the name.

The Moon Goddess sighed sadly. "Jennine was. . . difficult."

"In what way?"

"I will tell you, but it is complicated Violet. You must try to understand." She crossed her legs under her, leaning back on her hands. Her beautiful face was tilted up, looking into the sky. She looked so young, yet as old as the world itself. It was a dizzying experience.

"I had every faith in Jennine." She began softly. "She was so bright, so outgoing. Creative too. I know you all believe that I have a hand in your creation, but that isn't true. Not in the sense that *I* choose who is born and who isn't. When a child is conceived, I only hold the power to grant them a gift. For some, it is an animal with which they bond their souls with. For others, it is magic. And then there are the vampires, which I do love, but sadly, they pay a steep price for. So I do consider you all my children, in a way."

"When Jennine was born, I gave her the gift of Nia. A wolf as brilliant and creative as she was. She was such a good child, I had no doubt in my mind that she would do what I had set out for her to do." Her eyes closed, her fair lips turning down. "I'm not sure where I went wrong. I've had so long, too long, to think that if perhaps I had visited her, encouraged her, things would have turned out differently. But it is what it is, and I cannot change the past."

"I don't think you should beat yourself up this much." I offered. "You can't help what people do with their freewill."

Celeste peeked at me through her long lashes. "Maybe you are right. But even a Goddess can feel remorse."

"Why? Because she went crazy with jealousy?"

She laughed once, but it was not music like. The sound grated against my eardrums, making me wince.

"If it were only jealousy that drove Jennine to where she is today, I would not feel as I do. You see child, I neglected Jennine. I neglected to tell her how special she was to me, neglected to set her on the right path. And in my ignorance, she started listening to another. I knew it, but I did not nothing to stop it, having faith that she would continue to walk in the light."

"Bastian?"

"No. A far more sinister being. It was whispers at first. I cannot tell you when they became more than that, but eventually, Jennine started to turn away from me. She no longer looked to me for advice or good will. She became driven by greed, and selfishness. Her life became about what she *wanted*, instead of what she could *do*. Her mind was poisoned against me, but still. . ... I had hope. That hope disappeared when she sent Nia back to me." A lone tear that shone like a crystal ran down her pale cheek.

☐ "Who poisoned her against you?" I whispered.

"A demon." She spat. "As cold and cunning as a snake. His name is Phoebus. And. . ." She turned her face to me, stealing my breath with the anger only a Goddess could possess, "He is my brother."

CHAPTER 55
CELESTE

I'd been alive for centuries. Millenia even. Yet, it never got any easier to talk about Phoebus. But I had to make this right; I had to fix the mistake I'd made with Jennine. I could not allow the same thing to happen a second time.

"You have a brother?" Violet gasped.

"I do. Even deity's' have family." I smirked.

"Whoa." She took a step back. "So then, you must have Mother?"

"My Mothers name is Thia. My Father is, I suppose in simple terms, what you would call the Universe."

I didn't receive a reply, I assumed she was processing this information. So, I continued.

"I cannot remember a time when my brother and I got along. And I have been alive a *long* time. Where I prefer to quiet and peace of moonlight, Phoebus prefers to rage and burn like the sun. I content myself with caring for others, but he enjoys playing games. Horrible, horrible games." I let my eyes close, memories flashing to the beat of my words.

"The first creation of mine was werefoxes. Did you know that?"

"No."

"Stunning creatures. I cherished them so much; I went on to create more children. Bears, wolves. I should have stopped at the witches." I sighed. "But I created vampires too. I suppose some could argue I myself was greedy. Phoebus certainly thought so. I had so many children to adore and love, and they loved me as well. I use to come cloaked to bonfires where they would dance and sing my name to the Heavens. Perhaps that was also sinful." I mused out loud.

"My brother would frequent the mortal world, 'visiting' my creations. He would plant all manner of heinous thoughts in their minds, thriving on the chaos he caused. It wasn't until I created the Hybrids that I saw how truly evil he was."

Even with my eyes closed, I could sense the tension from Violet. Both her and Hala listened to my story intently, hanging on my every word. Their heartbeats were in sync, accelerated from the anticipation.

"Your histories will never show how amazing the Hybrids were Violet. That knowledge has been wiped from any memory, every parchment. Once, they were harmonious, living in peace with other species. That all ended with Arthimeus." His name burned on the way out. The memory was so clear, even now. I forgot about the girl and her wolf, forgot about the forest. I was reliving my worst mistake now, my chest tightening with every breath.

"He was a vampire wolf Hybrid. One day, he led a group of hunters into the forest. He was so strong, and quick. Agile. A true leader. Phoebus was also in those woods though. Never in the hundred of years of my life would I have guessed what he had planned. His anger and envy towards me drove him to confront Arthimeus that day. He gave him a 'gift' of his own, one borne by hate and blood. He turned my child into a monster, right under my eyes. When I next decided to look in on the village, I was horrified to see it had been razed to the ground. Women lay amongst the rubble, holding their offspring in eternal embrace. Men had had their hearts torn from their bodies, limbs strewn about."

My head fell forward, a desperate cry of anguish falling from my lips.

"I found Arthimeus. Eventually. He was in a cave, his teeth sunk into the neck of his Father, drinking his blood to sustain himself. I seeped for the loss of so many precious souls. So many innocent souls. . ." I drew my knees up, resting my chin on them. "When next I saw my brother, he gloated at having appropriated one of my creations, shaping them into his own. He vowed that the love I had enjoyed would be snuffed out, like a candle in the wind. And so I watched as my once peaceful children terrorized each other. Murdering one another. It is true the Hybrids fancied themselves above all other species, but that was only planted by Phoebus in the first place. As if the nightmare could not get any worse, the vampires turned against me, joining the Hybrids."

"Now I understand why they did. You see Violet, I live by the rules set in place for me, even when I don't want to. I *cannot* interfere with the freewill of my children. The consequences would be disastrous. I watched helplessly as one after another vampire was slaughtered, until finally, they lost hope in me. So they did what they thought they had to do in order to survive."

"What did you do?" Violet asked. She was leaned against my rock, her eyes misty and wide. I reached one had out to gently caress her cheek.

"I had a daughter." I told her.

Hala whined under me, the sound ending in a broken cry.

"I don't understand." She placed her had over mine.

"Just as I bestow gifts on you, my Mother bestowed a gift to me. I bore a daughter, a true daughter, of my own flesh and blood. She was my greatest love. I raised her out of sight of the carnage below, and the watchful eyes of my brother. I made her strong, but gentle. Loving, but unyielding. A princess, and a warrior. Like anyone of you, I gave her a gift. A black wolf, marked by me and me alone. Against my own heart, when she ready, I sent her down to the mortal world. I watched over her, always. She held true to me, fighting amongst allies and ending the war."

"Arthimeus had passed already, leaving his cruel mission to his son. And then to his son after him. By the time my daughter was ready to leave me, generations had passed on Earth. The grandson was the last Hybrid to exist, until they no longer existed at all." I laughed mirthlessly.

"Maybe I was wrong. Maybe what I did next is my biggest mistake."

Violets hand trembled over mine, her breath shaky.

"I could not find it in myself to forgive the vampires. Their betrayal of me was of their own doing, not by any means of Phoebus. It was petty of me, foolish even. In my anger, I took the *gift* that Phoebus had given Arthimeus, giving it to them. I watched in silence for centuries as they drank the lifeblood of others to survive. When they could not, they weakened, suffered. I truly felt it was a fair punishment." My hand slipped away from Violet, falling to my side loosely. "Until I realized I was no better than my cruel, merciless brother. But it was too late; Once a gift is given, no matter how cruel it is, it cannot be taken away."

My vicious tale came to end, the memories subsiding, but leaving behind the pain. Always pain. It was as much a part of me as the love I showed to my children. Never ending, never fading, a constant reminder of what and who I was, and what I had done. Beside me, Violet sank to her knees, weeping quietly. Hala echoed her cries, despair wafting in the air around the three of us. But I knew I could keep them here much longer. She needed to hear it all before I sent her back.

"Do you understand now?" I asked her.

She nodded, wiping her face. "You are not evil Celeste." She raised her head. "You made a mistake."

"One of the many repercussions of watching over mortals. They make frequent mistakes." I smiled humorlessly. "Sooner or later, I was bound to make a few too."

"Phoebus is talking to Jennine, isn't he?"

I nodded once.

"Who am I to you?"

"You are my child, but not my daughter. I will never have another true daughter." I blinked tears away. "But you are special Violet. You are the key to the war that hasn't happened yet."

"My pack is barely surviving, even now, with Jasper and I at the head. How can I prevent a war?" She cried desperately.

"I cannot tell you what I do not know. I don't know my brothers plans. I wish I did. All I know is that he has Jennine's ear, and sooner or later, he will show himself to her, if he hasn't already."

Violet jumped to her feet. Hala echoed her humans movement, ears flattening and a snarl ripping between her teeth.

"You have no information for me at all!" She shouted at me. "You saddled me with this responsibility, when I am literally the *worst* person for the job!"

Her eyes held an amount of fear that broke my heart. My feet slipped off the rock, hovering inches above the ground. I stood before her, unknowingly just as afraid as she was.

"There is no time to be wasted doubting yourself." I let a tiny bit of my aura fill my words. It had the desired effect; Violet quieted, staring at me with awe. "You are the one I trust with this Violet. You and those closest to you. I have faith you will not fail!"

"What if we do?" She whimpered.

"That is not an option. Phoebus must be stopped! Jennine is simply his puppet this time. But don't underestimate her either. He is no longer playing games; Failure this time means the end of all of us."

"I can't do it Celeste." She stepped further away from me, her head shaking side to side. "You have to chose another. I'm not strong enough."

"Doubting yourself, again!" My voice filled the forest, the branches of the trees bowing to my authority. Hala fell to her knees, her head to the ground. Violet, on the other hand, stood straight and tall, a look of steel in her eyes. My heart and aura settled as I watched her withstand the power of a Goddess. My expression softened, my feet moving towards her. "You are your Mothers daughter. So much stronger than you realize. You will succeed, just as she did."

415

I cupped her cheeks, leaning in.

"What was your daughters name?" She asked quietly. I froze.

"Elsa."

"What happened to her?"

My lips touched Violets forehead gently. I whispered against her skin, "This you must remember child; She died."

There was the familiar shimmer of the air. When I opened my eyes, I was alone in the forest.

CHAPTER 56
JASPER

I stared, wide-eyed, at my mate, along with everyone else. We'd reconvened in the living area, with the doors shut, and had Gideon soundproof the room as an extra precaution. Vie had mindlinked me in a state, saying we needed to talk urgently. Of all the things she could have told us, the Moon Goddess's story didn't even make the top ten on my list.

"Poor Celeste. . ." Tracy wiped her eyes for the hundredth time.

The mood in general was solemn, everyone taking their individual time to process the information Violet had brought us. Eventually, I opened the conversation up with a question.

"So, Jennine was what? Her first choice?"

Vie looked at me. "You mean, before me? I think so."

"What's the end goal?" King asked. "For this Phoebus guy?"

"She said it would mean the end of us all. And I don't think she meant the end of werewolves, specifically. I think he wants to destroy everything Celeste created. The wolves, werebears, werefoxes, witches. Maybe even the vampires, who knows."

"That's so weird." Tracy said. "If he's so jealous, why not just create something of his own? A species of his own children?"

"Maybe he can't." I thought aloud. "Maybe it's not part of his power."

"So he manipulates the creations of his sister into getting rid of themselves out of spite." Ashwell added.

"Or maybe he's just a prick who gets off on mass genocide." King spat.

"Whatever his motivations, he has to be stopped. This is now way bigger than just a problem with Jennine; Like Celeste said, she's just his puppet this time. But whatever he's planning, we can be sure that she's a main player." Vie pinched the bridge of near nose. "I need to talk my parents."

"I was just thinking the same thing." Gideon agreed. "Shall I?"

"Please." She nodded.

He vanished with a slight *pop*.

I folded my hands together under my chin, waiting. According to Violet, she'd been with the Goddess for only a little while, but in reality, she'd slept for hours. It was twilight outside, the shadows of the setting sun streaming in through the windows. My eyes followed a bird flitting from tree to tree in the yard, my inner thoughts a jumbled mess. My sole focus right now was trying to figure out how I could protect my family. I was about to have two children, born into a world that would soon be thrown into chaos, and my guts twisted and knotted at the thought.

It wasn't long before Gideon reappeared in the center of the room, holding hands with Dimitri and Lily. Both of them looked somewhat dizzy, settling into the nearest chairs.

"We can't be gone long." Lily told us. "Dad said you have information about Jennine." She said the name like it was poison.

"You might want to call Ben and tell him to look after stuff for a couple hours." I suggested to Dimitri. "This is a lot."

He raised an eyebrow between me and his daughter, but nodded, pulling out his cell.

"Did you find her?" Lily directed the question Violet.

"No. But we know more than we did."

Dimitri ended the call, leaning back in his seat. "Go ahead." So, for the second time tonight, Violet recounted her meeting with the Goddess, sparing no detail. Tracy teared up all over again, while the rest of us listened closely to anything we might have missed before. Dimitris expression remained neutral, while his mates displayed various emotions as she listened. When she was done, the room was quiet, save for Tracys sniffles.

"It makes sense now." Dimitri spoke into the silence.

"What do you mean?" I asked.

He glanced at Lily. "Jennine wasn't always the way she is. We grew up, not together, but in the popular clicks you could say. Her parents were once very influential in the pack. She was a sweet girl, very helpful, very happy."

"When did that change?" King asked.

"Around highschool. But that happened with most of the girls. Boys too. People change as they grow up; Honestly, I'm sure most people thought her attitude stemmed from her parents, particularly her mother. Why would anyone assume, or even think, that an evil God had anything to do with it?"

"Dad. . ." Lily looked at Gideon with a strange expression. "You don't think. . . Bastian. . .?"

"I've been considering it." He nodded. "But it also might be unfair to assume that every single evil person was influenced by Phoebus. I'd like to believe that Bastian was, but maybe he was just simply evil, of his own freewill." He sighed.

"But we know for sure that Jennine is being influenced." I said. "And that makes her more dangerous than we originally thought."

"Agreed. Who knows if Phoebus decided to give her another gift of his." Ashwell said.

I stood, gathering everyone's attention.

"We need to focus on finding Jennine." I turned to King and Ashwell. "I want our training doubled. I also want you to pull back on border patrol; No point in putting pack members lives at risk. We have the shield up now, so put those men into training with the others. And I want you to put the word out that any women who want to train, have the right to."

"Yes Alpha." They replied in unison.

"Vie, I want you to train with Gideon, as much as your able. You might have different magic, but he can still guide you. Tracy, stay with her. Help me look out for my family."

Both the girls nodded. Violet rubbed circles over her stomach.

"You're talking like you have a plan son." Dimitri said slowly.

"I do."

"Care to fill us in?" Gideon asked.

Starting to pace, I walked them through the theory I had.

"Vie, you said Celeste told you to remember that her daughter died, right? Well, Elsa was a Goddess, wasn't she?"

"It stands to reason." Lily answered the question. "She was born from the Moon Goddess, and her grandmother was also a Goddess."

"But she still died." I stated firmly. "So, that means it's possible. Which means it's also probably possible that Phoebus can be killed too."

"You're right." Ashwell said slowly.

"I can only imagine how hard it's going to be to kill a God." King crossed his arms.

"Our first plan of action is to capture Jennine." I explained. "I'm betting that if *she* knows we know about Phoebus, he'll know it too. Knowing we know about him, and have general idea about what he's planning might throw him off a little."

"So, to summarize, you want to capture a Dark Witch, tell her we know her grand scheme, and then try to kill her God boss?" Tracy wrinkled her nose. "No offense, Alpha, but that's pretty out there."

"It's better than sitting around and waiting for a war." Lily spoke with authority. Tracy sank back into the sofa.

I looked at the other Alpha present. "Dimitri, I'm going to need you too."

"How can I help?"

"I'm going to need you to help me get in touch with other packs. And, if I remember correctly, you have an old werebear friend?"

He smirked. "He's not going to believe any of this."

"He might. After all, this family has not only a Mother Wolf, but a Midnight wolf too." Violet mirrored her fathers smirk.

"I don't suppose anyone knows how to get a hold of the foxes." Gideon looked around. Everyone shook their heads. "Perhaps Alistaire has contacts." He tapped his chin thoughtfully.

"Bring him here, if you can." I said.

For the next hour, we came up with a rough sketch of a plan. Despite sleeping for most of the afternoon, Violets eyelids started to droop, and Tracy was yawning. Around ten, our group split off, King and Ashwell heading to their respective floors, while Gideon took Dimitri and Lily home. Dimitri was to tell his Beta and Gamma what was happening, as well as fill them in on the plan so far. Everyone had their roles, and the sooner we got started the better.

Taking my mates hand, we walked through the house until we got to the kitchen. Vie sat at the island, resting her head on the cool marble surface. I pulled varying food items out of the fridge and cupboards, working to make us a light dinner.

"It's crazy, isn't it?" She said quietly. "A few months ago we were bickering with each other at school. Now we're mates, Alpha and Luna, and preparing to fight a God." She laughed. "Crazy."

I flipped the chicken in the pan, joining in her laugh. "Crazy indeed."

"I'm glad though. Glad I don't have to face it alone. I'm glad I have you."

I looked at her, my face serious. "You'll always have me Vie. No matter what."

She sat up tiredly when I set her plate in front her. We ate in comfortable silence, occasionally glancing at each other. My thoughts drifted back to my conversation with my wolf the other night.

"Ehno."

"Yes?"

"Did you know all this? Is this what you've been talking to Celeste about?"

"No."

I set my fork down. *"If you have any information that can help us, I'd really like it if you didn't keep it to yourself."*

"I know as much as you do Jasper."

Violet groaning pulled my attention to her.

"What's wrong?" I asked instantly.

"Hala is bugging me to go for a run. But I'm tired." She grumbled.

"I want to go for a run." Ehno piped up.

"She just said she was tired."

"Hala isn't."

I could feel his intention in my head and I rolled my eyes.

"Do you ever not think about sex?"

"It's been forever Jasper." He growled, surprising me. *"I want to mark my mate too! I want to complete the bond."*

"What are you talking about? Violet and I marked each other, the bond is *complete."*

He growled again, louder. Pushing forward, Ehno tried to take control; I gripped the countertop to steady myself, shocked by his behaviour.

"What is the matter with you?!" I yelled at him.

"I need to mark her Jasper!"

"Not tonight Ehno! In case you didn't notice, we're all stressed. Especially Vie, and-"

He tried to take over again. I pushed back, keeping him at bay by a thread. I couldn't understand where this sudden need came from. Our wolf counterparts marked each other, not out necessity, but more to show other wolves they were taken. But Ehno was acting as if this was life or death, snarling and clawing inside my head.

Violet stood, looking as frazzled as I was. "Hala is *insisting* we go for a run." She rolled her eyes hugely.

"So is Ehno."

"Let's go. Let them get it out of their systems." She scooped up the dishes, dropping them in the sink. We took the closest exit, the backdoor of the house. Another improvement by Gideon, and fairly convenient. I discarded my shoes by the stone steps leading into the yard, and then my sweater. It was especially bright out tonight, and looking up I saw why. It was a full moon, with not a cloud in the sky. It shone brightly, perfectly round with a white halo glowing around it. The stars around dulled in comparison.

Violet shifted, and I a few seconds later. Ehno instantly forced me back, having more control in this form.

"At least wait 'till your in the forest!" I sneered at him. The last thing I wanted to have to explain to anyone who happened to look out their window was why my wolf couldn't control himself. If I couldn't have sex in the open, neither could he.

To his credit though, he did manage to get to the trees, but not very far. As soon as the two made it past the first five, Hala crouched, her tail in the air. I turned my attention elsewhere, letting him have his moment, which he was all too eager for. It was a little unsteady at first, Hala was a big wolf after all. The thing that took me off guard was how good it felt; Ehno was in Alpha mode now, the beast coming out. But I felt everything, willingly giving myself over to the pleasure. It had never felt like this before. Our wolves had mated, a few times, but held back on marking. I knew Ehno wanted to, so I assumed it was Halas decision.

Usually I would mind my own business, give them a semblance of privacy. Of course, I could feel what he felt, but this was different. This was so much more intense, and I couldn't figure out if it was because they intended to mark each other this time. Eventually, I stopped thinking about it, caught up wholly in the sensations I was feeling. If I didn't know any better, I could have sworn it was *me* making love to Violet, not Ehno and Hala. As we neared closer, I had an unexpected urge to push forward. Ehno didn't fight me; He invited it. Instead of taking control from him though, I was in a sense merged with him. Seeing through his eyes, moving with him.

Together, as one mind, we went for Halas marking spot.

A fierce, guttural growl emitted from us as we pierced her skin. Our vision blurred, and then it was blinded by a piercing white light. It was just like what had happened when Violet and I had marked each other. The moment was pure ecstasy, beyond anything I could describe. Hala then stood, practically throwing us off. A second later, she was over us, her teeth exposed. There was pain, and then another wave of bliss. The light around us faded, and she pulled away, licking the blood from mouth.

Ehno shoved me back so suddenly, and forcefully, I was shocked I didn't lose consciousness. My anger flared, my intention to lash out at him. Until I focused on our mate. The words died on my tongue, every thought going blank. Hala stood tall, her head lifted proudly. There was visible golden glow around her, making her black fur shine. She might have even been bigger than before, too. But the thing that stood out the most was the mark on her side. It was no longer white, but a beautiful, brilliant gold, the glow around her only enhancing it. It matched our human marks perfectly.

I had a gut feeling. Following my instincts, I pushed forward again. Ehno let me, and I thought maybe he felt a little smug. Turning my head as far around as I could, I looked at my own fur. There was no glow around me, but, like I had suspected, I now had a mark to match Halas.

"Our bond is different from others." Ehno told me. I couldn't form a reply for him. *"And now, it's complete."*

Throwing back their heads, our wolves let out joyful howls.

CHAPTER 57
JASPER

"How do you feel?"

Vie and I were in the elevator, both of us completely drained from what had happened in the woods. Ehno was in the back of my mind, communicating with Hala. His ego had grown ten times in the frame of an hour. I had a feeling he was going to become insufferable to have inside my head for the foreseeable future.

"I'm exhausted. But I don't feel much different. You?" She replied.

"Same. I wonder what it means. Ehno said our bond is different from others."

She yawned. "Is there anything that *isn't* different about us?"

"I'm starting to think not."

She giggled as we stepped off the elevator. Her smile slipped when she looked at the door; I followed her gaze to find a folded piece of paper taped to the door.

"Not again." She groaned, ripping it from the wood. Unfolding it, her eyes scanned the page.

"What is it?" I asked curiously.

Wordlessly, she shoved the note at me, throwing open the door and stomping inside. Holding the note up I read:

You're not good enough. Feak. Monster. Failure. You'll be the downfall of Silver Moon. Do us all a favor and go back to own pack. FREAK!

I frowned deeply. Inhaling, I caught a few different scents around our door. One I recognized as Emma, a maid who worked here before Warrick got rid of her. I'd recently given her old job back. Besides hers, there was mine and Violets, a fading sense of Gideons, and an overly sweet

425

scent of strawberries and. . ..coconut? But there was something else in that mix that put me off, making me wrinkle my nose. Is was much too sweet, and had a hint of chemicals. Perfume, probably.

"Vie, do you know who put this here?" I asked her as I shut the door behind me. She was sitting on our bed, arms crossed.

"No."

"Why did you say 'not again'? How many of these have there been?"

"Only one."

"Why didn't you tell me?"

"I've been a little distracted Jasper." She took a breath. "And it doesn't matter anyway. I don't know who's writing them, and I don't care. I've got bigger things to worry about than someone writing petty, immature notes to me."

Her tone was dismissive, but I could tell this was really bothering her. Her jaw was clenched, her shoulders tensed. Her fists were clenched under her arms. Sitting next to her, I pulled her in for a side hug.

"You should have told me. I can find who wrote this, make them stop."

"I said it doesn't matter."

"It *does*." I tilted her chin, forcing her to look at me. "Someone is harassing you, making you feel unwanted. That's not okay, Violet. I wouldn't stand for it even if it weren't directed at you."

"Two notes doesn't exactly qualify 'harassment'." She argued.

I sighed. "Why are you always so stubborn?"

Her lip twitched in the hint of a smirk. "Afraid I'll pass that trait on?" She glanced at her belly.

"Goddess, I hope not."

We laughed together, the mood lightening a degree.

"I'm going to look into this." I held up the note. "Just because we're on the verge of a potential war, doesn't mean I ignore the little problems."

"Alright. If it'll make you feel better." She pulled away, but she looked relieved. The girl was too proud sometimes.

Getting up, I turned off the lights. Vie was already under the covers, lying on her side with her arm hanging over her stomach. I got in next to her, placing my hand on her bump, grinning when I felt tiny kicks on my palm. I scooted down the mattress, resting my forehead against her skin. Then I began to sing softly.

"Beddy-bye, butterfly, tuck into your flower,
Dream butterfly dreams, 'till the morning hour.
Beddy-bye, baby bear, lay down in your den,
Until the sun rises, and it's morning again.
Beddy-bye, bunny rabbit, close your eyes and dream,
Of all the games tomorrow we will play by the stream.
Beddy-Bye little squirrel, curl up in your nest,
You've gathered acorns all day long and now it's time to
rest.
Beddy-bye slithery snake, curl up nice and tight,
We'll meet again tomorrow in the early morning light.
Beddy-bye, tiny turtle, rest inside your shell,
Slowly you will fall asleep, we hope that you sleep well.
Beddy-Bye, friendly frog, let's not a make sound,
In the morning you will rabbit, and hop all around.
Beddy-Bye, little bird, though the night seems long,
Soon it will be morning and we'll wake to your song."

"That's so sweet." Violet whispered. "What is the song called?"

"I don't know." I admitted. "My Mom, my biological Mom, used to sing it to me at night."

"I love it. Will you sing it again?"

I repeated the song. And then again. I sang until Violet was sleeping deeply, the twins no longer kicking under my hand. I remained where I was, content to fall asleep near our babies.

When I woke up, it was with a start. Someone was knocking loudly at the door. The clock above the fireplace read six forty five. Rubbing a hand over my face, I rolled out of bed, glancing at my mate. She hadn't moved an inch

427

all night. Dragging my feet, I opened the door to a anxious-looking Ashwell.

"Is there a reason you're banging on my door this early?" I grouched at him.

"A very good one." he spoke quickly. "You need to get downstairs. And you should wake Violet too."

I was instantly more awake. "What happened?"

I left the door open, gesturing for him to come in. Leaning over the bed, I shook Vie's shoulder. Her eyes peeked open, her expression annoyed.

"What!" She whined.

"Ashwell is here. Somethings happened." I explained. She sat up, finding him standing a few feet from the bed.

"What's going on?"

He spoke to Violet. "Your brother is here."

"Garrett?"

"He's waiting outside of the border. He's demanding to be let into the pack. And he's angry, *very* angry."

Violet threw the covers off, swinging her legs over the edge of the bed. I was in the closet, throwing on fresh clothes, and tossed her a light jacket and a pair of running shoes. Slipping on a pair of my own, the three of us left the room, getting into the elevator.

"Did he say why he's here?" I asked Ashwell.

"Not in so many words."

"What *did* he say?" Violet demanded.

"He said, and I quote, 'Get that motherfucker out here. Today is the day he dies.'" His face was filled with questions. And I'm positive mine was too. I shared a look with my mate.

"He couldn't possibly remember." She said slowly.

"Mind catching me up?" Ashwell nudged me as the doors opened. I quickly told him a summarized version of the history between Garrett and I and Sophia. I explained about Gideon erasing their memories before we came to Silver Moon as well. He whistled lowly when I finished.

"Damn. Sounds like it might have been the best option."

"I can't think of any other reason he would come here looking for a fight." I sighed.

"Well, you did do the deed with his girlfriend."

"Shut up, Ashwell."

"I'm just saying, I'd want to mess up your face too. Even more, considering she turned out to be his mate."

"Ashwell." I gave him a look, which he studiously ignored.

"Did anybody think to get my Grandpa?" Violet stepped between us, rolling her eyes.

"I did."

We turned around, seeing King and Gideon hurrying up to us. Violet sighed in relief.

"I thought he should be made aware, since it's family." King explained.

"Good thing you did." Gideon said. "Let's go see what this is about."

My Gamma led us through the pack, past the rural areas and into the woods. We took the path through, walking about twenty minutes. I could start to make voices ahead; One of them was much louder than the rest, and far more agitated. Coming to the a break on the trees, we came upon a group of six warriors. Three of them were attempting to talk to Garrett on the other side. The others stood back, eyeing him warily.

"Garrett." Gideon called his name, getting his attention. His eyes scanned his grandfather, then moved onto King. Then Ashwell. Then Violet, and finally, rested on me. An unnerving grin spread across his face.

"Well, well. You actually came. I thought you'd send more goons to get rid of me." Garrett said.

"They have orders not to cross the border." I replied.

"And why can't I get in?" He growled.

"I placed a protective shield around the pack." Gideon told him. "Garrett, what are you doing here?"

"Didn't the dumbass there tell you?" He jerked his chin towards Ashwell. "I'm here for Jasper."

"Why?" Violet stepped forward. "What did Jasper do?"

"Like you don't know!" He yelled at her.

"Garrett." Gideon walked to the edge of the border, the warriors backing off. "What do you think he did?" His tone said he knew the answer, just waiting for Garrett to confirm it aloud.

"He slept with Sophia!" He snarled. "But that's not the only reason I'm here."

"Garrett, listen-"

"Shut the fuck up Violet! You're no better than your *mate*! I know what you did. I know what *all* of you did!"

"What did we do?" Gideon's calm exterior seemed to only fuel the anger coming from his grandson. He stepped as close as he could, raising his fist, and slamming it forward. It stopped mere inches from Gideon's chest, hitting the invisible wall that separated them.

"You erased my memory." He pointed a finger at Gideon. "And *you*," He pointed at Violet, "Knew about it, and covered for him! Even Mom and Dad knew!"

"That's not true!" Violet cried. "*You* agreed to it! You're the one who went to Grandpa's house."

"Liar!"

She threw her hands up, turning away from him.

"And there she goes, acting like a bitch again." Garrett clapped his hands in mock applause. "It's something you're really good at Violet."

"Garrett, you're acting like an idiot." I snapped at him. His eyes turned on me, hate filling them.

"You're words don't mean shit to me." He spat on the ground. "You turned my sister, my twin, against me. You had her cover for you like the pussy you are, trying to cover up what you did."

"If you really remembered what happened, you would know that's not true." I said.

"When did you get your memory back?" Gideon asked him.

"Last night." He stepped back, scoffing. "You seem irritated Grandpa. Worried about why your magic wore off? Maybe you've lost your touch. Or maybe you've always been shit at it."

"What about Sophia?" Gideon continued, ignoring the jibes.

"Oh yeah, she got her memory back. Begged and begged for me to forgive her, like she wasn't a lying slut."

Violet swung around. "What did you do?"

"What do you think?! I rejected the bitch!"

My gasp echoed Vie's. Gideon stared at his grandson as if he hadn't heard him correctly.

"You. . .You rejected her? How could you do that!" Violet screamed.

"Easy. I said the words, and then kicked her ass to the curb." Garrett laughed, the sound sending a shiver down my spine. "At least she was smart enough to accept the rejection. Now I can focus on you." He looked at me. "You turned my whole family against me. You convinced them to erase my memory, make me pretend to love that whore. All because it was easier for *you* not to accept the consequences of your actions."

"Garrett, Sophia loves you." I tried to reason with him.

"Yeah?" He shot back. "Did she love me when she was filled with your dick?! Did she love me when she was moaning your name while you fucked her?!"

I paused, my head cocking to the side. I replayed the memory of my encounter with Sophia that night.

"That never happened." I told him. "She never said my name."

Gideon looked at me sharply. I nodded at him, letting him know I was sure of what I was saying. Garrett, on the other hand, went red in the face.

"Fucking liar, I saw you two! I heard you two!"

"Really? What exactly did you see?" I smirked at him. Violet grabbed my arm.

"What the fuck Jasper?! Don't fucking egg him on!" She hissed at me.

"Relax." I whispered low, for her ears only.

"Don't fucking tell me to relax!"

431

I moved away from her, feeling shitty about stressing her out. But if Gideon and I were thinking the same thing, I had to know. I stepped to the border, leaning in. My expression was smug, cocky.

"Come on Garrett. What *did* you see me doing with Sophia? It must be eating at you." I chuckled.

Garretts face was now a light shade of purple, a vein in his forehead throbbing.

"You know what I think? I think you just didn't want to be with her anymore. I think you made this whole thing up as an excuse to reject her. Because I know I would remember a night with Sophia." I made my face thoughtful. "Yeah, I definitely would. With those legs. . . and that *ass*. . ."

"You son of a bitch!" He ran at me. His fists pounded against the shield over and over and over again. "I saw her on top of you! I saw her enjoying it! I heard her saying your name instead of mine!" He clawed at the wall, desperate to get through to me. "How dare you talk like that in front of my sister! You're a piece of shit, I'll kill you! I'll rip your fucking throat out!"

"I'd let you." I said. Garrett's attack paused. "If any of that had actually happened. You're being played Garrett. Someone tampered with your memory."

I heard a sigh of relief behind me, making a mental note to apologize to Vie afterwards.

His laugh echoed. "Oh that's rich! But I'm done playing your games Jasper. I'm done talking. Let's say you come to my side, and we'll see who walks away?"

"I don't think so. But you're invited into my pack."

He grinned, stepping over the line. I turned away, hearing his body drop.

"Bring him back with us. I want him confined until I get a hold of Dimitri." I told King. Wrapping an arm around my mate, I led her back to the path in the woods.

CHAPTER 58
VIOLET

"Have you talked to Sophia?"

Mom, Dad, Jasper, Grandpa, Ben and King and Ashwell were in Jaspers new office. I guessed the old office downstairs had been converted into another bedroom. The four rooms on our floor were our bedroom, the babies' room, and two offices, one for me and one for Jasper. It worked conveniently well, especially at times like this. I was seated on the sofa Jasper had requested, whilst everyone else either sat in chairs or stood. Mom rubbed my shoulder.

"I talked with her parents this morning." She said.

"How is she?" Jaspers face was concerned.

Mom sighed. "Not well, to put it mildly. Her Mother allowed me to check on her; She wouldn't speak, wouldn't look at me. She's essentially comatose, and I don't know when she will get better. If she will at all."

"They'd already accepted and marked each other." Dad rubbed a hand through his hair. "The pain must have been. . .. excruciating. If she wasn't a born Luna, she might have died."

I cringed at the word. Sophia may not have been my favorite person in the whole world, but she wasn't a *bad* person. I didn't want her to die.

"This has Jennine written all over it." I spat.

"It's the only answer. Nobody could have undone my spell. Not even Clara. No, this was Dark Magic. That bitch undid my spell, and then tweaked the original memory. Goddess knows what else she planted in Garretts brain." Grandpa slammed his fist against the wall. I'd never seen him so angry before.

433

"She was so *close*." Mom hissed beside me. Her hand clenched, nails digging into my skin. "She was *in* the pack! She got to my son. . ."

"Mom?" I nodded at her hand, now starting to become painful. She immediately let go of me.

"Sorry!"

"So what are we going to do now?" King asked.

Everyone started talking at once, throwing out different ideas, theories. I paid no attention, knowing exactly what had to be done, but also knowing nobody in this room would go for it. Especially because I was pregnant. Still, I tried.

"Uhm, guys?" I raised my hand a little, getting everyone's attention. "I think we're all thinking the same thing. Just nobody wants to say it." I looked around the room.

"What are you saying?" Ashwell asked.

"Well, it's obvious what her game is, isn't it? She went after Garrett to get to you two." I nodded at Mom and Dad. "I think it's obvious who her next target is." My tone was obvious, if it my words weren't.

Moms eyes widened. "No, not necessarily. It could be Sophia." She quickly argued.

"I think she's done with Sophia Mom. And Sofia isn't going to be of any use to anyone; We all know how being rejected takes a physical toll."

"So, we put extra security on you." Jasper stated. He narrowed his eyes when I shook my head.

"I don't think we should."

"I know what you're thinking, Vie, and the answer is no." He hissed. I caught him in a steely glare.

"Do you want to hear my plan, or not?" I argued.

***

A few weeks had gone by since the meeting in the office. To say that Jasper wasn't happy about my plan was an understatement. I knew why. So many things could go wrong, but taking down Jennine was priority number one. In order to stop Phoebus, we had to stop her first. My parents had taken Garrett back to Blood Moon, under confinement until this problem was resolved. Grandpa didn't feel right using magic on him again, as he didn't know exactly what Jennine had done with her Dark Magic, and didn't want to risk hurting him. Which was fair, in my opinion.

To distract myself from my mates moodiness, and worrying about my brother, I gathered Tracy and a few other girls to help me prepare the nursery. It took us a week to finish, but it was worth it.

I'd chosen elephants and giraffes for the theme, finding really cute wall sticks online. We'd painted the walls a neutral green instead of blue, and Tracy surprised me again with her artist abilities. By the time we were done, she'd painted what looked like a realistic version of the Savanah, with trees, tall grass, a watering hole and the setting sun. It reminded me a lot of the Lion King, and I loved it.

The crib had been placed to the side of her mural, with a large, wide dresser against the wall. Toys and clothes had been put away, and the closet was filled with unopened gifts from the pack that I would go through later with Jasper. I wouldn't have minded a baby shower, but this felt just right too. All in all, the room turned out better than I'd hoped, and I was excited to show Jasper. So after a hearty lunch, I went in search of him, finding him in his office.

"Hey." I opened the door, smiling softly.

"Hey." He looked up, setting down his pen.

"I was wondering if you had time to come see the nursery?"

"Sure." He stood, pushing his chair back. I took his hand, pulling him to the door. Turning the knob slowly, I let the door swing open, watching his face. He blinked once, stepping into the room. "Wow." He breathed.

"Do you like it?"

"I love it." He walked up to Tracys artwork. "Who did this?"

"Tracy. Apparently she had a hidden talent."

"Apparently. It's amazing." He grinned at me. "The boys are going to love this."

"I think so too."

He wrapped me in a hug, and I could feel the tension coming into his body. Rubbing his back, I pulled back to look at him.

"Everything is going to be fine." I said quietly.

"You don't know that." He ground out.

"I *do* actually." I placed my hands on either side of his face. "Because I trust you Jasper. And I trust that you would never let anything happen to us."

I pulled him down for a kiss. His shoulders relaxed as he sighed against my lips, drawing me in further. It was *I* who winced, pulling away. The next second, I had the strangest feeling that I'd wet myself. Jasper gasped, stepping back.

"Vie." He looked at the floor. I followed his gaze to see a puddle between my feet.

"Shit." I whispered.

"Was that. . .?"

I nodded. "Good thing I finished the nursery, huh?" I laughed anxiously. "I'll mindlink Kettler. Can you call my parents?"

"I will, when we get you settled at the hospital." His words were rushed. I watched in dazed amusement as he began to rush around the room, muttering about the diaper bag.

"Jasper, the bag is in our room." I told him.

"It is? Right, yeah. Okay." He dashed out the room. A minute later, I saw him rush past the door, bag in hand. Then I heard the elevator door sliding open. Had he really forgotten me? I shook my head, mindlinking him.

"I think you forgot something."

"Wha-? Oh fuck!"

I laughed. More liquid ran down my legs as I did, adding to the mess on the floor.

"Tracy? Can you do me a huge favor, and come mop the nursery floor?"

"Sure! Did you drop a glass?"

"Uh, no. My water broke."

"What?!"

"Yeah. Remember what all you have to do?"

"Absolutely! Don't worry about anything!"

Jasper appeared in the door, an apology written on his face. He quickly came to scoop me in his arms, bridal style.

"So." I started.

"Don't." He deadpanned. "Not a word."

I giggled. "Were *you* planning to have these babies while I stayed home?" I said anyway.

He groaned, rolling his eyes. "You're never going to let me forget this, are you?"

"Never."

We stopped only briefly to ask a warrior to notify my Grandpa, and then we were outside, Jasper setting me down gently in the back of Kings car. King was sitting in the drivers seat, his lips pressed into a firm line and laughter in his eyes. Jasper climbed in beside me, taking my hand.

"Ready to go now?" King glanced at us in the mirror. "Made sure you have everything?" He couldn't hold it in now, letting out a loud peel of laughter.

"Just drive!" Jasper said.

During the five minute drive, I was hit with my first solid contraction. I breathed through it, as Mom had told me to do, and then it was over. But I knew it was going to get a lot worse. In no time at all, we were parked, and Jasper was helping me out. Kettler and team of nurses were waiting for us inside, one coaxing me into a wheelchair. Jasper rolled me to the delivery room while Kettler walked beside us, asking the basic questions.

"How long since your water broke?"

"About. . .half an hour, maybe?" I guessed.

"What took you so long to get here?"

My lip pulled up. "Jasper forgot me upstairs."

Kettler laughed. "I wish I could say that's a first, but it's not. The guy always tends to freak out more than the woman."

"That actually doesn't make me feel better." Jasper sighed.

"Funny story to tell the kids someday." Kettler patted him on the back once. "Anything unusual about the liquid? Smell, color?"

"Uh, no. It was clear."

"Good, good."

"Kettler, isn't this too soon?" I asked worriedly. "I'm not due for another three weeks!"

"Yes, but you're having twins. They come earlier generally. Trust me, they will be fine." He assured me. My chest loosened at his words and I nodded. Somewhere in my head, I knew this information, but my mind was understandably frazzled. We got to my room just as I heard my Moms voice.

"That's my parents."

"I'll go get them. You get comfortable." Kettler said.

I'd just gotten into the bed when Mom, Dad and Grandpa entered. I tried to smile, but another contraction made me wince instead. Mom came to stand on the other side of the bed that wasn't occupied by Jasper, taking my hand.

"Oh Vie. I'm going to be here the whole time honey." She said.

"Thanks." I sighed as the contraction subsided.

The next couple hours were on and off. A nurse came in to give me ice chips, and check on the babies. She also attached a monitor to my stomach with some bands to keep an eye on the heart rates. At first, the contractions were fairly far apart, and not so bad. Mom was a little concerned with how slow my labor was progressing, her Doctor side kicking in. She re-checked everything the nurses did, until they finally just let her take over. It might have been funny, if I wasn't in so much pain.

Just as she promised me, the contractions were now only minutes apart, and fucking horrendous. I almost preferred my first shift at this point. Jasper was always right by my side, always touching some part of me. I had no idea when or how I got into a hospital gown, and I didn't care. I figured the dress I was wearing earlier would have sufficed but I guess someone else thought differently. I screamed, I cried, I cursed. The only definite sounds was Jasper in my ear and Mom on the other side.

"She's ready." Through blurry eyes, I saw Kettler at the end of the bed. Bringing up the stir-ups, he positioned my feet. Mom ran to get pads and towels, arranging them near my butt. "Violet. On my say, I want you to start pushing, as hard as you can. Ready? And. . .push!"

I held my breath, my eyes squeezing shut. I pushed down as hard as I possibly could, but nothing seemed to change.

"Good. Good! Okay, stop. Breath."

"You can do this Vie. You're doing so good love." Jasper said beside me.

"You really are sweetheart. Take a deep breath, and on the next contraction, push again, hard." Mom ran a damp cloth over my forehead.

When I felt the pressure coming, I repeated my actions, bearing down. A slice of pain so intense made me gasp, tears running down my face.

"I can't!" I sobbed. "He's not coming!"

"He is!" Jasper said. "He's almost here Violet. Just a little more baby, you can do this!"

"I need you to push Violet. One. Two. Three-Push, now!" Kettler's voice left no room for argument, so I did what he said on instinct. I felt a huge pressure in my lower region, and then-nothing. I blinked my tears away, raising my head to see a blood-covered arm. Mom left me to take him from Kettler, wrapping him in a blanket and working to clean him up. I wanted to see him so badly, but I could feel the urge to push again, knowing our second son was coming.

"K-Kettler." I breathed heavily. "I-I need to p-push again."

"Alright. On the next contraction-"

I started before he was done, the feeling overwhelming. The second baby came a lot easier, and a lot louder. He was barely out when he started wailing. Wrapping him up, Kettler joined Mom a few feet away, cleaning him and weighing him. Jasper kissed me lovingly while I caught my breath.

"I love you so much." He whispered.

"I love you too." I closed my eyes, utterly and completely exhausted.

Until another contraction hit.

My eyes flew open, panic filling me. Automatically, I started to push again, crying out.

"What is happening?!" Mom rushed to my side, one of my sons wrapped up in her arms.

Kettler was back in position in seconds, his face filled with worry. He examined me quickly before looking at her.

"There's another baby." He said.

"What?!"

"You missed that?!" I shrieked.

"He must have been hidden behind the other two!"

I screamed again, my body now running on its own. Two minutes later, the room was filled with another loud cry. I sank back, done. Mom and Kettler were checking the baby, Jasper seemed to still be in shock. And my eyes were closing no matter how hard I tried to keep them open. I felt something warm placed on my chest. Peeking through my lashes, I stared into the face of one of my children- He was beautiful. Beside him, someone placed my other son. Jasper helped me hold them, talking quietly to them. I cooed at them, smiling when they stirred.

"Violet."

My head lolled to the side. Mom held our mystery baby, gently rocking him. Jasper took on of our sons so Mom could set him on my chest.

"It's a girl." She whispered to me.

CHAPTER 59
VIOLET

King helped me bring the load of bags down to the car. I'd recovered very well, considering the surprise birth of our daughter. I'd chosen not to bring tradition and named her after a flower. We'd chosen Drew and Carson for our boys, and Camellia for our girl. She truly was a blessing, an unasked for gift.

Drew, our first born, was a quiet baby, except when he was hungry. He had Jaspers brown locks, and his silver eyes. I had a feeling he would take after his Dad a lot. Carson, on the other hand, had rick, deep blue eyes with just a tiny hint of the silver. His little tuft of black hair came from me, and probably his attitude as well. He was our grumpy baby, insisting on being held almost all the time, unless he was snuggled in his crib with his siblings. Tracy was always more than willing to carry him around with her while she tried to do her work, but mostly she was keeping him entertained with lots of peek-a-boo and tickling.

Camellia, she was stunning. I knew she was going to be a true heartbreaker when she got older. Two weeks ago, we'd all gotten the shock of our lives when she'd finally opened her eyes for the first time. They were a bright green, like emeralds. But she'd also inherited the silver. It made them pop, exponentially so, with a shine that was almost otherworldly. They were brighter than her brothers. Even brighter than her Dad! She had a little hair too, soft brunette curls that I loved to run my fingers through. She was such a sweet girl, and super cuddly.

I fear I might have been neglecting Jasper lately, but I loved them all so much. Just yesterday, Jasper had woken up and came to find me sleeping on the plush carpet in their room, surrounded by our babies. Carson had been hungry, and afterwards, I just didn't want to leave them.

Today was difficult for him, I knew. It was time to put my plan into action, and that meant leaving Silver Moon. My nerves were on edge as we packed up Kings SUV.

"Is that everything?" He asked.

"I think so. Are the kids ready?"

"Tracy was just bringing Carson downstairs, I think."

As if he'd manifested her, Tracy appeared at the door, waving and smiling sadly.

"Baby number one, right here!" She called. Setting it down, she adjusted the cover.

"Technically, he's baby number two." I laughed, taking the car seat from her.

Jasper stepped out of the door, holding one car seat in each hand, each with a different colored cover, and frowning deeply. Without a word, he strode to the vehicle, beginning to buckle them in.

"Is Grandpa ready to go?" I asked Tracy while watching my mate.

"Mr. Gideon said he would be down shortly." She nodded.

"Good. Thank you Tracy."

"What for?"

I turned my head, meeting her eyes. "In general, for everything."

She blushed a little but waved me off. Jasper walked back to us, taking my arm.

"Can I have a minute with Vie?"

"You don't need to ask Alpha! She's your mate after all." She giggled, walking back inside the house.

Before I could say or do anything, Jaspers lips were on mine, his hand gripping my waist. I could feel every emotion in his kiss, every ounce of fear, tension, anxiety. It did little to calm my own nerves.

"You," He breathed against my lips, "Promise me you will all be safe." His tone left no room for argument or naysayers.

"I promise." I gasped. He kissed me again, pulling me against his chest. I lost track of where I was for a moment, until someone cleared their throat loudly beside us.

"We should get going Violet." Grandpa stood, smirking at the two of us. I pulled away, but not before another quick kiss. He walked me to the car, saying good-bye to the kids.

"We'll be back before you know it." I said as I hopped in the passenger side. King started the engine.

"Call me when you get to Blood Moon."

"I will. Promise."

"I love you."

"I love you too."

He reached for my hand through the window. When King started to drive, I let go, blowing him a kiss. The absolute fear in his eyes made my stomach roll, but he was soon left behind. I turned my attention to my Grandpa, seated behind the kids.

"Thank you, for coming with us." I said.

"Anything for these little angels." He smiled towards the car seats. "Besides, they are much too young to be teleported yet."

I rolled my eyes, turning my attention to the road.

"He will be fine." King said softly. "The Alpha is just worried about your safety."

"I know." I sighed.

"Your parents will protect the little ones." Grandpa chimed in. "Lily is over the moon about the kids. You know she always wanted grandchildren."

"I know." I repeated. "And I know Blood Moon is the safest place for them right now. I just wish Jasper could come with us."

"Like you said, we'll be back before you know it."

"And the warriors?" I looked at King.

"Behind us. They took two separate trucks."

Glancing in the mirror, I recognized Ashwell behind the wheel of a giant truck. We lapsed into silence, scanning the road and the trees that surrounded us. Usually, it was a short drive from our pack to my old one, but we'd decided

443

to take a longer route. The detour would take us through the woods, bringing us closer to Uncle Killians pack. Right on cue, King took the turn, and our ride instantly got bumpier. The 'road' here wasn't was basically dirt and rock. I glanced anxiously at the car seats, worried they would be jostled too much.

"Shit!"

I jumped as King shouted, grabbing the armrest of my seat as the car swerved violently. My heart jumped into my throat as I turned, grabbing for my kids.

"Grandpa! Do something!" I yelled.

Before he could raise a single finger though, we came to a jerking, painful halt. My body was thrown forward, my back banging against the dashboard. At the same time, the airbags went off, barely cushioning the assault and also propelling me back into the seat. My ears were ringing, and it took a few seconds for me to register the cuts and blood on my arm. Glass lay everywhere, the windshield completely smashed in, giving a full view of the oak tree we'd hit.

"Grandpa?" I pushed against the airbag, trying to see him. "Grandpa! The babies!"

"T-they're fine. We're all fine." He said from the back.

"King? Are you okay?" He was holding his head, slowly shaking it from side to side. A line of blood ran from his temple to his chin.

"Think so."

"What the Hell was that?!" I demanded.

He looked through the hole where the windshield had been. "There." He raised his other hand, pointing.

Standing a few feet away was a cloaked figure. The build was enough to tell me it was a woman. Blonde hair was falling from the shadow where her face was. The hood covered her face completely, but I knew who she was. Anger and panic gripped me as I stared at her.

"Jennine." I whispered.

A deafening crunch had me wincing, covering my ears. I watched in shock as the doors of our vehicle peeled themselves off, falling to the forest floor. My seatbelt clicked, sliding back up into it's holder. My head whipped to the side as I heard her voice. It grated against my eardrums.

"Come on out Violet. We need to talk."

"Don't." King grabbed my arm. "Luna, don't."

"I don't have a choice King." Wrenching my arm away, I slid out of the SUV, landing on the door. Jennine raised her hand, crooking her finger for me to come closer. Giving her my best glare, I picked my way around the damage, coming to a stop on the edge of the road. We stood facing each other silently. I chose to break the tension.

"You could have killed us." I spat.

She laughed lightly. "I may not be a wolf anymore, but I do remember it takes more than that to kill one."

"My babies are in the car, you bitch!" I shouted at her.

"Oh, I know." Her tone held a smirk, and my hand twitched, ready to just kill her already.

"You're an idiot Jennine. The warriors-"

"Took a drive the other way." She interrupted. "It seems your Gamma forgot something at the pack, and had to turn around."

My stomach dropped. She'd sent Ashwell and the warriors back to Silver Moon. We were literally alone with the sociopath and no backup.

"Why are you here?" I asked.

"For you."

I took a step back. "Whatever you're thinking of doing with me, forget it. I'll kill you first!"

She laughed again, louder this time. "You can try! Really, I'd rather do this the easy way- It'll save a lot of time."

"Fuck you." I spat.

"Still a coward, I see." Grandpas voice came from behind me. "What kind of a coward can't even show her face?"

"Grandpa! Go back and protect the babies!" I yelled.

"No, he's right." Jennine trilled. "And I am no coward."

She pulled the hood back, revealing herself. I kind of knew what she looked like from Mom and Dad, but to see her in person was still unexpected. For some reason, I'd been imagining a slender, young, and attractive blonde girl. The person in front of me was, yes, thin, but she definitely wasn't a girl. This was a woman, her face tight and narrow. Her eyes were flat, cold, but held a distant emotion I couldn't quite decipher. Insanity, maybe. I could see where she might have been attractive once, but the aura she gave off now repelled, sending all sorts of red flags up in my head. Even if I didn't know who she was, I would know by instinct; This woman was dangerous, a threat.

"This is the bitch that's causing all the trouble?" King hobbled up to my left. "I don't see anything special about her."

Jennine hissed unimpressively at him.

"Grandpa we've got this. Go." I said.

"Really? You're bodyguard seems to have a twisted ankle." Jennine sneered.

"Like that's going to stop me from tearing your head off." King replied with a snarl.

"Male wolves are always so dramatic." She rolled her eyes. "Fine. I tried to do this the easy way. But clearly, you're all gunning for a fight. So. . ."

She snapped her fingers, grinning. A scream built in my chest as I saw the three car seats float over our heads, landing at her feet. Carsons green cover rippled in the breeze.

"I never was a fan of babies." She wrinkled her nose at the seats. "Too loud. And messy."

"Stop!" I forced the pressure in my chest out. "Please, give them back!"

"If you cooperate with me, I will leave them unharmed."

"Fine! What do you want?" I gasped.

"I told you. You."

I gulped, not taking my eyes off my children. "So you can fuck with my head too? Just like you did to my brother?"

"No, we have something else in mind for you." She examined her nails casually. "I will admit though, watching Garrett break that girls heart was *marvelous*."

My hands trembled with rage. I was very close to shifting.

"Come now Violet. Unless you want me to kill your babies?" She raised an eyebrow mockingly.

I stepped away from King, stopping a few feet from her.

"King." I ground out. "Come get them."

I heard him take three steps before Jennine held up her hand.

"Actually," I was suddenly pulled to her side, her hand reaching out to catch my arm. I winced as her grasp clamped down on my wounds. ",I've decided Lily doesn't get this either."

My knees buckled as the car seats went up in flames.

Tears sprang to my eyes and Hala jumped forward, merging with me while I tapped into our magic. A guttural, ear-splitting growl left my mouth, my hand whipping out to catch Jennine by the throat. All I wanted was to rip her throat out, and be done with it. Sadly, I knew I couldn't do that.

"Grandpa!"

He appeared on Jennine's other side, grabbing her shoulders. As soon as he started the spell, I jumped back, landing unsteadily in Kings arms. Jennine shrieked, throwing Grandpa off. He stumbled back, but the smirk on his face told me he'd been successful. Jennine raised her hand, winking at me.

"This isn't the last time you'll see me." She snapped, disappearing momentarily- Only to pop back exactly where she was before. She tried again, with the same result. The horror and confusion on her face was almost worth the emotional turmoil I was feeling right now. "What the fuck?! What is this?!"

"A loophole." Grandpa said. "You can try to teleport anywhere in the world Jennine, but you'll end up right back here."

"You're lying!"

"Go ahead and try."

She did, several times, in fact. With a piercing shriek, she threw her fists down, flames erupting around her. Her heated glare fell on me.

"You stupid *bitch*! You sacrificed your own children for this?!" Her laugh was hysterical. "Was it worth it?!"

"Yeah, about that." Walking to one of the charred seats, I bent down, removing the last of the cover. Grabbing the doll inside, now almost completely melted, I held it up. "Turns out Mom was right Jennine. You are kind of predictable. And stupid, if you seriously thought I would ever even entertain the idea of putting my babies at risk. But thank you, for walking right into our trap. It made our jobs *a lot* easier."

I dropped the unsalvageable toy, walking away from her, pulling out my cell to call my mate.

CHAPTER 60
JASPER

I nearly had a fucking heart attack when Ashwell and the warriors returned, *alone*. Fortunately, whatever Jennine had done to them wore off soon. We predicted she might try something like this. The worst case scenario, she would simply kill the backup. I was beyond thankful that she'd chosen the non-violent route. However, Ashwell didn't feel the same. Since Vies' phone call telling me she was fine and Jennine fell for the trap, he'd been ranting in the Jeep beside me.

"Cowardly bitch. I swear-"

"No offense, Ashwell, but can you just not? I'm a little more concerned about my mate right now."

"Yeah, sorry. I am too. Just don't like the fact that she magicked me so easily." He huffed.

We turned on the dirt road, anxiously searching for Violet or King. When I saw the wrecked SUV, my throat tightened, and I was out of the car before Ashwell even stopped.

"Violet!" I hollered.

"Over here!"

Hearing her voice had my knees going weak. I saw her waving at me, catching the scent of blood in the air. *Her* blood. Ehno and I growled at the same time. I ran to her, pulling her close and taking deep breaths, filling my nostrils with her scent.

"I'm so glad you're alright." I whispered.

"I told you I would be."

"Ugh. I'm going to puke."

Raising my head, I located Jennine sitting on the ground, arms crossed. Her expression reminded me a pouting child. For whatever reason, that pissed me off even more than I already was. Stepping around my mate, I took three confident steps towards her. Someone had drawn a circle in the dirt, indicating where her temporary prison was. Jennine looked up at me as if I was the most boring thing she'd ever laid eyes on.

"Yes?" Her tone was petulant.

"You understand this is over right?" I barked. "You're caught."

She exaggerated a yawn. "Whatever helps you sleep at night."

"You wouldn't be this calm if you knew who was on their way here."

"Is it dear old Daddy? Oh, that's right. You killed him." She grinned.

"You can't make me feel guilty about that Jennine. He was a monster, and deserved to die." I crouched down, getting at her eye-level. "Just like you."

She leaned forward, a mischievous glint in flat, blue eyes. "Who said anything about feeling guilty? Quite the contrary, in fact. I won't give you the whole 'we're more alike than you think' speech, but the fact that you can kill those who only *you* deem monsters, without thought or remorse really says something to your character, doesn't it?"

"You're going to argue that Warrick wasn't a monster?" Violet scoffed behind me. "That's a bad angle Jennine."

"Oh, no he was. All the way." She sat back. "But he *was* also your Dad. Father to your half brother too. Where is he by the way?"

"Shut up." I spat.

"One might think the fact that you're still hiding him at Blood Moon says something about you too. He already gave up any rights to be Alpha, so what's your excuse? Or do you just not want the reminder that you killed *his* Dad too?"

"I said shut up." I warned.

"Not to mention running the boys Mom off. You think she died as rogue yet? How will you explain that one to poor little Kiren?"

I lunged for her, but sadly, I was harshly pulled back by both Violet and King.

"Jasper, no! She's just baiting you!" Violet said. "You can't cross the line, or you'll be trapped in there with her!"

"She will meet a worse death than the one you want to give her." King reminded me. His words pushed through the anger I was feeling. Taking a breath, I glared at the girl in front of me.

"I didn't come here to argue with you. I want answers." I told her as calmly as I could.

"Answers for what? My big bad plan?" Jennine laughed bitterly. "Sorry kiddo. I'm not saying shit."

"Is that because you don't know the whole plan?"

"What are you talking about?"

King let me go, but stayed close in case I lost it on her again. "*We* know the plan Jennine. I was just wondering if *you* do."

"You're making less and less sense kid."

"We know that Phoebus wants to exterminate all of Celestes creations. Wolves, bears, foxes- everything."

She blinked at me a few times. Then she began to laugh again-Louder this time, uncontrollably. The sound gave me chills.

"Well!," She gasped, "You're really ahead of the curve, aren't you? I'm impressed that you know about Phoebus! But honestly, no, I had no knowledge in that plan. My only goal was to fuck up your Mothers life." She looked at Violet.

"Tell me where he is Jennine." I snarled.

"As if I know! He's a fucking *God*! He comes and goes as he pleases." She waved her hand at me.

"Then tell us where you meet up." Violet said.

"He meets me where ever he wants, there is no set place." She looked between us. "I will tell you this though- You're fucking morons if you think you can defeat him. You may as well just roll over and accept your fate. You won't win."

451

"Interesting." A new voice sounded behind us. Jennine's eyes lit up, a wild, crazed fire in them. Lily stepped forward, her piercing gaze solely focused on Jennine. "You did always have a way of overlooking those you considered beneath you."

Jennine looked at me. "Is this who I'm suppose to be afraid of? Lower this shield and I'll show you exactly who's beneath whom."

"I don't think so." I shook my head.

"Violet, I want you to leave now." Lily said. Her voice was so smooth, so calm. That only made her sound more dangerous.

"Why?" Vie replied, confused.

"Because what I'm about to do. . . Well, I don't want my daughter to see me like that." She stepped closer, just barely behind the circle. Now she was speaking to Jennine. "You stalked me and my mate. My children. You made my son reject his mate, and you were going to kill my grandchildren." She kicked at a car seat I hadn't even noticed until now. It was black, burnt almost to ash. The emotion that burned in my veins when I realized what Jennine had tried to do had no name.

"I've done more than that Lily."

"Anything you say now will only inspire me to draw out your death!" Lily hissed.

"I had a good run." Jennine shrugged. "In the interest of closure, you might also like to know that Jasper and Sophia were under my influence when they slept together."

"What?" I gasped.

"Fucking bitch!" Violet shouted.

Lily just stood there, shaking from head to toe. Jennine grinned at her.

"I've been slowly breaking your precious little boy for a long time. The next Alpha in line- The important one. But you," She waved a finger at Lily, "You broke your daughter all by yourself. What kind of Mother keeps her child on lockdown? Each time she snuck out, to *get away from you*, I had the opportunity to hurt her, even kill her if I wanted."

"So why didn't you?" Violet spat.

"Where's the fun in that? I was already fucking with Garrett. But then you got pregnant, and I wondered just how much it would hurt if you lost, not only your son, but your daughter and her babies too?"

"You're fucking insane." I said.

"Jasper, take Violet now." Lily ground the words out. I turned my mate away, hearing the distinctive sound of shifting. The Mother Wolfs tail brushed against my back.

"Jennine." Violet suddenly turned around. "I just want you to know. If you had any hope of seeing your wolf again when you die? That's not going to happen."

Jennine's body jerked, as if Violets words had physically hurt her.

"What do you know?!" She screamed. It was clear her old wolf, Violets wolf, was a touchy topic for her.

"I know that the Goddess decided to give Nia another human. Someone who would look after her, love her, and care about her. And I know for a fact that she is happy now."

Vie smiled knowingly at her. Jennine's eyes filled with so much hatred and rage, I felt an automatic need to shield my mate. I stepped in front of her as Jennine started shrieking.

"No! *No!* She didn't give her to you! She can't! You fucking bitch, *I'll kill you!*" Her words ended on a sob. Lilys wolf jerked her chin at me, so I took Violets arm, turning just before the screaming started. Only this time, it was a scream of agony. Ashwell was in the Jeep, watching the scene behind us with wide eyes. King took the passenger seat while I helped my mate into the back. I glanced back only once as we started driving away. The sight was enough to make my stomach roll.

***

The ride back to Silver Moon was quiet and tense.

"Let me see your arm." I took it without waiting. "Does it hurt?"

"Not so bad." Vie shrugged.

"There's glass in some of the cuts. You need to see Kettler."

"Alright."

King escorted us to the hospital, where nurses flocked. I shooed them off, taking Vie to an empty room to wait for Kettler. She hadn't looked at me this whole time. After our brief exchange on the way back, she hadn't spoken to me either. And I was beginning to get frustrated. When Kettler arrived, he immediately got to work pulling out glass shards and cleaning the cuts. I waited rather impatiently, leaning against the wall.

"That should do it." He set aside the last of the bloody pads. "Nothing too deep. They should heal quickly."

Vie nodded, flexing her hand.

"If that's everything, I have another patient I need to check on." He nodded at me as he left.

She was still sitting on the bed, head down. Her black hair made a curtain around her face, making it impossible to tell what she was thinking. The air around us was thick, and finally, I couldn't take it anymore. Pushing away from the wall, I came to stand in front of her. Placing my hands on either side of her face, I tilted it up so she would look at me. Shock and concern took over as I saw the tears running silently out of her eyes.

"Talk to me." My voice was a whispery rasp.

"I. . ." Her chest heaved as the first sob broke through. "I'm so sorry!" She clutched the front of my shirt. "A-all I can t-think about. . . is when she.. set the seats on fire!"

"Vie-"

"It was a s-stupid plan!" She wailed. "I c-can't get that i-image out of my head!"

My hands fell from her cheeks, reaching around to grab her in a hug. I held her tightly, letting her cry into my chest.

When her sobs had turned to hiccups, I pulled away so I could look at her again.

"It wasn't a stupid plan. It worked, didn't it? Jennine is gone, and she will never, ever be able to hurt our kids. Or anyone else. Okay? I'm sorry you had to go through that."

"I want to see our babies." She murmured.

"Then let's go see them."

I helped her off the bed, keeping an around her waist. Nurses glanced at us as we passed, but I ignored them. When we got outside, King was standing by the door, along with Gideon. They both took one look at Violet and understood what she needed.

"Tracy, can you bring the kids to our room please?" I mindlinked her.

"No problem Alpha."

"Thanks."

I didn't know if it would help or not to tell Vie that I'd also had terrorizing images in my head. Of course, she'd seen it first hand, and I'd only seen the aftermath. Still, it was not something I wanted to picture, but now it felt like I no choice. The more I tried not to, the more my brain conjured up images of my babies being killed. We both stepped up our pace, leaving Gideon and King behind. I reached the door first, wrenching it open with a loud *bang!* Violet shot past me, almost tripping on the stairs.

It was torture waiting in the elevator; It seemed like the ride up was years long. The door seemed to take the same amount of time to open. Finally, we were in front of our bedroom door, our hands reaching for the knob at the same time. But the door opened from the other side.

"Hey. I thought that was you-"

Vie took Drew from Tracy's arms, her face pressing against his tiny cheek. Tears leaked from her closed eyes, a small hiccup escaping. Tracy observed with a curious expression. I stepped past her, finding Camellia and Carson on the bed, pillows placed around them so they wouldn't fall off. Kicking off my shoes, I crawled onto the bed, scooping them up and snuggling them close. Their mother

455

and brother joined me shortly after, while Tracy quietly and discreetly left the room.

We stayed in our room all day, playing with the babies, soaking up their love and attention. When night fell, we moved back to the bed, the triplets holding onto each other as they slept. We stayed awake for a long time, just looking at them and holding hands on the pillows. Somewhere around two in the morning, Vie fell asleep, her nose against Carson's back. And I stayed up, watching over my family while my tears stained the fabric of the bedsheets under me.

CHAPTER 61
JASPER

I made a pack-wide announcement the next day. Along with clearing up Violets non-Hybrid status, I was glad to tell my pack that Jennine was gone. The relief was nearly tangible in the air. However, that relief didn't last long- It popped like a bubble when I explained about Phoebus, his past with Celeste, and the incoming threat *he* posed. I could see the same question on every face I looked at; How were we supposed to defeat a God?

I didn't have an answer for that.

For the rest of the week, I focused on my children and my mate. In our downtime, usually when the kids were napping, Vie and I would brainstorm together. Sometimes King and Ashwell would join, and Gideon, who said he rather liked Silver Moon. He was thinking of moving here, being as it was close to his daughter, but more 'open', as he put it. As of right now, he was using his skills to fix up the rest of the houses for the pack. I didn't mind, and he was making good use of the materials Dimitri had purchased for us.

I had to admit, although my pack was frightened, there was a semblance of peace right now. After all, we had no idea when Phoebus planned to attack, or how outright that attack would be. There wasn't much we could do in the way of preparing ourselves, so most, if not all, of us were focusing on our families. I'd come to know each of the triplets as individuals, learn their growing personalities. I loved spending the days with them, playing with different toys and watching them play with each other too. Camellia was extremely bold, usually taking it upon herself to lead the three of them in whatever activity.

She was definitely a Daddys girl too. Whenever I was near, she would find me, clenching and unclenching her tiny fists with a whine until I picked her up. Carson was more than happy to spend the majority of his time with Violet, while Drew preferred Tracy. As werewolves, they developed faster than human babies; Camellia was already rolling over, attempting to crawl, while the boys watched and giggled. Things were going to be interesting when the three of them learned to walk.

Right now, we were in my office. Camellia was on my lap, her stunning eyes searching everything in the room while she played with the pull string on my sweater. Vie was feeding Carson and Drew on the sofa, murmuring to them quietly. It was a tad difficult to type, write or answer the phone with one hand, but I was managing. Besides, if I put Camellia down, no doubt she would start to cry.

"So, I was wondering. . ." Violet spoke.

"About?"

"Do you think he knows? That Jennine is dead?"

I laid down my pen, stretching my fingers. "I think so. She was his go-to pawn in this scheme of his. If he hasn't figured it out by now. . ."

"He will soon." She finished for me. Her face turned thoughtful. "Maybe we've been thinking about this the wrong way."

"How do you mean?"

"We've been expecting Phoebus to attack outright now. But what if he doesn't? What if he just chooses another person to manipulate to do his will?"

I clicked my tongue, seeing her point. "Then we get rid of them too."

Violet sighed heavily. "He's a wimp, using others to do his dirty work." She made a face. "What kind of God hides behind a mortal?"

"Can't say I disagree with you there. Maybe there's a reason- Maybe he didn't have any choice but to do it this way."

"Maybe. . . Can you take them? Tracy is on her way up, and I have to meet Grandpa for a lesson."

"Sure."

I set Camellia down, and as predicted, she immediately started wailing. I smiled at her, taking the boys from Vie. They both burped simultaneously, making us laugh. Setting them down next to their pouting sister, I gave my mate a deep kiss before she left. Tracy chose that moment to make herself known.

"Do you have to do that in front of the babies?" She smirked.

"It's not like we're doing it on the sofa." Vie was blushing bright red and I chuckled. "Carson and Drew just finished eating, but Cam will need to eat in about half an hour. There's a bottle thawing out in our room."

"Okie dokie. Come here big boy!" She crouched down, holding her arms out to Drew, who instantly grinned his toothless grin.

"I think my son loves you more than he loves me." Violet frowned.

"Nonsense!"

"He is very attached to you." I mused aloud as I watched Drew flop onto his stomach, flailing his arms in a weak attempt to crawl. Tracy straightened, going to pick him up. As soon as he was in her arms though, he let out a deafening shriek. All three adults stared at him in shock.

"My Goddess, what's wrong Drew?! It's me, Aunt Tracy." She rocked him, but he continued his meltdown.

Violet narrowed her eyes, stepping closer to her. "Tracy, what is that smell?"

Now it was her turn to blush. "Oh, uhm. That's uh, probably. . . my mates." She finished in a whisper.

"You met your mate?! When?!" Vie exclaimed.

"Yesterday." Tracy sighed happily. "His name is Andrew. He's really sweet, and *super* hot!"

"Where did you meet him?" I asked. It was great she'd finally met her mate. Of everyone I knew, Tracy deserved that happiness.

"Actually, in the kitchen. He was getting a case of water for the warriors and I went in to make a sandwich."

"So, he's warrior?" Vie asked excitedly. Clearly, she'd already forgotten her lesson with Gideon, too wrapped up in the news.

"Yeah! But not one of ours." She looked at me. "He's one of the temporary ones from Blood Moon. I can't believe we only crossed paths yesterday!"

I searched my mind, eventually putting a face to the name. There was only one Andrew here for Blood Moon.

"Andrew Ruric?" I asked.

"You know him?"

"A little. We sparred a few times when I was training. He's a good warrior."

"I know him too. He was on his way to becoming head warrior in the next few years." Violet nodded.

"Oh, wow." Tracy blinked.

"I'm so happy for you!" The girls hugged. "Maybe that's why Drew is off today. Clearly, he doesn't want to share you." She giggled, and I joined in. Tracy looked at Drew, who was still pouting, and kissed his cheeks.

"I'll take you to meet Andrew." She told him. "You'll see how great he is. But you're still my number one guy."

Drews cheeks plumped as he smiled adorably at her. Camellia grabbed my pant leg suddenly; I bent down to scoop her up.

"Alright, I'm out of here. But you should invite Andrew over for dinner. We can do a double date." Vie said as she opened the door. "See you guys later."

We called our good-byes, and then it was just us and the kids. Camellia yawned in my arms, fussing a bit. Deciding she could probably use her bottle a little early, I walked Tracy out. She headed for the kids' room while I opened the door to ours. Locating the bottle on the counter, I checked the milk's temperature before settling down in the armchair. She drank greedily, her eyes starting to close before she was halfway done.

A knock sounded at the door, pulling my attention away from my girl.

"It's open." I called.

I heard the door open and close. And then my nose wrinkled as a too-sweet scent invaded the room. It was distantly memorable, as if I'd scented this particular smell before. But I couldn't place it.

"Hello Alpha."

My head turned to see Stacy standing behind me. She was smiling widely at me, her blonde hair done in loose waves. The blue dress she was wearing was *way* too revealing, and *way* too short. Ehno growled in my head, uncomfortable having another female other than or mate or Tracy in here.

"Uh, hi. What can I do for you?" I asked politely.

"I have a problem. Do you mind if I sit?"

"Sure."

I wasn't thrilled to have her here, and Violet was definitely going to freak. But if she really had a problem, I owed to her as Alpha to listen. She moved slowly, getting close to the chair as she made her way to the sofa. The scent of her perfume overwhelmed me, and I had to clench my jaw from gagging. Plopping on the sofa across from me, I looked away as I accidentally caught sight of her black lace thong. Though, she was taking her time to cross her legs, so perhaps that wasn't an accident at all.

"Get her out of here. I don't want her around my pup!" Ehno barked.

"I'll make it quick, and then she'll be gone." I promised him.

I waited for her to speak. She didn't. I cleared my throat, adjusting the bottle in my hand.

"So, you have a problem?" I asked.

"Yes." She sat back, her leg sliding down. I kept my eyes looking forward, knowing her panties were on display again. "You see, I haven't found my mate yet."

I wondered how that was my problem. Ehno grumbled the same question as she continued.

"I've looked everywhere in this pack. Obviously he's not here." She pouted, her bottom lip sticking out. "I was hoping to look at other packs."

461

"You're asking my permission to leave?"

"Kind of."

Camellia sucked at air. I removed the bottle, bringing her up to my shoulder to burp. "What exactly are you asking Stacy?"

"Well, everyone has noticed how close you and Alpha Varlos are. I was hoping you could escort me to the Blood Moon pack, so I can try and find my mate."

I felt warmth on my shoulder, indicating Camellia had spit up a bit. I sat her on my lap, her chin covered in drool and milk. Stacy glanced at her, an emotion playing across her face too quickly for me to identify. Then she was smiling again.

"Uhm, why do you feel you need an escort?" I avoided her eyes by using my sleeve to wipe up Cam. Goddess, I really wished she would move her leg.

"That should be obvious. There's a God out to destroy us! I wouldn't feel safe leaving the pack without an escort."

"I guess that's fair. I can send King or Ashwell with you."

"No offense Alpha, it's not that I don't trust them. . . I would just feel a lot more comfortable if *you* came. You know the pack, you know the Alpha there. And you grew up there, you could show me around, help me meet people. Hopefully one of them turns out to be my mate." She leaned forward, her breasts almost spilling out of the dress.

I knew I only had one card to play, and I played it.

"You make a good point Stacy. If you're able, we can leave on Monday. I'm sure the kids would love to see their Grandmother, and I know Vie has been wanting to visit our old pack too."

Just as I thought, her whole demeanor changed at the mention of Vie coming with us. She sat back, *finally* covering her exposed underwear.

"Is Monday not good for you?" I asked innocently.

"It is. I just don't think we should bother the Luna with this. I'm sure she's still recovering from birth. . ."

"Actually, she's recovered amazingly well. Totally able to make the trip with us."

"She must have things to take care of here. I'd hate to pull her away from her work." She tried a different angle.

"What's a few days? The work isn't going anywhere." I shrugged. "And, Vie was quite popular at school. I know she could introduce you to more people than I could. I was honestly kind of a loner."

"I bet she was." She clipped out. She looked at Camellia again. "I didn't the chance to tell you congratulations. You're son is adorable Alpha."

"This is actually my daughter." I corrected her.

"Oh. Sorry, babies all look the same to me." She laughed.

I almost pointed out that Cam was wearing a pink dress, but I held my tongue. Ehno was growing more and more agitated, and I was trying to figure out a way to get Stacy to leave.

"Well, why don't you take a few days to think about wether or not you want to go with us. If so, I'll arrange it with Alpha Varlos."

"I'll do that."

I stood, making sure not to disturb the sleeping girl in my arms. Stacy came to stand in front of me, batting her lashes and sticking out her chest.

"Walk me to the door?" She trilled.

"Uh, sure. . ." The door that was fifteen feet away? But, whatever got her to leave.

I led her out, waiting impatiently. Of course, she couldn't just go right to elevator. Instead, she stepped into the hallway, turning back to me. It was then that it clicked. The scent. Her scent. I had a moment of Deja-vu, standing by our door, reading one of the hateful notes left for my mate. It had been *Stacy's* scent out here! With the realization came anger. I interrupted whatever she was ranting on about.

463

"Say, have you heard of anyone leaving notes in the packhouse? I've been getting complaints of nasty messages taped to doors." I gave her a knowing look.

Surprise flashed in her eyes quickly, but I caught it. "No Alpha. But I'll let you know if I see anyone doing that."

"I hope you will." I stepped closer to her, lowering my voice. "Because someone left one for my mate. Maybe you can spread the word- If I or my Luna find another note on our door, *I* will personally hunt down the culprit. And they won't like the punishment. I don't tolerate that kind of behavior in this pack. Am I clear?"

My Alpha voice slipped in at the end, essentially freezing the girl in place.

"Am I clear?" I repeated harshly.

"Y-yes Alpha! " She squeaked.

"Good." I stepped back, closing the door in her face.

CHAPTER 62
VIOLET

I came home to the utter *worst* smell I'd ever smelled in my life. Jasper was lounging on the sofa, a glass if whiskey in his hand. Lazily, he lifted another to me.

"I shouldn't. The kids will need to nurse soon."

"Right." He poured the alcohol into his almost empty glass, taking a sip. I sat next to him, kicking off my shoes.

"What is that smell? And why is it stronger here?" I patted the sofa.

"Stacy was here." He replied casually.

My mouth fell slack, and anger immediately overtook me.

"Excuse me?!"

"Yup." His mouth made a *pop* on the p. "She wanted me to escort her to Blood Moon so she could try and find her mate there. I told her she could come with us on Monday."

"Jasper, what the fu-"

He held up his hand. "As soon as I mentioned you were coming, she changed her tune. Then she asked me to walk her to the door. And that's when I realized she's the one who's been leaving you those notes."

I was staring at him, trying to process too many things at once. It didn't surprise me at all to find out Stacy had left those awful messages on our door. She seemed like the type of hateful person to do just that.

"Why are you so calm about this?" I demanded.

"One, because I let her know without saying that I knew it was her. And I told her to spread the word that I would be *very* angry if I caught who was doing it." He smirked. "And two, because I really doubt she'll pull something like that again. She's been caught, and she knows it. More importantly, she knows that *I* know it."

"Fucking bitch." I muttered. "I knew I hated her."

"I called Gideon to come up here. There has to be some spell that can make this smell go away." He wrinkled his nose, effectively breaking the tension. I laughed, holding onto his arm.

"You're so cute!" I gasped. "It does smell pretty terrible though."

"Seriously. Camellia had a poop, and I'm not ashamed to say I left the diaper open on the bed for a while. It was a bad idea; Instead of covering the stench, it just mixed in with it."

I laughed harder. "You didn't!"

"I did." He took another drink.

A sudden thought had me sobering up. "Wait. . . Was Stacy here will Cam?"

He nodded. "I'm sorry about that. But she didn't touch her; Ehno wouldn't have allowed that anyway." He chuckled. "She thought Cam was a boy."

I snorted. "What?! She was wearing a dress!"

"Which I very nearly pointed out."

This time we both laughed. I leaned in to peck his cheek. "Thanks for telling me. Please don't let her in here again though- it makes me uncomfortable."

"I promise."

I stood. "I think I can help with the smell though."

"Please."

I giggled, closing my eyes, and reaching for that feeling inside me. When Hala and I were merged with my magic, I raised my hand, waving it around me. Grandpa and I were learning just how different my magic was compared to his. Where he needed incantations, I simply had to focus on what I wanted, willing it to become reality. So I focused on one of my favorite scents, Lavender, and in no time at all our bedroom smelled like an open meadow, filled with flowers.

"Thank you." Jasper sighed.

I sank back down. Only to get right back up as the baby monitor went off.

"I'll be back."

"I'll come with."

We left the room together, walking the three steps to the kids room. The door was open when I walked in. Tracy was holding Drew, but Carson and Cam were crying on the floor. I took our son while Jasper picked up our daughter. Tracy looked exhausted.

"You okay?" I asked with a smile.

"You know, I love this kid." She replied. "But he hasn't let me put him down at all! My arms are numb."

"That might be the first time I've ever heard you complain about something Tracy." Jasper said.

"Ouch! Drew, please stop doing that!" She took his hand away from her shirt, groaning when he grabbed it immediately again.

"How long has he been doing that?" I asked.

"Since we got in here. He's pinched me good a few times."

I handed Carson over, taking Drew from her. Instantly, he screamed, reaching for Tracy again. I kissed his cheek, singing softly, but he just shrieked over me. I looked at Jasper, bewildered.

"Sweet boy, it's okay! Aunt Tracy is right here, see?" I cooed.

He cried, and cried, until finally we gave up. I handed him back while she gave me his brother, and he settled into her arms, pulling at her shirt again. I shook my head, accepting the fact that my baby might actually prefer Tracy over me. Oh, well. At least he had good taste.

Settling into the rocking chair, Jasper handed me Cam so I could nurse. Tracy already had a bottle ready for Drew, and before long, all three were sound asleep. We put them in their crib, grinning when they cuddled into each other. Backing away, we quietly left the room.

"There are some forms that need to be organized in your Office. I'll get on that now." Tracy said.

"Oh, Tracy, take a break." I said.

"Are you crazy? This *is* my break!" She laughed. "You hired me, so let me work. I'm helping myself to whatever is in the mini-fridge in your office though."

"By all means."

She went on her way, whistling softly. I turned when the elevator opened, Grandpa walking out.

"I heard you had an unwanted smell." He greeted us.

"I already took care of it."

"Oh." He smiled at me. "Good. I'm glad to see you becoming more comfortable using your magic."

"It does feel that way." I returned his smile. "Sorry you came up here for nothing."

"Not for nothing. I also came to tell you that I'm going home for a day or so. Rose will be missing me, no doubt, and I want to ask her about moving here."

"I hope she's alright with it. I miss her."

"Me too. I'll be back in a few days."

He shook Jaspers hand and gave me a warm hug. Then, with a snap of his fingers, he was gone. I nudged my mate.

"So, how should we spend this lovely afternoon?"

"Hmm. . ." He wrapped his arms around me, leaning in to kiss my neck. "I can think of a few things I'd like to do."

I giggled, turning my face so I could kiss him. Heat and electricity shot through my veins.

Clumsily, we made it to our room, shutting the door and locking it. We reached for each other at the same time, clothes coming off and tossed to the floor. By the time we made it to the bed, we were both naked, eagerly devouring the other. We hadn't made love since I gave birth, and everything felt super sensitive to me. Especially my breasts. Jasper was gentle though, taking his time with me and making me feel loved and beautiful. He kissed each new line on my body, telling me how much he adored the marks that were proof of the lives we'd brought into the world. His words made my heart melt, made me even more sure of how much I loved him.

When we finished, we lay together on the pillows, my head on his chest. The rhythmic sound of his heart lulled me into a peaceful daze, adding to my ecstasy.

"I love you." I sighed.

"I love you too. So much." His fingers combed softly through my hair.

All was quiet until he sat up, throwing the covers off. I watched, confused, as he hurried into the closet. A minute later, he tossed a red, floral printed dress at me.

"Get dressed. I want to take you somewhere." He ducked out of sight again.

"Now? What about the kids?"

"I mindlinked Tracy. She's got them." He called out to me.

"Okay. . .."

I slid out of bed, searching the floor for my bra. I quickly put it on, then threw the dress on over top.

"I'm not going anywhere without panties." I said. A second later, A pair hit my head. I scooped them up. "Wow, you really want to go out."

"Yes, yes I do." Jasper emerged from the closet wearing a black button down shirt, with faded blue jeans and sneakers. His hair was still messy, but he looked. . . Hot. Sexy.

"I feel underdressed." I giggled.

"You look gorgeous." His voice held such a note of sincerity that the blood rushed to my cheeks without warning. Taking my hand, he led me out of the room and into the elevator. I glanced at him every few seconds, wondering what could have brought on this sudden urge to go out.

Things got even more suspicious when he led me to the garage next to the house. We'd been here exactly once, to check out Warrick's cars and decide which ones would be sold and for how much. All that was left was Ashwell's Jeep, Jaspers car, Kings SUV, and the trucks the Blood Moon warriors had come in. Jasper led me to his car, opening the door for me. I gave him a look as I got in, my

469

eyes following him as he walked around the hood and got in the drivers seat. He had a strange little smile on his face.

"Are you going to tell me where we're going?" I inquired.

"Nope. You'll have to wait and see." He grinned, pulling out of the garage.

He was whistling while he drove, tapping his fingers on the steering wheel. Soon, we were coming up to the border. And then we were driving past it.

"You know," I said, "I'm a little hurt. We have great sex, and then you shoo me out of bed to go on a random adventure." I smirked at him.

"It'll be worth it love. Trust me."

I leaned back in my seat, looking out the window. We were headed to Blood Moon, I knew that. But I couldn't think of any reason he would spring a trip out of the blue to our old pack. I tapped my foot in time with his fingers while I watched the trees go by in a blue of yellows, oranges and reds. A smile touched my lips as I thought of taking the kids out soon and playing in the leaves, just like Garrett and I had done when we were little. I remembered Dad throwing us into ginormous piles that he and Uncle Ben and Uncle Luke had raked up.

Thinking about Garrett made me wonder if that's where we were going. Grandpa hadn't been sure, but we were all intensely relieved that Jennine's magic had worn off with her death. Mom and Dad took him home, where he was trying to work things out with Sophia. He hadn't been in great shape when he'd left Silver Moon, but I'd promised to be in touch. He was my twin, after all, and no matter what I would be there for him.

Jasper took a sharp right turn, just before the border of the pack. I didn't ask, because I knew he wouldn't tell me where we were going until we got there. The area looked familiar though.

"We're almost there." He said.

"I believe you."

Twenty minutes later, he took a slow turn left, the road nearly disappearing. I looked around as he parked, cutting the engine. I reached for the handle but he stopped me, getting out and coming around to open the door for me.

"Such a gentleman today." I teased him.

"Just today?"

"Well, more than usual today."

"I'm honestly shocked you haven't figured out where we are yet."

I took in the trees, the bushes, the sky. I did feel a sense of being here before. I shrugged, gesturing for him to lead the way. Holding hands, we strolled through the woods together. Ten minutes later, I felt like a complete idiot.

Standing alone, looking just as I remembered it, was the cabin. Memories of our time here flashed through my mind, back when I wasn't completely sure if he was the right man for me, mate or not. It felt so weird, to be standing here now, in such completely different positions and statuses than we were only months ago. We'd been two teenagers, trying to figure out how being mates would work. Now we were Alpha and Luna, Mother and a Father. Uniquely marked by the Moon Goddess herself, and prepared to fight for the very world we lived in and for those whom we loved.

"Violet."

I turned, expecting to see Jasper standing behind me. I got another surreal shock when I saw him on one knee instead. In his hand was a box, housing the most beautiful piece of jewellery I'd ever seen. My hand went to my mouth and tears brimmed my lashes.

"Jasper." I gasped.

"Vie," He smiled up at me, "I love you. I've loved you since I was a kid. From the very first moment I saw you, standing up to that bully who was teasing me about my awful artwork."

A laugh bubbled up in my chest.

"You are the most beautiful, decent, strong, caring, amazing person I have ever known. In the short months

471

we've been mates, we've been through a rollercoaster of ups and downs. But you were there with me, and for me, the entire time. I want to be your rock, your support, like you've been for me, forever. I want to love you, forever. Longer, if the Goddess will allow it. I don't know where the future is going to take us. I don't know how bad the war is going to be. But I *do* know that I want to be the one by your side through it all. I love you. Will you marry me?"

For a few seconds, I couldn't form a single word. I was screaming the answer inside, but when I finally found my voice, it was filled with tears of joy, coming out no more than a shaky whisper.

"Yes."

Jasper jumped to his feet, pulling me in for a long, passionate kiss. He slid the ring on my finger, a single tear sliding down his cheek. I wiped it away with my fingertips. Acting on impulse, I closed my eyes, raised my hand. For the second time in that clearing, fresh grass and wildflowers grew beneath our feet.

"Beautiful." My mate whispered. I opened my eyes, finding him gazing at me with absolute love.

Unleashing the joy inside myself, I wrapped my arms around his neck, bringing his lips down to mine, and we sank to the ground together. As we made love on the forest floor, I silently vowed that whatever happened, when ever it happened, we would be together, looking after one another. And if by chance, we were apart, I would always, *always* find my way back to him. My love. My heart. My mate.

THE END

FOR NOW

ABOUT THE AUTHOR

S.V. Smith is a Canadian Indie Author based in Nova Scotia. She is the author of 'The Kingdom of Light Series,' an ongoing young adult fantasy romance, and a non-fiction work, 'An Honest Guide to Self-Publishing.' S.V. is passionate about her work and takes pride in her stories. Her favourite genres to read include fantasy, historical fiction, and romance.

Follow S.V. Smith on her social media for book updates, releases, giveaways and more.

Made in the USA
Monee, IL
23 November 2024

70935526R00260